Published March 2021
by Indies United Publishing House, LLC

Cover art designed by Damonza.com

ISBN: 978-1-64456-220-8
Library of Congress Control Number: 2020949703

INDIES UNITED PUBLISHING HOUSE, LLC
P.O. BOX 3071
QUINCY, IL 62305-3071
www.indiesunited.net

VOID OF POWER

FROM THE ASHES

ANDREW C. RAIFORD

INDIES UNITED PUBLISHING HOUSE, LLC

Void of Power - From the Ashes, book two of the VoP series, is dedicated to my children. All five are superheroes in my heart.

I also dedicate this book to my wife Beverly who tirelessly helped me through the preliminary editing processes and also for her love and support throughout the writing of this book.

PROLOGUE

Breathing wasn't difficult, it was impossible. Yet the naked figure continued to smile through the thick Plexiglas at the scientist holding a clipboard outside the water-filled tank. The smile was superficial, however. Beneath the calm exterior, her anger boiled with disgust for having been stripped, hog-tied, and connected to dozens of electrodes from scalp to toe, then mercilessly lowered into a water tank. Despite the fierce hatred she had for these people, she experienced no sense of panic and no fight for survival. She knew exactly how this episode would end. Things always happened exactly the way her visions indicated unless she took steps to change them. Even she could not understand this conundrum of time, cause and effect, and the ability to see outside of the temporal construct to which we seem inextricably fastened. If she could change it, why is it she couldn't foresee the results of her interference? Even the scientists were baffled by this. Heather rarely revealed every detail of the things she saw to the scientists under whose nasty care she lived and even lied on occasions to prevent them from carrying out their devious schemes. They concluded her visions were never 100 percent accurate, while only Heather knew the truth.

In Dr. Slater's twisted mind, the object of this particular experiment was to determine whether Heather Hollings' visions would intensify under life-threatening circumstances. His staff, including the lab assistants, had enough common sense to understand one cannot threaten a true clairvoyant with death. They suspected Dr. Slater had other motives for trussing Heather up this way.

Heather was confident she would not die now, so even as she neared the point of losing consciousness, she continued to smile at the researchers. The last thing she saw before she succumbed to a lack of oxygen was the door to the lab opening.

"Pull her out of there. Now."

The lab technician standing to one side had already begun to hoist the subject out of the glass enclosure. Heather choked and expelled water as her head cleared the surface and revived rather quickly. Her face glowed with anticipation of what was about to transpire. Water cascaded from her body as the attention of every soul in the room was riveted on her. The present tension however, was broken when the newcomer spoke again.

"Whose infantile brain concocted this little experiment?" the newly arrived stranger asked without looking up from the tablet he held.

A tall, unshaven, obese man wearing a white lab coat handed his clipboard to an associate then moved menacingly towards the smartly-dressed critic. The large man's intention, as he lowered his face to within inches of Dr. Harvey Tanner's, was to intimidate.

"Who the hell are you to judge my work, stranger?"

"I'm the one who will remove you from this facility if you don't get out of my face, Mr.," he paused to read the towering man's security ID, "Slater. Now, I will ask again. Whose infantile brain concocted this experiment?"

Doug Slater reached for Dr. Tanner's tie and gripped it in his massive fist. "I happen to run this laboratory, tiny man and I don't apprcciate your tone," he said in an amused, yet threatening manner.

Dr. Tanner placed his hand over Slater's wrist who began to scream as his hand glowed, then burst into flames. The fire spread quickly up Slater's arm and then consumed his head and shoulders. The younger assistants recoiled in horror as their boss's cries for help filled the lab. The screams stopped soon enough, but the fire grew hotter and soon all that remained of their universally disliked boss was a smoldering corpse on the floor. The lab technician who controlled the hoist was on his knees vomiting while the rest covered their faces with handkerchiefs or lab coats to block the stench of burning flesh.

With a loud hiss, the Halon fire suppression nozzles began spraying in response to the heat, smoke, and flames. Dr. Tanner produced a small travel umbrella which he flicked open to keep the halon from hitting him. Waiting patiently for the fire system to do its work, he then motioned to his assistant to shut it down. Glancing up at Heather, who was smiling even more than before, he said, "You saw this coming."

Heather didn't respond yet maintained a satisfied grin. After being released from her bonds she was helped to her feet and wrapped in a thick, cotton robe. Pulling the robe tighter, she turned to Dr. Tanner.

"I did. But that's not all. I saw a child killed in a car accident." Her eyes moving across every individual in the lab, she said, "I have no idea whose child it is."

With that, all but one person ran from the lab, desperately thumbing their cell phones. Dr. Tanner never took his eyes from her.

"That's not true, is it," he said more as a statement than a question. She tilted her head, then shrugged her shoulders before being led back to her cell.

Dr. Tanner turned to the only person remaining in the room who shook as he gawked at the smoldering mass. "Get rid of that," he said pointing to the corpse.

A senior staff member poked her head into the room and attempted to speak but withdrew for a moment due to the smell. When she had gathered her control, she said, "Excuse me, Dr. Tanner, your visitors from D.C. have arrived. Should I show them to the observation room?"

Tanner nodded as he wiped his hands on a handkerchief which he then tossed onto the black-charred, former lab scientist. Exiting the room and entering an elevator, he used his hand to brush any soot remaining on his jacket. He removed a communication device from his belt.

"Samuel, please bring patient number 34 to the observation room. Make sure he is presentable, then ready patient 23."

The indirect lighting and comfortable stadium seating of the medium sized observation room were designed to put the occupants of the room at ease, a necessity because the subjects on the other side of the large plate glass wall were often disturbing.

Dr. Tanner greeted every guest as they entered the room, with a smile and a handshake with the enthusiasm of a politician, yet the coolness of a Hollywood celebrity. He, like every other person entering the room, ignored the guards who stood to either side of the entrance. People rarely paid the slightest attention to the dozens of security personnel at this facility, tucked neatly in a remote corner of what is known as Area 51. Not even Dr. Tanner knew one of the guards didn't belong there.

Tanner noticed the tiny woman with dull brown hair seemed bothered that she was required to attend this meeting. The timbrel of her voice corroborated this fact.

"Are we going to be watching alien autopsy movies, Doctor? Because we might have saved ourselves a lot of travel-time by viewing those on a dozen websites."

"No aliens today, I promise. But before you leave this room, you'll understand the importance of our work here."

"I certainly hope so, Dr. Tanner, because I'd be very disappointed if we have to look at one more dead squid."

"Patience, Dr. Muller. Patience."

Dr. Tanner counted only nine individuals in the room, including the guards when the doors were closed and he took the podium.

"Thank you for coming and welcome. You are all familiar with this facility and our purpose here, so no introductions or explanations are necessary. You have been sent here by your respective organizations or summoned here by me to coordinate in efforts to gain access to certain assets vital to our national security. These assets are two nine-year-old children. After we lost major assets during our initial attempt to gain custody of these children, the military was then given primary responsibility to capture or kill Coraline Paden and Eli Jennings."

Dr. Muller interrupted, "Yes, Dr. Tanner, we are very aware the military lost a large fortune in equipment, as well as many lives." She read from a notepad, "Numerous F-40s, Ospreys, attack helicopters, drones, Tomahawk Missiles, tanks, Hummers, anti-aircraft, GVCs, including hundreds of soldiers, pilots and crew members. A large loss with nothing to show besides the total humiliation of the Central Government and an impetus for the state militias to begin stockpiling weapons."

Dr. Tanner's countenance didn't change whatsoever. "Had they succeeded in taking out these two children, the cost would have been considered negligible."

"But they didn't succeed, Dr. Tanner. If the Central Government could not eradicate these threats with air-force and military strike teams that included sophisticated warplanes and mechanized units with the latest in technology, what makes you think you can make a difference?"

"That is why you all were summoned here today," he said abruptly. "I certainly hope we are smarter than the generals who earned their humiliating defeat. We have talent here the Central Government does not possess."

At this point he gestured toward the glass wall at the front of the room. Lights slowly illuminated the spaced behind the glass revealing two separate cells, containing a woman on the left and a man on the right. Each sat shackled to a table. The man stared blankly at one of the side walls. The woman, however looked directly at the glass wall with a knowing smile on her face.

"Can she see us?" asked one of those seated.

"No. But she knows we're here. The assets we possess here may not be equal to the extraordinary powers of Coraline and Eli, but working together, we stand a chance."

A thin man with coke-bottle glasses, a goatee and mustache wearing a dusty old suit stood to speak. "And these assets you speak of, will they help us willingly?"

"Oh, they will help us. Remember, we have members of their families in holding cells. They will cooperate."

"I'm sorry, Dr. Tanner," interrupted the frumpy Dr. Muller, "but the last time we checked, the family members of your 'assets' were liberated from your facility in Oklahoma by the very children which are the targets of this mission!"

Harvey Tanner's face finally revealed some weariness of being questioned by those sent to aid his efforts. He looked at the floor for a count of three, then made eye contact with each person in the room. "That is correct. We no longer possess hostages. But our assets do not know this. As far as they know, their mothers, fathers, brothers, and sisters are still being held by us. They will aid us."

The man with the coke-bottle glasses cleared his throat and interrupted. "Dr. Tanner, excuse me, but I think she knows."

Every eye went to the attractive woman attached to the table in the cell before them. Her smile turned into a grin, one that did not bode well for Dr. Tanner's scheme. Dr. Tanner quickly moved on with his train of thought.

"Also... Also, we have not been idle these past few months. Since the incident in the Void, we have gathered information necessary to accomplish our goal: the capture or destruction of Coraline Paden and Eli Jennings. Our task is to concentrate on the children, Central Government will focus on the so-called Defenders. Even as we speak, military personnel are meeting to discuss how to handle this group. We know their names and faces. What we don't know is how they happen to possess technology more advanced than anything we've thrown against them."

A young man with longish hair and three-day growth on his face raised his hand.

"Yes, Mr. Rodriguez."

"I was under the impression the children and these Defenders were united now. How can we focus on one without running headlong into the other? Shouldn't we be meeting with the military in a joint effort? Anything we plan must include trained military personnel!"

"You are absolutely correct. I'd like to introduce to you Major Barrett Ratcliff. You will refer to him as 'Major'."

A sunbaked man with close-cropped hair stood and faced the group. His fatigues were clean and new, without the usual rank insignias you see on the men who guarded the base, yet his overall impression was that of someone accustomed to being in command.

"The Major and his team have been placed under my command and are here to assist us in any way we deem fit. Is this not so, Major?"

His response was a simple nod.

CHAPTER ONE
ADAM

West Texas winds could scarcely cover the sound created by heavy boots breaking through the dry, crusty earth as the muscular runner made a desperate attempt to move out of his pursuer's weapon-range. Carrying only his backpack, he moved steadily up and down the rugged landscape as the occasional bullet zipped past him. This only caused him to hasten his pace and perhaps duck lower.

Adam felt a sense of relief with the knowledge that his enemies were dropping farther and farther behind. It had taken an inordinate amount of time for his dim-witted assailants to figure out that taking potshots at a running person so far away was a waste of time and ammunition. He had only another three hundred yards to go before he reached rocky terrain, which would offer him cover and concealment as well as make tracking more difficult. Not that those giving chase were likely to be expert trackers, but even a child could follow the deep footprints in this crusty earth.

He had begun to reconsider the wisdom of leaving home for the sole purpose of paying a visit to the long-haired brunette he'd met during the appreciation ceremony in Austin a few months back. At this point he had only been struck by one of the dozens of rounds fired in his direction. Fortunately, the only damage was to his backpack, so his visit to the spectacular April Brice now seemed well worth the trouble.

Adam's thoughts drifted back to the first time he laid eyes on her. She caught his attention when he and his siblings were taking in the sights on 6th Street in downtown Austin the night of the festivities. Among the thousands of unknown faces Adam had seen that night, only one made him stop what he was doing to gawk. It was obvious to his siblings something or someone had temporarily robbed Adam of his senses. He appeared transfixed. His brother's girlfriend, Sarah, had to nudge him when he failed to notice there was a small, bright-eyed girl tugging on his arm to get his attention. Only then did he see the smiling face looking up at him.

"What's your name?" he asked as he took the Celebration Day pamphlet from her hand and began to sign his autograph. She tried to answer, but no words came out.

"Her name is Rita," laughed the blue-eyed girl standing behind her younger sister. "And as you can tell she's a little nervous about meeting you."

"How about you? Are you nervous?" he asked the beauty curiously.

"Nervous? No. Happy though. Oh, by the way, I'm April. April Brice," she said with a devastating smile.

Adam introduced April and Rita to his brother Alex, Alex's girlfriend Sarah, and sister Hayley, then invited them to join his group as they explored 6th Street.

"We'd love to, but we can't. Those are our parents waiting for us," she said pointing to a couple standing across the street. "We're looking for a place to eat, so we won't hold you up."

"You would not hold us up a bit! Please ask them to join us; we're starving, aren't we guys?" Adam said turning to Alex.

Alex nodded in agreement. "Of course! We seem to be popular today, so I think we probably stand a good chance of being placed at the front of whichever line we choose. Well, maybe."

The parents walked over after being frantically waved across by their daughters. Hayley and Sarah later said they had never seen Adam on better behavior than when he was working to impress April's parents. Finding their way to the most popular restaurant on 6th Street, where the line wrapped around the block, the four New Castlehale icons gazed longingly at the restaurant menu board when the doorman who kept order outside the establishment recognized them. In a thunderous voice he called to them, "If ya'll are The Defenders, and I know you are, ya'll are more than welcome to a table right this minute! We've got a corner table we save for celebrities and we just threw that little creep Troy Jenkins out on his ear for mistreating the staff! Whataya say?!"

Adam, held out his arm for April to take hold, then stepped forward and said softly, "Defenders. Party of eight."

Alex tapped Adam on the shoulder and jerked his thumb toward the six Texas State Troopers who had been shadowing them all evening to aid in their protection. "What about them?"

Adam turned to the maître d and asked, "Is there any way you guys could wrangle up some sandwiches for our State Trooper friends here and put it on our tab? I promise they'll stay out of your way."

The maître d snapped his fingers for waitstaff and spoke to them as he pointed at the six Troopers.

"Now then," said Adam, "let's eat!" With that, they entered the restaurant through the thunderous applause of those standing in line. They were quite the awesome sight that night. Hayley wasn't particularly comfortable being the center of attention at any time, but here the feeling was accentuated by the fact they were shoved to the front of the line. Her wave at the crowd was more of an apology than a celebrity wave.

Every minute Adam spends with April Brice makes him feel like he is walking on a cloud. For this reason, it is difficult for him to remember the details of that night in Austin. A bullet whizzing by forced him to concentrate again on his escape from these bandits. He knew they couldn't possibly catch him in a foot-race and was even less concerned about them acquiring a new vehicle on short notice. The jeep they had used in their attempt to run him down now sported a broken axle after hitting a tumbleweed-covered hole that Adam had easily vaulted. The driver of the vehicle scornfully laughed when he saw Adam jump the dead weed believing it would simply disintegrate on the bumper of the 4-wheel drive vehicle. Had the occupants been wearing seatbelts, the driver might have prevented impacting the steering wheel with his chest, and the front-seat passenger may not have been ejected through the windshield when the vehicle came to an abrupt halt. The tell-tale sign to Adam that his chances immensely improved was the flight of the two men who had been standing in the back seats hanging onto the roll-bar. They catapulted forward in twisted spasms through the air, smashing into the dirt with a breathy thud. Several minutes passed before they gathered their wits, collected their weapons, and stagger forward in a feeble attempt to follow their prey. They were a sorry lot firing their guns indiscriminately, although, at that point, Adam felt the jarring impact of a bullet striking his backpack. The Kevlar material and the contents of the pack saved his life, but he instinctively knew something inside was ruined.

Adam's long legs and excellent physical conditioning allowed him to quickly reach the ruins of an old stone building. Crouching low behind a partially destroyed wall, he paused to take stock of his gear. From his pack, he retrieved his tablet but found the impact of the recent bullet had smashed the glass. This reminder of his present danger caused him to stand and poke his head above the stones for a quick glance at his pursuers, who were still at a good distance. From his holster Adam drew a large-caliber handgun and after taking careful aim, he lobbed one of the . 50 caliber projectiles in their direction. The meteoric strike of the bullet into a rock and the horrendous sound that followed caused them to turn tail and stagger back to their vehicle. Being in open terrain and being fired upon by someone tucked behind stone walls was not their idea of smart fun.

Upon inspection of the tablet, he realized he would not be able to access the faux-GPS system he and his siblings had devised, allowing them to triangulate the position of any aircraft or vehicle used by the residents of New Castlehale. Included in the system was an S.O.S. signal. Once sent it would summon a swift rescue mission. Early in the chase, Adam decided not to use it so long as he maintained the upper hand. Given the lack of skill in his pursuers, there was no need to scramble fighter aircraft. Besides, he'd never hear the end of teasing from the rest of the Walsh family that he had to be rescued because of a girl. The tablet was beyond help. He stuffed it back into the pack anyway.

After taking stock of supplies, he drank from the water bottle, quickly put his arms through the straps of his pack and buckled it around his waist. Drawing the large revolver from its holster again, he replaced the two empty casings with fresh rounds from his belt. He immediately set out at a trot heading directly west to avoid the bandits. The Brice home was visible to him, but only as a wavy blob viewed through the rippling heat waves coming from the earth. "Only a mile and a half," he thought, which was about the same distance as a couple of laps around the hanger bay. Adam ran a lap at least once every three hours when he was working at home just to gather his thoughts.

Moving at a steady pace, it didn't take him long to reach the Brice property. He crept silently to the barn and peeked inside just to make sure the Beast was still where he left it, then walked casually to the main house.

He was within ten feet of the house when the screen door flew open and April launched herself onto Adam, who caught her in his arms. He closed his eyes, relishing this moment of the first real contact he'd had with her. When he opened them, he saw Trevor and Ruthy Brice, along with his own mom and brother Alex, who was grinning ear-to-ear. He dropped April quickly.

"Mom? Alex? What are you doing here?"

"Well, you may not have felt it necessary to broadcast an S.O.S. when you, on foot, are being chased by two vehicles filled with bad guys, but Mr. and Mrs. Brice here had enough sense to contact us! What were you thinking?"

"Do you see two vehicles chasing me, Mom?" He turned and pointed to the empty landscape.

"Explain yourself right now, mister!" demanded the worried mom.

Alex was beside himself with glee now that the tables were turned on his younger brother. Alex was usually the one in the hot seat, desperately having to explain himself to his mother while Adam stood by enjoying the spectacle. It was with a great deal of satisfaction he asked Adam, "What *did* happen to the bad guys?" The humor of the situation was not lost on Adam, yet he knew better than to white-wash facts to his mom.

"April and I took a walk into town to get a bite at the little diner," he said, pointing to a structure on the far side of a field east of their location. "We were the only ones in the place when three characters walked in and sat at the table right next to ours. They could have chosen any table in the place, but they had to plop themselves down right beside us and just sat there staring. I whispered to April to walk back through the kitchen and out the rear exit, then run home as fast as she could. I would follow soon. She did as I suggested and excused herself to use the restroom, but one of the guys stood up to follow her. I gave him a rough shove back into his chair, then I pulled mine up to their table and sat down.

"The guy on the right said, 'It's three against one, boy.' I back-fisted him into oblivion before he could get another word out of his mouth and turned to the others. Then it was two against one and there was zero chance these guys could get the best of me."

"What did they do?" Mr. Brice asked.

Adam smiled. "They ran, and at that moment it seemed a good idea to give chase. Only when I reached the street, there were two vehicles and several armed individuals waiting outside. I turned tail and did some running of my own, straight back into the diner to grab my backpack and headed out the back door. There was no time to send an S.O.S. if I was going to stay ahead of this bunch. I did my best to lead them away from April, whom I could see already halfway across the open area there. She's fast!" he said smiling at her as he lost his train of thought.

"Continue," Evelyn Walsh said with a touch of amusement.

"The first vehicle drove right through the fence to chase me down. I took out their engine with one shot from my fifty and ran for the hills. The other vehicle followed me for a distance, and almost caught up, but broke their axle. I reached cover soon enough. One more shot sent them scurrying, and here I am. How did you get here so quickly?"

"Mr. Brice called Junction. Junction radioed Command while mom and I were airborne testing the new injectors in Flyer One. Hedgehog relayed the message when we were only minutes away. From altitude, mom spotted you sitting behind that stone wall. We could see you were in no danger, so we landed here at once."

"Where is Flyer One?" Adam asked looking about.

Alex pointed straight up. Far above their heads the jet aircraft appeared as a tiny dot, hovering silently and almost invisible.

"You used my app! That's great! Bring it down!" Adam bellowed out.

Alex thumbed a couple of icons on his wristband and the hovering craft descended rapidly, deployed its landing gear, and touched down lightly in front of the barn.

Adam turned to April and said, "I wrote that app."

Evelyn stepped in front of Adam and grabbed him by the ear. "Adam Walsh, you listen to me. You might think you are Superman, but you're not. When you get into trouble, you send out an S.O.S. Do you understand me?"

"Yes ma'am, but I couldn't. A bullet took out my tablet."

He pulled off his backpack and pointed to the strike point. Evelyn put her head down and leaned into Adam's chest. April looked like she was going to faint, while Mr. Brice admired the way Adam regarded the danger about as much as he would a mosquito bite. Alex broke the uncomfortable silence.

"Yah, Adam, you should always send an S.O.S. when you get into trouble like that. Always!" agreed Alex in mock superiority.

"Oh, look who's talking! You've never sent an S.O.S. in your life!" said Adam calmly.

"That's not true! I sent an S.O.S. to Sarah to save me from my loneliness yesterday, but she didn't respond. She

14

and Hayley are too busy in China to bother with me."

Ruth Brice cocked her head sideways at Evelyn with a questioning wonder, "China?"

Evelyn nodded. "Yes. Long story. She is studying there. But we shouldn't take up any more of your time. It was very thoughtful of you to call us. I'm glad somebody did."

"It was the least we could do," said Trevor Brice. "We're happy no harm came to Adam and April."

Evelyn paused for a moment to ponder the casual use of "Adam and April" in a sentence. What did she know about this family? They seem nice enough. Their property and home appeared organized and neat and it is completely understandable why Adam would be so attracted to this young woman. She's intelligent, beautiful, well-mannered, physically fit, and certainly seems to be enamored with him. But Evelyn had only recently begun getting used to Alex and Sarah together with the accompanying hugs and kisses. At least Sarah was a known factor, and a loved one at that! It is difficult enough for a single mother, but now to see the baby of the family paying so much attention to this stranger who lived in a remote section of the Void was uncomfortable. She glanced at Adam, who at 6 foot 4 inches tall could hardly be thought of as a baby.

"Well it means a lot to us, Trevor. I also appreciate the fact you were immediately willing to go after my Adam yourself when you learned what happened in town. Thank you. If there is ever anything we can do for you, please let us know," she responded.

"Actually, there is something you can do for us," Ruth Brice chimed in immediately. She exchanged glances with Trevor and April while she seemed hesitant to say what she was thinking aloud.

"Please, Mrs. Brice, anything you need. Just ask," Adam interjected.

"Well, this incident sort of made us more vulnerable than we were before. It's nerve-wracking enough being out here, even with Kermit so close. Those men now know where to look for your son, and I'm afraid they'll try to find him through us."

"Oh Ruth! I do apologize," said Evelyn. "Please forgive

my thoughtlessness. What would you like? We can install a security system if you'd like. We have cameras, sensors, all sorts of devices to give you better security. We have weapons and people to train your whole family."

Trevor Brice nodded in surprise at such a generous offer. "Well, Ms. Walsh, that... all that...would be...well, more than generous!"

Ruthy Brice interrupted, "Ms. Walsh, I do appreciate your offer, but that is not exactly what I had in mind."

Between Adam, Alex, and Evelyn, they all chimed in with responses that were all in agreement with, "Whatever you'd like. Please. Ask."

"I'd like one of those S.O.S. signal devices. If the probability of those people coming after us is great, I'd rather have the air force and cavalry come to our aid than fight these people alone. I hope that's not too much to ask."

Evelyn immediately moved forward and placed her arms around Ruth. "Of course, that's not too much to ask. We'll have one out to you within twenty-four hours, along with the other things. Adam will supervise the installation himself."

April's mom responded by unleashing a torrent of emotion. For too long she had lived in fear for her family, existing on the edge of nowhere with no real help nearby. This was true even though her husband was a major in the Texas Militia. He had kept them safe to this point, but now that the danger had increased, she was grateful to receive the gifts the Walsh family offered.

Adam held out his hand to Trevor, who had his arm around his teenage daughter. "Mr. Brice, please forgive me for placing your daughter in danger today. It was never my intent. Sometimes we just forget our very presence can stir up hornet's nests. In my vehicle, I have weapons and a couple of sweet devices that will give you a distinct advantage over your average bandit or group of bandits. With your permission, I'd like to install them before I drive home to collect the rest.

"Apology accepted, Adam, and thank you for leading those men away from April. That tells me everything I need to know about you. Please stay for supper tonight?"

"Mr. Brice," interrupted Alex, who took a few steps

closer, waving his hand back and forth as if to squelch a bad idea. "Um, I'm not sure you understand what it means to invite Adam for supper. I hope you have more cattle than those six in the pen out back. You'll need them if you're planning to feed my little brother."

Evelyn laughed. "Don't be alarmed, Trevor. Alex is exaggerating. You'll only need two or three head, max."

Adam glanced away into the distance to ignore them. April felt as if she'd died and gone to heaven.

CHAPTER TWO
SLICE AND DICE

Recent snow-storms had blanketed the Himalayan region, making any form of climbing activities impossibly dangerous. Even at lower elevations the cold winds forced the population to bundle up at night, though it was only the beginning of fall. Despite the cold, the white-haired, elderly monk seemed impervious to the winds as they cut unmercifully across the covered top floor of the monastery.

Four guards wearing charcoal grey uniforms also ignored the inclement weather to keep watch over their master. Each of the four had been awakened long before dawn at the sound of a hand-written note being slipped under their door, instructing them to join their teacher before sunrise. The invitation indicated they were to attend, speak no words, and merely witness the event about to transpire.

Master Cheng was the embodiment of patience as he centered his attention upon the neat rows of trainees seated on the cold stone pavement of the courtyards below. Uniformed instructors paced slowly up and down rows of novices, issuing commands. In unison they stood, bowed to the instructors, then spread out in organized fashion for the morning rituals.

Beside the master on the wind-swept rooftop stood a tall, slender female wearing a closely wrapped uniform enabling her to keep relatively warm, yet also assured her the freedom of movement needed to spar. Being one of only seven individuals allowed to wear weapons in the presence of the Master, she proudly wore a katana slung across her back with the handle protruding above her shoulder.

From this towering height, Hayley Walsh could distinguish Sarah from the other students below. It wasn't that there were only two students with any hair, but that Sarah had the only phosphorescent pink hair within three thousand miles.

Hayley stood quietly as she waited for Master Cheng to break the silence. It was custom to allow the teacher the first and last words in any situation. She wondered if he often tested the patience of those around him by being silent for so long, but at last he spoke.

"Sarah shows great promise, little one. Yet, she harbors great pain," said the bright-eyed monk who was a head shorter than Hayley.

"She continues to heal from the loss of her family, Sifu Cheng. Yet, she has come far since their deaths over two years past." Hayley turned to her teacher. "Her desire to learn is greater than any I possessed on the day my father delivered me to Shaolin."

"That is true, Hayley. But your gift of learning gives you an advantage. You only had to be shown something once, and you performed it perfectly from that day forward. You mastered in a few short years what others take decades to perfect. You are my star pupil, yet there was never a desperate quality in your desire. You have never known the usual struggles of achieving balance because you were born with it. Sarah has not been blessed that way, but yes, she does have great desire. See how she performs?" he said gesturing toward the courtyard below.

Hayley nodded with approval as she watched her best friend and almost-sister smoothly transition from one form to another with skill far beyond those around her. While the youngest of the trainees watched Sarah for a clue as to which move came next in the graceful forms, Sarah's eyes were half closed as if concentrating on an energy yet discovered by her fellows.

Hayley longed for the end of each day when Sarah finished the chores every student must perform, and after the evening meal, she would then have Sarah demonstrate what she learned that day. After gentle instruction and tips for improvement, Hayley would end the evening by soothing Sarah's aches and pains with deep tissue massages and ancient Chinese medicinal practices. While it was customary for Shaolin trainees to bunk in the long single room together, Master Cheng had agreed while Hayley was there, Sarah and the other female student, Guan Yin, could share her quarters. Sarah and Guan Yin were only the second and third female novices admitted to training in the past century, Hayley being the first.

The old teacher turned to Hayley, who continued to watch the students below. "You have done well since the day you took your leave of us. I observed new techniques as you sparred with Chi Wah and Kwai Po yesterday. Together, my two most experienced warriors could not best you. Please spar with me now that I may learn from my student."

The aged master took a step back, placed his right fist into his left palm and bowed. Hayley reciprocated, then transitioned to a crane stance. Master Chen crouched low in the classic tiger, and the fight was on. A flurry of blows, blocks, kicks, and grappling techniques continued for minutes, with the teacher audibly shouting the name of each technique and style Hayley used in attack or defense followed by, "Show me something new!"

"Eagle Claw! Bamboo Leaf Palm! Very good!"

Although the master used techniques only a very advanced sensei would know, he found he could not land a blow on his best pupil. Nor could she strike him as long as she utilized techniques known to the aging warrior. The four witnesses to the bout experienced varying degrees of shock and wonder as their eyes followed the dueling pair across the rooftop.

The Master pressed forward using an attack he had personally developed. Having never revealed this technique to any living soul, he believed she could not possibly anticipate it. Closing on his opponent, he executed the savage blow but discovered she was simply not there. A powerful kick came from behind, sending the grey-bearded man flying forward. As Hayley expected, he flipped and skidded to a stop on his feet in a strong stance. He remained in that pose for a moment before standing erect to bow. Hayley had not expected him to end the match so soon.

"So, the student has surpassed the teacher. Good. But where did you learn this technique? It was a mere footnote in a scroll written by a 14th century monk. The ability to..." he paused to fish for the words, "... be not there, has been regarded as myth by many. My teacher thought it so, as did I until this moment."

"Sifu, I read that scroll and pondered the footnote for many months before I made inquiries. There were no answers from those within our discipline, but I did find the answers I needed from an unlikely source." She paused for a moment. Her countenance revealed what she was about to say would seem incredulous, even to a man with deep metaphysical roots.

"Speak it, little one."

"The answers I sought came from a nine-year-old girl, Master."

The master's eyes brightened. "A golden child?"

Interlocking arms with Master Cheng, she smiled as they walked slowly to the steps that would lead them to the lower floors. "Golden Child is for movies, Sifu Cheng. There has never been a child such as Coraline. She's more of an awakening for the human race this planet has not seen. I doubt the world is ready for this child. They'll kill her before they start adoring her."

"Such high praise, little one. I often thought the same thing about you, even though you were much older than nine when you first came to us."

"This is different, Master. I inherited my ability to devour knowledge from my parents. A child prodigy, perhaps, but nothing remotely close to Coraline. My brothers inherited the same traits. Alex, although an accomplished scientist in his own rite, is gifted in a different way. He leads a charmed life. We've been amazed at his ability to 'be not there' when the hammer drops."

"He drops hammers?"

Hayley laughed. "Forgive me, Sensei; it is an American expression meaning when danger is imminent. I've seen him 'be not there' during a hail of bullets and I've seen him do it in air-to-air combat. He almost seems invulnerable, yet I know it is merely talent accompanied by incredible luck. No, this child Coraline Paden is more than simply gifted or charmed. It's almost as if the universe itself gave birth to a child that embodies the next stage in human evolution. Those not like her will fade away like the dinosaurs."

"Ah. But you contradict yourself, Hayley. You said, on one hand the universe gave birth to this child, but on the other hand, you said the world is not ready for her. The world must be ready if she is truly a child of the universal field. But as you said, humans will always fear and resist what they do not understand. Perhaps this Coraline is here to teach us not to fear."

They paused before a shrine dedicated to a previous Master where the elderly monk offered incense. Hayley stood back and patiently waited for him to complete his ritual. Master Cheng moved respectfully to a shelf beneath the shrine and pulled out a neatly folded hand-embroidered sash from below a likeness of the deceased. He held it at arms-length for a moment before pressing it to his forehead, then turned to Hayley.

"This sash, or a copy of it, has been passed on from master to master of Shaolin for 14 centuries. Every living master is its keeper but may not wear it unless the previous master acknowledges while he was yet fit; his student surpassed and bested him. This sash has not been worn in eight centuries, until today."

Hayley was stunned. She could not form words for a few moments, looking from the sash to her master and back again. She even turned to the four witnesses standing silently behind her, hoping for support for what she was about to say.

"But Master Cheng, I can't be the Master of Shaolin! I...I cannot! I will not! I have tasks away from here. You have aged instructors who are more than worthy to take your place!"

"You misunderstand little one. The sash does not make

you Master of Shaolin. The sash merely indicates you have surpassed the master and bested him. It does not happen very often. You may take this sash with you in your tasks. We will have another made. If I am bested again, I will give that one away also. But none may wear this but those who have surpassed their living master while he is fit. Lastly, the wearer of this sash may open his or her own school."

"My own school?"

Master Cheng nodded. Hayley was relieved and humbled. She carefully wrapped the sash around her waist and tied it off with gratitude. While living in New Castlehale, she had continued her training through knowledge gained from books and ancient manuscripts, applying the techniques to the things she learned during her earlier years at Shaolin. She felt all her personal efforts now paid off, not just because of the sash, but because she had pleased Master Cheng. She leaned forward and hugged her teacher.

"And now, little one, please excuse me as I go about my duties. I suggest you go about yours."

They bowed and separated. She moved as if in a dream as she walked down the wide staircase. In a flurry of fresh thoughts, she wondered how the other instructors, some thirty or forty years her senior, would react when they laid eyes on the ancient sash. Many, whom she had grown close to, would celebrate with her. One or two felt she was even too young to be allowed to wear weapons in the presence of the Master. These would outwardly congratulate her yet begrudge her secretly.

Stepping into the courtyard, only one instructor noticed her initially. His eyes passed over the sash and continued on as if he had seen nothing out of the ordinary. The students glanced at it as she walked up and down each row, but no one understood the significance of the intricately woven sash. Stopping occasionally, she would give instruction to a trainee who was making obvious mistakes. Raising a fist here or kicking a calf muscle there to force a student into a wider stance, she kept an eye out for anyone entering the courtyard. Only once did a runner stop to relay a message to the class instructor and then hurry on. There was no acknowledgment whatsoever anything was different about her attire. Moving from courtyard to courtyard she would occasionally pause to inspect weapons-racks or watch the third-years spar. It wasn't until she reached the largest of the courtyards, where the advanced students were seated in neat rows before five elderly instructors, that she noticed the first iota of recognition. Master Cheng stood at the top of the steps with his advanced instructors looking down on the courtyard. He clapped his hands once as she approached the steps. All five ranking instructors, along with every student present, stood and bowed to Hayley. The Master clapped his hands again and the trainees moved to tighter rows in the center of the open area. From two directions, students came trotting into the large courtyard, Sarah among them, and made neat rows. With a grand gesture Master Cheng invited Hayley to stand at his right hand. She moved with deliberate strides to the spot indicated, then turned to face the filled courtyard as he spoke.

"This morning I ask you join with me in celebrating a remarkable event. The sash worn by Hayley Walsh has been passed down from master to master for hundreds of years for presentation only to individuals who have surpassed the Master of Shaolin while he is still fit. It has only been worn by two individuals in 14 centuries. This day, Hayley Walsh has earned the right to wear this sash. You all have been witness to her skill in defeating each of my instructors, and even her mastery at besting two of my instructors simultaneously. That is a feat rarely accomplished, yet this very morning I proudly acknowledge she bested me in a contest. These four guardians are my witnesses. Please honor her for her outstanding and rare accomplishment."

In unison, the assembly of teachers and students bowed yet again, then began to applaud and shout their congratulations. When the accolades subsided, he continued speaking.

"With this sash comes not only honor, but the great opportunity of opening her own school back in the United States, should she choose this path. To aid her in this task, I am offering her seven individuals to accompany her to her home in Texas. Those who would add their name for consideration will indicate so to your instructor. The final decision of choosing applicants will be Hayley's with my recommendations."

Sarah's face lit up. This changed everything, she thought. As happy as she was to train at Shaolin, she also missed her sweetheart. On top of that, if Hayley opens her own school, Sarah would be a pupil with favored status. It also meant they would be leaving Shaolin to return to Texas soon. Very soon.

CHAPTER THREE
HOME AGAIN

In what could only be described as a meteoric descent, the aircraft fell to earth at a rate that caused every fluid in the body to race toward the brain. The advanced hoverpad technology that allowed the aircraft to accomplish this maneuver also allowed Alex to arrest the seemingly reckless descent quickly and safely. Evelyn Walsh, even though warned ahead of time, still found the drop quite distasteful.

"Don't ever do that again when I am in this aircraft with you," she said with eyes closed and clutching her safety harness.

"Mom, you asked me to demonstrate the new hover technology's capabilities. Didn't you find that in the least bit exhilarating?"

"I did not."

"Okay. I'll pass the word to Hedgehog, Hayley, and Sarah when they get back. No rock-drops while the Queen is in the aircraft."

"Hedgehog executes this maneuver? Surely not!"

"Mom, this maneuver may one day save his life. I can think of several situations where it would mean the difference between living and dying."

Evelyn sighed deeply and shook her head. She wondered what it would be like to live a normal life. 'Well,' she thought, 'as normal as most citizens in the Void live.' The thought only lasted a few moments before she realized her children possessed the training, education, and technological edge to keep them alive and healthy. She would acquiesce to this *rock-drop*.

"Make sure he's fully trained before he attempts it, please," she said in resignation.

"Too late. He's the one who showed me how to do it."

The laugh came slowly but soon turned into the type that wouldn't stop because she had expended a mountain of emotions in her attempt to keep her children, including Hedgehog, in check when it came to risk-taking. The laughter, mixed with tears, was the realization that to continue would be an exercise in futility.

"That boy tries very hard to be just like you, Alex. Please be mindful of that at all times."

For his mother's sake, Alex executed a gentle turn into the canyon. Floating gracefully between the colorful stratified walls revealing ages of erosion and upheaval, he began checking for intruders who might be near the entrance to their hidden complex. In the decades since New Castlehale had been built, not one soul had ever discovered her secret location and they hoped to keep it that way.

"Vigilance," Alex said softly to himself.

Approaching the hanger bay entrance, the large, camouflaged doors slid back smoothly, allowing him to hover his aircraft into the gaping mouth set into the cliff wall. The formidable fighter moved carefully to the landing pad as three children came sprinting from the opposite door of the hanger bay.

The tallest of the young ones ran to a computer console nearby, making quick motions over the touch screen before he joined the others in the 'safe zone' marked off by paint on the concrete floor. The trio then waited patiently for Evelyn and Alex to deplane.

"Hedgehog, who is minding security while you're lollygagging on the flight deck?" Alex asked as he moved toward the group.

"It's Brian's watch, but I'm keeping an eye out."

Hedgehog thumbed over his shoulder to the wall monitor on which friend Brian could be seen waving into the camera. Evelyn and Adam had given Hedgehog permission to train his friend on the security systems to free up his own time for flight training. It was also a great opportunity for Brian. Working in the manufacturing labs was standard fare for most New Castlehale families, enriching residents by providing not only education but monetary gain far above the citizens who lived in the Void. However, being honored with an invitation to join Command might be a route to adventure. The chance of being invited to become a part of Command were greatly improved now that the needs were greater. Alex needed more pilots, more ground crew, and now the creation of an official ground force necessitated qualified soldiers. There was talk of recruiting from the settlements to bolster their numbers. Nick Hollings had already received several requests from seasoned Texas Rangers to become a part of the effort.

Hedgehog was very proud of his position as one of Alex's fighter pilots and it showed when he stood at attention. The transformation of the boy since being rescued in the desert over two years ago was astonishing. Coincidentally he was in a growing phase and seemed to add an inch to his height every month now. He was taller, but still very thin and wiry. The most notable change in him was his movements were no longer boyish. Lost was his youthful meandering and constant running up and down stairs and through the corridors. He now marched with a purpose, with a touch of Alex's swagger in each step, or so Sarah claimed. The Walsh family and New Castlehale staff immediately noted the difference in him after he actively participated in the air campaign during the Battle of Junction. He may not have engaged in a head-to-head dogfight as had Alex and Hayley, but he did chase down and destroyed several Tomahawk missiles in flight. The exciting things he had seen and done over the past year would mature any young person quickly. Having received medals from the Governor of Texas for his actions during the brief conflict, he wore them to the breakfast table for weeks until the family spoke to him about it.

Alex and his mom walked directly to the safe zone they themselves had created to prevent non-essential personnel from wandering onto the flight deck. Hedgehog, Coraline and Eli all received hugs from Evelyn.

The children and their mother Kate had been immediately welcomed into New Castlehale as family by the entire Walsh clan. And while both children missed their home in Llano, along with their favorite pastime of sitting in the branches of the great oak tree there, those things seemed a small price to pay for living in this secret underground dwelling. Besides the sunset views, which was mostly the purpose of tree-climbing, were even better sitting atop the tall mesa that formed the roof of their complex.

In addition to the great adventures and exciting places to run, play and even work in their new home, it was the residents of New Castlehale Coraline and Eli appreciated most. Eli had become good friends with Hedgehog and Brian, while Coraline was partial to spending time with Evelyn and Adam. There was a special bond between Evelyn and Coraline neither could explain, but they reveled in each other's company.

Adam was a different story. He was Coraline's fun big brother, a role he enjoyed since she was one of few who really got his humor. He could make Coraline laugh so deeply, its healing effect could be felt throughout the complex.

Coraline and Eli were now central to the dynamic of this underground community. Every soul in proximity to the tiny red-haired wisp of a girl experienced personal change. Evelyn noted without exception the residents made quantum leaps in mental capacity, learning, concentration, and creativity. The clarity of thought brought rapid advancements in both personal growth and scientific discovery.

Eli also was a major game-changer at New Castlehale. The medical doctor experienced the greatest change of all. Since Eli could heal with a touch, the doctor had no patients to deal with and was free to focus on research. He only asked that Eli allow him the opportunity to gather cultures from patients before and after healing from major diseases. There were plans underway to allow Eli and Coraline to leave the complex with the medical team to visit towns and settlements in the Void. Evelyn Walsh and Kate Jennings both insisted the doctor and his staff act as a front, so when diseased individuals come to them, any healing the children perform would appear to be the work of the team. Such was their concern for protecting the gifted pair.

"Is Adam okay?" Hedgehog asked.

"He's fine, sweetheart," Evelyn responded. "He was having lunch in Kermit when he ran into a few bad guys. He taught them a lesson in good manners and walked away without a scratch."

"He was hit by a bullet," said Coraline.

The group stood there for a moment, amazed she could know such things, but as always, they simply accepted the fact whatever she said, you could bet your life it was so.

Understanding the reason behind their facial expressions, Coraline said, "I just know. But it stopped on his backpack and broke his tablet."

"That's right, Little Ginger," said Alex. "The bottom line is, he's okay. He's helping a rancher make his property safe from bandits; he'll be home later this evening. Tomorrow he will return to Kermit to complete the task. Eli, Coraline, if you'd like to go with him, and it's okay with your mom, you can ride along to help; I'm sure he won't mind. Hedgehog, you'll be my wingman on escort duty to Kermit, then we fly a patrol mission that will include a brief stop in Junction for a meeting with Jennifer and Madison."

Evelyn added, "And I will approve this mission so long as Hedgehog is back by 1800 hours to do homework."

"Deal," replied Alex and Hedgehog in unison.

CHAPTER FOUR
RANGERS

Only the billions of stars that comprise the Milky Way, punctuated by Saturn and Jupiter, gave any light whatsoever to the night sky in the Nevada desert. In the years before the Cultural War, the city lights of Las Vegas, 83 miles to the southwest, created a glow that broke such dark nights considerably. The city never recovered from the destruction of that war, resulting in a reappearance of deep, velvety black, starry nights. In such absence of light, Nick Hollings' thermal camouflage fatigues and painted face made him practically invisible to the naked eye and thermal imaging equipment alike. This was not a guarantee he would not be discovered since they could use those devices to spot his equipment. This particular facility, the object of their mission, called Research and Development Command, is more commonly known as Area 51. To prevent RDC drone-mounted infrared cameras from detecting his equipment, he covered it with a material that rendered it invisible to nighttime detectors. The material was strapped to a collapsible frame that formed a mini-tent, wide enough to accommodate a sniper and spotter, and long enough to cover the barrel of his rifle.

Nick's spotter wore a pair of virtual-reality goggles that displayed live camera views of the buildings. The actual telescopic camera sat just inside the flap of the small tent pointed at the nearest building.

She whispered, "So, what's the deal with you and Evelyn?"

"You don't speak for six hours and that's the first thing you ask?" Nick said without taking his eye from the scope.

Ranger Madison Jameson smiled beneath her huge goggles. "Why not?"

"I can feel that grin on your face. I don't even have to see it; I feel it. But, if you must know, I'm not sure where things are between Evelyn and me. Several weeks after the celebration in Austin, she started acting differently towards me."

"How so?"

"I was under the impression we were beginning to be..." There was a pause.

"To be what?"

"You know."

"Pretend I don't. To be what?"

"An item."

"An item. There are so many ways to describe relationships and the best thing you can come up with is 'an item'."

"Sure."

"Well I have news for you, Ranger. You two are still an item. If you can't figure that out based solely on the way she looks at you, you need to have your head examined."

"If you say so."

"Of course, I say so. HOLD!" There was a pause before she continued. "Activity at the east door. Two guards exiting. One of them is Pete."

Nick cycled through the zoom feature on his rifle scope.

"Confirmed. That's Pete with his back to us. He's signaling. Subject alive. Sub-Level 4 East side. Plan B. Will exit in ten. Rendezvous waypoint 3."

"Plan B," murmured Madison. "If Pete recommends no forced entry, then they must have some pretty tight security in there."

"Would you have less?" Nick asked.

"No. I would not."

"Let's saddle up. Calling Remo Two," he said, stabbing

the small pad strapped to his left forearm with his finger. "ETA, 6 minutes."

"Roger that," she responded as she stripped the goggles from her head and stuffed them into a backpack. Together they disassembled the telescopic camera and stowed the components.

The vibration of their wrist devices indicated a drone would overfly their position in fifteen seconds. They remained perfectly still until the sound of the retreating drone faded. Another would not appear for ten minutes. If all went well, they would be long gone before then. The Rangers quickly collapsed their concealment kit and stuffed it into one of their packs, then knelt, weapons ready as they waited for Remo Two.

"I hate being out in the open like this," Madison whispered as she adjusted her position so she was back to back with Nick, both scanning the surrounding area with night vision. "All it would take is one unscheduled patrol to breeze by and we're toast."

"You mean, *they* are toast. Correct, Ranger?"

"Yeah. That's what I meant."

"Relax. The security here is nothing compared to what it was before the war. We wouldn't have gotten anywhere near here back in the day. They were on constant alert back then. Mostly to keep curiosity seekers out. A large number of people thought the government kept extraterrestrials here."

"Pah! Little did they know it would become a place to experiment on children. I can't wait to get in there."

"We'll get our chance. Plan first. Payback later. Here's our ride."

From the southeast, a saucer-shaped disc moved silently only a few meters above the sandy desert floor and glided to a stop just feet from their position. With a whispering swish, a door slid open and the Rangers jumped aboard. Stowing his gear and taking a seat, Nick took control at the console and the craft moved away into the darkness. The inside of the craft was dimly lit in a red glow, enough to reveal there were only four seats forward and an open area for cargo aft. With no pilot and no windows, Remo Two is an updated version of Remo One used to autonomously supply ground-troops during the battle of Junction. It was a remarkable test of New Castlehale technology during a time when the Central Government threw considerable military assets against them. This newer version used advanced hover-pad technology, making it much faster and much quieter than the prototype. Remo Two also had defensive capabilities which could be operated from within. Built for stealth and not maneuverability, the passenger's safety depends mostly on not being detected. Plasma guns notwithstanding, they knew they could never prevail in an eyes-on assault by armed fighter aircraft. Consolation hinged on the fact the chances of being spotted visually at night was almost zero.

Only a few minutes passed before they arrived at the designated coordinates, a low-lying area surrounded by small hills. From even a quarter-mile away, their aircraft was well-hidden.

When Remo touched earth, the door opened, both Rangers quickly moved to scan the perimeter. Satisfied there were no nearby threats, Nick moved to the top of the westward hill while Madison took east. Upon reaching the crest he began searching for signs of approaching vehicles. Touching his communication device, he spoke, "West clear."

"East clear."

"And now we wait."

"So, where were we?" Madison asked. "Oh, I remember. You needed to get your head examined."

"This is not the time, Maddie."

"To get your head examined?"

"You know what I mean."

"I do. But listen, Nick. Evelyn Walsh has grown rather attached to you and you need to get it through your thick skull. Right now, she's worried about the future. She wishes now she had never agreed to the whole awards ceremony in Austin last year. It painted a huge target on her and her family."

"Maybe so. But it also bought us some very strong allies. It cemented the relationship between New Castlehale, the State of Texas and the Texas Rangers. You know as well as I do there is not a Ranger or Texas Trooper alive who does not wish they could have been a part of the battle of Junction.

You and I are gods to them!"

"God and goddess."

"Whatever. Plus, the Texas Militia and the Void dwellers have begun joint construction of a base in Mason just to be closer to the action next time. They now have funding from the state of Texas to modernize and train new troops. That's a first. The next time the Central Government decides to send ground forces into the Void, they're going to face a little stiffer competition than a bunch of teenagers driving antique Abrams tanks."

"Those antiques kicked butt, I might remind you."

"How could I forget? Hell, I was there!"

Nick raised his binoculars to his face and clicked through the menu until he reached infrared. "Maddie, get over here. We've got company!"

Just above the horizon there appeared a sporadic flicker of light. It was very dim but easily detected using night-vision. After a minute or two, far off and traveling at a high rate of speed for a desert vehicle came a rider on a dirt bike. Driving over small hills the bike took air for several seconds before landing with perfected skill. The rider pushed his machine to its limit. A mile or two behind him were several helicopters, now using their spotlights and scouring the open expanse.

Madison moved to a position beside Nick and lifted binoculars to her face. "That's got to be Pete. Look at that guy. He's nuts!" said Madison.

"Tell me you wouldn't be doing the same with three helos after you. Get ready to move quickly. He'll be here in one minute. Open the large cargo bay. As soon as he's in, we're out of here."

"Roger that." She turned and ran down the short hill as fast as she could in darkness. As she approached the craft, she touched a button on her right forearm and two doors slid back. A ramp automatically extended to the ground, ready for the third Ranger to drive directly into the hold.

Nick continued to watch as Pete raced in at breakneck speed. "Pete, watch your speed as you top the next hill. We're at the base of the other side. Ramp is out."

"Yes sir, Captain."

The pursuing helicopters were only a mile out now. Nick ran down the hill and leaped into the saucer-shaped craft, strapping himself into a seat. Madison was already in the adjacent seat and had buckled her harness when Pete topped the hill. He drove straight up the ramp ducking low as he and his bike entered the cargo bay doors. Making sure the tires hit the brightly painted groove in the floor plates, he drove into a set of tire clamps. The bike was tightly secured even before he killed the engine. Diving into one of the remaining seats he yelled, "Go! Go! Go!"

Inside the craft the sound of power surging was loud and growing louder by the second. Outside the craft, except for the low, deep hum of the hover-pads there was very little sound created. The g-force applied to their bodies was gut-wrenching as Remo shot straight up into the air far faster than any helicopter could possibly follow. To his regret, Pete had voiced the go signal before he had completely buckled himself in. Now that they were ascending at an ever-increasing speed he could barely control his arm to complete the process. Madison attempted a laugh as she witnessed his inability to accomplish such a simple task, but her laugh ended up in her stomach. The ascent to 5000 feet took only a matter of seconds, but it seemed an eternity to those being pinned to their seats. They all knew it was a risky thing to take an aircraft this high so close to a military installation. Fighter jets would be scrambled immediately, if there was something to be seen on conventional radar. Because Remo was completely stealth, once they were away from the immediate threat of attack copters, they were invisible. The aircraft now slowed its ascent and turned east at cruising speed. Pete was finally able to snap the buckle on his harness and Madison was finally able to laugh.

"I thought you'd never get strapped in."

"I was thinking the same thing. You should have gotten out of your seat to help me."

"Not likely."

Nick rotated his seat to face the others as soon as he could. "Report!"

"Well, Captain," Pete answered as he removed his fake mustache, "Heather is alive. I can't speak for how well her captors have treated her over the past fifteen years, but if what I saw in the past couple of hours is any indication, we need to rescue her and every other soul in there."

Pete expected immediate questions but got none. Ranger Hollings' features were frozen, as if he had turned to rock and there was nothing in the universe more important than the thoughts running rapid-fire through his brain.

"I think things may change for the better for her after the new guy arrived from Washington D.C., one Dr. Harvey Tanner. This guy killed the man he was sent to replace! From what I saw, Dr. Doug Slater was one great big pile of smoldering ash by the time Tanner got through with him. Apparently, there was some disagreement about Slater's harsh treatment of the prisoners, and Tanner lit him on fire."

Both Nick and Madison scrunched their expressions, indicating half revulsion and half disbelief.

"I'm not kidding! That's what I was told. I saw the corpse myself. Anyway, I followed the new guy Tanner to a meeting room and from what I heard, our little war is not over. There are plans in the works to come after New Castlehale and those kids of ours."

"Okay. I want a detailed report," Nick said leaning forward. Everything you saw. Everyone you met. Everything you heard. I want a recommendation on a plan of rescue, and I want it in 24 hours. That'll give you time to get some sleep. I want you to remain in New Castlehale for the next few days."

"Yes sir, Captain."

"But right now, tell me what you know about my sister; what you heard and saw and how she looked."

Madison listened to Ranger Keller tell all he knew of Heather Hollings, but at the same time watched Nick's reactions closely. She worried about him. He'd had more than his share of grief in recent years

CHAPTER FIVE
WINGS OF AN EAGLE

Adam arrived home late in the night and proceeded to load his vehicle with the things he needed for the return to Kermit. He also put a few things in there he thought April and her mom might enjoy. After confirming his check-list, he crawled into bed only to awaken a few short hours later. He was anxious to start the day. After dressing in his most appealing work clothes, he strapped on his favorite large-caliber handgun and spare ammunition and looked in the mirror. He had never looked at himself in the mirror the way he was now seeing himself. In the past, his glances looked for changes in his muscle or body mass after a particularly hard work-out routine, with little thought as to how he appeared to women. Now he looked at his hair and wondered if he should keep it as is or do something different. He wondered if the handgun he carried was too large, perhaps giving a wrong impression. Shrugging his shoulders, he concluded it was the weapon he trusted, as well as the only one that truly fit his large hands. The other standard military or police side-arms seemed tiny in his massive paws. Satisfied, he exited his quarters and paused in the hallway to pat himself down one more to take a mental inventory of the things he carried on his person first thing each morning.

"Com-badge, gun belt, gun, spare ammo, watch, knife,

flashlight, backpack," he said to himself. "I'm ready to go now. This should be a good day. Better than yesterday catching a bullet in my tablet. But that was way worth it. And I'm talking to myself."

Lilly, the family cook and sometimes nanny, sang out a rousing Spanish ballad as she scrambled eggs for breakfast. Kate Jennings stood over another stove frying up bacon as Lilly's husband, Cholo filled pitchers with water and juice. The intense fragrance of freshly brewed coffee, bacon and biscuits in the oven permeated the mess hall. The Walsh family made it a habit to eat their meals together. This was a practice Evelyn was raised with and she saw it as instrumental in keeping a cohesive family unit.

As usual, Adam was the first of the family to the breakfast table. For the last few months he was almost always accompanied by his new buddy, Coraline. She climbed into the chair beside him, watching every move he made as he poured juice for them both.

"What are you grinning at baby sister?" he asked as he slid the apple juice over to her.

"I'm grinning at you, Gulliver. You seem to be in a big hurry today. Are we going to see anyone special?" she asked as she pushed her plate toward him. "Toast please."

"Yes, I'm seeing you. You're special, aren't you?"

"I am special. But not special-special," she said with a giggle.

He easily reached the stack of toast in the middle of the table and plopped one onto her plate, then scooped up the butter and jam to place before her. "I'm sure I don't know what you're referring to."

"I'm sure you do."

"I'm sure I don't."

She poked him in the ribs with her tiny finger. "Yuh huh."

Adam quickly wrapped his massive arm around her head and held it there as he tapped the red hair on top. "Nuh UH."

"Mmmm hmmmm."

"Spit it out, baby sister. What do you think you know?"

She sang the words, "Adams in luh-uv. Adams in luh-uv."

He peaked under his arm to see her pretty, smiling eyes peering up at him.

"Okay. But don't tell anyone. It's our secret, agreed?"

"It'll cost you."

"What?"

"I'll tell you just before we leave to see your girlfriend," she said as others began to enter the mess hall.

Hedgehog and Eli sat down at the table on the other side of Coraline, who was still smiling and humming a tune to, "Adam's in luh-uv."

"When are we leaving to see your girlfriend?" Hedgehog asked as he watched Lilly put a plate of bacon and eggs before him.

"We've not reached the point yet to call her my girlfriend, Hedgehog," Adam said before shoving an entire slice of toast into his mouth.

"Yes, but we've reached the point you're driving for hours a day just to see her," said Alex as he and Evelyn walked into the mess hall. "And to answer your question, Hedgehog, we're wheels up at 0900 hours."

A mouth full of eggs prevented Hedgehog from giving Alex a verbal response so he resorted to a simple thumbs-up.

Evelyn walked directly behind Hedgehog and leaned over to whisper loudly, "Hedgehog, please do not stuff your mouth like a pig! You've got plenty of time to eat before you leave. Just slow down and enjoy your breakfast. We're civilized here and will remain so."

Because his mouth was so filled with breakfast, he could only respond with a questioning grunt sound as he pointed at Adam, who had a mouth full himself. Adam quickly swallowed and turned to Hedgehog.

"Mom's right. Don't do as I do. Do as she says."

Lilly whacked Adam with the large wooden spoon which was never absent from her apron pocket. As usual, this resulted in an intense burst of laughter from Eli and Coraline.

Adam, who was eager to change the subject to something other than his eating habits or April Brice, asked,

"Mom, what's Ranger Hollings up to? We haven't seen him in weeks!"

Evelyn was not pleased with the sudden change in topic. Her expression communicated everything Adam needed to know. Adam leaned over to Coraline, who was daintily spreading jam over her toast and began humming the tune that would have gone perfectly with "Mah-ahm's in luh-uv. Mah-ahms's in luh-uv." Coraline smiled as she kicked him under the table.

Evelyn Walsh, who misses nothing, saw the exchange between Adam and Coraline. It was with a touch of exasperation she responded to his question. "Nick is wrapping up personal business; then he'll be back here for a while. I spoke with him briefly four days ago."

"What business is that?" Alex asked as he scooped fresh fruit onto his plate.

"Personal business."

Adam recognized the grave concern in her voice and countenance and concluded it would be best to let it go. "The equipment we need for the trip to Kermit is already loaded up and ready to go. I have only to meet with the engineers in Lab 3 at 0800 hours for a briefing on a new asset; then I'll meet you all at the vehicle at 0845. Eli and Coraline, pack your tablets in case you get bored."

Eli being anxious to speak, raised his hand as if he were in a classroom.

Evelyn smiled for the first time since she walked into the dining facility. "You don't have to raise your hand to speak at the breakfast table, Sweetie. This is not the classroom. What is it?"

"Is my mom coming with us?"

"Yes, dear. She is. Isn't that right Kate?"

"Yes, I'm happy to tag along! I love riding in that beastie thing Adam drives. It's like a luxury tank! I'll be waiting with the rest of you at 8:45. Evelyn, is there anything I can bring? A snack pack for instance? Sandwiches?"

"That would be lovely! Please coordinate with Lilly since she's already preparing a food package we'll take along."

Kate Jennings loved being included in the Walsh family plans. Living in New Castlehale was not only socially rewarding for her, but also exposed her decades-old, self-imposed, glass ceiling. Living with people who never stop learning causes one to take note of one's own personal growth. She woke every morning with a keen sense of gratitude for being allowed to remain with this family, especially after they risked life and limb to break her out of her prison cell in Oklahoma.

Breakfast went quickly since everyone had something important to do before they left for Kermit. Adam leaned over and spoke softly over Coraline's head of flaming red hair.

"So, tell me now, baby sister, what cost you have in mind to keep my secret."

"Not so secret."

"Okay. Tell me now what cost you have in mind to keep my not so secret."

She gently folded her napkin and placed it on the table, then stood next to Adam's chair and cupped her hand next to his ear and whispered. He had been carefully wiping his hands with his napkin but slowed to an absolute stop as he took in her proposal. Eyes wide and eyebrows up, he turned to face her and made her stand right in front of him with his hands pinning her arms.

"You are NOT going to try this," he said whispering quietly.

"I've already tried it, and it works. I just want to surprise everyone with it."

Adam's eyes took in each family member at the table and thought he will certainly have his butt in a sling for knowing this ahead of time and not saying anything.

"Are you sure about this?"

"I'm sure. Remember where to stop and wait for me."

"Alright, Coraline. I don't have to tell you mom and Kate are not going to like it. Me? I'm going to enjoy the heck out of it. Especially if it works," he said winking at her.

The flight deck echoed voices coming from those patiently waiting near Adam's vehicle rightly referred to as the Beast, as the last of the provisions and gear were being packed into its spacious cargo bay. Adam was bent over placing each item in its predetermined spot as Kate read off the checklist. Organization was a rule with this family. Food items were neatly arranged in a refrigerated section of the compartment while the rest were fastened down in separate boxes. Secured to the inside of the cargo hatch itself were two rifles, a grenade launcher, a large fully-automatic shotgun, and enough ammunition to hold off a small army.

"Ok guys, back up a bit," Adam said as he prepared to close the hatch. "We're good to go. Mom rides shotgun. Mrs. Jennings and Eli in the back."

"Where is Coraline?" Evelyn said as she looked around the vehicle.

"Oh. Uh, Coraline is outside the complex. We'll pick her up down by the draw on our way out."

"What's she doing out there?" Kate asked.

"She said it was important. We'll find out when we get there," Adam muttered quickly, trying not make eye contact.

Interrupted by a low-frequency beep, every head turned to watch for the arriving aircraft as the large landing bay doors slid aside. To Evelyn's delight and dismay, Remo Two hovered across the threshold. She felt delighted because she knew Nick might be on board. Her dismay was due to fear something could have gone wrong with the mission and his well-being was never guaranteed. The strangely shaped craft floated four feet above the floor with a pulsating deep hum to a spot adjacent to the safety zone, settled down and automatically cut the engines. Three Texas Rangers stepped out and onto the flight line. Adam heard his mother catch her breath when she caught sight of Captain Hollings.

"We weren't expecting such a grand reception!" said Madison.

"Maddie, you all deserve a grand reception whether it was planned or not!"

Not knowing the nature of the mission, Adam asked, "I'm guessing your trip was a success?" he asked.

"Mostly successful. We couldn't rescue my sister, but Pete came out with good intel," replied Nick. His eyes had not left Evelyn once since stepping out of the aircraft, and she reciprocated. This was not lost on Madison who whispered the word "item" to Nick as he moved forward to hug Evelyn. His facial expression did not change a bit.

"We were about to embark for Kermit. You are all more than welcome to come along with us," said Adam as he shook hands with Pete and Madison.

"As much as we'd love to join you," said Nick with a quick glance at his Rangers, "The sergeant has a report to write, Maddie is needed in Junction and I have a teleconference with headquarters and we could all use a couple of hours shut-eye. Will you be there most of the day? I may be able to join you later."

Evelyn's eyes lit up. Even a casual observer could tell this was the best news she'd heard in days. "That would be wonderful, Nick! You can find us on faux-GPS. We've brought enough food for lunch and dinner, so yes, we'll be there for a while. You should be able to get a few hours of sleep and make it in plenty of time for supper tonight, then ride back with us in the Beast. Now that we have Remo Two back, we can deliver a care-package to the new base in Mason today, and you, Nick, can hitch a ride if you don't mind riding with the cargo."

Adam spoke up. "Maddie, Flyers One and Three will be escorting us to Kermit, then proceeding to Junction. You can ride with one of them if you're ready to go now."

"That'd be perfect! Thank you!"

"What would be perfect?" asked Alex as he and Hedgehog strode through the entry arch wearing the new flight suits designed for handling g-forces.

"I get to fly with one of you to Junction."

"Fly with me!" shouted Hedgehog.

"Now wait just a minute," Alex replied leaning down over Hedgehog. "I'm in command here. I'll decide who flies with whom," said Alex as he pointed to the rank insignia on his collar.

"What? I don't get a choice in this matter?" asked Madison.

"Oh. Yes. Please do," replied Alex with a sheepish look.

Madison dug deep into a vest pocket and produced a coin. Flipping it high into the air she caught it and slapped it onto the back of her other wrist. Peaking beneath her hand she said, "I ride with Hedgehog."

"That's decided, so let's saddle up! We are wheels up in 5 minutes," said Alex winking at Madison. Hedgehog turned to jog away towards his flyer, waving Madison to follow.

"Alex! Can I talk to you for just a second before you go?" Adam said as he took his brother by the arm, leading him a few feet away from the others.

"I'll see you later," said Nick as he gave Evelyn one more hug, who in return whispered, "I was worried. I missed you."

"I missed you too. We'll talk later."

From an observer's standpoint it was hard to tell who kissed who, but the fact is both Evelyn and Nick had the notion at the exact same moment. They kissed softly for two seconds. Everyone watched. Two seconds doesn't sound like a particularly long span of time but count it out for yourself and imagine kissing the person you have fallen in love with. Those two seconds can carry you emotionally through a bad day, or week, or month. Kate Jennings teared up. Eli sensed the overwhelming wave of grief she felt over the absence of her own husband and took her hand. Madison watched the kiss from her perch on the wing of Flyer Three. She turned to Hedgehog and said, "Item." Hedgehog responded with, "Yuk" as he donned his flight helmet. Adam and Alex, who had stopped their conversation, stared with half-smiles on their lips.

After he finished his conversation with Adam, Alex shouted out, "Let's saddle up, people! We've got citizens of the Void waiting on us! We've got goods to deliver! We've got people depending on us." He turned to Hedgehog, waiting patiently in his cockpit and gave a twirling wave of his index finger. Flyer Three's engines came to life as Alex made a dash to Flyer One.

Adam made one more check of his sidearm before getting behind the wheel of the Beast. After making sure the passenger doors were secured, he checked his own, buckled his harness and spoke to those in the back seat. "Is everyone ready? Eli? Did you bring everything you wanted?" he asked while looking into the mirror.

"I did," Eli responded. "All we need to do is remember to pick up Coraline."

"On that topic, Adam, what exactly is she doing outside

the complex by herself? You failed to tell me that," asked Evelyn.

A bead of sweat rolled down Adam's brow as he replied, "Mom, I think it'd be best if she just surprised you. I'd rather not say a thing until she shows us her, uh... discovery."

"Why do I have the feeling I'm not going to like this surprise at all?" Evelyn asked.

"Eli?" Interrupted Kate, "Do you know what Coraline is up to?"

"I don't, Mom. She only told me she discovered something she said was 'delightful'."

Adam watched in his side mirror while both flyers hovered toward the hanger bay doors, then turned over the engine of the powerful desert vehicle. He had made modifications to the Beast over the past few months that transformed an already formidable vehicle into something akin to a comfort battle-tank. It was faster, had thicker armor, more effective weapons, and a surprise only he and three technicians down in the labs knew about.

Just thinking about it made him smile to himself as he steered toward the ground exit. The tunnel leading to the outside was eerily lit by red LEDs that flashed by as the Beast picked up speed. Long before they reached the doors, the four-inch-thick steel panels receded into a space cut from solid rock to accommodate them. At nine o'clock in the morning the west side of the complex was still deep in the shadows of the towering mesa above. Every neck in the vehicle was straining to see the dry creek bed ahead in hopes of finding Coraline. It didn't take long to cover the quarter-mile distance to the draw where Adam stopped the vehicle.

"This is where we get out and watch," Adam said with a touch of concern in his voice. Evelyn picked up on that concern as she opened her door. Every eye was fixed on the two flyers hovering nearby. Alex and Hedgehog remained 100 feet off the rocky terrain with only fifty feet between them.

"Where is she?" Evelyn demanded.

Adam simply pointed to the top of the mesa. Each of them turned to the spot he pointed. All were appalled to see the tiny girl standing on the edge of the cliff waving down at them from hundreds of feet above.

"What is she going to do, Adam?" asked Mrs. Jennings. "What is she doing up there?"

"Just watch."

Back-lit by the morning sun, Coraline's silhouette was easily discerned even from this distance. She spread her arms and held her hands up as if she were going to fly.

"Oh, God, no. Please don't tell me she's going to try to fly," said Evelyn. "Adam, you contact her and tell her to wait there for Alex to pick her up. You do it right now."

"It's too late, Mom. Watch."

Eli recognized what was about to happen before anyone else because he had done something similar with Coraline when they created energy bubbles to travel/float across central Texas during their escape from government searchers. The difference here though was instead of a bubble to ride in, she generated energy fields in the shape of a large bird's wings. As Coraline's arms were held out, the marvelous translucence of those wings was revealed when the morning rays refracted into bright and beautiful colors. Flapping two or three times to get a feel for them, she leapt head-first from the cliff and dropped precipitously toward the earth below with her wings trailing behind her. Except for Eli, they were all horrified by what they were witnessing. The Jewel of Texas seemed doomed to certain death on the rocks below until she spread her wings and pulled out of the dive, soaring high into the air above them. She flew directly between the two flyers whose pilots and passenger sat with wide-eyed astonishment. Both pilots immediately landed their aircraft to watch what was happening from solid ground.

Mixed with the slight sound of the morning breeze came the intense laughter of a child relishing every moment of her mysterious and awe-inspiring exhibition. At the sound of Coraline's laughter, every person present cheered with glee after witnessing human flight that was not dependent on a human-made device manufactured from textile, wood, or steel. Coraline performed a barrel-roll and loop before turning toward the group of thoroughly amazed friends and family. She came in like an attacking eagle, fast and silent.

As she neared their position, she opened her wings to check her speed and with a great show of bird-like behavior, she settled to earth gently only fifteen feet from them.

There was silence for a few moments before the entire group surged towards her to cover her with hugs and kisses. Kate and Evelyn were hugging each other while Adam knelt before her and pulled her to himself in a tender hug. He swept her up and threw her onto his shoulder.

"That was magnificent, baby sister! I knew what was going to happen, and I'm still in shock!"

"That was SO much fun. I know we don't have time now, but later I'll show you guys how to do it!"

That got their attention.

"But sweetheart, we … well … we don't have your gifts! There's no way!" said Kate.

"I can help you," she said looking down on the astonished bunch. "I didn't know I could teach others to do the things I do until I found I was able to share with Hayley a gift which makes her unbeatable in a fight. She kind of had it in her already, but I awakened it. You all have this in you. I'm sure of it."

They exchanged looks of uncertainty and dismay. Adam shook his head and said, "If anyone can make us fly, Little Ginger, you can. I'm so proud of you! Now, let's get on the road!"

"Yah. Let's go. We shouldn't let the little missus (meaning April) wait on her precious sugar-booger, now can we?" said Alex as he gestured for Hedgehog and Madison to follow.

"Sugar-booger!!!" shouted Hedgehog as he laughed uproariously. That is until he caught sight of Adam and Coraline giving him the eye. Madison thwacked him with a finger and reminded him, "Don't you have piloting to do?"

CHAPTER SIX
THEY NEVER LEARN

Spending the better part of every day in a windowless bunker is not high on anyone's list of desirable work activities, but Skank seemed to thrive in this environment. His few friends had been extremely concerned about his emotional state during the Battle of Junction, when he was buried for two days under the rubble of the Trading Post with the odd-ball woman named Pearl. An air strike by federal aircraft collapsed the entire structure on top of the entrance to the steel-reinforced basement. Because radio contact with Skank confirmed he and Pearl were safe and sound, rescuers in Junction focused their efforts on those whose fates were uncertain. When they finally got around to clearing the entrance to his bunker, he came out for five minutes to see what kind of damage had been done to the town, then went right back down there. Skank is a special person.

Wearing his trademark headband with binocular loupes and LED lights, he peeked around the large pile of electronic components to see what his friend and now co-worker Pearl was going on about.

"Skank, I'm lookin' at a couple of fellas out front and they don't look like they're from around here."

He slid in behind her to see her monitor screen, placing his hands on her shoulders. Her eyes glanced down at the dirty fingernails draped there, but her countenance betrayed the fact she might be slightly stimulated. In her 32 years of life, she'd never actually had a man voluntarily put hands on her, so this was a treat. Not being accustomed to smiling in public, due mainly to the fact she only had five or six good teeth in her head, she allowed herself a brief smile before she resumed her closed-mouth glee.

"You got that right, Pearl. That suit probably cost more than everything I own."

"Including your engraved Colt Python?"

"Including that."

One didn't encounter shark-skin suits very often in Junction or any other settlement in the Void. A person would more likely cross paths with someone wearing scuba-gear on a mountaintop. Skank took note of the way these two loitered out front and took a disliking to the furtive over-the-shoulder glances. Removing his headband, he tossed it aside and retrieved an old sawed-off pump shotgun from the rack. Cycling a round into the chamber, he turned to Pearl as he added one more shell to the magazine tube.

"Stay down here. Button up as soon as I'm out."

"You bet. Do I call Jennifer?" She drew her own side-arm and pulled the slide back far enough to see the round in the chamber.

"No. I'll take care of this. And I meant what I said. Holster that pistol and stay here. No matter what, you stay down here."

"You bet, Skank."

Exiting the bunker, he stood for a moment and waved at the camera. The steel doors slid back into place, turning it into a locked fortress once again. He took a moment to drink in the beauty of the new Trading Post, which had sprung up quickly from the ashes of the old.

The materials used in rebuilding were donated by the State of Texas at the request of the Governor himself; Red granite exterior, harkening to the Capitol offices in Austin, mosaic tiles brought from Spain, solid oak counters and hand-crafted shelves. This new structure was larger and taller than the old Trading Post with a helipad on the roof and actual air-conditioning.

In gratitude for what the citizens of Junction had done defeating the technologically-advanced armed forces of the Central Government, the State of Texas rebuilt not only the Trading Post but the Town Hall as well. The Governor made sure truckloads of lumber and building materials were delivered for the repair of any and every home damaged in the battle. In addition, a new water tower stood at the town's center as well as five large windmills to supply the town with a clean source of electricity, enough to alleviate the usual brown-outs common to Junction. The State of Texas also saw fit to build a tall steel communications tower that included an active radar system and an observation post now manned 24/7. If any of the nefarious gangs scattered through the Void had been desirous of taking over this town before, they were nose-deep in jealousy now.

Skank walked onto the sales floor where Stan and Marcia Burroughs were organizing products on the new shelves. He beckoned for the two new employees to get behind the counter. Before they could reach it, the heavy oak doors swung inward as two men meandered into the store. The first took a position next to the front windows as if to keep watch while the other walked to the back sporting a wide yet disingenuous smile.

"Good morning."

"What can I do for you?" asked Skank as he fingered the shotgun hidden under the counter.

"I need to speak to the owner of this establishment. Is she here?"

"Who's asking?"

It was evident the man was not accustomed to being questioned by shopkeepers yet persisted in his temporary politeness.

"My name is Arturo Ramos."

"And your business with the owner of The Trading Post is..."

"Between me and the owner."

"Well, why didn't you say so before!" said Skank with a huge grin as he drew the shotgun from under the counter and pointed it at Arturo Ramos' head. The man standing near the door reacted by pulling a handgun from his waistband but was countered by weapons pointed at him by both Stan and Marcia, neither of which looked uncomfortable with the current confrontation.

A small bell tinkled, indicating someone entering the front door. The man who was supposed to be keeping watch for Arturo turned just in time to see the business end of a rather large heavy handgun, which was the last thing he saw before being knocked unconsciousness.

"Skank, why do I come back to find an armed stand-off in my brand-new Trading Post?" asked Jennifer as she moved quickly behind Arturo, relieving him of his 9mm pistol.

"Your question is better answered by Mr. Sharkskin here. He claims to have business with you."

"My name is Arturo Ramos, and I..."

"Shut up," Jennifer said, cutting him off as she reached for the communication device on her belt.

"Command post to tower."

"This is tower, go ahead."

"Perry, go to condition Yellow. I want a report in two minutes."

"Roger that," came the crackly response.

"I know who you are Mr. Ramos."

Arturo Ramos did not like the sound of that. Casting a nervous glance between Jennifer and Skank's 12-gauge shotgun, he asked, "If you know who I am, then you'll know I'm just a small fish in a big pond. Why go to yellow alert for such a small fish?" he asked with a slimy charm. Jennifer never took her eyes from him.

"Skank. What do you use small fish for?"

"Bait."

"That's right. Bait." Jennifer glanced at the camera in the corner of the room. "Pearl?"

"Yes ma'am?"

"Pearl, don't call me ma'am. Just Jennifer, thank you. What do you see on the road?"

"Just our patrols."

"Get the Sheriff down here. Tell him we have two guests for his little steel bed and breakfast. Also, run our friend Arturo Ramos here through the state database and display here in the store."

"Will do, Jennifer."

"Skank, I'll take care of Mr. Ramos here while you fingerprint his friend. Take them to Pearl. Let's find out as much as we can about our mystery guest on the floor there."

"You've got to know my boss will never allow me to stay in your jail cell for even one night. They will come here in force to get me out, and you think you're prepared for that, but you're not," Arturo said at almost a shout.

"I reckon you haven't been keeping up with current events, Art. May I call you Art? We successfully fought off an entire Federal armored battalion protected by attack fighters, helicopters, and survived Tomahawk cruise missiles. Do you honestly think we're going to quake in fear of seeing a Chevy full of outlaws?"

"How did you recognize me? We've never met."

"I collect wanted posters as a hobby, little fish. Just so happens I read yours yesterday."

"I didn't come here for trouble. I was sent here to work a deal with you, but no one told me I'd have to deal with a n..."

Jennifer reached out and clamped her fingers around his neck, effectively cutting off his air supply as she lifted him just high enough to keep his toes from touching the floor. Frantically grasping her arm and wrist in a feeble attempt to escape her grip, he began turning a shade of deep blue. He tried his best to say "stop," but he couldn't.

"You were just about to call me something that will upset me. You don't want to see me upset. Now, when I set you down, you will finish that sentence with more respect. Do you understand me? Just nod your head."

The nod was vigorous. After setting him down, she made a concerted effort to smooth out the wrinkles in the shiny new suit and generally aid in bringing him back to a state of equilibrium.

"Good, we understand each other now, Art."

There was more vigorous nodding by the snappily-dressed man as Maria and her husband exchanged a relieved glance. They had seen Jennifer react to that sort of racism in the past and were glad this one might have a happier ending.

"Now tell me again what you were about to say," she said with a manufactured smile.

"I was about to say I did not know that you were a black woman. That's all."

"Now why would my color make a bit of difference, Art?"

"I'm sorry. My bad. I just came to deliver the message from my boss."

"Apology accepted. Now, who is your boss, and what is the deal?"

"My boss is Jesus Carrillo. You may remember that you killed his brother last year."

"I did not actually see the man die, but I did get to witness his entire compound disappear in a cloud of fire and smoke. One of the highlights of my life," she said with a sigh. "What does Jesus want?"

"Jesus wants payback in a bad way, but he is willing to give up his desire to avenge his brother for some favors."

Jennifer's face lit up in a beautiful smile. "Favors. Well you know, it's good to know that in order to stop this incessant quaking in our boots, all we need do is grant Jesus some favors. Please, tell me it's not that easy!"

Arturo knew sarcasm when he saw it, and he did not take it well. He scowled at Jennifer and the Burroughs', but knew he was in no position to do anything about the obvious rejection of his boss' offer. "Yes. It's that easy. I have not even told you what favors he seeks! He only wants one thing really."

"And what would that be?" she asked leaning forward.

"He wants the large black desert vehicle that launched the rockets the night his brother died."

"Is that all?" she asked looking to Skank for a reaction.

"That's all. And if he doesn't get it by the next full moon, he'll take his revenge on some small, unsuspecting town; then he'll move on to the next town and so on until he feels we're even. If I don't return with a response within 48 hours, he'll begin. Their blood will be on your head."

"Pearl! Is the Sheriff on his way?"

"Yes ma'am. He's pulling in now."

"Well, Mr. Ramos. Thank you for that information and now I am going to turn you and your friend there over to the town Sheriff. He'll give you a place to sleep and three squares until we decide what to do with you."

"Remember, you have 48 hours," Ramos said with a sneer.

The thick oak doors opened as the sheriff with a deputy in tow stepped into the trading post. The no-nonsense, seasoned lawman stepped over the unconscious man on the floor and asked without even a hint of a smile, "Did I come at a bad time?"

The deputy stood shaking his head as he nudged the man on the floor with the toe of his boot. "They just never learn, do they?"

Just then the loud-speaker came on and Pearl's voice sounded clearly in the Trading Post. "Jennifer, we've got an unidentified aircraft coming in from the east."

CHAPTER SEVEN
DISTRACTED

Adam always enjoyed road trips with the family, and especially since his newly acquired baby sister Coraline arrived. The two of them teased each other incessantly while Eli rolled with tearful laughter at their antics. Every soul in New Castlehale loved these tease sessions for no other reason than to hear Coraline's healing laughter.

When the luxury desert vehicle of Adam's was ten minutes from Kermit, Command at New Castlehale transmitted a warning concerning an unidentified aircraft approaching Junction from the west.

"Coyote to Roadrunner."

"Roadrunner. Go."

"We should check that bogey."

"We agree, Coyote, but leave Hedgehog with us. We'd feel safer if he was overhead. Besides, he's got Maddie backseat," Adam replied at the prompting of his mom.

"Negative, Roadrunner. Radar shows only one bogey lit up, but there may be hidden aircraft. I recommend he fly my wing, passenger or not. If you get into trouble, we'll be on top of you in no time."

Adam turned to his mom. "I think he's right, Mom. Besides, if anything were to happen at either location, Hedgehog will be a lot safer with Alex than he could be flying over us with no wingman."

Evelyn nodded reluctantly.

"Coyote, the Queen acknowledges your plan. We'll be fine."

"Roger that. Hedgehog, bat-turn and go buster."

"Affirmative Coyote. I'm on your wing. Maddie, hang on tight!"

Both aircraft made high-g turns toward Junction to the southeast. Hedgehog checked a cockpit mirror to check on Madison, who for the first time since he'd known her looked a little shaken. "Ranger Maddie, are you going to be okay?"

"Just do your thing, Hedgehog. Pretend I'm not here and do whatever you have to do."

"Roger that."

This was Hedgehog's chance to go head to head with a possible manned aircraft, yet there was no trace of fear in him. They were only minutes from striking distance as Hedgehog worked furiously running scans.

"Coyote, I just ran a full-spectrum. I'm only seeing the one bogey."

"Roger that, Hedgehog. I've got this bird painted and it appears to be a bot."

"Coyote, I've got lock. Permission to fire."

"Flight, this is Command. Let's get a visual first before you shoot."

"Roger that, Command. Hedgehog, go right. I'm going straight in."

Alex flew straight for the ROA (remotely operated aircraft) while Hedgehog maneuvered for a shot from behind.

"Affirmative. It's a bot. Command, Hedgehog has his fangs out."

"Roger that, Coyote. You are cleared to engage."

Hedgehog fired a short burst from his plasma cannons and the unmanned craft exploded and fell from the sky. Although he gained a lot of satisfaction at shooting down the unmanned aircraft, it just wasn't the same as shooting down the Tomahawk missiles last year. This felt more like target practice than anything else. It was with less than total excitement that Hedgehog radioed his success.

"Boola-Boola. Bird is down."

"Way to go, Nugget!" shouted Alex. "Now, Stay on station. I'm taking her down to investigate the wreckage."

Alex followed the fluttering debris to the ground, then performed a low pass over the scattered pieces. There appeared to be no markings whatsoever on the fuselage or wings. Meanwhile, Hedgehog was searching the skies with eyes and radar when an alert tone sounded loudly in his headset.

"Warning. Ground to air missile locked on," came the voice through his headset. Hedgehog's display indicated the direction as his aircraft began dispensing chaff and flares. Turning hard to starboard, he searched intently for the ascending missile.

Madison held tightly as he went through these maneuvers. Her only words were, "Oh God," as she spotted the ascending missile.

"Hedgehog, when it's close, pucker up and use your hoverpads as you out-turn it!" shouted Alex. "Wait on it!"

"I know! I know! I've been here before, remember!"

"Wait on it!"

"I know!"

The aircraft spewed chaff and flares generously as a gut-wrenching maneuver kicked Hedgehog's fighter so far from the blast there was zero chance of damage.

"We're okay!!" he screamed as he turned immediately into the direction of the launcher just as another ground to air missile was launched. The memory of the day he and Hayley came under this same attack gave him total confidence as he prepared two missiles: One for the approaching SAM and one for the launcher.

"Hammer away." He counted to three before he launched an air-to-ground high-explosive warhead. Watching his display carefully, he counted the seconds. "Three, two, one, boom." There was flash below as he allowed his plane to drift starboard to ascertain whether the missile would continue to track him. It didn't. Flying in weird spirals it sailed harmlessly past, having had all its electronics fried by the Hammer. His high-explosive missile continued toward the launcher, but seconds before it hit its mark, the launcher along with two other trucks disintegrated in a large ball of flame. If anything survived that hit, it certainly didn't after Hedgehog's missile followed up with a second horrendous blast. Alex's flyer passed over the carnage only a few seconds later.

"Hedgehog, that was excellent flying. Couldn't have done better myself. Looks like our Federal friends are back."

"Don't you mean they *were* back?" replied a smiling Hedgehog.

"Roger that, they are history. Stay on station. I'm going down for a quick look."

"Roadrunner to Hedgehog."

"This is Hedgehog. Go ahead."

"Is Madison okay?"

"She's doing great, Roadrunner. We're fine."

With a sick look on her face, Madison looked out onto the horizon and said to herself, "Yeah. I'm just peachy."

Alex descended to the semi-arid terrain as his wingman circled high overhead keeping an eye out for threats. As he neared the wreckage he noted there were no markings on the pieces scattered over hundreds of feet. Unlike the video footage from Hayley's encounter with mobile anti-aircraft vehicles, he saw no bodies. Something seemed very wrong. Hovering slowly over the area he took a mental note of how easy a target he would be from anyone on the ground and was already in the process of leaving when his headphone screeched a warning. He had no time to glance at his display before his aircraft rocked from a loud explosion, jarring him in the cockpit. Desperately, he fought the controls to keep from crashing to earth. He knew one of his hoverpads was toast. The aircraft bucked and spun like a helicopter without a tail rotor for a few seconds before he could regain better control.

"I'm hit! Mayday! Mayday!"

From above Hedgehog and Madison watched as Flyer One spun out of control, belching flame and smoke. He instinctively moved his aircraft closer to Alex.

"I'm coming down!" said Hedgehog.

"NO! Don't come down. I've got this!" said Alex.

With a helpless feeling, Hedgehog and Madison watched Alex fighting to stay in the air. A second missile was launched, taking out the aircraft's rudder and a second hoverpad. This time Hedgehog saw the origin of the rocket. He quickly lined up on that location and unleashed a torrent of plasma rounds and high explosive rockets. There were no more missiles coming from that area. As he banked, there was a horrendous explosion from Alex's location. He turned only in time to witness a thousand pieces of Alex's aircraft falling to earth.

"Command, this is Hedgehog. Coyote is down! Coyote is down!"

CHAPTER EIGHT
BRICE RANCH

The desert vehicle skidded to a stop on the graveled area in front of the Brice home. The front passenger door flew open as an emotionally distraught Evelyn Walsh exited. Frantically, she thumbed her communication device.

"Queen to Hedgehog, come in!"

"Hedgehog. Go ahead, Queen."

"Did Coyote eject safely?"

"We don't know. He was very close to the ground when his flyer exploded. We saw no chute, but he may have already reached the ground. If he ejected, he was low when he did it. We're searching now."

"If he is hurt, you pick him up and fly him here as fast as you can. Seconds count, Hedgehog. Please hurry."

April Brice burst from the Brice home, sprinting to Adam who was already busy tossing things around inside the open rear hatch. As she reached him she threw her arms wide for a hug but was handed a plasma rifle instead. A look of hurt appeared on her face for a moment but changed when he said, "Get this to your dad and fetch him here. We have trouble." She turned to run to the house with the rifle without asking another question. She barely covered a few yards as the force of a powerful explosion knocked her to the ground. The barn had been turned to matchsticks by a missile launched from an aircraft. Every head turned to the west to see an Osprey coming in low, weapons firing. Adam yelled for everyone to stay in the Beast as he dove behind the wheel. Tires spinning, he positioned the vehicle next to April to block the incoming fire as she struggled to regain her feet. He jumped from the vehicle and tossed her into the rear seat. Raising a plasma rifle, he sent a full-auto burst of green fire towards the enemy aircraft. His accurate fire tore the windshield from the Osprey as it touched ground about three-hundred yards out. Unexpected gunfire erupted from his right. A glance revealed Trevor Brice sending out a hail of bullets from an ancient M4 carbine. Soldiers poured from the rear of the federal aircraft, spreading out for an attack just as the Osprey's fuel tanks exploded. The aircraft's armor was no match for Adam's plasma rifle.

"Let's get these kids to the basement!" Evelyn yelled as she herded the two away from the Beast along with Kate toward the ranch house. From behind the Beast, Trevor watched as the group ran and was shocked to see bullets disintegrating upon impact with a translucent force field that encased the small group. He even slapped Adam on the back to get his attention to view the event.

"I've seen it before, Mr. Brice. What we should concern ourselves with right now is the fact we're about to be flanked." He pointed left and right of the burning Osprey. Men were maneuvering towards the safety of deep trenches that bordered the western edge of the property. From those positions they could direct fire onto anything on the property, including the Beast, which sat in the middle of the large open area between the burning barn and the house. Even the thick armor of Adam's desert vehicle could not withstand the withering fire of the stormtrooper's plasma rifles. Several rounds had already passed completely through the Beast, causing Adam and Trevor to hit the dirt. At that moment, the ground shook as large amounts of dirt and rock spewed from the earth to form a thick barrier between the attackers and the Beast. Trevor's face revealed a depth of shock and disbelief. Standing directly behind them, Eli and Coraline were holding hands as they created a protective barrier around the Beast and berm.

Without hesitation Adam stood and grabbed Mr. Brice

by the suspenders, lifting him from the dirt as they both moved to the open hatch at the rear of the vehicle to retrieve weapons. Adam shoved a large automatic shotgun into Trevor's hands, snatching up the grenade launcher for himself. Together they poked their heads over the newly created earthen barrier to reconnoiter and witnessed the effectiveness of Eli and Coraline's protective shield. Tracer rounds zeroed in on their position but splattered upon the nearly invisible shield in much the same way as an insect would on the windshield of an automobile.

Adam pressed his communication device. "Roadrunner to Queen."

"Yes! Are you alright?"

"We're okay, thanks to Eli and Coraline. But I need you to do something quickly!"

"What is it?"

"On the control system I installed in the basement last night is a perimeter map. Highlight the western trenches, click on 'Battery One' and launch. Do it now!"

Within thirty seconds, the bolts which secured the roof to a small nearby shed exploded, sending the corrugated tin flying. From within the shed a battery of high-explosive rockets launched into the air, climbed to about 200 feet, then took a sharp turn west. Trevor Brice said, "I really didn't think we were going to get to use those for a long time. Hell, the epoxy on those bolts may not have even set yet."

They watched as the missiles rocketed toward the entire perimeter with devastating results. The volume of fire that had been coming from those trenches dwindled to almost nothing. They could see darkly clad figures moving away, carrying both the wounded and dead. Adam's mortar rounds had taken the fight out of them and sent them fleeing with no other means of escape than on foot. Eli and Coraline relaxed and knelt together, hugging each other as Kate, Evelyn and April came running from the basement toward them.

"Roadrunner to Hedgehog."

"Hedgehog here, go."

"Sitrep!"

"We've got Coyote. He's hurt bad. Flyer One is toast. Nothing left of her. We're full-throttle to your location now."

"Roger that, Hedgehog. Over."

Adam walked over to Coraline and lifted her into his arms. "Thank you, both. I owe you one baby sister. That was very close indeed. I guess we now know how effective your shields are against plasma rifles."

"We were able to stop this attack, but I'm not sure how long we can hold out against what's coming," she said as she pointed westward. Every eye went to the sky on the western horizon, but they couldn't see a thing.

Just as they spoke, a deep humming sound drifted over their heads and they all turned to see Flyer Three with a colorful hedgehog painted on the nose cone coming in fast. With expert ease, it set down only fifty feet from them. The bullet-proof canopy rose slowly from the flyer as Ranger Madison called out for Eli who ran as fast as he could toward the craft with Coraline right on his heels. Alex was unconscious in the rear seat of the flyer with gaping wounds in his scalp and shoulder. It appeared his arm was also broken. With Adam's help, Eli and Coraline climbed up the side of the jet and reached over to lay hands on Alex's chest. A golden glow began from Eli's fingertips and engulfed Alex's entire body as Madison, who had been cradling him during the flight, sat marveling at the thing she was witnessing. Coraline held her tiny little hand on Alex's forehead. Never once did Madison concern herself that the glow of this healing had encompassed her own body as well. During the healing process she learned a lot about Coraline and the depth of the danger they were all in at this moment.

"Eli, will he be alright?" Evelyn whispered over his shoulder.

Eli nodded yes but continued to press his hand to Alex's chest.

"We need to get Alex back in the air soon," Coraline pointed out as she looked down at Evelyn. "I will give him what he needs to protect us from above, but it must happen quickly. We only have minutes."

"What is coming?" asked Adam.

"Many planes and more soldiers. If we can get away in

the next minute or two, we should."

Evelyn, for the second time this day, was forced into a situation to place her trust and faith in Coraline's abilities. Cor's leap off the cliff earlier put only her life at risk, which was hard enough to endure, but now all their lives were dependent on trusting this beautiful child.

She looked into Coraline's eyes. "Make it happen. Hedgehog, take the rear seat as soon as Alex is ready. I'm going to trust you to be his second set of eyes." She turned to Adam, "Let's try to fit everyone in the Beast and make a run for it. Do it now."

Alex opened his eyes as if he had just awakened from a nap. "Mom? What's happening?"

"There's no time to explain. We're about to be paid a visit by more federal aircraft. Try your best to distract them or stop them any way you can. We're making a run for it."

Alex looked over his flight suit covered in blood as he removed himself from Maddie's lap and climbed into the front seat. He was already throwing switches as Madison deplaned and Hedgehog took her place in the rear seat.

Adam helped Eli and Coraline from the flyer as everyone made a dash for the tank-like desert vehicle. Large weapons were quickly stowed away into the rear compartment and they began the process of loading seven adults and three children into the vehicle. Trevor, Ruth, Kate, Madison, along with April and her little sister stuffed themselves into the rear seat, which was more spacious than they imagined. With Adam at the wheel, Evelyn and two kids with her in the right front passenger seat, the Beast began to move swiftly away from the Brice ranch. Ruth and Trevor looked longingly back at the ranch house as they pulled away. They watched as Flyer Three leaped from the earth straight up into the air just as the Brice home exploded in a ball of flame. The ground where Flyer Three had been only seconds before was now a huge crater.

Alex's fighter reached five thousand feet in seconds using hoverpads only. With very little loss of momentum, Alex then turned the nose of his craft straight up and threw the throttles forward. The fusion engines propelled him vertically to ten thousand feet so quickly the enemy pilots could hardly follow the movement. Leveling out, he knew he would soon have the speed to survive this fight. The opposing aircraft could not possibly match the velocity of this craft. Hedgehog had eyes on the radar as Alex scanned the skies for enemy aircraft. Four fighter jets zoomed by at supersonic speed only three hundred feet below them.

Hedgehog spoke clearly and calmly from the rear seat. "Coyote, the only aircraft we have on radar are slow-movers moving to flank the Beast which is moving east at 100 mph. Looks to be helos. These fast-movers are stealth. Junction is not picking them up and neither are we. We're visual."

"Roger that. Good thing they can't light us up either. It's all eyeballs now all around. Lose sight, lose the fight. We've got them on speed and agility, not to mention weaponry. Let's do this."

As he turned his nose toward Adam's vehicle, alarms went off indicating multiple missiles were launched at him. Alex didn't even bother to look at his radar. He knew exactly how the attacking fighters would turn into him and knew exactly when they would launch. His response was simple; go full-throttle. His craft was remarkably faster than anything the enemy pilots had ever known and they were dumbfounded to find the air-to-air missiles could not possibly turn with this strange aircraft. There was no surprise to Alex and Hedgehog over the fact the missiles found only empty space where their calculations had anticipated finding a fighter.

"Coyote, we've got a lock on four helos."

"Fox Two," stated Alex in a calm voice as he launched infrared air-to-air missiles. Neither of them looked to see if the missiles were on target while Alex performed an aileron roll before changing heading.

"Bandits, ten-o'clock high. Bandits on our six."

Alex acknowledged Hedgehog with a 'roger that' before maneuvering his jet to go nose-to-nose with the fighters coming in from above. Alarms in their helmets told them they were locked on from ahead and behind. There was no waiting on these missiles to get close; they were already so close that only Alex's reflexes saved them. Flyer Three dropped chaff and flares plus one other strange object that lingered only for a moment before exploding. The EMP canister did its work. It effectively killed the electronics on the incoming missiles plus one of the fighters that did not attempt to match Alex's turn. All fell to earth.

Taking his craft vertical with hoverpads run to their maximum certainly saved their lives but put tremendous strain on their bodies. The vertical thrust alone was horrendous, but the fact the craft had to roll to keep the hoverpads from ripping the plane to pieces as it rocketed upward caused Hedgehog to pass out momentarily while Alex seemed to have been unaffected. As he positioned his craft for a kill, he wondered if Coraline had done something to him to enable him to withstand the g-forces.

"Fox Two."

His two remaining air-to-air missiles sped away and found their targets.

"Two bogeys down. Hedgehog, are you okay?"

There was no response. A visual check revealed six more aircraft maneuvering to box them in. The sheer number of crafts surrounding him caused him to doubt for the first time, his ability to out-maneuver his opponents. Escape was his only option. As he turned to take the path of least resistance, his radio crackled to life.

"Unidentified aircraft. You are surrounded by a Federal Air Service fighter squadron. You cannot hope to escape. If you turn to heading 270 we will escort you to our nearest base to take you into custody. Please acknowledge."

Alex threw his throttles forward, ignoring the request. He now had multiple enemy aircraft close on his tail. Some had already launched missiles closing on him even though he was nearing his theoretical maximum air speed.

"What's going on?" came Hedgehog's voice from the back seat.

"We've got missiles pointed up our tailpipe and it looks like we may not gain airspeed fast enough to lose them. Sorry Hedge."

"Dropping flairs. Dropping chaff. EMP canister away," said Hedgehog as he worked as fast as his could on his console.

Suddenly, everything in the aircraft except flight control

went dead. No communications. No radar. A visual check behind him brought more confusion than anything. Everything that was not them was falling from the sky. Fighter jets, missiles, all spiraled to earth. Surely the tiny EMP canister meant only for incoming missiles had not caused this. The only reason they themselves were not going down was the avionics and flight controls on their new generation fighter were hardened against even the strongest electromagnetic pulses. The puzzle here was what had produced such a strong pulse to take everything down for thousands of feet. The only one he knew of that could do that was one of their own.

"Coyote, check starboard," said Hedgehog.

Glancing off his wing, he found his answer. There was Sarah flying her delta-winged fighter, minus her only large EMP missile, he guessed. She waved furiously at them with a beautiful smile that made Alex shout with joy. On their port wing, Hayley in Flyer Two with an unknown passenger in the back seat, gave a serious thumb up. His sister and girlfriend apparently made it back from China just in time to save him and Hedgehog from almost certain destruction. Almost.

Using hand signals, Hayley indicated they should clean up the remaining bogeys. Alex indicated he would go after the slow-movers. Sarah followed Hayley.

"Hedgehog?"

"I'm working on it!"

"Work faster!"

Hedgehog had pulled spare computer boards from beneath his seat and was quickly discarding the burned ones and replacing them with fresh copies.

"I've got guns. Thanks Hedgehog. Give us coms."

"Give me a minute."

"We don't have a minute."

"We're going in. You focus on the boards; I'll take care of the slow-movers."

To his left he saw two enemy aircraft falling to earth on fire. Hayley and Sarah were making good progress. He could not make out what was going on below and had no way of differentiating between the Beast and other vehicles without his radar and faux-GPS trackers.

"… Slice, peel right! Now! Now! Now!" sounded the radio as it came back online.

"Thanks, Dice. That was close. He's history!"

Alex's radar was back up and now able to locate his family on the ground. The situation was serious, but thankfully the Beast was able to withstand the fire coming from the sole remaining attack helicopter. One long burst from Flyer Three made short work of the remaining attacker.

"Coyote to Dice."

"Dice, go ahead, darlin'."

"I missed you too, but for now, go to altitude and give us wide eyes."

"Coyote to base."

"Command Base here."

"Dice is going to altitude. Let's take a look at the entire region. Tie us in. Coyote out."

"Coyote to Roadrunner."

"Roadrunner here."

"Sitrep."

"We're all cozy together in here. We need a relief vehicle dispatched ASAP. I like a tight community, but this is unsatisfactory."

Adam slowed the large vehicle to a stop and turned to Coraline.

"Baby sister, is it safe for us to step out of the vehicle?"

Coraline's reply was a simple thumb up. She was exhausted after having maintained an energy shield around the Beast for as long as the attack lasted. Even with her shield, it was evident their ride had taken some serious damage. The rear hatch was damaged. Thanks to Eli, the only two ground vehicles that gave chase had been rendered useless by creating a large chasm in the earth directly in their path.

"Coyote, this is Command. Dice has given us wide eyes. Enemy aircraft have bugged out."

"Roger that, Command. Coyote to Slice."

"Slice here."

"Welcome home and thanks. I'm setting down at the

Queen's location. Join us. Area is clear."

"Roger that. Coyote. It's good to be back. Can't wait to introduce you to my new friend, Guan Yin!"

CHAPTER NINE
INTRUDER

Hayley landed her aircraft near the Beast and deplaned with her new pupil. The family watched curiously as Guan Yin approached the group following closely on Hayley's heels. Hayley had tried to persuade her to walk by her side, but life-long habit made doing so difficult. Evelyn thought Guan Yin might be a little shaken after having to endure the aerial combat in the back seat of Flyer Two, but she appeared okay.

Hayley greeted and hugged her family as Guan Yin stood with head bowed. When all the hugs were over, she walked to her new friend/student and led her by the hand to meet Evelyn. It must have been very intimidating for Guan Yin to see the beautiful lady surrounded by giant men. Adam especially.

"Mom, I want you to meet Guan Yin of Shaolin Temple. I have invited her to live with us in New Castlehale."

Evelyn opened her arms to greet the young girl with a hug, but Guan Yin got down on her hands and knees to bow down before her with her face to the ground. Eyebrows went up all around. Hayley attempted to pick the girl up out of the dirt, but she resisted.

"Guan Yin, what is wrong?" Hayley asked in perfect Mandarin Chinese.

"Nothing is wrong. I am showing respect to your queen,"

she answered in her native tongue.

Hayley laughed and looked at her mother. "She thinks you are a real queen. She must have overheard our communication in the air!"

"Guan Yin, yes we do refer to her as 'Queen' when we are speaking to one another over the radio, but she is not actually a queen. She is my mother and the leader of our community. Stand and greet her."

Guan Yin stood looking just a little embarrassed. When Evelyn hugged her she still seemed just a little frightened.

Hayley put her arm around Guan Yin and said in Chinese, "You'll get used to it. We're big on hugs around here. But, in the meantime, we've got to work on your English."

"I can help there," said Coraline as she approached Guan Yin.

"Coraline, what did you have in mind?"

"I can teach her to speak English. That would help everyone, wouldn't it?" she said as she reached out a hand to shake. As soon as she made contact, Guan Yin fell to her knees. Coraline placed her forehead onto Guan Yin's and held it for less than ten counts. When she was through, Guan Yin stood shakily to her feet. Hayley held onto her arm tightly.

"That was amazing!" said Guan Yin in a very thick Chinese accent. "What just happened?"

"I taught you to speak English!"

"I understand every word you spoke! I am speaking English! I can also fly that!" she said pointing at Hayley's flyer.

"Fly what?" asked Hayley.

"Well, yah," said Coraline. "I, uh, kind of passed that along to her. Stuff I've learned from Hedgehog in the past year. You can test her in the simulators. I think she'll be good."

Both Evelyn and Hayley were speechless.

Deep within the mesa that was home to New Castlehale,

a room full of scientists and technicians busied themselves making last minute calculations, reexamining their check-lists and double-checking safety protocols. Secretly, they wished for the luxury of twenty-four hours of preparation before launching the reconnaissance craft named Hermes, but this crisis in the Void expedited matters.

This advanced piece of equipment would allow Evelyn and her team in Command to monitor the movement of any aircraft, stealth or not, in addition to any vehicle on the ground. Calculations were made to place Hermes in a geostationary orbit. The oddly shaped space vehicle would not only be able to achieve orbit on its own without the aid of booster-rockets, but it would be able to change its orbit and move closer to an area under surveillance when called upon. Hermes could also return to its original stationary orbit or return to base to be immediately replaced by one with replenished power cells. With the improvements to the fusion engines, this satellite could be on station and functioning within twenty minutes of launch.

The lead scientist on the Hermes project called for a pre-launch check and received positive responses from each section. She turned to the communications officer on watch and instructed them to give Adam Walsh and the family the heads-up.

"Command to Roadrunner."

"This is Roadrunner, go ahead Command."

"We are prepared to launch Hermes on your order. Confirm launch sequence."

Adam glanced at his mom who nodded in agreement. "Launch sequence alpha, one, nine, one, one, dash, four, five, bravo. Queen gives the go. Roadrunner concurs."

"Hermes sequence confirmed. Launch in progress. Twenty minutes to station. Good luck, Roadrunner."

"Roadrunner, out."

Hayley cocked her head as she turned to Adam. "What's a Hermes?"

"Hermes was Zeus' youngest son. He carried messages. The Romans called him Mercury."

"Adam, I know the myth. What was it you just launched with the name Hermes?"

"Ah. That's right. You've been gone a while. We missed you both." He reached inside the vehicle and brought out plastic bottles of water, handing one to Hayley, Guan Yin and the other to Alex.

"Our latest toy from air group is a remotely operated eye-in-the-sky. Only this one goes a bit higher than we've ever sent Sarah, and it stays in space. We now have 24-hour surveillance. No longer will the feds catch us unaware. We now have something else they don't have."

"Then let's get Sarah on the ground. It gets lonely up there flying in circles."

"She is on approach to our position now. Our plan is to modify Sarah's craft for other roles. Hermes will have total vision within the next 20 minutes. Believe me, there isn't a piece of technology this sophisticated anywhere on the planet. If we can build these fast enough, we'll have eyes over the entire continent in short order. It also means we've got to expand our technical group. We need people, Mom."

"I know, honey. We're in contact with settlement leaders now to put together a list of somewhat qualified people."

"I can help with that too!" Every head turned to see Coraline sitting contentedly on the roof of the Beast. Her smile assured them she believed her idea to be simple and effective. Evelyn was beginning to understand Coraline's every facial expression as easily as she would any of her children. "Starting with that man over there." Every eye followed her arm and finger pointing off into the distance. There stumbling along the crest of a hill, a quarter of a mile off, was a lone figure who appeared to be disoriented.

Adam immediately grabbed his long-gun and drew down on the distant figure. Squinting in the sun, he turned to the others. "He's a fed."

Evelyn raised binoculars to study the lone soldier for a few seconds. "Adam, would you and Hayley please fetch that man? Eli, darling, would you go with them to make sure our new guest is not wounded or suffering. Coraline, would you mind shielding them as they approach?"

Adam held out his arms to signify catching Coraline. With the blind trust she placed in her big brother, she leaped from the roof of the desert vehicle right into Adam's arms.

Alex laughed. "The Amazing Flying Walsh Acrobats!"

They all laughed as the children climbed into the rear seat of the Beast. Adam hopped in and gunned the engine once as the four headed out in the direction of the federal soldier. As they approached, he turned and raised his hands high over his head and knelt on the ground.

Using caution, Adam opened his door and using it as a shield, leveled his rifle on the man who seemed anxious to live. Hayley approached slowly with her sword held as she would a knife, only the blade portion was hidden behind her back. From the man's perspective, she appeared to be holding an ornate stick in her hand. Eli and Coraline followed closely on Hayley's heels, a shimmering bubble-shaped shield enveloped the three of them.

Hayley moved quickly to snap a set of bands around his wrists as she pulled his hands behind his back. Without saying a word, she lifted him to his feet and began to search pockets and waistband.

Coraline stood directly in front of the man as Hayley continued her search. Gazing into the man's eyes for any sign of subterfuge, she declared, "He's unharmed and poses no threat."

"What is your name?"

"Reynolds, Charles A. Aerial Gunner. ID number F159-0506-029."

"Hello, Reynolds, Charles A," said Coraline as she touched her finger on his forehead.

It took only a minute to load Charlie Reynolds into the Beast and get back to the main group.

A low tone sounded several times, indicating an incoming message. "Roadrunner, this is Mason HQ. Be advised you have a friendly aircraft approaching your position. On board is Ranger One."

"Roger that, Mason HQ. We are expecting Remo Two."

"Roadrunner, also be advised, air defense is setting up along your path home. Will wave as you pass by."

"Roger that, Mason, and thank you. The shield is much appreciated."

Sarah stopped hugging Alex long enough to say, "Adam, you've got three fighter craft to escort you home. I doubt ground-to-air defense will make much of a difference."

"Adam was right in accepting their help, Sarah," replied Evelyn. "Right now, we need a tight coalition between the state of Texas, the Texas Militia, and every settlement in the Void. This is not over. It's good to see them responding without being ordered to act. Let's just hope their IFF is up to snuff. I'd hate to have them accidentally fire on one of ours."

April had to ask, "What is an IFF?"

"I'm sorry, April. That's a device that recognizes and differentiates between friendly and enemy aircraft. It's a handy little piece of hardware. I just hope Mason HQ has an updated unit."

"No worries there, Mom. I installed the chips into their fire control systems myself," Alex said as he kissed the top of Sarah's head one more time.

"As soon as Ranger Hollings arrives, we're off for home," Evelyn stated. "Trevor, Ruth, I cannot find the words to express the sorrow we feel for the loss of your home. On behalf of New Castlehale, I would like to offer your family three choices that may help you look more brightly at the future. One, we can send in teams to rebuild your ranch better than we found it this morning, or two, we can move you to a safer location such as Junction and build a home for you there. There are a lot of wonderful folks in Junction that will welcome you with open arms. We cannot replace the home you had, but we can certainly help you rebuild your lives."

Ruth took Evelyn by the hand. "I don't know what to say! That is a very generous offer! But what is the third choice?"

"Come and live with us in New Castlehale. I know that is a hard thing to ask of you, sight unseen. You may not take to living in an underground complex after living in the wide-open spaces of the Void."

"Can you give us a minute to talk it over as a family?"

"Please take your time."

Evelyn turned to scan east for the incoming flight. She

couldn't wait to see her Ranger again. It had been a long day. The Brice family moved away thirty paces and stood in a tight circle. Every few seconds, one of them would lift their head and glance over at the waiting Walsh clan. April made eye contact with Adam while her younger sister Rita gave Hedgehog a blushing glance. Hedgehog never noticed. Trevor and Ruth tried to keep them on track. It only took a couple of minutes before they returned with determined faces.

Trevor stepped forward. "It was unanimous. We're tired of living sixty miles past nowhere, and with the possibility of another war coming, we'd rather be with you. If it's all the same to you, we'd prefer to live in the safety of New Castlehale, wherever that is." The whole family nodded in agreement.

"While we can't promise you New Castlehale will stay safe forever, you are all most welcome," replied Evelyn as both families converged in hugs and handshakes.

"And you are all going to ride in style to New Castlehale. An aircraft is about to land with enough room to carry you all to your new home. Perhaps in a day or two, we'll return to your property to determine if anything is salvageable, but for now we'll take care of your immediate needs upon arrival at home base. Lilly and Cholo will meet you in the hanger bay to show you to your quarters. You'll be supplied with clothing and other necessities until we can get you all outfitted suitably. Alex will be your escort home. We'll join you for dinner tonight at 1800 hours."

Trevor held out the automatic shotgun that had been thrust into his hands during the fighting, but Adam waved him off. "You keep it Mr. Brice. It's the least I can do to thank you for your help back there. That is one mean weapon in a pinch. I'll make another for myself."

"You made this?" he said as he turned it over in his hands for a closer inspection.

"Sure! I'll teach you how to make them or any other design you care to come up with!"

Handshakes and hugs were still being exchanged as Remo Two made a soft landing nearby. The loading door opened and three Texas Rangers stepped onto the ramp.

"I always seem to arrive just in the nick-of-too-late," he said smiling as he wrapped his arms around Evelyn. "We need to get moving. You can fill me in on the ride home. But I should tell you Jennifer is requesting Coraline catch a lift to Junction with Ranger Madison. She's got a prisoner there she'd like Coraline to... uh... meet."

"Coraline, would you like to visit Jennifer with the ladies?"

Coraline nodded aggressively.

Evelyn bore a contented smile as she held out her arm towards the Brice family. "Nick, I would like you to meet Trevor and Ruth Brice and their daughters, April and Rita."

"Pleasure to meet you folks. I'm sorry for the loss of your home. I was looking at the photos of your property on the way down, and by the looks of it you all had a difficult morning."

"Ranger Hollings, we've met before," said Trevor with extended hand. "It was in Junction after the battle last year. My battalion helped in the cleanup."

"Ah! XO Brice! Yes, I remember you. Your help was greatly appreciated in Junction. I'm glad we're able to return the favor!" He turned to Adam, "We are going to return the favor, right?"

"No worries, Ranger Hollings. Mom has already invited the Brice family to become a part of New Castlehale. We're way ahead of you."

"Nick, I'd also like you to meet Guan Yin. She came from Shaolin Temple with Hayley. She'll be staying with us at New Castlehale."

"Guan Yin. Hěn gāoxìng rènshì n," Nick said as he bowed slightly.

The smile on Guan Yin's face made her beam. "You speak Mandarin! Very good!" she replied.

"Well, no. That's actually all I know. I am happy to meet you," he said sincerely.

The prisoner sat cross-legged on the ground with his back against one of the Beast's gigantic tires. He seemed oblivious to any conversation around him as he stared off into the distance. He could just as easily have been waiting for a bus.

ANDREW C. RAIFORD

"Adam, who is our friend here?" Nick asked nodding toward the man.

"We picked him up earlier. Apparently, he survived his chopper crash and lived to meet our Little Ginger here who convinced him to stay with us."

Ranger Hollings turned to the two Rangers with him and pointed to the prisoner. Immediately the two gently raised him to his feet. One did a thorough search of his uniform, removed his belt and shoes, and walked him to Remo. The interior of the craft had been transformed into a passenger vehicle. Putting a blindfold on him, they placed him in a small seat to one side and handcuffed him securely.

Alex gave Sarah one last hug before he went into command mode. "Hedgehog will pilot Remo Two with the Brice family, the Ranger escort and the prisoner. I'm flying escort to the Queen. Guan Yin, if you don't mind, you'll ride with me in Hedgehog's flyer. Saddle up, people."

Guan Yin whispered in Hayley's ear, "What does mean Shadow Yup?"

Hayley laughed again. "Ah. Coraline only taught you the basics. Saddle up. I'll explain all these things later, but right now it means climb into the back seat of that aircraft. You will ride with my brother, Alex."

"Yes. Okay. He handsome."

Sarah showed no response to hearing that. She merely turned toward her aircraft and sashayed away with only one backward glance at Alex. Trevor Brice and his family were motioned into Remo Two, where they found reasonably comfortable seats. April and Rita's wide-eyed stares at the strange craft were probably due to the fact neither of them had ever flown before and had no idea what to expect. Adam helped Rita buckle in as he made eye contact with April.

"Don't worry about a thing. Remo Two, as we call him, is so safe he doesn't even require a pilot," said Adam.

Ruth began to stand up, exclaiming, "There is no pilot?" Trevor gently pressed her back into her seat.

"Not to worry, Ms. Brice. Hedgehog will be your pilot today and fly you straight to your new home,"

"Relax," Trevor interjected. "I watched one of these things deliver tons of supplies for weeks. It always arrived full of supplies and departed empty. I think we'll be safe for a quick trip across the Void with a fighter escort on our wing. Besides, didn't you hear what he said? Hedgehog will be piloting the craft."

"But this thing doesn't have wings!"

"It'll be fine, honey. Trust me. Trust Evelyn. Trust Adam."

Adam took his sweet time strapping April into her seat. "It's a short flight. This aircraft is so smooth you'll barely even know you're in the air. Hedgehog will take good care of you. Just between you and me, and please don't tell him I said this, but he just may be the best pilot we have, next to Alex." Upon hearing that, Rita leaned over to look down the makeshift aisle to see Hedgehog seated at the controls, then let out an imperceptible sigh.

"Ranger Madison, you still have a meeting in Junction. Evelyn, perhaps one of these guys could ferry her in?"

Hayley put her arm over Madison's shoulders. "I'd be happy to give you a lift, Maddie. It'll be a good chance to catch up."

"I'll get my things from the other flyer."

Evelyn turned to Adam, placing her hand on his arm. "Adam, I know I have always asked you to keep your speed to a safe pace, but I think it's important to get the whole family home as quickly as possible. Do you understand?"

"I do understand, Mom. And I have a great big surprise for you. I intended to wait until we were in grave danger before using the latest upgrade to the Beast, but I guess this is as good a time as any. I'll get you home quicker than you think. Everybody pile in!"

Evelyn gave Adam one of those looks that said, "I don't like surprises," but she trusted her youngest son. With everyone accounted for and in their vehicle or aircraft, Adam cranked up the engines on the Beast and thumbed his comDev.

"Roadrunner to all aircraft. Before you lift off, turn your attention to the Beast and enjoy being the first to witness the latest technological upgrade to my vehicle."

Every eye was on the desert vehicle when it hovered off the ground and lifted thirty feet into the air.

"The Beast on steroids!" he said as he headed off toward the panhandle at a good clip.

Evelyn had to ask, "Why on earth didn't you use this when we were escaping Brice Ranch?"

"The skies were filled with advanced fighter aircraft. We wouldn't have lasted thirty seconds against them. Our best bet was to try to outrun the slow movers using Coraline's shields as protection. It paid off."

Remo Two, Flyer Three and the Beast were now in formation heading home as Hayley and Sarah headed southeast to Junction. Adam's newly revealed secret would most likely be the central topic of discussion at dinner tonight. Meanwhile, in the cargo space of Remo two, Aerial Gunner Reynolds listened intently to every conversation in the aircraft and allowed himself a self-satisfied grin revealing he too had secrets.

CHAPTER TEN
KEEPING THE EDGE

"Yes, sir. It has been confirmed the 12 or 13 aircraft destroyed near Kermit were federal military assets consisting of troop transports, fighter jets and attack helicopters. Wreckage pieces with serial numbers from the destroyed aircraft are enroute to Camp Mabry even now. I'm afraid of what will happen when word of this gets out to the patriot states."

Evelyn Walsh studied the faces of all who were in attendance at the video meeting. The Governor of Texas, Aaron Hammond, appeared a bit pale at this point, while Major Johnston of the Texas Rangers, Major Carol Peters of the State Troopers and General Ben Medford of The Texas State Guard seemed only angered by the news. The others involved in the video conference looked as if they might be ill.

"I'm sorry to say, Ms. Walsh, the news has already gotten out. Only a few hours has passed since the incident and news of it has spread all the way to Washington. I was immediately contacted by President Taylor's staff and informed this also was a rouge operation. We have not heard directly from the President. If I may be so bold as to say, the rouge operation excuse is certainly wearing thin. The senior staff at Fort Hood has released a statement she and her officers no longer consider their base to be a part of the

Central Government and has pledged their support to the patriot states," replied the Governor.

Evelyn turned briefly to glance at Nick and Alex. There was a genuine look of astonishment but also a bit of anxiety written across her countenance. "Governor, is this the same Fort Hood that sent mechanized units to make war on Junction? Remember things did not go well for them. Surely they can't be anxious to join us."

General Medford was quick to answer. "Ms. Walsh... Evelyn, Washington replaced the entire upper echelon of leadership from every base in Texas and surrounding states who participated in that operation. The consensus is the attack on Junction was a true rogue operation conducted without involving Washington D.C., as far as anyone knows. Fort Hood is under the leadership of a super-patriot today. I know this person. She's a rock not to be trifled with.

"Surely, Washington is not going to allow her and her staff to get away with mutiny?"

"What do you say to the person in charge of the largest military base on the continent? I'm coming down there to take it back?" Major Johnston had a half smile on his face when he said the words. "Besides, two Air Force bases down here have followed suit. Pretty soon, Texas will have the most powerful military force in our hemisphere. Today's attack, so closely on the heels of Junction, has resulted in states and military bases moving to one side of the line or the other."

Evelyn, ever thinking 'family' responded, "Not every soldier or airman living on those bases has family down here in Texas. What will they do?"

"Buses have already been dispatched to those bases to evacuate those who do not share their commander's geopolitical sentiments. Surprisingly enough, it won't take many busses. I'm afraid Central Government has kicked a hornet's nest," General Medford stated with a touch of pride.

"What about support for those bases? You must know what's left of the Pentagon will cut off all support for them!" exclaimed one of the other attendees at the meeting.

Governor Hammond responded immediately, "I have already been contacted by the Governors of every patriot state, and they have all agreed to throw their state's weight behind the support of those bases. Fortunately for us, the patriot states have historically been givers, while the Central Government states happen to be takers. We've got the resources and the mindset to protect our territory. The greatest fear Washington D.C. has right now is to lose the support of the only states that aren't going broke."

"What are we doing to prevent another full-scale conflict?" Evelyn asked. "Surely, neither they nor we can afford to repeat catastrophic war. It's insane, what they have done, but by now they should know if they attack us, we will respond with equal or greater force."

The Governor answered quickly. "Our message to President Taylor was for them to stand down. He has not responded, most likely because they are trying to decide what to do about their bases down here as well as scurrying to prevent another civil war. I know President Taylor personally. He will not leap into a fight that will destroy the progress we've made these past 50 plus years, but right now, the leadership of the patriot states is hopping mad. Most of them have mobilized their militias and have set air defenses to cover their assets. I myself have announced a no-fly zone around our ports and oil refineries. We have created an air shield that will be almost impenetrable. Three nuclear attack submarines surfaced off the coast near Galveston flying Texas flags. Things are happening quickly. Now, if you would be generous enough to share some of your own advanced military assets with the State of Texas, we would be invulnerable to attack."

"I'm sorry, Governor Hammond. There are many technological advances New Castlehale would be more than happy to share with you, but our military assets are not among them at this point. I'm sure you understand."

"I do understand, but I had to try."

"Thank you, Governor. I must take this time to notify you of a very important move The Defenders will be taking from this day onward until we feel safe. According to the Cultural War Treaties signed by all parties involved, the Void is free of any control by either Central Government or the State of Texas. We rule ourselves. From this day forward, the airspace over the Void is restricted. Any aircraft entering our airspace will be shot down unless its transponder is recognized by our IFF system as being a friendly. The codes for admittance to our system must be applied for and installed by one of our technicians."

General Medford leaned forward toward the camera to ask, "Evelyn, is that a necessary move? We have aircraft in and out of the Void in support of your new militia facilities on a frequent basis. We'll have fifteen or twenty flights going into the Void in the next three days!"

"It's alright, Ben. We have already begun updating your IFFs. Technicians are on their way to you this very minute. You'll be good before the sun comes up in the morning."

"Thank you, ma'am."

"Major Johnston, Major Peters, any aircraft with a Texas Ranger or State Trooper transponder will come and go freely, day or night. I apologize to those organizations who have flights in and out of the Void for other purposes, but you may apply to our office in Junction, which will be quick to respond and get you set up for access to our skies. We're serious about those violating our air-space. Our anti-aircraft batteries will be mobile and undetectable by conventional means. Those violating the airspace will be dealt with swiftly with only one warning."

Ms. Walsh felt horrible taking such a defensive stance on behalf of the region, but to safeguard her family and friends dedicated to the notion of independence from those who wish them harm, she had no choice.

"I apologize if our actions seem drastic, but we have our families to think about. Thank you all for joining this meeting. We'll be in touch and update you on any changes."

"We understand completely, Ms. Walsh," said the Governor before signing off.

Evelyn turned to those around her and said, "We have no idea who we can trust, but for now we're going to have to cautiously pretend to trust the Governor and the others. The one thing we should do now is try to impress upon them, using our technology that we are not to be played with."

"Agreed," said Nick Hollings as he eyed Roland Davis, Calista Heinrich, and Andrea Trevino, who had entered the control room as Hayley was speaking. They seemed to be waiting for a break in the conversation. "I think they will be impressed sufficiently when they see we will soon have three stationary satellites overlooking both Texas and the Void. And let's not even mention the fact another will be stationed over Area 51 in Nevada. If Central Government ever gets wind of that, it will certainly precipitate war."

"Speaking of satellites," interrupted Roland Davis, "now might be a good time to introduce an idea that came up during the Research and Development's meeting this afternoon. It is so simple, doable, and potentially effective, it would be worth ten new-generation fighters."

Alex leaned back in his workstation chair and put his feet up on a side-table. "We are definitely all ears."

"This should be good," said Adam.

"Of course, when we say *simple*, we obviously mean simple for the New Castlehale science team; otherwise Central Government would already have this technology," injected Andrea Trevino.

"Of course. That's a given," smiled Hayley.

Calista Heinrich stepped forward and began. "Once we were able to solve the issues related to miniaturization and implementation of our hoverpad technology, it was a logical step to equip our aircraft. The success of that phase was both necessary and timely. The next step was to adopt these technologies to a satellite platform. During a brain-storming dinner tonight we came up with ideas for future uses ranging from wheelchair technology, to automated waiters and transportation of crops and goods. Then, it dawned on us we could save a lot of near-future work for the manufacturing labs if we were to create something new to augment our Air Force. All it would take is four satellites like Hermes tethered to a missile launcher we send into orbit. It can be moved at will to an optimum location for launching space-to-earth missiles for aircraft interception, preemptive strikes on federal targets, or simple deterrence. With a large enough payload, and believe me, these power systems have what it takes to carry it, we could take out an entire airbase before they even knew anything was happening. This might make them think twice about doing what they did yesterday.

One might say we *upped the ante*. Is that the right phrase, *upped the ante*? Did I use it correctly?"

The command center fell silent as heads nodded.

"Please forgive my forwardness," said Sarah, "but in my reading I came across historical references to the militarization of space. That was a controversial topic before the Cultural Wars. According to what I read, the governments of China, Russia, and the United States, signed a treaty prohibiting weapons in orbit or on the moon. Why was it a bad idea then, but a good idea now?"

The room remained quiet for a few moments longer, mostly because it was a teenager who pointed out the elephant in the room.

"I can answer that," Roland Davis responded. "During that time period, all three countries were capable of placing weapons into orbit. We didn't want China or Russia to gain that superiority and they didn't want us to have that advantage over them. The best solution was signing a treaty that disallowed it across the board. Today, every country that was affected by the devastation of the Cultural Wars is directing more of their limited resources toward rebuilding infrastructure than going into space. Besides ourselves, only the reorganized Federation of States has communication satellites, which are being shared by every country on earth. There is no space race. We have technologies and personnel assets the Central Government wants badly and are willing to break treaty to obtain. We must break treaty to defend. We must maintain our edge as best we can just to survive this."

"Besides, every treaty established by those countries are no longer valid since they no longer exist as constituted. Our current government isn't exactly run the same way as it was before the war, and although China is still a communist country, their devastation was worse than ours. In terms of people, they lost more of their population than actually live in the continental U.S.," injected Alex.

"But the ideals of the space treaty are still valid," retorted Evelyn Walsh. "We should always keep that in mind. On the other hand, the need to contain the Central Government and prevent them from violating the current treaties is great. If we are to prevent another continental war, we need to teach President Taylor there are serious consequences to breaking the treaties."

Alex walked over to the console and switched the main viewer to a security camera keeping watch over the latest satellite being built in the labs. "As far as the Space Treaty is concerned, remember the Void did not sign that treaty. We are outside the reach of the Central Government and are under no state control. What we do is our business. Besides, the huge difference between what New Castlehale wants to launch into orbit and what they put into orbit back then is, ours are totally retrievable. When they are no longer needed, we can pull them back at a moment's notice. At this very moment, there is a threat of all-out war. The dividing lines are being established even as we speak. If a missile platform, or even a squadron of them is doable, let's get it done quickly and keep them in orbit until this threat of war is over. At this time, we've got the edge; let's keep it."

He turned to the scientists and asked, "How long?"

"Sooner than you think," answered Calista Heinrich. "We have everything we need at hand. The first platform can be in orbit in a matter of days."

He looked at Evelyn who nodded. "Make it happen."

CHAPTER ELEVEN
DEFINING SUCCESS

"Stop the video."

Major Barrett Ratcliff lifted himself slowly from his seat near the large monitor that revealed blurry footage of an unusual aircraft ascending rapidly. An eerie light emanated from the bottom of the fuselage and wings of this craft. The major stood before the monitor with his nose nearly touching. He jabbed his bronzed pointer finger at the area of the glow.

"What is this, Captain?"

"We don't know sir. The best photos we have of these aircraft were taken of the five that landed in a public park in Austin last year. Up until the Junction incident, we had never seen anything like it. Until yesterday, we had never seen aircraft with these amazing maneuvering capabilities. Most of what we know about the aircraft and the Walsh family themselves, we know from that event. The craft we encountered yesterday seemed even more advanced than last year's model. The only thing we really know is it is a vertical takeoff and landing aircraft; we know it transitions rapidly to fixed-wing flight, and we know it kicked the hell out of the best aircraft we own."

"Tell me about the losses," the Major asked but never took his eyes off of the monitor.

"We lost 12 aircraft, sir, including F-40s, attack

helicopters and an Osprey. Our mission team was aboard that aircraft. Most were killed on the ground, but those who survived withdrew to the extraction point with their wounded."

The captain giving the report shook his head in disbelief. "What about the fighter pilots? They ejected, right?"

"We don't know. They could have made it safely to the ground, but we can't fly in there for extraction. If they survived, they are walking home now and it's a long walk. We just don't know."

"Captain, what is your best guess about this," Major Ratcliff asked as he accentuated every syllable with a jab to the glow under the wings.

"Sir, the pilots who bugged out said the vertical takeoff was unlike anything they had ever seen. It was faster than anything we've ever conceived. When the craft went nose vertical, our pilots reported the glowing pads you see there, which we guess are some type of boosters. Whatever they are, they seem to have solved the unstable characteristics our VTOL aircraft experienced."

"Tell me about the boots on the ground," the major commanded as he turned away from the wall.

"That story is almost as unbelievable as the aircraft. They barely made it out of the plane. Before the craft touched down they were taking plasma rounds. Almost all our men made it out of the Osprey before it exploded."

The captain used his pointer to change the image on the front wall. The photo was obviously shot from high altitude and revealed the entire Brice Ranch. He showed the locations of the barn, the main ranch house, and other outlying buildings. Drawing a quarter-circle he revealed the trenches on the western edge of the property.

"Taking cover in these trenches west of the target, they immediately laid down suppressing fire to diminish the enemy's capabilities, but it proved to be quite ineffective," the captain stated with a hint of a blush.

"Ineffective how?" ordered the major.

"Ineffective as in..." he hesitated, wondering if he should even speak the words. "...the earth erupted around the armored vehicle where the targets took cover. It concealed the vehicle from their view but they continued to fire. The men swear something surrounded the target and appeared to be a force field. Bullets, plasma rounds, even a couple of 40mm grenades could not penetrate it."

"Captain, that makes no sense at all. How did we lose so many men?"

"Well, sir, Gunny reported a battery of rocket launchers located in this small structure covered every yard of the trenches. The first volley was devastating. Sir, they had to know we were coming. They would never have had the time to put together such an effective defense. They were armed with plasma rifles, sir. Advanced aircraft? Force fields? Rocket batteries? What kind of farmers are these? The mission was Charlie Foxtrot. A total failure, sir."

"Thank you, Captain. You are dismissed," came a voice from the back of the room. The captain stood, then paused as if to say something to the Major but thought better of it and left the room looking defeated.

"Dr. Tanner, this is the second time we've had our asses handed to us on a great big silver platter. First in Junction, now here. You said there was a 100% chance of success if we followed your plan. This is not what I would call a 'success'."

"Did you leave Reynolds on the ground near Kermit?" Dr. Tanner asked as he cleaned his fingernail with a pocket knife.

"We did. We can assume he was taken prisoner."

"Then, the mission was a complete success."

"A success," responded the Major as he turned his back on Dr. Tanner to face the monitor on the wall. "We lost most of our men and a mountain of dollars' worth of aircraft and you call it a complete success. Although, in the end, it is your definition of success that matters here, it will be yours Washington will call into account."

"You let me worry about Washington."

"Roger that, sir. What do we do now?"

"We wait. You take care of your wounded. Make arrangements with the Pentagon for replacements. I'm going to read a book, enjoy my very expensive brandy, smoke a cigar and wait."

"Wait for what?"

"For word from our man Charles Reynolds."

"Is he as good as you thought he was?"

"Better. As a matter of fact."

With that, Dr. Tanner dismissed him with a wave of his hand. He enjoyed having a well-trained dog he could give commands to with hand signals and smiled as the door closed. The smile was due to the fact neither the Major nor anyone else knew he had more than one well-trained dog. After introducing Charles Reynolds to President Taylor earlier this week, he not only had a well-trained dog in the White House, but he had control of every branch of the military. He would have to work fast. If he could steal the technology of this group called *Defender*, and gain control of Coraline Paden and Eli Jennings, he could rule the planet.

The illumination in the corridors of New Castlehale was dimmed considerably between 2300 and 0600 hours every night, yet the security cameras operated normally to ensure movement of any kind was monitored. Any motion activated scanners read and identified that person's com badge. The ID was added to a database and reviewed by security personnel in the morning. Given the nature of the work in the underground labs, no one living in the complex saw this as an intrusion into their privacy. However, if the hall scanners failed to access a com badge, security was immediately notified and a team dispatched. Com badges were to be worn at all times.

For this reason, the darkly clad figure wore a badge that was not his own. During a brief encounter in the hall only minutes earlier he managed to exchange badges with one of the maintenance crew as he handed a wire-stripper to the man in a tight space. If his plan worked out well, he would send his transmission and have the man's badge back in less than ten minutes.

Checking the hall one last time, he slipped into a room adjacent to the control center and worked his way through the row of servers till he came to the rack labeled 'communications'. His eyes inspected every shelf looking for the laptop used by Paige in IT. She freely gave him the password without an argument after he placed his hand upon her head. Doing so, he was able to make her believe he was Adam Walsh and had need of her laptop later. She even blushed as she gave it up, thinking perhaps this could be the beginning of something special.

Charles Reynolds had an unusual talent Dr. Tanner and the others at Research and Development Command thought would be a counter to the mental abilities Coraline possessed. From what Reynolds had experienced thus far, Tanner was 100% correct. During his capture near Kermit, the scene played out much as Dr. Tanner predicted it would. As the tiny, red-headed child placed her finger on his forehead, he was able to compartmentalize his mind to protect everything of importance yet fed her only what he thought she wanted to know. Convincing those present he was somewhat mind-numbed after the fact was an easy bit of acting. It took a lot of self-control not to react as he overheard Coraline telling Ms. Walsh, "He's harmless. He joined the military as a mechanic, but after he worked on aircraft for a while he grew tired of it and asked to be a door gunner. He's on our side now."

Finding what he needed on Paige's laptop, he typed this message: "Captured. Exact location unknown. Mind block successful. Working as repairman. C and the others convinced of my allegiance. Important VIP meet scheduled soon. Will be in contact. CR"

The message was encoded and sent. He did what he could to erase his tracks, then closed the laptop. Returning Paige's computer to the shelf, he returned to the maintenance man's last location. Finding him still squeezed into the small wall panel, he reached in and touched his finger to the man's head, then exchanged badges again.

"How easy can it get?" he asked himself as he headed back to his quarters.

The glow of the computer monitor was the only source of light in the room. It's soft white rays illuminated the teeth of the man reading the screen. His smile was that of a Cheshire cat as he manipulated the mouse. Feeling good about himself, he clicked 'Print', then listened for the whirring of the printer only feet away. There was spring in his step as he leaped from the chair and snatched the printout as if it were the brass ring of the ancient merry-go-rounds. This message was reassuring and gave him great hope for the future. This is a game-changer.

CHAPTER TWELVE
SURPRISE VISIT

Hedgehog dominated the conversation with a grumbling rant as he, Coraline and Eli walked to the galley. "There is entirely too much kissin' going on around here. Mom's kissin' Ranger Nick; Alex is kissin' Sarah, and I saw my friend Brian's big brother kissin' the girl from the hydroponics bay. The other day after I landed Remo, Hayley and mom gave me kisses right here (pointing to his forehead), and now Adam will be joining the club with April! Yeeesh!! Next thing I know, I'm going to walk into a room and find you two locking lips!"

Coraline elbowed Eli and pointed at her lips. Eli knew exactly what to do.

"Hedgehog, look!" shouted Coraline.

When he turned to look, Eli and Coraline performed a brief peck on the lips.

"I don't want to see it!" shouted Hedgehog as he turned towards breakfast.

Eli blushed as Coraline laughed and called out to Hedgehog, who was already twelve feet down the corridor, "Be careful what you wish for, Hedgehog! I know someone else here at New Castlehale who wants to kiss you. I'm just saying. I think she really likes you," she nearly sang.

Hedgehog paused, with shoulders drooping and head down. "Who?"

"Open your eyes and you'll figure it out," she said as she ran ahead to beat them to the galley.

"Coraline! Come back! Who are you talking about?"

She waved her hand over her head as she slowed down to make a dignified entrance into the galley. Eli followed her in, hoping no one noticed how flushed he was.

Coraline took her usual seat next to Adam, which forced April to take the next one over. Coraline had in her mind to milk as much fun out of this romance as she could while it was still young.

"Did you two sleep well?" Adam asked of April and Rita as they chose their seats.

April's smile was worth the firefights he'd been embroiled in recently. "These past couple of days I've slept better than I have slept in my entire life! I'm so used to waking up several times a night to the sound of my father making his rounds through the house. I'm sure he probably made a few rounds of the corridors these past few nights out of force of habit, but out there in the Void, we never really felt completely safe. Thing is, you get used to anything. Home is home."

"You have a new home now," he said with an unusual softness.

The grin on Coraline's face was enormous as she looked up at him. Her giggling made it difficult to spread the butter onto her toast.

"Baby sister, would you like me to do that for you? Are you having trouble?" he asked looking down his nose at her.

"I'm all good, Gulliver. I just think it's going to be a fun day," she said, continuing a giggle that spread across the table. It was a welcome sound as Evelyn and Nick, along with Trevor and Ruth Brice, entered the room. Behind them were Kate, Hayley, Guan Yin, Sarah, and Alex.

Kate turned to Evelyn and Ruth and whispered, "It's good to hear laughter after all we've been through. I am amazed at the collective resilience we exhibit after enduring such pain. We come back from war and strife and wounds, but it's hard to come back from loss. Don't you still feel it after all the years your Charlie has been gone?"

Evelyn nodded her head. "Let's eat. I'm starving."

With a great deal of dish clashing and silverware clinking, breakfast was served up in grand fashion. Trevor and Ruth found themselves a little amazed at the food placed before them. It had been ages since anyone in the Brice family had tasted a real cup of coffee. The 'coffee' they were used to was actually chicory. But here, real coffee, orange juice, apple juice, thick-sliced bacon, eggs, biscuits and toast, marmalade, jellies, hash browns, and even fresh fruits were laid out upon the table. There was even a pot of grits on the stove. The children were not very fond of it, but Adam and Alex had a taste for it since it was one of their father's favorite morning dishes.

Adam was on his best behavior during this meal, not wanting to seem either overanxious or uninterested. There was no face-stuffing with whole pieces of toast, finger licking, or talking with his mouth full. His usual banter with the kids was not happening this morning because Coraline was absorbed in conversation with April. What concerned Adam most was the fact they would put their heads together and whisper, then, occasionally, both of them would stop and turn to look at him.

"Good grief," Adam murmured into his breakfast. In an attempt to interrupt their whisperings, Adam spoke to Coraline, "Baby Sister, did you have a good conversation with Jennifer's prisoner in Junction?"

"I did! I was happy to help Jennifer and the Sheriff. They now know where Jesus lives."

The reaction around the table was just short of a burst of laughter.

"Jesus?" responded Adam.

"Yes. Jesus, but not the Son of the One. This one is Jesus Carrillo."

"Ah! You had me going there Little Ginger," he said as he turned to Nick Hollings. "Nick, what's going to happen there."

"Well, we have a little surprise planned for Mr. Jesus Carrillo that I'm afraid he's not going to like. No, sir. Not one little bit," Nick answered, then went back to the private conversation he was engaged in before.

Ranger Hollings and Trevor Brice were more interested

in a scratch pad one of them carried from an early morning meeting. Apparently, they were planning something special. Anyone who watched the two at breakfast (and there was one in particular who was watching) could see the respect each held for the other. Evelyn knew from the beginning the Brice family would be a good match for the New Castlehale community.

When it appeared, most were finishing up their breakfast, Alex began rapping his half-full orange juice glass with his spoon. "May I have everyone's attention, please? As you all know, I have joined the ranks of New Castlehale pilots who have the distinction of being saved on the battlefield by our little angels," he said nodding his head towards Coraline and Eli.

"On behalf of the Walsh family, the staff and residents of New Castlehale, I would like to thank three individuals in particular." He turned to the children. "Eli and Coraline, thank you for healing me and making me fit for the finale of the fight over Kermit. Over the past year there have come to be hundreds who owe you both a debt of gratitude that could hardly be repaid in an entire lifetime. First Hayley and Sarah in Oklahoma, then countless others in Junction and, again, at the skirmish at Kermit."

There were a few chuckles. "I know, that rhymes! Thank you from the bottom of our hearts."

There was applause all around, then lots of touching and hugging. You know, the stuff that makes Hedgehog uncomfortable.

"The third person I would like to thank this morning is Hedgehog. Hedgehog, front and center!"

Hedgehog's head snapped up off of his plate with a strip of bacon hanging out of his mouth, staring as if Alex had just popped out of a jack-in-the-box.

"Hedgehog, front and center!" Alex nearly shouted.

He dropped the bacon onto his plate and ran to stand before Alex, who was trying to fish something out of his own shirt pocket.

"Stand at attention, little brother."

He had only been made to stand at attention six or seven times in past year, but those were to be chewed out for some crazy stunt he pulled, like getting caught performing ultra-dangerous aerial maneuvers in his new flyer. He had a penchant for pushing everything to the limit. He was just like Alex.

"In recognition of your outstanding performance of late, you are being promoted. You successfully evaded a ground-to-air missile launch meant for your tailpipe, engaged the enemy, and destroyed him. Then, at personal risk, you accomplished an extraordinary dust off."

"What's a dust off," asked Kate Jennings.

"It's what they call it when some crazy pilot flies onto a hot battlefield to pick up casualties," answered Hayley.

"That's correct. He landed, carried me to safety, disregarding the danger to himself and his aircraft. Together, he and Madison delivered me to our two angels near Kermit. As if that wasn't enough, his cool and flawless performance in aerial combat against an enemy who outnumbered us a dozen to one, as my back-seater, topped it off. Congratulations, Hedgehog! You deserve these."

Alex pinned a pair of silver rank insignias to his collar. "You are hereby promoted to the rank of lieutenant in the New Castlehale Air Force." Alex saluted Hedgehog and offered a hand to shake.

All were on their feet applauding. This was Hedgehog's moment. Coraline jumped up and down and clapped harder than anyone there. Well, almost anyone. Standing in the background, Rita Brice, almost at swoon-point, banged her hands together so hard she might have bruised them. Coraline and Eli gave each other an acknowledging nod. They both picked up on the intense emotion coming from the young Brice sister.

Again, there was a round of hugging, which Hedgehog didn't seem to mind so much for this occasion. He received hugs from the ladies and hand-shakes and back slaps from the men. The last in line to congratulate him was Rita Brice. She smiled sweetly and said, "Congratulations, Hedgehog. I think that's awesome." As he shook her hand, his eyes went wide at the sudden awareness of who Coraline might have been speaking about on their way to breakfast. His suspicion was confirmed with one glance at Coraline standing behind

Rita.

"Uh, thanks..... Rita..... I... uh .... glad. Cool. Thanks."

He felt the need to remove himself from this situation before he made a further fool of himself. Turning on his heels to return to his seat, Sarah immediately snagged him for a hug, then whispered in his ear. "My, my, how much you've grown in the months I was gone. We need to catch up sometime soon, Phillip. Today, if possible. Oh, by the way, very smooth there with Rita. I'm sure she didn't notice the gravy on your chin. Way to go."

He was reaching for his chin when the klaxon alarm sounded.

"Pilots to their aircraft. Unidentified aircraft due west." came from the loudspeakers.

Alex shouted, "Let's move!" as he headed for the door. Hayley, Sarah, and Hedgehog were right behind him.

Evelyn touched her communications badge. "Command, what is it?"

"Military fighter aircraft. 179 miles east south-east. Heading takes them to Junction."

"I'll be right there," Evelyn said as she and Adam walked swiftly from the gallery to the command center. April followed close behind.

The Major in command of seven F-35's glanced off his right wing to find an aircraft, the likes of which he had never seen before. "What the hell is that?" He thought he'd seen everything that could possibly fly, but this one was other-worldly. His radio squawked.

Alex flew closer than necessary to the lead F-35. "Panthers, you are in violation of restricted airspace. There is an armed Void fighter on your right wing. Acknowledge or rock your wings."

"Dot Chaser, Lima Charlie. This is Arkansas Air National Guard - RZB Squadron, destination, San Antonio."

"RZB, you are off-course for San Antonio. Change heading to One Three Five. I say again, change heading to One Three Five immediately. Acknowledge."

A woman's voice came over the wave, "Void ATC to RZB Squadron leader. State your mission."

"Void ATC, RZB is here at the invitation of the State of Texas. Dallas/Fort Worth ATC reports temporary restrictions. RZB was ordered to this heading. Turning now to heading One Three Five. Sorry for the intrusion. It was our privilege to be chased by The Defender. RZB Out."

The flight of seven rocked their wings and changed their heading to the southeast as Alex and his Flyers turned west-southwest.

"Coyote, that was a relief."

"Slice, agreed. I was relieved not to have to shoot down those old Panthers. I'm surprised they still fly. But, thankfully, they are on our side now. They may be ancient by our standards, but they dominated the skies worldwide for half a century. Dice, let's go home. Slice and Hedgehog will continue southwest to rendezvous with Remo Two heading back to base."

"Coyote to Command, Flyer One and Delta are returning to base."

Evelyn turned her chair to face Nick. "What's happening at Dallas/Fort Worth?"

The Ranger was speaking into his headset at that precise moment and held up one finger as he glanced her direction.

"Roger that, sir. We are advised." He stabbed the console with his finger and smiled at Evelyn. "That was Major Johnston. Word has it Air Force One landed at Dallas/Ft Worth just seven minutes ago. Once the President's helicopter is clear of the airport, they will pull restrictions off of that airspace."

"Do we know his destination?"

"Texas Ranger Headquarters."

"Waco? And the reason for his visit?"

"Apparently, the President is trying to smooth things over. He asked the Governor, the commanding officer of Fort Hood, our Major Johnston, and General Medford, meet at Texas Ranger Headquarters, which for some reason he considers to be neutral ground."

Nick had not seen this particular look on Evelyn's face since the day they met. It was part confusion, part amazement, and part they-gotta-be-out-of-their-minds.

"Neutral ground? After their aircraft bombed Texas Ranger facilities across the state killing dozens? President Taylor must have an extremely short memory."

"Nonetheless, that is their request. And that's not all. He is asking to meet with The Defender."

"Why have we not received an invitation through the Governor?"

The conversation between Evelyn and Nick was interrupted by the communications officer. "Evelyn, Governor on the line."

"Speakers."

"Ms. Walsh, I'm sorry to contact you so late but there will be a meeting at the Texas Rangers Headquarters this evening at 7:30 pm. In attendance will be..."

"I already know, Governor. Is there anything you'd like to tell me before we meet with President Taylor?"

"No. Just your presence has been requested. You are limited to an unarmed entourage of 4 and only one unarmed aircraft."

"Are these your rules or the President's?"

"Does it matter?"

"Yes, it does Governor. If we are going to work together in the future, you must allow me the privilege of having an armed escort. I do not take orders from you and I certainly don't take them from President Taylor. Now, knowing you do not take orders from me, I am requesting the President be limited to his personal guard and no fighter aircraft over Waco. We will provide air cover for the entire meeting, and I am coming with an entourage of eight or nine. My guards will be armed. If President Taylor does not accept that, then tell him the meeting is off. The person who may be responsible for killing so many innocents in the Void last year does not deserve to dictate terms. You tell him that. We want a show of good faith. I'll be right here waiting for your answer."

"Ms. Walsh, Evelyn, I know you are in a position to do

whatever you want. The treaties prevent him from taking action against you, but…"

"But nothing. Military aircraft and heavy armor with federal brands have already broken the treaties and we stopped them dead in their tracks, including an all-out Tomahawk missile attack. We will not be dictated to by President Taylor. Allowing our request will be a start in reparations between us and his administration. You tell him exactly what I said."

"I will do that. Please stand by."

The monitor screen went to the seal of the State of Texas as Evelyn turned to Nick.

"I love it when you put Presidents and Governors in their place," said Nick as he moved close to her to take her in his arms. She laughed.

"Was I out of line?"

"No, you were not. We lost a lot of good people. He deserved that, and more."

Evelyn turned to the communications officer. "Where are my children?"

The officer punched a few buttons then announced, "Coyote and Dice are fifteen minutes out heading to base, Slice and Hedgehog are approaching Remo carrying the Junction delegation. They will rendezvous and be home within the hour."

"Ask them all to increase their air speed and get here ASAP. We'll need some time to prepare for the meeting with the President."

"Roger that, ma'am."

CHAPTER THIRTEEN
CONFERENCE

Adam adjusted his heading slightly as they approached Texas Ranger Headquarters in Waco.

"You know your places; let's make a grand entrance."

Flying side-by-side ahead of Remo Two, Alex and Hayley increased speed and began to move apart from one another. Hedgehog and Sarah raced by Remo Two to take the positions Alex and Hayley vacated.

"Coyote to Ranger One, I'm seeing heavy guard on your helipad, just as you said there would be."

"Roger that, Coyote. Be aware Secret Service are occupying adjacent rooftops. Flyers One and Two, make one low pass over the closest adjacent buildings before you set down atop headquarters. Let them know we are aware of their presence."

"Roger that, Ranger One. Making our pass."

Alex and Hayley broke formation to make a circle of the adjacent buildings using hoverpads only. This meant there would be very little noise save the low humming emitted from the aircraft as they passed nearly over the heads of the secret service detail on top of each building. Hayley took note of the number of cameras and cell phones taking photos of their craft as they drifted by. After Alex made his pass, he flew directly to the Texas Ranger helipad and landed as Hayley hovered nearby. He recognized the

Governor and Major Johnston, who flanked President Taylor as he opened his canopy. There were two military officers and one well-dressed individual standing behind the President. Tossing his helmet onto the seat, he deplaned.

The President and entourage watched Alex curiously as he stepped away from the craft. The President's security team reacted visibly at the presence of Alex's sidearms. They quickly spread out in a 'just-in-case' posture. Secret Service did not like this arrangement, but the alternative, they were informed, was to go to war. To their astonishment, the heavily-armed aircraft took off without a pilot and ascended into the air without warning. Alex made a hand-sign to Hayley which brought her in to land in the same spot. The President's team was even more curious about the latex-clad figure who stepped out of the second plane. Wearing a sword across her back, she joined Alex and together they took note of every person on the helipad. After a satisfying look, they took a dozen steps in opposite directions as Hayley's flyer took up a position close to the rooftop, then turned to face Remo Two. That was Adam's signal to land on the helipad.

"Who are these two, Governor?" asked a disquieted President.

"Alex and Hayley Walsh, sir. Besides being the son and daughter of Evelyn Walsh, they are also the backbone of The Defenders. Tonight, they are Evelyn Walsh's security team."

The President glanced up to see three more aircraft approaching their location. "Where does this technology come from?"

Major Johnston chose to answer that question. "Sir. Everything you see here was built by these people. Suffice it to say, sir, The Defenders, which includes the entire family and a number of others, have more brain-power concentrated in their group than exist on the entire continent. Maybe the world, sir," he said with a hint of pride. "They are not to be trifled with and cannot be played. They possess technology we can't even imagine."

The President looked annoyed at that response. "Thank you, Major." His frustration wasn't with the Major as much as it was he was uncomfortable with this whole situation. He did not enjoy being dictated to by private citizens, common or otherwise, but especially when they possess technology such as this. Still, he was very curious to meet this Evelyn of the Void. He knew next to nothing about them except they could be very dangerous when provoked.

Remo Two moved in silently with two escorting fighters. The ordinance hanging from the bottom of the fighters was nothing short of intimidating. Once Evelyn's aircraft had landed the two fighters flew in opposite directions and began flying slow close circles around the building.

"Hedgehog to Coyote."

"Coyote, go ahead, Hedgehog."

"Do we have eyes overhead?"

"Affirmative, Hedgehog. Hermes will transmit, now."

Alex clicked yet another icon on his arm band and Hedgehog and Sarah both began receiving information from their satellite.

"Coyote, we have eyes on."

"Dice?"

"Roger that, Coyote. Confirmed. We have eyes on."

"Keep your head on a swivel, both of you."

"Roger that."

Alex felt uncomfortable for the first time in ages. His hands felt clammy and he found himself wiping them on his flight suit. So many things could go wrong here. The only thing that gave him any degree of comfort was the fact Texas Rangers were more plentiful than the President's men. The Rangers had his back.

The low humming of Remo Two's hoverpads ceased as a section of the side opened and an automated ramp appeared from the aircraft. The first to exit the craft were Rangers Jameson and Hollings, who stood to one side as Evelyn moved gracefully down the ramp. Behind her walked Coraline and Eli. Lastly, Adam, who insisted on wearing battle armor, emerged from the door of the aircraft. He took on gigantic proportions wearing that gear. His aim was to impress, and he succeeded. The Secret Service detail could not help but notice the strange looking weapon he carried.

"What the hell is that thing he's got strapped across his back? Is it a freaking phaser or laser-rifle of some kind?" asked one agent to another. They both looked at the unusual weapon, then at the hovering aircraft above, then back to the laser rifle.

The group made their way toward the Presidential entourage. A member of Secret Service stood between Evelyn's group and the President with his hand held up. "I'm sorry ma'am. But the two children will not be allowed near the President. Orders. I'm sure you understand why."

"Yes, I do. I will ask them to hold back until we have entered the building." She spoke briefly with Nick and Maddie who agreed to stay with the children, then turned to approach the President. Nobody seemed offended.

"Mr. President, I am pleased to meet you at last. I am Evelyn Walsh. This my daughter, Hayley, and these are my sons Alex and Adam. Thank you for inviting us. I would introduce you to our two adoptive children, but you have given orders to not allow them in your presence."

"I am grateful to you, Ms. Walsh for agreeing to this meeting. There have been some terrible misunderstandings and I have confidence together we can clear them up. The issue of the children will be discussed," he said as he glanced in their direction.

"I was also under the impression, Mr. President, General Medford of the Texas Militia and the commanding officer from Ft. Hood were to meet with us."

"They are waiting for us inside, Ms. Walsh."

Evelyn moved past the President to shake hands with the Governor and Major Johnston. The major received a hug, which caused some eyebrows to raise. The President looked a bit uncomfortable standing there with Adam, Alex and Hayley staring at him with very serious looks on their faces. He turned to move down the stairwell that led into the building. Waving an arm toward the door, he smiled at Evelyn as she brushed by, then turned in behind her along with his Secret Service. The last two of the President's security detail to bring up the rear took a moment to glance up in the sky at four strange silent fighter aircraft above them.

"Who the hell are these people?" one asked the other. When they lowered their gaze to scan the rooftop one more time, they discovered two children standing three feet away with two Texas Rangers behind them. Coraline put out her hand to shake his, which he accepted.

"We are just plain folks, Zach," said Coraline. "Just plain folks who don't like being bombed."

"How do you know my name?" the man responded.

"It's what your wife Helen called you when she kissed you goodbye last night," was Coraline's reply before she turned to walk down the stairs. She paused for a moment before she continued to say, "Zach, your friend there still owes you $35 for the meal you bought him last week. He's good for it."

The security officers now understood why the President didn't want to be anywhere near these children. Madison shrugged her shoulders and gave them a 'that-was-predictable' look as she walked by. Nick led them directly to the security offices where a wall of monitors displayed the conference room. They watched as the President, the Governor, the Major and Evelyn entered the room and sat at their assigned seat. Hayley was seated to Evelyn's right while Adam and Alex stood directly behind their mother. The two military officers from Texas were seated near the end of the conference table. They greeted Evelyn and her group, then sat and remained silent.

Eli and Coraline smiled at one another as Evelyn turned to look at the camera in the corner opposite her.

The President followed her gaze and saw the camera. "Forgive me, Evelyn, but one of the stipulations of our meeting was it would not be recorded."

"And you are correct, sir. It is not being recorded. Due to your order that the children be kept at a distance, I think it only right they be allowed to watch via closed circuit. I hope this meets with your approval."

"What possible need would children have in listening in on this meeting, ma'am? I fail to see the point."

"The point is since the purpose of the attack on Junction and the second attack near Kermit was to kill them and us, and instead they saved hundreds of lives, we are here to find out why you want them dead."

The President looked perplexed for a moment. "I appreciate your candid response, Evelyn, but as we have stated, the attacks on Junction and Kermit were carried out by a rogue faction within our armed forces. We have been very clear on this point. Neither I nor my administration had prior knowledge of these attacks and did what we could to find out who carried them out and why."

"And your findings being?" asked Hayley, who spoke for the first time since arriving.

"What we know at this time is the attack on Junction was carried out by a group led by General Turner."

"Excuse me, Mr. President, but we already know this since General Turner is still under lock and key in Texas," said Governor Hammond. "What we would like to know is how it was repeated last week in Kermit."

"We do not know who ordered that attack; therefore, it must be a rogue operation."

"We know who did, Mr. President," stated Evelyn.

"We are open to all theories," said the President.

"I have no theories, Mr. President. I have facts. Fact number one: It was a federal missile launcher that shot down one of our planes near Junction this week. Fact number two: It was a federal Osprey that burned the property of Trevor and Ruth Brice near Kermit. It was federal troops who disembarked from the Osprey and were killed on the same property. It was federal F-40s that were shot down in the vicinity by our planes. Quite a few of them, according to the wreckage we picked up across the countryside. And fact number three: we know the name of the individuals who ordered that attack."

"H-how could you possibly know that?" stammered President Taylor.

"Do the names Dr. Tanner and Major Barrett Ratcliff ring a bell for you, Mr. President?" asked Alex.

At this point the man in the suit seated behind the President leaned forward and whispered in his ear. There was a pause, then President Taylor leaned forward. "We are aware of Major Barrett Ratcliff, but we cannot comment on Dr. Tanner because his work is classified."

Evelyn leaned forward. "I would suggest, Mr. President, you declassify that information here and now. You see, we have an eye-witness who was present in the room when Dr. Tanner and Major Ratcliff revealed plans to capture or kill the children. Shortly thereafter, we were attacked."

"That is just not possible. Dr. Tanner was with me in Washington D.C. last week."

"Would you mind telling us who accompanied Dr. Tanner during that meeting?"

The President turned to his assistants seated behind him. The three whispered back and forth for a minute as they consulted their tablets. The President nodded and turned to Evelyn.

"That is classified information," said the President as he looked at his folded hands.

"I respect that, Mr. President, but Dr. Tanner, as you know," responded Evelyn, "is the man in charge of your 'super-secret facility', Research and Development Command, otherwise known to civilians as Area 51."

"We cannot speak with you on the matter of RDC in Nevada."

"That's quite all right, Mr. President. If you can't speak to me about it, then listen to me while I fill you in on the activities of that facility. Dr. Tanner replaced the previous director, Dr. Doug Slater, after burning him to a crisp in the presence of staff and one of their prisoners, one Heather Hollings."

Major Johnston leaned forward, placing his hand on the table. "Excuse me, Evelyn, but would this Heather Hollings be related to our Ranger Captain Nick Hollings?"

"Yes, Major. She is Nick's sister."

"Why did he never mention her to me?"

"Ranger Hollings plays his cards close to his chest, Major. He felt the fewer who knew this information, the better for her. But now, in this room with us is the one man with the power to free her. Is that not correct, Mr. President?"

Coraline tugged on Ranger Madison's shirtsleeve and whispered, "I need to go to the bathroom."

"Of course, sweetheart. I'll show you where it is."

Madison poked Nick once and mouthed the words 'ladies room'. He nodded as Madison and Coraline stood up to move to the door at the rear of the room. Exiting the room, she found two Secret Service agents were standing outside the door. "I'm sorry, ma'am. You cannot leave while the President is in the building."

"But my little friend here has to use the restroom," Madison pleaded with big eyes.

The agent looked down at Coraline, who was holding herself and jumping up and down.

"Ok but come right back. Agent Bender will accompany you."

"No problem," smiled Madison as she led the way to the elevator.

"Ranger Jameson, there is a restroom right down the hall that way," the agent pointed.

"Silly, that's the men's restroom. Down here in Texas we have rules," Madison said curtly as she continued to the elevator.

When they entered the elevator, Coraline looked up at the agent and said, "When I grow up, I want to be a Texas Ranger like Maddie or maybe one of you guys. Do you think I could do that?"

"I think so, little one. What's your name?"

"Coraline," she said with the cutest smile she could muster, then stuck out her hand to shake his. "What's your name?"

He looked at her hand for a second but then took it. It was all she needed to gather quite a lot of information from him. The elevator stopped and the door opened. Madison led Coraline by the hand to the ladies room. There was another Secret Service agent standing outside the restroom when they got there. He reached out and opened the door for them. They didn't stay in there for very long, but that didn't keep the security agent from glancing at his watch every thirty seconds or so. Finally, the door opened. As Coraline walked out she turned to the agent and said, "I washed my hands just like my mom taught me," as she held them up. "My name is Coraline. What's yours?"

"I'm agent Jones."

Again, she stuck out her hand to shake. "I'm happy to meet you Agent Jones! I got to ride in an airplane today!" she said as she shook his hand also. Looking down the hall to the stairwell she noticed there were three or four more agents loitering around.

"Let's take the stairs!" she cried out to Madison who chuckled, then put out her arm as if to say, "after you!"

Coraline skipped down the hall, acting like she was the happiest girl on planet earth, shaking hands with every Secret Service person present. When they got to the stairwell she announced to Maddie, "I'll race you!" and shot through the door with Maddie and two agents right behind her. They made it back to the security floor and headed back to the door where Agent Bender was back at his post.

"Thank you for taking me to the bathroom, Maddie!" she said as she pushed past the detail. "I really had to go bad!"

Madison glanced at the agents as she walked past. "Kids."

When they got back to their seats, Madison leaned over to Coraline and whispered, "Did you learn a lot?"

Coraline replied, "Loads," with a serious look on her face.

President Taylor, who had been consulting one of his advisers, leaned forward and said, "Ms. Walsh, we will look into this very soon. I promise you."

"You will look into it now, Mr. President. This is something I must insist upon. None of us are leaving this room until I have your assurance Heather Hollings is released. She has been held against her will for fifteen years. She will be released today. You will use the phone in your pocket, call Dr. Tanner and have him release Heather now. We can have an aircraft there to pick her up in two hours."

"These things take time, Ms. Walsh. You cannot demand her release and have it happen immediately. Dr. Tanner must be consulted. He would know better than anyone about Heather and her state of mental health."

"So, you know about Heather?"

"Well, not about her personally. I'm only saying Dr. Tanner is a gifted doctor."

I agree with you Dr. Tanner is a gifted person, but only in the same way as Heather, Coraline and Eli are gifted. The difference is our children use their gifts to save lives and not to murder colleagues. Your Dr. Tanner, sir, is a killer. He has, in his dubious care, a number of gifted individuals that were taken from their homes and families and are abused in lab experiments. Surely, you sir, do not condone these actions. The parents and relatives of your prisoners were held as hostages at the Billings Institute in Oklahoma. These we rescued ourselves. You lost a few of your aircraft there, I recall. The directors of that facility, Patricia Faulkner and Carolyn Franklin are in the custody of the State of Texas. As far as Dr. Tanner is concerned, he has nothing of relevance to say about the state of mental health of any of his captives. Release Heather Hollings now. If she is not released, I can promise you there will be retaliation for the attacks on my family over the past year. You started this war. You have it within your power to stop it."

"Madam, you are in no position to make threats. What do you have, five or six aircraft? I have at my disposal hundreds of aircraft that would be...."

"Mr. President," the Governor interrupted. "Ms. Walsh, we agreed to meet here to make peace between us and prevent another catastrophic war. It would be a grave mistake to resume hostilities over one patient. The patriot states are itching for a fight after finding out what happened in Texas and the Void."

"I agree, Governor. The ball is in the President's court. My family was attacked. It is up to the President to make things right. It is not out of bounds or unreasonable to ask him to release an innocent family member from captivity. Mr. President?"

President Taylor turned to the men behind him for consultation for fifteen or twenty seconds. The Governor, Major Johnston and the Walsh family exchanged glances across the table during this short period. When he finished speaking to his men, he turned and folded his hands before him on the table with his eyes closed. The room was silent until he spoke.

"While I acknowledge you are an innocent party, even victims of wrongdoing committed by our government forces, I continue to maintain I and my administration are also innocent victims in this whole affair. In a show of good faith, I will arrange to have Heather Hollings released from RDC this night. I will make the call immediately following this meeting. We will arrange for her to be outside the facility three hours from now."

"Thank you, Mr. President. On behalf of the Walsh family and the Hollings, we sincerely thank you."

"It is the right thing to do. Although, my General here asked if there's a chance they could take a look at some of your technology."

"Mr. President, that may be possible in the future. Perhaps when there is a resolution to the entire 'gifted children' issue, there will be a sharing of technologies. But not yet."

"I understand, madam. When we have earned one another's trust. But now, I must excuse myself. I have phone calls to make."

CHAPTER FOURTEEN
A SECRET PLACE

Secret Service personnel, along with four Texas Rangers led Evelyn and her family to the roof. As they rounded the corner to the stairwell they met up with Coraline, and Eli along with Rangers Hollings and Jameson.

"I can't wait to hear your comments," Evelyn said to the group as a whole.

Nick and Madison merely nodded, but Coraline said, "Boy Howdy."

After Alex and Hayley recalled their aircraft one at a time and took up positions nearby, Remo Two landed again to pick up the remainder of the party. Secret Service Agents, as well as Texas Rangers on every roof in the area, had their eyes glued to this technological ballet, as the five aircraft maneuvered into formation and flew silently into the night.

Coraline was the first to speak once they were underway.

"Ranger Nick, it would be a good idea for you to call home and have Charles Reynolds put into your jail thingy as soon as possible. Tell whomever you speak to they must be careful not to touch him or let him touch them."

"Why, darlin'?"

"I'll explain after you make the call," whispered Coraline.

Ranger Hollings touched his comDev. "Adam, please patch me into Command." It only took a second or two before Adam nodded.

"Ranger One to Command."

"This is Command. Go ahead."

"Patch me in to Ranger Keller. Urgent."

"Keller here, go ahead."

"Pete, find Charles Reynolds immediately. Put him in the brig. Do not do this alone. Do not touch him with bare hands and do not allow him to touch you. This is of utmost importance. Place two guards on him. We will deal with him on arrival. Acknowledge."

"Acknowledged. Charles Reynolds. Do not touch. Do not allow him to touch us. Two guards. Out," replied Pete.

Evelyn turned to Coraline. "What is it, Coraline?"

"The President didn't want to answer your question about who was at the meeting with Dr. Tanner, so I thought I could get the answer to that question by touching his guards. Three of them saw Charles Reynolds shaking hands with the President."

Nick leaned over. "Sweetheart, why weren't you able to see that when you touched Mr. Reynolds near Kermit?"

Coraline teared up a bit. "I don't know. He seemed like a regular person I could read. Maybe I just didn't dig deep enough. Maybe he blocked me?"

Evelyn looked a little disturbed by this. "It's okay, Coraline. How could you have possibly known you were dealing with another reader. What do you think should happen when we get back?"

"I think I should try again."

"Is that wise?" said Madison. "I mean, if this guy knew someone with Coraline's ability was going to read him upon capture, doesn't that automatically mean his abilities are beyond hers?"

Nick interrupted. "Not necessarily, Maddie. It could be they assumed our Coraline's abilities were not quite developed based solely on her age. Obviously, their strategy was not to control Coraline but to simply conceal and deceive. Sweetie, do you have any idea how he kept you from discovering his intent and information when you touched him that day near Kermit?"

"Yes. I have to put everything I want people to see or

know in a special box or room in my mind and only show them that, just like I did when I first showed mom everything that happened to us before we met her for the first time on the road that night." Coraline looked directly into Evelyn's eyes. "I gave you only what is in that box. He must have done something like that. I thought he was just a regular guy." Her shoulders dropped as she bowed her head. "I'm sorry."

"That's okay, darlin'," said Nick. "We move on from here."

"Adam, let's make best speed. Inform the others," said Evelyn as she exchanged glances with Nick.

"Coraline, one more question. Do you think it's safe to try to read him now?" asked Nick.

"I think so. I know how the boxes work. But after we're done with him, he should never be allowed to leave."

Air Traffic Control at the Dallas/Ft. Worth watched as Marine One made its way to the airport. In the skies above two F-40s kept watch as two helicopter gunships flanked the President's aircraft. The man in the suit standing over the shoulder of the controller leaned in and poked the screen saying, "That's him," he said as he touched his comDev. "Air Force One, be advised; Rudolf is on approach. Prepare for transfer. Detail, take your positions."

"What the..."

"What? What just happened?" ask the Secret Serviceman.

"We have lost contact with Marine One. No sign of the two escorts. They've disappeared."

"Disappeared where?"

"Hawk One, do you have a visual on Marine One? Come in, Hawk One."

"They are... hold. No joy. Where the... Mayday, Mayday, Mayday. Marine One and escorts are down. Three fireballs below. I say again, three helos down. Taking a closer look. Hawk Two, on me."

The man in the suit began giving instructions to his

team on the ground as the operational manager pushed his way in close to the controller.

"Everyone back to your station! Account for every aircraft in the area. Every aircraft! Stan, report."

"Two military aircraft present, Hawk One and Two. Rescue aircraft departing now will make four."

"What happened?"

The controller glanced back at his supervisor and shook his head. "They just dropped out of the sky, sir."

***

"Command to Roadrunner."

"This is Roadrunner. Go ahead."

"The President's helicopter went down at 2208 hours. The President and his detail are dead."

"Command, repeat message," Adam responded as he put the communication to speakers.

"The President is dead. His aircraft, along with two escorts went down just miles from Dallas/Fort Worth."

"Adam, what is our ETA?" Evelyn asked immediately.

"We're six minutes out."

"Command, where did that message originate?"

"Ma'am, from the commander of Ft. Hood. Texas Rangers headquarters and the Governor's office have also been informed. They await a response from you."

"Inform them we will be in contact in ten minutes. Thank you."

"Ranger One to Coyote."

"This is Coyote. Go ahead Ranger One."

"Did you copy that?"

"Affirmative. Ranger One. We will be blamed. Remo Two should continue to base, we will remain airborne. Suggest activating New Castlehale perimeter defenses."

"Roger that, Coyote. Texas Militia is being notified and put on alert. Will be in contact. Out."

***

The wide, brightly lit corridor was a welcome contrast to

the hour and a half ride from Waco in Remo Two. Coraline and Eli walked side-by-side following closely on the heels of Rangers Nick and Madison. Nick stopped and turned to Coraline.

"Will you wait here for a moment before you go in, little darlin'?"

Coraline nodded her head and waited with Eli and Madison.

Nick approached the cell and nodded to Pete Keller. The Ranger removed an electronic key from his belt and held it before a sensor. The bars sounded off with a loud clank and slid aside. Charles Reynolds sat up from the flat surface meant for sleeping. A slight smile covered his lips. Confidence, perhaps a touch of arrogance, exuded from the man.

"You're going to threaten me. I don't threaten easily," he said as he stood. Pete moved to the opposite side of the cell with his handgun pointed at Reynold's face.

"What are you going to do, shoot me? I'll have you know I have powers far beyond your child. You have no idea who you're dealing with or what I'm capable of," he said as he shook his head.

"Are you done talking?" Nick said as he produced handcuffs from his belt and turned the prisoner around to cuff his hands behind his back. He paused a moment as he noticed a bead of sweat on Reynold's brow. "You talk and sweat a lot for a man who thinks he's in total control of this situation. I'm just going to say this once. Our little 'child', as you call her, is going to come in here and communicate with you. If I get the slightest hint you are harming her in anyway, my friend Pete here is going to put a large bullet through your brain pan. Can your mind read that? If you want to remain alive, you will submit yourself to her probing. You see, we don't absolutely know whether she is more powerful than you, but after following her around for the past year or so and witnessing first-hand what she's capable of, I'm willing to bet she is. You may think you are the first and greatest, but I'm guessing you are about to meet the final product. Now, be seated and do your best to stay alive."

Nick stepped to the door of the cell and motioned for the kids to enter the cell. Coraline showed absolutely no fear as she walked confidently to stand two feet from the prisoner. Eli looked terrified. She reached over to touch his arm and smiled at him. Nodding, she said, "It'll be okay. He won't elude me this time."

Her small, delicate hands went up to cover his temples. From the perspective of those in the room, nothing was happening. Charles Reynold's perspective was entirely different. The room disappeared and he found himself in the center of a cyclone of rushing images. Some he recognized from far in the past, others were only recently acquired memories. He saw this week and the week before in one single timeline rush by like a train passing through a railway station. Everything he saw was him. The girl was invisible to him. This was different than anything he had ever experienced. He was used to being in control. He had always been the reader and not the read. Suddenly, everything stopped and he found himself standing on a garden path bordered by rose bushes. He looked closely and noticed the roses were multi-colored. Red, pink, and white roses shared a common plant. Down the path he could see an opening ahead with a great stone dais in the center. At the pinnacle of the structure sat a young red-headed girl. Comparing this scene to many he himself had conjured for individuals for the purpose of taking advantage of them, he thought she was simply doing the same thing, and he smiled to himself.

Approaching the steps, he noticed the two large fruit-bearing trees to either side of the structure, the beautiful, velvety dark, star-filled sky. Coraline, he thought, had a much more creative artistry in her illusions than he usually presented to himself and others. As intriguing as the dome-like sky was to him, it was the horizon that grabbed his attention. While it gave the impression it was either dusk or dawn, he couldn't tell because this golden gradient light appeared in every direction he looked. Although he really did admire what he was seeing, he pretended otherwise.

"I have a place like this too, you know. You are not the only person so gifted," he said looking up at Coraline, whose eyes never left him.

"Can you go there now?" she asked.

He closed his eyes to try. He shook his head once or twice trying to awaken in him the power to summon his secret place. He did not succeed. "What did you do to me?" he asked in a desperate whisper.

"I did nothing to you. You have no power, no say in my secret place. Just as I would have none in yours. You cannot summon yours from here," she said with no hint of emotion.

"Ah, but I can block you from tapping my thoughts and memories. I did it before when you picked me up near Kermit and I can do it again. Nothing you try can open those doors."

"Nothing? Are you sure?"

"Try."

A translucent bubble appeared around Reynold's head and dragged him up the steps of the dais to a place at Coraline's feet. He panicked when he saw himself displayed in another bubble. He saw himself shaking hands with President Taylor as Dr. Tanner from the Nevada facility stood behind him. Another bubble appeared next to that one revealing all the devious instructions he relayed to President Taylor and their deadly results. Coraline now knew President Taylor himself ordered the large explosives-filled briefcases to be placed aboard Marine One and the two accompanying escort craft.

"Dr. Tanner used you to kill President Taylor," said Coraline as a matter-of-fact.

"You'll not get more information. I'm more than just a reader," he said desperately. "I'm more powerful than you can imagine!"

She sat staring at Reynolds with her hands folded and her feet crossed before her. She seemed to be studying him. The images of Tanner and the President disappeared and another bubble took its place. This showed Charles Reynold's as a young boy being taken from his family in West Virginia. They placed him in a vehicle and made promises to him all the way to the airport. He had never flown. They promised him a window seat and lots of candy. He would never have to eat broccoli again, they said.

"This isn't so bad. Besides, I was really tired of my

sister and her friends. I had grown tired of reading their simple minds. I was constantly in trouble with teachers and psychiatrists who thought I was an arrogant little git." Reynolds smiled. *"I was an arrogant little git, but what does that matter? That was how I reminded myself I was powerful. Being powerful was more important than feeling accepted or loved."*

"Dr. Slater was a pig, but he always let me get my way. He used me to control the staff and to get anything he wanted from people. He let me do the same thing. I always got my way. It's too bad Dr. Tanner burned him to a crisp. I thought I would miss Dr. Slater, but I don't. He cared more for himself than he cared for me. Dr. Tanner has plans to rule the country. He wants to rule the world and I'll be right there with him. There is nothing we can't accomplish together."

Suddenly, he realized he wasn't alone. Coraline remained seated on the dais with an unflinching stare. He panicked when he realized she would extract every bit of information from a brain he thought was impenetrable.

"Stop. Please stop! I don't want you to see the things I've done!"

"Why does it bother you that I can?" Coraline asked.

"I don't know! But stop! You must not! You can't. Nobody can know what I've done!"

Another bubble appeared. He didn't want to look at it but couldn't help himself. Whether the struggle was caused by shame or pride or such a fear as he had never experienced in his life, he could only give in to the impulse to turn and see what the bubble contained. Even though he promised himself since the day he was taken prisoner in Kermit, he would refrain from reading and/or controlling the inhabitants of New Castlehale, there were a few he took advantage of.

"I needed access to the communications system in order to make my reports to Dr. Tanner. I had no problems controlling the maintenance man; and controlling the girl in IT was necessary also. She is such an intelligent and kind girl. I actually did feel bad taking advantage of her. Access to her laptop was all I really wanted. I should not have taken advantage of her in other things. I'm used to getting my way. She was just another toy. The guy in charge of the ordinance lockers was easy too. He thought I was just another coworker in need of explosives. He even showed me how they worked. I am a god compared to these people. I can use people like chess pieces."

Coraline was on her feet causing him to shake loose his musings.

"What did you do with the explosives?" she asked, showing the first hint of emotion.

"It doesn't matter now. You can't stop it. It's too late."

"Stop what?" Coraline's eyes grew wide.

Another wavering energy field appeared and this time they both watched as the vision revealed him placing explosives onto one of the flyers. It didn't matter to him which flyer it was; he simply picked one at random, gave the timer a crank and went back to his room. He didn't know how soon the bomb would explode because he didn't care. All he cared was it would. It was war and one of their pilots would die.

Coraline desperately sought to discover which flyer it was but there was no hint. He didn't know himself. She made the bubble that encased his head drag him to one side of the dais. The translucent membrane encompassed his entire body and he seemed to go to sleep. She ran from the dais back to the garden path.

In the cell where Nick, Maddie, Eli, and Pete stood they only saw Coraline and Reynolds close their eyes for mere moments. Coraline opened her eyes and pushed Reynolds backward onto the mattress behind him, then turned and yelled, "Alex needs to land those planes now! Land them up top! Don't bring them into New Castlehale! They must get away from those planes. One of them has a bomb!"

"How soon will it go off?" asked Nick.

"Even he didn't know," she said as she glanced back at his sleeping body.

"Command, patch me into all aircraft."

"Go ahead, Nick."

"Alex, you have to land those planes immediately. Land

them apart from one another up on top of the mesa. One of them has a bomb set to explode. Don't ask questions. Do it now."

"Let's do it, people!" Alex called over the air.

Hayley and Sarah's flyers were the first to reach the mesa. Both exited their aircraft and ran to the small house that served as a secret entrance to the underground facility. They watched nervously as Alex and Hedgehog made their approach from the north. The sky instantly became as bright as daylight and the earth shook with an explosion that knocked them both on their backs. Struggling to regain their feet, Sarah and Hayley forced themselves to shake off the ringing ears and fogged brains.

CHAPTER FIFTEEN
GOODBYES

"Governor Hammond, we were on approach to New Castlehale when word of the assassination reached us. Every plane we own can be accounted for; I assure you we had nothing to do with the killing of President Taylor and his entourage. You must believe this."

"Evelyn, I do believe you. Everyone here believes you, but the mysterious circumstances are causing many in Taylor's administration to believe that in the absence of missile trails and the fact the deed was carried out right under the nose of his Air Force escort, that a high technology weapon had to be used. Your technology surpasses anything they've ever seen. I cannot control what they think. What assurances can we give them?"

Evelyn hung her head as she listened. She paused a few moments before answering.

"Governor, Major Johnston, Ben, General Stokes, I'm afraid I can give no assurances that will assuage their fears, but I'm going to try by saying this. During our meeting with President Taylor, we asked him who was present in the recent meeting he had with Dr. Tanner from their not-so-secret Nevada facility. You were there. You recall his answer was this information was classified. We now know who that individual was and we have him in custody in our brig."

"Who is he? And how do you happen to have him in your

custody?" asked General Stokes.

"His name is Charles Reynolds. We picked him up on the ground after our battle with Federal aircraft and ground forces near Kermit. His story was he is a helicopter door-gunner. Our Coraline gave him a cursory reading and deemed him harmless. He has been at our facility working on a maintenance crew," she said, unsure of how they would receive this.

Governor Hammond had a quizzical look on his face when he asked, "I don't understand. Why would this Dr. Tanner be interested in having a door-gunner meet with President Taylor?"

"Because Charles Reynolds is a reader."

"I'm sorry, Ms. Walsh, did you say 'reader'?" asked Ben Medford of the Texas State Guard.

"I did. Like our own Coraline, he can read your mind if he has physical contact with you. Our own Coraline can plant a thought in your head that you will act on whether you like it or not. We suspect his powers are similar. The only reason we know about Charles Reynolds is because Coraline excused herself to use the restroom during our meeting with President Taylor. She shook hands with half a dozen Secret Service Agents. Some of them witnessed Charles Reynolds shaking hands with the President. Afterward, Dr. Tanner, President Taylor and Charles Reynolds met privately in the Oval Office."

The pause was palpable. The implications of exposing the President to a person with such powers are shocking. The military, political and economic ramifications alone are staggering to the imagination. Everyone on the call seemed to be taking time to process these thoughts.

Evelyn broke the silence. "He is being interrogated even as we speak. We do not know the extent of his gifts, but we should have our answer very soon."

"Ms. Walsh. Evelyn, in the meantime, what do we tell Acting President Michael Cott?" asked Hammond.

"Tell him...tell him..."

The control room shook, accompanied by a deep muffled roar that seemed far off. Adam ran to his control station as he asked the communications officer, "What just happened?"

"It felt like an explosion!" replied the man.

"I know that! Where did the explosion take place? Labs? Landing Bay? I want answers!"

"Not in Labs. Not in Landing Bay. Somewhere outside."

"Roadrunner to Coyote, come in Coyote."

There was no answer.

"Roadrunner to Slice! Hedgehog! Dice! Come in."

"Command to any aircraft. Come in."

The wait for a response seemed to last a lifetime. Every person in the control room was on their feet with frightened expressions. They exchanged glances with one another in silence as if they were a submarine crew standing by anxiously awaiting depth charges.

Adam's commanding voice broke the tension. "Radar. Report."

"Nothing on radar," the operator answered in a whisper.

"Roadrunner to Coyote. Anyone. Come in."

Finally, the speakers in the control room stopped transmitting static. In a slow, tortured voice, Hayley responded.

"Adam. Mom," There was a long pause. "Hedgehog is gone. His flyer.... exploded... He's dead."

Evelyn cried out through her comDev, "Hayley, we can send Eli!"

"It's too late for Eli, Mom. There's nothing left to heal. He's gone."

The control room went quiet again, except for the static from the speakers. Adam cut communications, then walked over to his mom and took her hand. She stared at the speakers for a moment until she realized the conference call she was on was still live. She turned slowly to the front wall, where four pale faces watched.

"Evelyn, I'm sorry. If there is anything we can do, just ask. Hedgehog was special to us. He...he was ... special," said a mournful Major Johnston who had gotten to know the Walsh family intimately over the past year.

"I don't know what just happened. But I will fill you in as soon as I know. Governor, tell President Cott we both lost loved ones today. My gut tells me Dr. Tanner murdered both of them. Tell him, we are being played against each other. We will have proof shortly. Please, allow us time until we know what has happened. New Castlehale, out."

Evelyn sank into her chair and covered her face with her hands. Adam stood behind her looking helpless, like he wanted answers. He put his hand on his mom's shoulder and said, "I'll look into this Mom." As he turned to head for the elevator he saw four figures filling the doorway. Nick had his arms around Coraline exchanging words while Ranger Madison held Eli's hand. Adam stopped on his way out and knelt as Coraline put her arms around him. She touched his face and at that moment, Adam knew everything she did about Charles Reynolds and the explosion. He kissed the top of her head and walked to the elevators located down the corridor.

"What do I say to them? Hedgehog was a brother to us. He was Sarah's flesh and blood brother. I have no idea," he thought to himself as he entered the elevator. It was the longest elevator ride in his life. When he exited to the top lobby he threw a switch on the wall. The winding staircase that leads to the secret entrance up top made the metal on metal grinding noise as it spiraled its way up.

When he opened the front door to the tiny house, he could see three figures searching the mesa top for any sign of Hedgehog. The fires from the wreckage were already subsiding, so he stepped back into the house and pulled out a pair of night-vision visors. Finding his way to Alex he thought he might have difficulty even gaining his attention. Alex cried as he moved frantically in his search, calling out for Hedgehog. Finally, out of breath and almost out of tears, he ran to Sarah and embraced her as they released a torrent of tears and sobs. Hayley and Adam stood by, both trying to wipe away the tears with their sleeves. Shortly, all four were embraced in a knot of arms and grieving. Adam told them what they all needed to hear.

"Dr. Tanner did this. He set us up. Charles Reynolds was placed on the ground near Kermit to be found by us. He used his abilities as a reader to blow up the President and he personally set the explosive that killed Hedgehog. Coraline put him into a coma in the brig until we can deal with him later."

Alex drew his pistol from the holster and started walking to the small house. Hayley stood in his way. "Alex, that won't do anybody any good! It won't bring Hedgehog back and it won't make you feel any better." She knew it was a cliched response, but for the life of her, nothing better came to mind. It didn't matter anyway since he pushed his way past her, but Adam was next in line to block his path. "Brother, set that thought aside. Putting a bullet in him would be a great mercy compared to what Coraline will do with him. She has plans. She let me know she can control him. With the knowledge she'll pull out of his head, we'll be able turn the tables on Tanner. Let her do her work."

Alex stood for a few moments looking undecided and confused. He had difficulty finishing his thoughts. But at last, as the other three looked on, he took a deep breath, holstered his weapon, and turned to Sarah, who was trying unsuccessfully to stem the flow of tears. "I'm so sorry, Sarah," Alex cried. "I'm sorry for losing Hedgehog. I'm sorry. We are going to finish this. You and I, and Mom, Hayley, Adam, and our friends are going to come up with a plan and then we are going to hunt down and stomp Dr. Tanner into the dirt. Coraline can have Reynolds, but I want Tanner. He thinks he will get away with all he's done, but we are going to find him. I promise. And when we do..."

"Command to Roadrunner."

"This is Roadrunner, go ahead."

"Roadrunner, this is Ranger One. Hermes has picked up fifteen Tomahawks heading directly for us. All aircraft need to be inside now. We're activating the dome. Move now!"

Adam ran for the house as Hayley, Alex and Sarah made a dash for their planes. Their wheels were barely off the ground when four hidden hatches near each corner of the mesa burst open. From each of the gaping hollows emerged a glass and steel technological monstrosity. Each laser weapon system consisted of a prominent large laser at the top designed to destroy aircraft. On each side were smaller lasers designed to take out incoming missiles, rockets, and drones. A plane might get close enough to launch its missiles but will never make it out of the area. The science team swore the chance of defeating this system was next to nothing.

Evelyn sat up straight and looked around the room. "Everyone, listen up. Security, once our planes are in the landing bay, we will go to red alert and lock this place down." She swiveled her chair as she adjusted her headset. "New Castlehale residents will move in an orderly fashion to their assigned posts or protected areas. We've got incoming missiles, but our science team assures us our Artemis System will destroy anything and everything they throw at us. Satellite team will meet in the defense center in ten minutes. Team leaders, let's keep everyone calm, listen for instructions. Evelyn out."

She got out of her chair and walked directly to Coraline and knelt before her. "Coraline, could you show me what you know about Charles Reynolds, sweetheart?" Coraline hugged Evelyn and held her head close to her own. There was the usual swirl of images and rushing sounds, followed by Evelyn holding Coraline at arm's length as she bowed her head. "Cor, darling, sometimes I think we ask too much of you. Are you alright?"

"I'm good. I'm a lot better than Charles Reynolds will be for a while and definitely better than Dr. Tanner when Alex, Hayley and Sarah get done with him. There's a lot of anger there. I can feel it from here. They are on the flight deck headed our way."

Ranger Hollings moved over to the communications station and tapped the officer on the shoulder. "Get Jennifer in Junction online. Also get Ben Medford back online, along with Major Johnston, and General Deborah Stokes at Ft. Hood. When they are live, patch them through to my comDev."

As Nick got to the entry to defense center, Alex, Adam, Hayley, and Sarah approached from the opposite direction. When they met, they all stopped and stared at one another. There was nothing to say that couldn't wait until the danger passed. Nick said, "Let's take these bastards to school." There was nodding all around as they entered the room.

Before Sarah, who was last in line, could walk in, she was stopped by Coraline who took her by the hand and said,

"I'm sorry we won't see Hedgehog for a while. Would you like to speak with him before he moves onward?"

"WHAT?"

"Before he moves onward, I can help you see him if that is what you would like," she said with sorrow in her eyes. "If anyone sees him, I think it should be you."

"Well, yah!" she said, her eyes still red from crying.

Coraline hugged her in the same way she hugged Evelyn a few moments before. However, this time it was different. Rather than an exchange of information, this was a transition to a different place. Sarah found herself standing on the same garden path Charles Reynolds took only twenty minutes earlier. The smell of roses was strong as she turned to see Coraline standing beside her. Down the path she spotted the dais on which Charles Reynold's comatose body lay bound in a bubble.

"What is this place?"

"Let's just call it a place between two worlds. Ours, which is seen, and the one unseen by human eyes. I have been given, or perhaps I should say 'blessed' to have use of it. Now," she said as she walked up the steps ignoring the sleeping Reynolds, "let's talk to Hedgehog."

Coraline held her hands up over her head and a bright glowing light covered the platform on which they stood. A figure wrapped in light stepped onto the dais. "Sarah? Sarah, is that you?" came a voice.

"It is, Hedgehog. It's me! Where are you?"

"I'm standing in light! I can see Mom and Dad, and Donald over there! They're waiting for me. A glowing person told me to wait here, and here you are!"

"I saw your plane explode, Hedgehog! Are you really dead?"

"Yes. To you, I am dead. But now that I'm here, I'm not sure *dead* really exists. I don't know what to tell you other than I'm okay. Keep Mom, Alex, Hayley, and Adam safe while you can, Sarah. Tell them I said thank you for their love. Everything is great here, Sarah. I already feel like I've been here forever. I'm home."

"I love you, Hedgehog! I'm so sorry you died!"

"I love you too, Sarah. I'm not sorry though. I'm not sure

anyone feels that here. It's all wonderful. Tell everyone I'll see them later." He turned his head to look behind him. "I'm going now. Goodbye for now, Sarah. We'll be seeing each other again."

The light diminished and the peace of that place enveloped them. Sarah turned to Coraline who had backed off a few paces. "Wow. It would have been great to see Mom and Dad and Donald too."

Sarah turned to look at the body of Charles Reynolds stretched out. "What is going to happen to him?"

"I'm coming back here to talk to him more. He may not like what will be required of him. But that's not up to me."

"Who else could it be up to, Coraline?"

"All I can say right now is, there are plans for Charles Reynolds."

"Ok. Anyway, thank you for bringing me here. Thank you for letting me see Hedgehog."

"You're welcome. Now come here," she said as she opened her arms for a hug. When they touched, the dais, the garden and the peace of that place disappeared and they found themselves hugging in the hall outside the defense center once again.

Hayley had turned to watch them hugging in the hall and understood right away Coraline was helping Sarah in ways she could barely comprehend. She was reminded of how Coraline had helped her over the past year. She would not have been able to beat Master Cheng on the temple roof at Shaolin had it not been for Coraline's ability to help her reach her 'untapped potential.' But all that seemed a lifetime ago and now everything was changed. She remembered Hedgehog's first words after a year of silence following their rescue in the desert from the bandits. She thought of the countless hours Hedgehog played in the flight simulators and the excitement he showed after they survived their encounter with surface-to-air missiles during their trip to Two-Towers. The joy he expressed upon receiving his own flyer will forever be locked in her brain. The memories then faded into the image of Hedgehog's aircraft exploding into tiny pieces. The strength of that memory rolled over her like a wave at that point. She wasn't aware someone was speaking to her.

"Hayley, are you okay?" asked her mother.

Hayley's countenance betrayed both intense anger and deep sorrow. Wiping her face upon her sleeve, she said, "I am. Let's do this."

CHAPTER SIXTEEN
ARTEMIS

The monitor on the wall displayed the live radar data feed from Hermes in orbit far above them. Bright yellow dots moving along a trajectory directed at New Castlehale revealed the locations of fifteen Tomahawk missiles."

"How soon will they reach us?" asked Ranger Madison.

"First strike, ETA ten minutes. The last in fourteen," said Adam sitting behind the console. They will be in range of Artemis when they reach this circle." He had a laser pointer in his hand as he pointed out the circle with New Castlehale in the center.

Alex, who had been silent since entering the defense center, seemed to be having difficulty compartmentalizing the loss. With an uncharacteristically shaky voice, he said, "There is no doubt about the fact Charles Reynolds got word to the outside of our location. The secret is out. We will protect New Castlehale. Violators of our air-space will be terminated with extreme prejudice. Get word of what is happening out to all settlement and township leaders, as well as militia units scattered about. The towns nearby need to know curiosity seekers infiltrating our area will be dealt with no differently than enemy combatants. If we are going to survive this, we need to send a strong message."

"It's already started," said Adam after listening intently into his headphones. "Bacon at Two-Towers is reporting they are under attack by what's left of the Carrillo family. Bacon says it's nothing they can't handle, but I'm afraid word may have gotten out that we may be too preoccupied to protect our settlements at this time."

"You may be right," said Ranger Hollings. "The good news is I was on the line just now with Ben Medford and General Stokes. The Texas Militia is bolstering our units in Fredericksburg. Remember our little friends who operated the Abrams tanks during the battle of Junction? As we speak they are moving to block I-10 outside of Junction. They have a couple of Ben's anti-aircraft units with them. Hornburg sent bull-dozers with them to dig tank emplacements. General Stokes is sending airborne troops to Lubbock along with helicopter gunships. Oklahoma's Governor informed us troops are rolling into Amarillo to strengthen our militia units there as well as putting their State Guard on full alert. Other states are following suit. We've got the Governor back online now. Adam, put him up. Along with Ben Medford and General Stokes."

The radar image moved to the left side of the large wall monitor while live-streamed video of Governor Hammond, General Stokes and Ben Medford appeared.

"Evelyn, I'm sorry for all this. I didn't think the reaction would come this quickly. Although I'm here to tell you the acting President is denying any involvement in this attack."

"That's not likely, Governor. What you're seeing on your screen is live radar of incoming Tomahawk missiles."

General Stokes interrupted. "Ms. Walsh. How can you be certain these are Tomahawk missiles and not aircraft?"

"Our down-looking radar system is in a stationary orbit above us. We see everything on wavelengths which your scientists cannot conceive of, both on the ground and in the air, and know by experience these are definitely Tomahawk missiles. Adam, show them."

An inset video frame revealed the shape of a Tomahawk missile as seen from space. The telemetry identifying it as a Tomahawk was revealed beneath.

"Do you have anything capable of stopping them?" asked the Governor.

"When Tomahawks were launched with the hopes of

destroying Junction, we tried our best to take them down using aircraft. That effort was unsuccessful. Thankfully Coraline and Eli were able to protect that town from certain annihilation using their remarkable gifts. That incident took a lot out of those children. We knew then the chances of being fired on in the like manner in the future was great. So, our scientists, who had been working on laser technology for decades, stepped up their work and came up with a defense system that will be tested in actual battle, moments from now. We brought Artemis online four months ago. This system will kill those missiles before they get close to this facility."

"Ma'am, you are placing a lot of trust and confidence in an untested system." replied General Stokes.

"It is not untested. It is simply untested in battle. We have a lot of confidence in our science teams."

"Teams? Plural? How many teams do you have?" Ben Medford asked.

"Let's just say we have enough science teams for advanced research into laser technology, defense technology, and most importantly at the moment, aerospace technology. Our planes, satellites and weaponry are decades in advance of anything the Feds can throw against us. We did not ask for this war, and yet they have intruded upon our lives and our freedom in ways that cannot be swept under the rug by 'these-were-rogue-actors' excuses. I would like you to stay on the line to witness our laser defenses in action. You must respond to the acting President and tell him we did not kill his predecessor. We know who did, and we are going after him. If he doesn't want war, he'd best stand down and put a leash on his war dog, Dr. Tanner. We are demanding justice with that man. If the President chooses to continue this aggression, we will end this war and rebuild this country from the ashes. You tell him our only wish is to be left alone, but if he can't do that, we suggest he pause for a moment to count the costs. The states have already made their choices after the attack earlier this week near Kermit. This coming war will be over quickly and with finality."

"Mom, we've got Tomahawks about to knock on our

door," said Adam with an angry look about him.

"Take'em, brother," said Alex with a voice filled with vengeance.

"Sharing the screen," said Adam. "Top view and radar. All four Artemis systems are activated. Ladies and gentlemen, what you are looking at is the latest in laser technology. Each Artemis unit consists of one 2-megawatt laser, with two 700-kilowatt lasers as backups, each capable of targeting threats independently."

The images on the right side of the large wall monitor were replaced by a live video feed from the top of the mesa. The use of night-vision cameras enabled the viewers in the defense center to see the large laser weapons turning together."

"Acquisition in five, four, three, two one...."

The eerie green landscape was interrupted by a series of bright flashes. No sooner had they illuminated the green world, the yellow dots on the radar began disappearing, one by one. The lasers moved quickly and took no time at all to recharge for a follow-up shot. This went on for four minutes as each Tomahawk entered the kill zone. When it was over, Evelyn looked over to Adam and simply nodded.

"Tomahawk threat is ended. For now," said Adam as he switched the video feeds back to see the Governor and others.

General Stokes was tapping her fingers on the desk in front of her. She then looked into the camera. "Very impressive, Ms. Walsh. I see now why you named her Artemis. Nobody is going to screw with her. Congratulations to your science teams. We have nothing like it. Very impressive. I'd like to know how you power such weapons."

"Thank you, General, but our power systems are classified. Now, Governor, please relay my message to acting President Cott. And Governor, please inform President Cott, we have a larger version of these Artemis systems in orbit. We call it Zeus. It can be redirected at the drop of a hat and arrive at any location over the continental U.S. in short order. Please inform him we're hurting from our losses. And as we all know, hurt people hurt people. Tell him – 'don't make us hurt you'."

"I will, Ms. Walsh. In the meantime, look for our air patrols overflying the Void over the next 48 hours. We're throwing a lot of planes into the air for the next few days. They have proper IFF thanks to your technicians. We'll be in touch."

"Thank you all. New Castlehale Command out."

"Uh, Mom, we don't have a Zeus in orbit," said Adam without even looking up from his console.

"No. We don't. But they don't know that. How soon can we have the missile platform we talked about yesterday?" she asked, but then paused with a confused look. "When did we talk about that? Was it yesterday or the day before? I'm losing track."

Alex put his arms around his mom and said in a calm voice, "That was yesterday, Mom. It'll take a day or more to build and test. We've got the materials and the missiles. The space team is working furiously on it, but they'll need to sleep sometime."

"Let's make that a priority. We'll need it when we go after Dr. Tanner."

"I have a question," said Ranger Hollings. "Did President Taylor make that call to Nevada before he was killed? I feel selfish even asking at a time like this, but if we're going after Tanner, we need to know. If he did, then Tanner will be expecting us."

"I wish we had the answer to that question, Nick," Evelyn said collapsing back into her chair. "I'm so tired."

***

"What happened to our Tomahawks?" Tanner asked Major Ratcliff.

"It seems they were destroyed, Dr. Tanner. I've been telling you we have no idea what we are dealing with. I'm not sure Washington D.C. could have stopped all those missiles. These people continue to beat us at every turn," he responded.

"We'll find out who and what we're dealing with soon enough, Major. When Charles Reynolds checks in again, we'll know more. His latest order was to report on their defenses and aircraft. He was due to check in an hour ago. Give him time."

"We should have waited for that report before we launched 30 million dollars' worth of Tomahawks at their command center. Most likely they are scattered over the countryside. What a waste!"

Tanner came out of his chair. "No! Not a waste! They are probably exchanging threats with Washington right now, which is precisely what I was hoping for. I only wish we could have introduced Charles Reynolds to Vice President Cott. It doesn't matter right now. I received a call from President Taylor just moments before he exploded." The look of satisfaction on his face was striking, being a mixture of happiness and evil intent that frightened even the battle-tested Major. "The last thing agreed upon between Ms. Walsh and the President was Heather Hollings to be released tonight. I seriously doubt they will be coming tonight after my little Tomahawk message. But they will try, and we will be ready for them."

"Ready how? We don't know their strength or plans! How do you get ready for that?" asked an impatient Major Ratcliff.

"We are moving way beyond technology, Major. Way beyond."

Dr. Tanner reached over to place his hand on a touchscreen before him. The monitor on the wall changed immediately. There on the screen before them was a man strapped to a Y-shaped platform suspended in a glass sphere. Electrical devices protruded from his head, neck, shoulders, and chest, connecting him to the sphere.

"Dr. Tanner, who is this person?"

"Major, meet our secret weapon. Mr. David Paden."

"Who?"

"Coraline's father."

CHAPTER SEVENTEEN
GIFTS

The first yellow rays announcing the dawn turned Coraline's striking red hair into a halo that framed her beautiful face. Bathed in peace, she welcomed the sun as she would a friend. Her knowing smile would have made any onlooker wonder if there was a personal relationship, almost a kinship with the Creator of the universe. But there were no observers with her as she sat cross-legged, mere inches from the edge of the cliff.

Everyone has a place or an activity that recharges their being. Some choose solitude to restore equilibrium to their life, while others are regenerated in the presence of others. Some sleep. Some swim. There are those who believe certain activities recharge them while just the opposite is true. Drugs, alcohol, power-trips, manipulation, and other vices are destructive to any soul. Those who claim these are regenerative only fool themselves. Coraline's recharge comes from two places - the time alone in her secret garden and the mornings or afternoons that she spends watching the sunrise or fall below the horizon. It's as if those photons, after their 8-minute journey to our earth, fill her soul and heart with light and strength. A deep sigh sets her being aright.

After sitting for ten or fifteen minutes, she glanced over her shoulder as if someone were close by. Lifting herself to her feet, she took one last long look at the rising sun, then walked across the top of the mesa where last night's tragedy occurred. Her head swiveled left and right as she walked across the flat surface, taking note of the debris left behind by Hedgehog's aircraft. Somehow, she understood what she saw could not be even a small portion of the craft, and the remainder must be scattered across the base of the mesa.

As she pondered this, a truck appeared from the long drive north of the mesa. Exiting from the back of the truck a small crew of workers surveyed the wreckage as they donned their gloves. When their eyes met with Coraline, they all seemed to freeze. Some whispered to the person standing next to them and there was a lot of nodding. The foreman of the crew waved to her, which she returned, then all were waving at Coraline. She smiled and moved on.

Walking to the northwestern corner, she leaned over to search the ground hundreds of feet below. What she did see was a lone figure poking through the wreckage. He stopped what he was doing long enough to look up to see her silhouette against the brightening sky. Coraline watched as Adam stooped down to pick up a large piece of sheet metal.

Sitting on a boulder, he held the metal before him as if he were admiring a book cover. What he saw was the art he had asked a New Castlehale artist to paint on the nose of Hedgehogs flyer. He recalled the day in Junction he chased Hedgehog down in a foot-race, only to catch him as he passed the aircraft that would soon be his very own. Adam remembered that Hedgehog remembered that day as the best day of his life.

"And now you're gone," Adam said out loud.

"He's not gone-gone," said the voice behind him.

He turned to see Coraline.

"But I thought I just saw you up... oh. Never mind."

He turned back to his sheet of metal. "What do you mean *not gone-gone*," he asked.

"Would you like me to show you?"

"Sure, baby sister. Show me whatever it is," he said without turning away from the painted sheet metal.

Coraline put her arms around Adam's neck from behind him and pressed her head to his. He saw, through Coraline's own eyes, what happened when Sarah and Hedgehog said their goodbyes. He felt the joy, the sorrow, and the peace of that meeting. When it was over he turned around with tear-filled eyes and asked, "Have the others seen this?"

"Yes. Except for Lilly, Cholo and Eli's mom."

"I'm glad for that because his loss has just about ripped my heart out. Knowing he lives on somewhere heals a lot of that. Coraline, he was like a brother to me," Adam wiped his eyes on his shirt sleeve. "Nobody had his enthusiasm and the effort he put into being the best pilot he could be was inspirational. I think he very well might have become the best pilot ever. Better than Alex even. I'm going to miss him. But thank you for sharing his goodbye."

He held up the piece of sheet metal with the hedgehog drawn on it. "This is going on the wall in the landing bay. Everybody who comes and goes on the landing deck will see it and remember."

"I think Hedgehog will like that!" Coraline said with a smile.

"Coraline, will you walk back with me?" He stood up with the aircraft piece in his arms then glanced up at the mesa before him. "Or better yet, if you can, will you give me a ride to the top?"

Coraline laughed. "I thought you'd never ask! Just take my hand."

Adam took her tiny fingers into his huge hand and held them gently. The world around him took on a shimmering electric blue tint as his feet left the canyon floor. He looked down to see they were hovering a foot from the dirt on which they stood only a moment before. The force-field-like wrap lifted them effortlessly skyward. He imagined this is what it must feel like to be weightless in space. Their airy chariot rotated as it lifted them hundreds of feet to the top of the mesa. With the gentleness of a mother placing a sleeping baby into a crib, Coraline deposited them close to the small house that doubled as a secret entrance to New Castlehale. When their feet touched the earth, their shimmering conveyance dissipated into thin air. The work crew sent up to clear the mesa-top of debris stood mesmerized at what they just witnessed. Coraline waved to them again.

"How'd you like that, Gulliver?" she asked with her endearing laugh.

"Now that, my Ginger Lilliputian, is how I wish we could travel every day."

"We'd never get anywhere on time, though. It's not very fast. You should stick to your jets."

"I reckon you're right. Let's get breakfast. I seem to have my appetite back."

"I'm hungry too. I could eat a pony," she said with a pretend serious look.

"HA! I've never seen you eat more than a mouse, baby sister!"

"Okay. Maybe a little tiny pony."

"Look there, Cor," Adam said pointing at the sloping northern edge of the mesa where the gravel road wound its way down to the desert. At the base of the road, construction was already beginning on gates to prevent unauthorized traffic from taking the winding road up to the top of the mesa. "Robotic sentries will be placed overlooking this road to stop any who get past the gates. I spoke with Sanders on my way down this morning. If his ideas work out the way he thinks, I doubt any tourists, friendly or not, will get through," said Adam. He paused to think through the risk management issues but was interrupted in thought by Coraline tugging on his hand.

"Let's go."

Together they rode the elevator down to the dining level but stopped briefly to place the aircraft piece against the wall in the command center. Then, hand in hand they walked silently to breakfast. As they entered the galley, they both noticed Lilly and Kate looked like they hadn't slept a wink in days. To get their minds off of their loss, they worked at preparing breakfast. Cholo, who usually occupied himself reading his tablet each morning, sat with his elbows on his knees and hands folded, praying as he stared at the floor. Occasionally, the sound of weeping came from the kitchen, which only made Cholo pray all the harder.

"Cor, I think it would be helpful if you showed these three what you showed me."

"I think so too. I'll do that while you set the table."

Coraline, who was beginning to show signs of weariness, walked over to Cholo and led him into the kitchen area. Lilly and Kate turned to see Coraline holding her arm out as if to beckon them. The four held hands, and with awkward kneeling or stooping, they did their best to put their heads together. They embraced for mere moments. Adam had just enough time to carry the toaster to the middle of the table and place bread and butter there, then take his usual spot. When Lilly walked out into the dining area she looked refreshed and at peace. That is the effect Coraline has on others at the best of times, but in this situation, her gift was a game-changer.

When the rest of the family, including the Rangers and Jennifer (who flew in with the cargo in Remo Two from a midnight run) appeared for breakfast, nobody seemed eager to talk, but they all gave Coraline curious glances with a mixture of awe and curiosity. Every one of them had now seen the exchange between Sarah and Hedgehog, thanks to Coraline who visited each one of them in the night. And although it filled them with hope, the vision left them with many questions that needed answering. Now didn't seem the time, but they all promised themselves they would ask. What they each felt, along with their pain, was a peace that was unexpected. The hurt of losing a cherished family member now seemed tempered with a joyful sadness, accompanied by an inexpressible confidence in the future. No sacrifice they could make in the days and weeks to come would be too great to finish the mission in which Hedgehog threw his complete devotion.

Eli sat quietly, taking in the emotions of his friends and family. He too saw what Coraline had to share of Hedgehog's goodbye. The peace the experience brought him was added to his own emotional state, having already experienced the passing of his father and the farewell moment in which Coraline included him. He glanced at Coraline across the table and saw she was already looking directly at him. They exchanged a brief knowing smile. Hope is an empowering thing.

April Brice entered the galley and walked directly to Sarah for an exchange of hugs. She whispered something into Sarah's ear and then moved to a seat next to Adam.

"How is Rita doing?" asked Adam.

"She took it hard. I'm pretty sure if it wasn't for the visit we received from Coraline last night," April said as she leaned over to see Coraline on the other side of him, "Rita might have spent the rest of the week hiding in the bathroom. Thank you, Coraline."

"Where is she now?" asked Hayley.

"She skipped breakfast to go upstairs to meet with Paige in IT. Last night she agreed to take on Rita as an assistant. We found the message on the monitor in our quarters this morning. I think Coraline had something to do with that."

Alex spoke up on the opposite side of the table. "Have you decided what you want to do?"

"Weapons Systems Research and Development."

"Weapons Systems?" asked Jennifer. "Have you done that before?"

"No. But last night, Coraline took me down to the labs and asked me what I would like to learn. I felt I could be the best help to Adam by learning about weapons, so she took me by the hand and introduced me to Andrea Trevino in charge of research and development, and... well ... we put our heads together. Literally. When we were done, I was filled with knowledge of engineering and manufacturing things I've never heard of. I could walk in there right now and build a plasma rifle, but Coraline tells me working with Andrea will help lock that knowledge into my brain." April looked up at the ceiling lights as if attempting to pull some inspiration from them. "I've already got some ideas on where to start."

Every eye went back to Coraline, who seemed oblivious to the attention. Adam chuckled as he shook his head. "My Little Ginger is capable of changing the world, and yet she sits there nibbling on her toast with her little pinkie sticking out all lady-like." He looked at April and said, "You gotta love her." That lightened to mood considerably in the room.

Coraline responded: "We will all change the world. We're changing it now. Guan Yin was just the start of what we can do. I was able to teach her to speak English, but she also learned how to pilot our airplanes. Now April will be able to build weapons systems. I'm not absolutely sure about this, but I believe I can transfer knowledge from any individual to another. We can build things twice as fast. We can have twice as many pilots."

Alex had to ask, "Can I learn Hayley's Kung Fu?"

Hayley asked, "Can I learn to fly as well as Alex?"

Kate asked, "Can I learn to do what you do Coraline?"

Coraline sat silently for a couple of seconds, then answered, "Yes, yes, and no. Yes, to Kung Fu and piloting, but you would still need to practice. Your muscles have memories. A mind transfer won't help those. You'd have to practice." Then she looked at Kate. "No, because what I have is a gift from the One. Some of you have gifts buried deep. I will help you there. One of you at this table already has a special gift but has never told another human being. I will not tattle, but the time will come when you should tell the others."

Everyone took a slow look around the table. The conversation stopped there. It was a quiet breakfast until Evelyn stood up to speak.

"I hope you all got at least some sleep last night because we have a big day ahead of us. A list of priorities is on the monitors in your quarters. There will be a memori..." She paused to looked down at her napkin for a second, then continued, "There will be a Celebration of Life service for Hedgehog on the flight deck tomorrow at 1100 hours followed by a reception. Ranger Hollings has something he'd like to tell us."

Nick stood as he placed his coffee cup on the table before him. "Listen up. Now that our location has been compromised, we must create a perimeter around New Castlehale to prevent ground assault. We have already invited the Texas Militia to move their camp to the west of this facility. Units are arriving this morning to set up a temporary camp and begin patrols in the area. We have arranged for work crews from Lubbock to build permanent structures for their base of operations. Because of the sensitive nature of the research that is being done here, only hand-picked and Coraline-vetted high-ranking officers will be allowed access to New Castlehale. Our internal security will increase substantially. XO Brice is taking charge of that. We're already covered from air assault. Nothing, and I mean nothing, will be able to compromise our air space. Artemis proved that last night. But we need a backup system. We will be positioning anti-aircraft missile launchers on nearby hilltops as well as mobile laser batteries. I was told last night the smaller 700 kilowatt lasers can be mounted, not only to mobile vehicles, but to aircraft. Our goal is to have total battlefield supremacy in the air and on the ground. Until that time, we'll be relying on the State of Texas and the Militia."

"What about Dr. Tanner?" asked Alex. "When do we go after him?"

"Soon. But not now. We'll shore up our defenses here and in the settlements first. Tanner may try to get to us through them. Let's make sure our people have reasonable defenses first; then we'll go after Tanner. Evelyn has posted your assignments. Let's get to it."

"Mom, my task list for today says 'escort - 1030 hours'," said Alex. "What's up with that?"

"Mine also," said Sarah.

"At 1030 hours this morning, Remo Two will carry me, along with our Rangers, Jennifer, Kate and Eli to meet with the Governor and other key players. Ranger Pete Keller was sent ahead in the middle of the night in Remo One to Waco to scout ahead of us. Our meeting will be at 1300 hours. Flying escort will be Alex and Sarah in Flyer One. And Hayley and Guan Yin in Flyer Two. Alex, I want both planes loaded heavy with air-to-air missiles. Before we go wheels-up, Hermes II will be launched this morning. We'll have eyes in the sky here and there. We're taking no chances. Adam, make sure Texas Air Reserve is notified of our presence. The new President will not meet with us, but he is sending his Chief of Staff. Hopefully, we can nip this war in the bud. Questions?"

Adam got up from the table. "Coraline will not be going? She made all the difference in the world during the first meeting."

"No. Coraline has asked to stay behind on this one. She has.....work to do."

CHAPTER EIGHTEEN
THE MESSENGER

The light above Charles Reynolds seemed far off and in a haze or fog of some kind. He shook his head slightly and squinted rapidly, attempting to open his eyes completely. When waking from a dreamless sleep the hands usually come up to the face to wipe away the sleep, but his hands would not obey this instinct. Struggling to find his bearings, his mind began to shed its muddled state. The light became sharper as his surroundings melted into view and he suddenly remembered where he was before this sleep overtook him.

"Do you prefer sitting or standing? You've been lying there for some time."

"I would like to stand, but... but I can't move."

"Try now."

He felt suddenly unrestrained and instinctively took a deep breath. Coraline's secret garden loomed large in his vision. The deep black dome far above was filled with stars that had the appearance of exquisite diamonds, sparkling in just the perfect type of light in which jewelers love to display their wares. The smell of the roses and the peacefulness of this small world swept over him to the point he felt he may not be able to breathe this air for much longer. Why such a heavenly sight would make him feel a depth of despair he did not know. This should have been enjoyable, but it was

148

not. He wanted to run and hide, but he couldn't.

The glowing golden tones that ribboned the horizon in every direction made him feel the anticipation of dawn, or dusk, or both. The fact he couldn't decide gave him the sensation he was in a timeless place. There was no future. There was no past. There was only right now. This made him feel even more uncomfortable because if there is no time, the only thing that matters is being. He knew his being was as out of place here as it was the perfect place for Coraline.

He turned to see who it was who spoke to him. It was not Coraline. Seated upon the stone-like bench was a figure that glowed. The radiance of its light concealed details such as facial features and even gender.

"Who are you?" Charles asked.

"I am a messenger of the One."

"For you, Mr. Reynolds, he is THE Messenger."

Charles recognized Coraline's voice and turned to confirm it. She was hovering in mid-air with her legs crossed. He studied her for a moment, then slowly turned to the radiant being. Inside, he shook with fear because he knew he was without power here. Trying his best to hide the fact, he decided to attempt to lighten the mood.

"What, you can't hover like our little red-headed friend here?" he asked in a demeaning tone. This obvious blustering for control was as ineffective as his question.

"Does hovering impress you?"

Charles pondered the brilliance of the question. An answer in the affirmative would be an admission of inferiority. An answer in the negative would be recognized as a lie in this place. He changed the subject.

"Who is the One?" he asked.

"In the One we live and move and exist by His will. In the One all things hold together. Even you, Charles Reynolds."

"That's nice," said Charles in a patronizing tone with a roll of his eyes.

A wave of the Messenger's hand suddenly transported Reynolds off of the dais to be suspended in the air twenty or thirty paces from them. The man struggled helplessly to make his feet touch the ground or at least move himself to an upright position. He was a pathetic figure writhing in the air, with no way to affect movement in any direction. It would have been entertaining to watch, but Coraline and the Messenger gave their full attention to one another. Happy for the temporary removal of the subject of this gathering, she floated down onto the dais and sat cross-legged before the Messenger as if to hang onto his every word.

"Coraline, how is Eli? I trust he is well."

"Very well, Messenger. He's growing and making friends. He hasn't been the same since you last spoke with us."

"I very much enjoyed talking with him. His innocence and child-like faith were refreshing. Very much different than this one," he said as he pointed his hand toward Charles.

"This one has no faith and long ago exchanged his innocence for the perception of power," said Coraline with a tone of uncertainty. "But....," she paused.

"Continue."

"I didn't feel comfortable bringing judgment to this one on my own or handing him over to those who would seek justice."

"Ah, but Coraline, you brought judgment to one other and you did not seek advice."

"Yes," she said glancing over at Charles Reynolds. "I didn't hesitate on that occasion, and I was correct."

"What is the difference here, child?"

"There is some good in this one," she said almost pleadingly.

"He killed one of your friends."

"He did," she said nodding with a purpose.

"And yet you did not act as you did before."

"This is different. The man I judged in Llano murdered Nick's fiancée because... well ... he was a killer. He... he enjoyed killing. Mr. Reynolds is a soldier. A soldier in a war. He believes he's fighting on the right side, but he feels regret for abusing his gift; for taking advantage of people."

The Messenger's eyes studied Coraline as if he were just as interested in her thoughts and character as a human might be interested in his. He understood completely there was much she needed to learn, but the fascinating thing to him was she had experiences that intrigued him. "Continue," he said.

"This one is gifted," Coraline stated as if she were defending a sibling.

"Now we get to the heart of the matter. You would like to believe all who are gifted must be good because all gifts are given by the One."

"As much as I'd like to believe that, I know it isn't true. The man responsible for this war, Dr. Tanner, is a gifted man. He abuses his gifts and the gifts of the people he has in his prison. I want to believe he has brainwashed this one." She again glanced at Reynolds who continued to struggle. "If I cannot convince him there is a better way than the path he has chosen, he will be handed over to the Walsh family for judgment. I suspect it will not go well for him. When I searched him to find what harm he has done, I discovered a deep shame for what he had done. As grievous as his evil actions have been, he felt remorse."

"Perhaps if I spoke with him," said the Messenger.

"That is what I was hoping for," said Coraline as she stood.

"Then, leave him with me. But, before you go, there is something you should know."

"What is it?"

"Your father is one of Dr. Tanner's captive. He will use your father's gift against you. Do not go blindly in. What is it you humans say? Look before you leap? Trust in the One," he said. He then whispered, "but, you may be able to find out more from this one," nodding toward Reynolds, "when I give him back to you. That is all I can say."

"Is my dad alright? Is he well? I can feel he is alive, but that's it," Coraline said taking a step toward the Messenger. There was no answer. Only a *look* that reminded her of the last thing he said. That was all he could say.

"Give my thanks to the One."

"Thank Him yourself."

"I do. Every day." She smiled at him and turned away.

Alex and Hayley raced their aircraft ahead to reconnoiter the Texas Ranger HQ helipad and adjacent structures. Once they were convinced it was safe, they flashed their landing lights, then moved aside as their searchlights scanned the grounds below. Remo Two made a rapid approach, then set down gently onto the rooftop. The ramp emerged from the saucer-like aircraft as the large door opened. Madison and Jennifer were the first to step out onto the ramp wearing full combat gear. Madison carried her suppressed, titanium, plasma machine-pistol, while Jennifer cradled her beloved Blackie, the largest rifle imaginable. Both women wore a poker face that did not convey the anger they were feeling at the events of the past 48 hours.

Major Johnston, standing beside one of his Rangers at the roof stairwell, grinned when he saw the two women and turned to his subordinate. "Well-protected, wouldn't you say?"

The Ranger smiled pleasantly. "Sir, may I have a transfer to Junction? We need an office there and I think I should head it up."

"Easy now, hot-dog. You may not be as qualified for that task as you think you are. Let me give you a bit of advice. Be very careful how you tread around that one. She's twice as dangerous as Hollings and Jameson, not because she's more highly trained, but because she is absolutely unpredictable. Yes sir, mind your P's and Q's around that one," the major said just before walking toward the aircraft.

Evelyn and Nick exited the aircraft with Kate and Eli close behind.

Major Johnston held his arms wide to receive Evelyn. "My deepest condolences for the loss of our Hedgehog. The entire state will mourn his passing. Every teenager in the great State of Texas wanted to be him, and I don't blame them. He was a remarkable boy."

"Thank you, Sam. That means the world coming from you," she replied.

Nick pointed to a row of packing crates lined up along the edge of the roof. "What are those, Major?"

"A helicopter landed just prior to the Chief of Staff's

arrival. They unloaded them, left four guys, then took off. I was curious, but they didn't stick around for questions. I was curious and was about to inspect them when the second helicopter landed.

"Tell me what you know about the Chief of Staff," said Evelyn.

"Their group landed just minutes before you. Had an awfully large entourage with him. Two dozen landed on the roof and a truckload or two came in through the front door. I expected to meet him here on the helipad, but the guys who landed said he was coming through the front door. I didn't bother to go downstairs to meet him. He's probably waiting for us in the conference room now. From what I've heard about him, he's tough. Retired military, four-star General. Nick, you've met him. According to records, he was the officer who recommended you for the Congressional Medal of Honor. He was standing right beside you in the photograph of the President putting the thing around your neck."

"Oh. Him," said Nick.

"I read the account of what you did to earn that medal. I'm as shocked as anyone you lived through that. You'll have to tell me the story one day."

"Yes, sir. Of course," Nick said looking up into the sky at the New Castlehale flyers circling the building.

Evelyn smiled as he broke into the humble routine he displayed often. In her opinion it was one of his most endearing characteristics. She patted him on the arm and said, "Nick, you'll have to tell us all that story. Now, Sam, please continue concerning the Chief of Staff."

"Well, ma'am, there's not a lot to say except the news media and the world is watching to see how he handles this situation. On one hand, he does not want to seem weak, but on the other hand, he does not want to restart a war that should never have happened in the first place. Stupid people did stupid things back then that ignited a war that changed the world. The only thing that hasn't changed about this world is there are still plenty of stupid people. I think you will do well meeting with him. I have to warn you though, he will not allow Eli to come into his presence."

"But Eli is not a reader! I purposefully left Coraline behind as a show of good faith."

"I'm not sure that will matter to him, but I'll ask. Follow me. I'll take you to the meeting room."

"Major, what about the men who came in through the front door. Are they scattered through the building?" Nick asked.

"Hell no. I gave instructions only the Chief of Staff and his personal guard would get past the first floor. I told the rest to sit down and grab something to read. His personal guard of fifteen escorted the Chief of Staff upstairs. Seems like a lot of security, but after what happened to the old President, well, they're probably just being cautious."

The group walked down the hallway to the entrance of the upper floor. Opening the door Major Johnson froze in place. He held up his left hand in a fist as he drew his pistol with his right. He pointed to the blood splatter on the wall behind the door.

"What's happening here, Major?" whispered Evelyn.

"There should be two guards here."

Evelyn turned to Eli. "What can you tell us?"

Eli closed his eyes for a moment. "There is danger here. Wounded on this floor. Men waiting in the rooms ahead. Fighting on the floors below."

Evelyn turned to Jennifer and said, "Quickly. Escort Kate and Eli back to the aircraft and wait there for Guan Yin. As soon as she arrives, you come back here."

"Queen to Flyers One and Two."

"Go ahead, Queen."

"Coyote, we have a problem. Cover for three as they run for Remo. Slice, put Guan Yin on the helipad. Have her take Remo Two a safe distance and wait for our word. We may need to exit quickly."

"Roger that, Queen. Slice on her way down."

"Coyote, contact home base, let them know we've walked into a trap. Waive the Governor off. He's walking right into it. Go to high alert. Queen out."

Major Johnston, Nick and Madison had their weapons raised as they moved to the first room on the right. The door was locked and rightly so. It was labeled *Weapons Locker*.

Major Johnston used a key to open the door and they all entered. Madison, already properly armed, stood by the door as Nick and the major loaded up with long guns of their choice. Nick grabbed a plasma rifle and placed grenades on his belt, while Major Johnston's choice was a 12-gauge auto-shotgun.

"I think whoever is waiting for us must want some of this," he said as he put on a harness that held quad-loaders for quick shell access. Evelyn walked past, eyeing the gun rack for a weapon when Nick said, "Evelyn, you don't have to do this. You should join Kate and Eli in Remo. We're suited to this kind of work."

She stopped and reached for a Beretta Plasma Carbine, then pulled a vest loaded with spare magazines from the wall. As she tugged up the zipper, she looked up at Nick and said, "These Rangers helped us when we were in the thick of it. It's time I repay their kindness. I can do this." Then she gave the charging handle a quick tug and released it with a snap of finality.

Nick took charge just as Jennifer came bounding down the stairs with her huge black rifle at the ready. He made hand-signs that indicated he would take point to be followed by Madison and the Major. Jennifer and Evelyn would take up the rear and watch their six. He then pointed to a room on the left with the door closed. Knowing it was a small conference room, he placed a wired device on the door itself and listened carefully in an earpiece. Using hand signals, he indicated the door should be covered before he dug into a vest pocket to retrieve a small device that looked like a simple cable connected to an LED screen. Pushing the cable in the gap between the bottom of the door and the floor, he could clearly see three men with rifles covering the door. Pointing to the Major, he indicated he wanted a sizeable hole in the door. The major smiled as he pulled a special 12-gauge round from his vest and inserted it into the magazine. Motioning for everyone to get low, he placed his left hand on the charging handle and nodded to Nick who pulled the pin on a grenade and squatted to the left of the door. The major racked the explosive round into the chamber and pulled the trigger. The blast created a hole about the size of a grapefruit. Plasma fire came through the wall at chest level over Evelyn and Jennifer's heads as Nick shoved the grenade through the hole, then pivoted on his feet and shielded his head. The explosion was deafening, but immediately the Major entered the doorway stooping low with his shotgun at the ready as Nick followed closely at his heels but maintained a high position. Four men lay either dead or unconscious on the floor. Outside in the hallway, gunfire ensued as men in fatigues poured from the rooms down the hall. The soldiers exiting the rooms had not counted on Jennifer laying down a large volume of fire with her .308 rifle as Maddie's plasma rifle spewed projectiles at 1600 rpm. The survivors did a lot of back-peddling as they realized the hall was the least safe place to be at that moment.

The building shook with a ferocious explosion that seemed to come from the rooftop.

"Queen to Coyote, report."

"Activity on rooftop. Watch your six. Men were hiding in the packing crates on the roof. They were firing as they emerged. Slice launched an HE. One or two did make it to the stairwell. Guns on your six, Mom."

Evelyn tapped Jennifer and pointed to the stairwell. Bringing her beloved Blackie to bear on the stairwell, she made sure she had a 40mm grenade round loaded in the tube attached to the underside of her barrel, then depressed the trigger. There was a deep 'THONK', immediately followed by a blast in the stairwell down the hall. From Alex's perspective hovering over the building he saw a body fly out of the stairwell.

"Coyote to Queen. Bad guys in stairwell are toast. Coyote to Slice, I will remain on station. You better get down there. Reconnoiter before you jump."

"Coyote, can you spare Dice?"

Alex thought about it for a few seconds before he answered. He had lost one family member in the past 24 hours, he was hesitant to lose another, but he knew Sarah was up to the task, especially after Coraline had done a joining of the minds with her and Hayley. In theory, Sarah should know what Hayley knows. In theory. He was going to trust Coraline on this one.

"Choose your floor; I'll send her down."

"Roger that. Watch my spike."

Both aircraft hovered down to the rooftop level exactly between the Ranger Headquarters and the hotel across the park. Hayley flipped up a monitor and powered up her array of specialized cameras. Using forward-looking infrared combined with other wavelengths, she could see the first floor was filled with soldiers trying to fight their way upstairs but were prevented by men and women who were obviously Rangers. The occasional cowboy hat was a dead give-away. The Rangers were pinned in from below and above. Soldiers on the third floor were tossing grenades down the stairs with hopes of dislodging their prey. Hayley chose the fourth floor. Placing the crosshairs on a window, she fired a spike through the glass which embedded itself into a concrete pillar. The result was a zip-line connecting her flyer to the building. She opened the canopy, slid down to the wing, connected a device from her belt to the cable and dove from the craft. Alex shifted his flyers to a position above Flyer Two and before Hayley had even reached the building, Sarah made the leap to Flyer Two and was almost immediately on her way down the zip line.

Hayley released her carabiner from the zip line and turned in time to help Sarah make the landing. Both had their feet planted on solid floor when Hayley sent a message to her flyer to release the cable and ascend.

"Slice to Coyote. We're on floor. First floor is bad guys, second floor Rangers, third floor bad guys. We'll take third floor; you take first. Slice out."

Sarah had already headed for the stairwell and stumbled upon one soldier guarding the exit. He was more surprised to see her since he had his head buried in his cellphone. It cost him his life. Her sword was completely through a horizontal arc before he could even raise his rifle. Hayley came up from behind just as the man's head went tumbling down the steps. Having shared experiences from Hayley's past during the mind-merge, she reacted exactly as Hayley would have: one enemy down. Together they moved down the stairs to the third floor. Shouted commands could be heard coming from that floor as they neared the landing. One soldier stood watch over the stairwell. This one however was giving his full attention to his task of guarding his team's rear position. The distance from her position to the guard was too great for stealth, or even a concerted rush. Hayley held a clenched fist up as a sign to Sarah they would pause for a moment to think.

CHAPTER NINTEEN
TRUTH BE TOLD

Alex hovered his craft mere feet above the lawn as he filled the first floor with fire from his aircraft's machine guns. Being careful to avoid hitting the structure's pillars, he made existence impossible for anyone on the first floor. His plane moved laterally across the lawn and around the corner of the building above the parking lot as he poured continuous fire into the building. Above the flyer on the second floor, he noticed a single Ranger standing in an opening created by broken glass. The man wearing the silver-starred badge was giving him the thumbs up. It didn't take long before the Rangers on the second floor took advantage of the situation and fought their way down to the first floor to clear it of remaining threats. Seeing that, Alex moved his aircraft up and over the building again to keep watch on the area. A quick check with Hermes told him the skies in the vicinity were clear except for the two flyers. He did take note of the Governor's helicopter and two escorts enroute from the south along Interstate 35 that had turned and were headed back to Austin. He knew in the next few minutes dozens of fighter aircraft would fill the skies over Waco.

On the center landing between the third and fourth floor, Sarah placed her hand on Hayley's chest and said, "Let me do this." With that she removed her harness and puffed up her hair.

Sarah sashayed down the stairs, smiling as if she were the princess of the grand ball. The soldier had his rifle trained on her immediately, but she made no threatening moves except to move steadily down the steps. Seeing this slender pink-haired girl coming down the stairs looking as she did, threw his mind into a tail-spin. He lowered his weapon. Before he could begin to raise the rifle again, Sarah drew her Glock and fired one round. He dropped to the floor. She turned as Hayley tossed her battle harness down to her.

"Now this is going to be a story for the whole family," Hayley snorted as she moved past. Poking her head into the doorway leading onto the third floor for only a brief second, she got a quick assessment of the situation. Apparently, the exchange of gunfire between the 2nd floor Rangers and the 3rd floor federals masked the single shot that took out their rear guard. As she formulated an attack plan, her eyes rested on the automatic rifle of the dead soldier at her feet. She picked it up and handed it over to Sarah. Sarah had already procured a grenade from the man's harness and held it in front of her with a very entertained smirk.

"I like the way you think," said Hayley, "I'll toss this. Wait for the bang. You go left. I'll go right. Are you ready?"

Sarah checked the rifle to make sure there was a round in the chamber, then nodded.

The grenade exploded with a deafening roar before Hayley moved to the right with her sword in hand. Sarah entered to the left, firing the rifle into the remaining men bunched up around the door of the opposite stairwell. Three of the men who escaped the initial blast took cover behind desks or support pillars. They would have easily pinned Sarah down to move in on her, had it not been for Hayley coming from behind; her sword's blinding flashes cut through them faster than they could react. The entire floor was cleared in a matter of a minute.

"Rangers below! This is Hayley Walsh, Defender. Third

floor is clear. Hold your fire!"

She walked down the staircase and was met by Ranger Janet Smithers, who embraced her. Even with the blood-splattered face it was easy to see Hayley reacted with a sign of recognition. "I remember you, Janet. Maddie introduced us. Speaking of Maddie, we should move upstairs to see if we can take some pressure off of her and Major Johnston on the top floor. As they turned to retrace their steps, Ranger Smithers was slightly shocked to see Sarah standing over a pile of federal storm-troopers cradling a rifle. She walked over to the slender teenager and touched her arm.

"I'm so sorry about Hedgehog," Ranger Smithers said, as her eyes passed over the dead soldiers lying about. "The kid was a hero of Texas if there ever was one. You know, they say dishing out retribution never makes you feel better, but I'd have to say at this moment, I think they're full of it. I've lost a lot of good friends this evening. Although I may not feel this way in the morning, right now, this feels right.

Sarah nodded, unable to add anything because she was a bucket of raw emotions. Everything that happened to her in the past week felt to her as if she was operating in a dense fog. Never was there time to prepare herself for what would transpire, but how could there be? Not only for her, but for anyone? The moment she returned to Texas from China with Hayley and Guan Yin, they were cast into the disorienting rush of war. Twenty-four hours had not passed since she lost her brother, and as reassuring as Coraline's ability to make good-byes possible was, she was again cast into this battle. There was hardly time to breathe before she was thrown into her first face-to-face encounter with flesh and blood enemies. The contrast between launching missiles from 12,000 feet and fighting face-to-face was stark, and in some ways, devastating. She marveled that she could do the things she had done in the past ten minutes. It was Coraline. Something in the mind connection between herself and Hayley prepared her for this. These thoughts flowed through her mind and heart as she ejected the near-empty magazine from her rifle and replaced it with a fresh one jerked from the harness of the soldier at her feet. She removed an ammo harness from another soldier and pulled it over her shoulder.

"Sarah, are we good?"

"What?"

"Are we good to go? There is more work for us above," Hayley said reaching out to touch Sarah's other arm. Hayley and Janet Smithers had made eye contact that spoke concern for Sarah's mental state.

"I'm better than good, sister. Let's kick their butts," Sarah said with smiling eyes.

Hayley was impressed. She'd seen Sarah put on a brave face, along with a supposedly reassuring smile in the past, and knew during those times she was forcing herself to feel better. But just now, she smiled with her eyes. She knew Sarah well enough to know things really were *better than good*. Hayley shouted gleefully, "Then let's do it!"

Together the three turned toward the opposite stairwell when they realized the other Rangers hadn't paused for even a second. Already, they were engaged in a gun battle with the federal storm-troopers above.

"Coyote to Remo Two."

"Remo Two here."

"Guan Yin, where are you?"

"We are on soccer field... across river!"

"Soccer field?"

"Yes. It says 'Beijing" on field."

"Do you mean Baylor?"

"Ah. Yes. Bay Lor. Soccer field."

"That's a football stadium. Different game. Listen up, Guan Yin. In just a few minutes the skies will be filled with friendly planes. Expect them. Anyway, get back up here and cover the roof with your guns. Listen for instructions and keep your eyes on that roof. Queen may need a quick exit!"

"Okay. Coyote. On way."

The storm-troopers on the floor below Nick's team

engaged the Rangers fighting their way upstairs. In the storm-troopers' minds something had to happen soon or they would be trapped. Besides, their objective from the beginning was to kill the Walsh family and anyone else who showed up to meet the Chief of Staff. Making a concerted effort to push Nick and his crew up toward the roof, they quickly made progress. Nick tossed a grenade down the hall which rolled past the storm-troopers and clanked down the stairs before exploding. He then used a hand signal that indicated retreat. The small band began a leapfrogging maneuver to escape what was coming. One or two would provide cover fire while the lead peeled back to take up a position behind to cover for those peeling off past them. If they could just make it to the roof, they'd have air cover while they made their escape. Everyone except Evelyn and Nick made it to the stairwell. Nick shoved Evelyn into the Weapons Locker and yelled for the rest of the team to make a break for it. He entered the locker room and slammed the door shut behind him. It was a solid steel door, but he knew it would not hold for long. He was hoping for enough time for the Rangers below to fight their way to him.

Ushering Evelyn to the back of the locker room, he asked her to get down into the corner, and began to cover her with flack vests. It took some grunting, but he managed to move a steel cabinet to at least provide concealment and temporary protection for what would be coming through that door. He knew a plasma round would cut through it like butter, but he noted most of the storm-troopers were carrying conventional rifles.

"Keep these protective vests over you. We just need to hold out long enough for the cavalry to arrive."

She didn't argue but watched him from beneath her cover as he pulled a large squad automatic weapon (SAW) from the wall. He loaded it with a bulky, double-drum magazine. The door to the weapons locker rattled, then the doorknob was blown away leaving only a hole there. He had put bolts in place to hold the door, so he still had time. Someone on the other side of the door was stupid enough to press his eye to the hole. The 6.8mm bullets from the weapon in Nick's hand found the hole and the face behind it.

Plasma rounds came through the door as Nick dove to the opposite corner. There were several attempts to kick the door open, but the laws of physics were having none of it. Nick traded his SAW for a plasma rifle and emptied the magazine into the door. There was a momentary silence.

The storm-troopers in the hall apparently found a better way to dislodge the door because it exploded from its hinges and hit the floor. Nick stood up and laid down fire through the opening. Evelyn continued to watch Nick as he directed his fire down the length of the room. She witnessed bullets hitting his flack vest, tearing chunks from it. His helmet was torn from his head and even his clothing was being ripped to shreds from his body, yet he continued to pour fire toward the enemy. The bullet impacts were pushing him back till his back was against the wall. It seemed like hundreds of bullets were tearing into him, even to the point of disintegrating the very gun he held in his hand. He forced himself forward to grab another plasma rifle and continued.

Evelyn could not understand what she was seeing. He should have been dead twenty seconds ago, but there he stood, his vest and shirt in tatters, pieces falling from him as he unflinchingly stood his ground returning fire. She noticed the volume of incoming rounds was diminishing. When they stopped, she looked up to see an unscathed Nick standing above her with a smile on his face. She pushed the covering of vests off of her and stood staring as if she saw a ghost. Looking toward the doorway, Hayley and Madison stood looking aghast over a pile of dead soldiers. The looks on their faces would not have been different had Nick been a newly-arrived extraterrestrial with six eyes and horns. Nick just waved.

Looking into Evelyn's eyes he said, "Truth be told ... I'm bulletproof. Coraline has her gifts, and I have mine."

CHAPTER TWENTY
REVELATION

"What?"

"Bulletproof."

Evelyn walked directly to Madison and pulled the .45 caliber automatic from her holster.

"Say that again."

"Bulletproof."

BAM! She shot him with Maddie's pistol hitting him square in the chest.

"Ow!"

"Bulletproof? And you never bothered to tell me?"

"Well, I had my reasons."

Evelyn took aim at Nick with Maddie's pistol and pulled the trigger twice. BAM! BAM!

"OW!! Bullets can't kill me, but they still hurt!" he yelled, obviously hurt more emotionally than physically.

Madison reached over and gently took her gun back as Evelyn turned and walked briskly up the stairs. The beautiful Ranger stared at Nick for a moment, then fired another three rounds at him. BAM! BAM! BAM!

"HEY!!!" Nick yelled.

"You couldn't even tell your partner?" she asked before offering Hayley a shot.

"I'm good," Hayley said holding her hands up to reject the offer.

Madison said, "Ranger Nick, you should find some clothes before you catch a chill in that almost-naked condition."

"I'll get clothes out of my locker downstairs. Hayley? Can we get Eli down here? I'm certain there are a lot of wounded here. Ours and theirs."

The thought registered heavily on both Hayley and Madison as they sprinted up the stairs. This left only Major Johnston, his friend Pete, and a handful of Rangers who were peering inside the locker.

"So, Mr. Congressional Medal of Honor. It now makes total sense how you survived the operation that earned you that medal. Yes, sir, it makes total sense," he said as he loaded another shotgun shell.

"Now, Major. A .45 slug hurts bad enough, but you are NOT going to shoot me with that 12-gauge."

"Well, sir. I figure you owe me one. You see, you always kept yourself between us and them tonight and here I was thinking, 'my God, this is the bravest man I've ever seen!' You could have said, 'I'll take this, my beloved Major, because, well… I'm bulletproof,' but you didn't. You let us follow you right into the enemy's face!"

"Are you telling me, Major, you would have believed me if I told you I was bulletproof?"

BAM! Nick was pushed against the wall by the blast from the Major's shotgun.

"OOWW!!!!" he shouted louder than anyone had ever heard him shout before.

Nick scrambled to picked up a handgun from the floor and said, "I swear by the One, the next person who shoots me will lose a knee!"

No one stayed. Nick kicked around the rubble lying about the floor for a few seconds till he found his personal sidearm. Upon inspection he discovered it had been destroyed by a plasma round. He tossed it onto the floor but soon found a temporary replacement on a shelf. Exiting into the hall, he turned just as Evelyn was stooped over checking for signs of life. Eli stood next to her but took time to timidly wave hello with a questioning look on his face. "It must have been my appearance," Nick thought. Evelyn and Nick's eyes met for a moment. He could tell there was a little hurt there. 'She'll get over it,' he thought as he headed for his downstairs locker. It wasn't until he got into the brightly lit part of the hallway he realized how much of his clothing had actually been burned away by the plasma rounds. He tried covering himself discreetly with his hands as he glanced this way and that to see if anyone was staring. They were. It's not often the Rangers in the Waco headquarters got to see one of their captains walking nearly naked with a gun in one hand and a badge in the other. There was hardly enough cloth left on which to pin the badge, which incidentally had a bullet hole through the center star. The belt around his waist held onto just enough material to make him look like he wore a loincloth.

The Rangers were too busy moving from body to body checking for life signs to continue staring at their captain. When Nick reached the locker room, he removed his boots and belt. Upon inspection, he discovered the boots were fine, but the belt would need to be retired. There were only a couple of leather flaps holding what was left of his holster. After years of innumerable firefights, both as a soldier and a Texas Ranger, he had never been shot up this bad that he could recall, and he had never been shot by a plasma round. Until this evening, he had no idea how his body would handle one but certainly knew now, having been hit by hundreds. Bullets normally just made small holes in his clothing, but the plasma rounds burned away much of the clothing at the impact point. He was glad to know the extent of his gift.

Reaching into his locker, he grabbed a clean shirt and removed it from its hanger. His mind went back to a time when he was a ten year old on a trip with his father into Austin. He was very excited because the happy purpose of the trip was his first visit to a gun store. After stern instructions from dad about not touching anything, he obediently shadowed his dad through the establishment. Standing at the gun case, his dad asked the salesperson to show him one of the dozens of AR-15s that lined the rack behind the counter. Listening carefully, the young Nick took in every bit of the information the clerk rattled off about the difference between the various manufacturers. Every head turned to a nearby counter where the salesperson gave a customer opposite her a loud verbal warning, "Please sir, do not put that loaded magazine into that pistol!"

"I know what I'm doing! I've been handling guns all my life," the offended man responded.

The accidental discharge gave evidence his lifetime of gun-handling was the perfect example of the wrong kind. It was obvious to all he had his finger on the trigger when the slide ran forward. The gun's report was nauseously loud as every individual in the store froze in place, hoping no one was injured. The offender carefully laid the loaded weapon on the counter and backed away saying, "That was not my fault! There's something wrong with that gun!"

"Stand right where you are!" said the gun store owner who came out of the back room. "Is everyone okay? Where did the bullet go?"

Nicks dad knelt before him and spun him around a couple of times. "Are you alright son?" Nick nodded in the affirmative. "Don't mention this to your mother. She'd just get upset, okay?" He nodded again.

The owner reached out to remove the loaded weapon from the counter. He ejected the magazine, then the round from the chamber. Inspecting the bullet, he saw it was a run-o-the-mill 9mm hollow point. "Keep looking! That bullet had to go somewhere! And YOU!" he said pointing to the offender. "You will produce some identification so we can bill you if we find a hole in a five-thousand dollar rifle!" The man quickly pulled out some ID and handed it to the clerk.

After ten minutes of searching, they gave up and threw the idiot 'gun-handler' out of the store with a warning to never come back. Conversations resumed and everyone generally ignored Nick. Here was his chance to feel what it was rolling around inside his shirt. He unbuttoned just one and reached his hand inside and came out with a mushroomed bullet. His eyes widened as he realized there was a hole in his shirt, but no hole in him. After buttoning up again, he walked a few feet and pretended to pick something off the floor. Turning to his dad, he said, "Look what I found!" and held up the bullet.

"Where did you find it?" asked the owner.

"Over there beneath the shelf," he answered with a look he hoped they would believe him. But why would they not? He found the bullet!

"Thank you, young man. I would have spent a week looking for that! Do you have a .22 rifle?"

Nick's dad answered, "He sure does!"

"Well, here's a box of .22 just for you," and he handed Nick the box of 50 rounds.

"What do you say to the man?" Nick's dad said.

"Thank you, sir."

The images of that day faded from his thoughts as he leaned his head against the locker. A lot had happened in his life since that day. He never mentioned that incident to a soul. It wasn't until he was in the military that he again discovered he was indeed impervious to bullets. He had no explanation other than the fact his sister was taken from the family because of a special 'gift.' She could predict events before they happened with uncanny accuracy. So, he assumed he must have received a 'gift' also. It certainly was different than Heather's, but it was a gift, nonetheless.

After pulling on a pair of jeans, he tucked in his shirt and then dug through his locker for a spare gun belt. The only one in there was one he wore only on dress occasions. It was fancy, but it would do just fine. He turned the Colt auto he carried from upstairs over in his hand several times to look it over. Walking to a table nearby, he field-stripped the gun to inspect it more closely. It had some wear on certain parts, but it looked to be a functioning weapon. He hated the thought of carrying an untested gun anywhere, but after he checked it over, he felt it would get him back to New Castlehale, where he had a good replacement. After tonight, he even considered the notion of carrying a 9mm from here on out. Being bulletproof, he always felt like he could absorb any number of hits from a criminal before he took careful aim and shot back with a big projectile in .45 caliber. But, going to war, he needed as many bullets at his disposal as he could carry. New Castlehale had an arsenal with many choices. He'd think about it when he got home.

"Home," he said to himself. It's funny how he's come to

think of that place as home now. He shook off the stray thoughts and figured he best get a move on. He didn't want Evelyn taking off without him and felt he needed to explain things. In the top of his locker was a spare cowboy hat. It looked entirely too new, but it was all he had. He put it on, looked in the mirror, and found all he could think about was Evelyn.

He walked from the locker room and took the stairs. Several groups of people carrying bodies down the stairs on stretchers looked at him as he passed. He even met a few federal storm troopers wearing handcuffs as they marched downstairs in the custody of Texas Rangers. Apparently, Eli had done his work on these guys because their clothes were soaked in blood but seemed healthy.

He stopped at the weapons locker again to grab spare magazines for his sidearm, and then found an undamaged plasma rifle to carry out. Taking one last look down the hall he was amazed his own people were not injured or killed during the fight. Major Johnston was right about one thing. He had made sure he was always between his people and the federal troopers. He took a lot of rounds that would have hit them.

Walking up to the roof, he looked around only to find Alex sitting in the cockpit of his flyer. Remo Two was nowhere to be seen and Hayley was gone.

"Are you it?" he asked Alex.

"Yup. Sarah went back with mom. Hayley and Guan Yin rode protection, and I'm here to give you a lift. I think mom is pretty hurt by your secrecy about being bulletproof. Are you really bulletproof, dude?"

"It's my gift," Nick said as he climbed into the rear seat of the aircraft.

"Yah. That's something mom would have liked to have known some time back. She's spent a lot of time worrying about you when you were off doing your Ranger thing. She loves you, you know. Helmet is back there. You can adjust it to your big fat head." Alex smirked as he reached down to flip a succession of switches on the controls panel.

"Big fat head, huh? Is that what your mom thinks?"

"I'm just saying, dude. You shoulda told her."

"I know. I know. I wish now I had. But when I spend time with her, the last thing I think about is the fact bullets bounce off of me. You know what it's like with you and Sarah. Doesn't being with Sarah make all cogent thought leak out of your brain and run off onto the flight line? Well, that's what your mom does to me. I'm always asking myself, 'Am I moving too fast? Am I moving too slow?' I think I'm a pretty bright guy. I wouldn't say I was inept around women. But she's not an ordinary woman, your mother."

"No, she's not. So, what are you going to say to her when you get back?"

"Thinking about what I'm going to say and what actually comes out at the moment never seems to be the same."

"What would you like to say?" Alex asked as he looked down at the light on his communications control panel.

"I know I'm going to have to do some groveling. I know that. One of these days I know I'm going to tell her I love her. I've got it in my head to marry her. What do you think of that idea?"

Alex was going through his flight-prep when he froze his hand in mid-motion. "Marry? ...my mom?" he said into his headset.

"Yah."

"You know, some people would call that an old-fashioned notion."

"Don't I know it. But I'm an old fashioned guy. Your mom deserves nothing short of total commitment, and I'm willing to give her that."

"Well, my Texas Ranger friend, I will get you home as quickly as I possibly can. I'm absolutely positively sure I can beat Remo Two back to New Castlehale so you are waiting on the flight line when she comes through the doors. It's groveling time, Ranger."

Flyer One shot into the air, turned west and took off like a rocket.

Aboard Remo Two, Maddie, Jennifer, and Sarah were going on about the trap that almost caught them. They talked at length about how to prevent walking into another in the future. Kate could not bring herself to feel anything remotely close to excitement about the whole ordeal. She sat with her arms around Eli, who seemed to be sound asleep. Earlier when she and Eli were forced to take refuge with Guan Yin in Remo Two, she wished she had never agreed to come at all. Now, having seen Eli heal so many of the wounded soldiers and Rangers, she felt remorse at that initial judgment.

Evelyn decided she would pilot the aircraft back to New Castlehale manually because there were so many things about the week that weighed heavily on her. She had no desire for talk, but when she noticed there was a communication coming in, she switched to it so it came through her headset. To her surprise, Alex was transmitting everything being said in his aircraft. Her finger hovered over the button for a moment and stopped. The glow of the console in the darkened aircraft lit her face just enough to reveal the level of interest she had in this conversation. Her conscience reminded her about the privacy rules she established at New Castlehale and made her finger move ever so closer to the off switch.

"We're not at New Castlehale," she decided to herself as she pulled her finger back.

When the transmission stopped, she turned on her faux-GPS. There on the screen was a moving dot that represented Flyer One. He was traveling parallel to her course, but 15,000 feet above her and moving five times faster. A slight smile revealed a different mood after listening to what Nick had to say to Alex. Instead of increasing airspeed, she left it just as it was. They would get home soon enough.

Alex and Ranger Hollings stood in the bright lights of the landing bay waiting for the doors to the south canyon to open, allowing Remo Two entrance to New Castlehale. When the low beeping sound commenced, Alex turned to Nick and said, "Do you remember the first day you stepped foot onto this flight deck?"

Nick nodded affirmatively.

"And do you remember you looked over my shoulder to see that camera there watching and listening to every word we said as I talked about Sarah?"

Nick again nodded, but with a little more worry on his face.

"Well. This is a payback of sorts. My mom will step out of that aircraft having heard every word you said when you climbed aboard Flyer One."

"What?"

"Yup. But listen up. Speaking from experience, I happen to know this will work out well for you. I know my mom."

Just then Remo Two entered the landing bay and put down softly onto its designated area. They could see Evelyn's face as she shut down the aircraft. She looked up briefly at Nick and Alex, then continued what she was doing. The door opened and the ramp moved out to allow the passengers to disembark. Jennifer and Maddie came down the ramp first. They both nodded their heads as they moved, arm in arm, past Nick and Alex.

"Would you like to take a dip in the pool?" Jennifer asked Maddie.

"O my God, that would be heaven," Maddie answered as they exited the landing bay.

Kate had hold of Eli's hand as they came down the ramp. Eli still had the same puzzled look on his face he had back at Ranger Headquarters as he waved at Nick. The Ranger waved back.

"That poor kid," Nick said to Alex. "He's been through an awful lot of grief over the past year."

Alex responded, "He has. But he's got an asset most kids don't have. Coraline. I'm sure she's helped him make sense of all this. She has a knack for that. Look at how much she has helped us over the past year."

"You got that right," Nick responded, nodding his head.

Sarah exited the craft and approached Alex with quiet dignity; a look of exhaustion encasing her entire being. Gently wrapping her arms around him, she realized this comforting action was as much for herself as it was for Alex. After a greeting kiss, she held him at arm's length and said,

"Everything will be different from this day forward."

They all turned to watch as Evelyn appeared in the doorway of the aircraft, paused for a moment to think, then, in confident strides, walked down the ramp as if she were now committed to a course of action. Nick felt his heart in his throat as he watched her getting closer. Everything he thought he wanted to say was already melting from conscious thought. This shook him to his core because he knew he was going to stammer, and the first words out of his mouth would make or break him.

This is what happened instead: She walked directly to him, took him by the hand and led him from the flight deck. Alex and Sarah watched as their mom pulled the Texas Ranger by the hand from the landing bay. Before exiting, Nick looked over his shoulder to Alex and Sarah who waved back with full hearts.

Sarah was correct. Everything would be different from this point forward.

CHAPTER TWENTY-ONE
MEMORIAL

Adam leaned his back against the Artemis unit on the north-eastern edge of New Castlehale's mesa, holding a diagnostic tool in one hand and his forehead in the other. A few feet to his left, a panel had been removed, revealing the electronics within, the obvious object of his repairs. Having replaced the part, he plopped himself down to think and remember. This morning he had a difficult time focusing on the electronic relays because of the heavy numbness he felt after the loss of Hedgehog. As much grief as that kid could give the rest of the Walsh family with his Alex-like antics, he was universally loved. Adam came to that realization in the past 24 hours as he had thrown himself into war preparations in the hope of making this numbness go away. He instinctively knew the entire community had been doing all that needed to be done to engage in this war, in spite of the weight of grief. Today they would stop. Today, at 1100 hours, was Hedgehog's Memorial Service. Adam felt that if he took this moment of time to grieve, perhaps the service itself would be bearable. For now, it hurt more deeply than he had ever felt, and he cried harder than he could remember. Grateful for his time alone, he poured his heart out over the canyons and mesas. Looking out over the majestic pre-dawn view, he felt for the first time in his life somehow connected to the beauty that surrounded the place

175

he called home. Was the feeling a result of the loss, or was this a by-product of the time he spent with Coraline? They were worth contemplating as the sky grew lighter and lighter. The bracing, gentle breeze dried his eyes quickly and enabled him to enjoy the sunrise for the first time in ages.

"Coffee?"

Adam turned to see April holding two cups.

"Sure. How long have you been standing there?"

"Only a second or two," she said as she sat next to him. "It's lovely here this early. Do you come here often?"

"Actually, no. I'm usually sitting in the galley at this time 'stuffing my face', as my mom calls it. I didn't sleep well last night, so I came up here to replace the primary relays in Artemis."

"Did they fry?"

"No. But I couldn't sleep thinking about them, so I thought I'd replace them and test these to see how they're holding out. We may need Artemis at any time, and I want to make sure these will hold up. April, we can't let one of those missiles reach the mesa. Not that I'm afraid they will do much damage to New Castlehale, but just because I want to beat these guys in every way."

"I understand," she said because she too felt the need for payback after losing her home.

"Adam, you and I haven't had any time alone since our family moved in. I understand the situation, but I've been aching to tell you... that I think about you every day. Especially after losing Hedgehog. I know how much you loved him."

Adam took her hand. "My whole life is turned upside down. Something about this seems harder to handle than the day I lost my dad. I can't put my finger on it. There was so much in life I cared about before the other day. I loved building machines and missiles and guns. I see now those arc just things. Everything I built, I built for people I love, and one of those people was murdered right here under our noses. I... I got too used to the Walsh family being the ones who dished it out and always came out on top. I thought we were invincible, but we're not."

"We're not," she echoed in a whisper. "But, we still have

people to build things for. Living in Kermit, my mom and I, and Rita, feared every day the wrong people would catch us with our guard down. Dad could protect us, but only if he were there. He often wasn't. We feared because the word 'invincible' wasn't even in our vocabulary. So, I understand why you would have that notion living here. Invincibility seemed a very appealing concept our first night here, sleeping in a steel structure, buried under hundreds of feet of rock. Hedgehog's death ended that for me, and now I'm back where I started; I am afraid again. Only now I have a family around me. A totally, bad-ass family. That'll change one's perspective if nothing else does."

Neither spoke for ten minutes as they watched the sun break the horizon. With the sun in his face, Adam stood, then reached for April's hand to help her up. He smiled and said, "We are a totally bad-ass family. And you're a part of it now. I can't wait to rain some of that bad-assery down on Mr. Tanner's head and pound him to dust. When that is over and we perhaps have some time to breathe, you and I are going to build toys that will change the planet. Help me get this panel closed up, then, let's go eat."

She tossed the remainder of her coffee onto the ground, then turned to Adam and pulled his face down to hers.

"I like your use of '*you and I*'. I'd say that's a deal."

There is no nicer way to seal a deal than with a kiss. They did.

Seated in her usual spot, Coraline observed the hustle and bustle in the galley with the same child-like curiosity that never seemed to leave her. This, in spite of the fact she had a greater grasp of the universe and its interwoven complexities than any adult alive, with the exception of her dad. She smiled as Lilly produced her usually splendid breakfast fare while Cholo sat in the corner reading his morning news from Austin. The customary noise levels were not present during this meal, however, quiet conversations took place between pairs at the table. Alex and Sarah whispered to each other sweetly, yet never ever missed the opportunity to pass this or that up and down the table. Jennifer, who commonly was the loudest voice at the table spoke in an uncharacteristically subdued manner with Ranger Madison, both of whom were already dressed in battle fatigues. Coraline noted that, thankfully, Jennifer adhered to Evelyn's 'No-grenades-at-the-breakfast-table' rule. Kate and Eli seemed to have a lot to whisper to one another concerning the loss of Hedgehog. Ruth and Trevor Brice were there with their daughter Rita seated between them. The three of them with their heads together, mom and dad convincing the young one she would feel better being here at breakfast with their entirely new extended family. Rita was suffering deeply.

Adam and April entered the galley holding hands. Everyone tried their best to act as if this was perfectly normal, but it was obvious some people are better actors than others. After greeting her parents, she and Adam moved around the table to sit in their usual spot next to Coraline, who in the past had purposefully sat between them to tease Adam. This time, she got out of her seat and moved over one chair so the two of them could be together.

"Thank you, baby sister. You are a sweetheart."

"It's where you belong, Gulliver," she said with her hand on his hairy forearm.

Coraline sighed as she sensed how grateful the whole family was she had shared Sarah's good-bye to Hedgehog with them. Occasionally, each of the whispering pairs would stop and glance her way. In spite of the horrible events of the past two days, she sensed the beginning of peace, the beginning of healing. She also knew she would have to spend a quality moment with Rita.

Evelyn and Nick entered the galley, stopping to give Lilly a warm, morning hug. Lilly always seemed to blush a bit whenever Nick greeted her each day. Cholo would be tempted to give her a teasing whack with her own wooden spoon had he been the caretaker of that instrument of instruction.

"Good morning," said Nick in a voice loud enough to get the attention of every person there. He paused for a moment, wondering how everyone was handling the revelation that one of their own had a fantastic gift but never bothered to tell a soul. "Evelyn has words for us that will be broadcast throughout New Castlehale."

Evelyn tapped the comDev that was pinned to her uniform. "Residents of New Castlehale, friends, and family, this is Evelyn Walsh. War has been declared on the Void, and we will answer that challenge. I received a message from the Governor of Texas last night. He has been in contact with the Governors of every patriot state and all their resources stand behind us. The State of Texas is with us. Young people and veterans who wish to join the fight are standing in lines all over the country to enlist. This won't do us much good over the next few days and weeks, but it demonstrates to Washington they have stepped over the line. Major military bases have picked sides, much like they did during the Cultural War sixty plus years ago. I personally believe there will be more saber-rattling for a few days before anyone decides to take large-scale action. We are going to take this pause to strengthen our position in a way we hope will cause the newly appointed President to refrain from further attacks for a while.

"But not today. Today will be a day of remembering and preparing. Recently, we have lost family, friends, and allies. They will live on in our thoughts and hearts. Today, at 1100 hours, there will be a Celebration of Life Service for Hedgehog on the flight deck. Dress will be according to each person's station and task here. Command will wear dress uniform. Air crews, space teams, ordinance crews, ground assault teams will wear what would bring the most honor to those who gave their lives. Speak to your section leaders. There will be a reception immediately following the service.

"This day, and tomorrow, will be filled with preparation because tomorrow evening we hit back. Tomorrow, we teach the Central Government and its minions, rogue or not, they cannot break treaty with us and not pay the price. I know many of you have been working non-stop for days on your contribution to the mission, which begins at 1900 hours tomorrow. Talk to your section leaders for instructions and tasks. May the One be with you and with us. That is all. Thank you."

Eyes exchanged glances all about the table. Not a cup clinked, or a fork moved for a minute. Evelyn and Nick sat down together at the table as Lilly poured them each a cup of coffee, the only sound in the room.

"So, Mom.... Nick, this is it? We are definitely at war?" Hayley asked.

They nodded their heads.

Eli broke the silence. "Everything will be okay. Because the president... is an idiot."

Coraline laughed so hard she nearly fell out of her chair, which of course got the entire room started. The room was healed. Even Rita laughed deeply, which is what Coraline was hoping for.

———————

New Castlehale personnel had been coming and going from the landing deck all morning in preparation for the Celebration of Life service. At this point there were 30 or 40 visitors gathered. Remo Two and Three had been ferrying in attendees from across Texas, including the Governor, his aides, and a number of military officers. Many arrived at the Militia base-camp to the west of New Castlehale by helicopters and delivered to the flight deck by Remo One, which had been retrofitted with hover pads. Adam thought it was perfectly suited for this purpose.

Those visiting New Castlehale for the first time were quite obvious. There was plenty of gawking and pointing as the arrivals exited their aircraft. Most of them had never seen anything even remotely as impressive as this vast cavern of steel and rock. The six armed, fighter aircraft that lined one side of the flight deck made quite the impressive sight to those gathered. Major Trevor Brice took his job as Chief of Security very seriously. Each plane was guarded by two men, as well as guards on every entrance and exit to the landing deck. Not all in attendance would be touring the inner facility.

Bacon Jorres from Two Towers leaned over to Sheriff Aaron Schiller from Junction and said, "Begorrah! Have you ever seen anything like this? I got the idea they lived large....

but this? I had no idea."

Sheriff Schiller responded with, "Who the hell cares how big it is. I'm just glad they are on our side."

Evelyn Walsh and Nick Hollings were in a tight circle with the Governor, Major Johnston of the Texas Rangers, General Deborah Stokes, and Ben Medford near the podium. No one had ever seen Nick in his Texas Ranger dress uniform besides Major Johnston. Evelyn eyeballed him up and down several times when he stopped by her quarters to walk her to the flight deck. He always found it amusing to hear this highly educated woman, who probably had the equivalent of two or three PhDs and ran a small city-state with an air force, an army and a space-team, say things like "Me likey!! Me likey!!"

When the couple walked onto the flight deck, Jennifer happened to be standing near Alex and nudged him to say, while nodding towards Ranger Hollings, "Now that, pinhead, is what I call a full-fledged Tasty Critter!"

"Vixen," he replied with a smirk.

Monitors set up on the edges of the landing deck assembly area displayed videos and photos of Hedgehog from his earliest days at New Castlehale until his death. Rows of benches were placed before a large, raised platform on which were 13 chairs and a rostrum for the speakers. Directly behind the platform was a brand new Flyer with the exact same hedgehog painted on the nose. It was apparent the aircraft had been polished to a high gloss by caring hands before the service. The actual landing zone for incoming and outgoing aircraft was kept clear so their fighters could be scrambled at a moment's notice, but there was probably no need for that at this particular time since the skies above New Castlehale were brimming with fighters from the Texas Air Guard, along with a squadron from Arkansas.

It became apparent the celebration would be starting soon, when droves of scientists, soldiers, husbands, wives, and children began to pour onto the flight deck from within the living areas of New Castlehale. In a quiet and efficient manner, they filled the benches that seemed to have been planned for an exact number. The children were especially excited to be on the flight deck because at any other time they were forbidden to be there.

The soldiers did not use the benches but formed two lines left and right of the seating area. Evelyn led the Governor, two generals, along with Rangers Hollings, Jameson, and Johnston up onto the stage. They were followed by Alex, Adam, Hayley, Sarah, and lastly, Jennifer. Jennifer was the only person on stage who was not in dress attire. She wore a tailor-made combat uniform with armor. She was awesome, and one of the generals even commented on that fact. Fortunately, Adam had talked her out of carrying her beloved rifle 'Blackie' with her onto the podium. She acquiesced, but only because she noticed neither Sarah nor Hayley were wearing their swords.

Evelyn noted the generals were scrutinizing every detail of the flight deck and every person they saw. The weaponry and technology of New Castlehale made them feel as if they had been transported to another planet. They all noticed the tables for refreshments had no legs or wheels. They hovered above the floor at a precise height and did not budge. One of the officers even tried to move the table, but they may as well had been trying to move a skyscraper. The tiny hoverpads on these tables were programmed to be in a certain place and would resist movement. Only a technician could move the table.

Feeling her wristband vibrate, she noticed every monitor in the area switched to what they all agreed was the best photo of Hedgehog. It was taken at Two Towers when he was recounting the tale of dodging anti-aircraft missiles over West Texas with Hayley and came out victorious. Everyone loved that photo and there was a noticeable reaction from all those in attendance when it popped onto the monitors. Evelyn paused for a moment as she remembered that day, then moved to the podium and touched the wings that were pinned to her uniform.

"We gather today to honor the life of Phillip "Hedgehog" Stark..."

CHAPTER TWENTY-TWO
MISSION DAY

Adam was shaken awake with gentle little nudges.

"What?" he said without even turning over.

"Wake up," said a tiny voice.

"Why?"

"I need you to take me somewhere."

"Where?"

"To Llano."

He rolled over to see Coraline's beautiful little face smiling down at him.

"Now? It's only 430 in the freakin' morning!"

"I know silly. It will take us some time to get there and back."

"We'll miss breakfast," he said with a look of faux concern.

"No, we won't. I've already been to the galley. Lilly has been there 30 minutes already. I asked her to make us breakfast tacos."

"What on earth is so important in Llano you feel the need to wake up the whole world in the middle of the night."

She answered with a faux seriousness, "Adam, you are a wonderful big brother, but you are NOT the whole world."

He snatched her up and threw her over his shoulder and carried her to the door of his quarters, saying, "No? Well, I know what to do with you then!" When the door opened, he set her down outside the door and said, "Go wake my sister. Tell her we need an escort to Llano."

Coraline glanced over to her right, and standing there already dressed and armed were Hayley, Sarah, Jennifer, and Madison. Adam blushed since he was standing there wearing nothing but his night shorts covered with bat symbols. "Uh, Coraline...why are we going to Llano?"

"To get Sugar, of course."

He slowly turned back into his quarters talking to himself. "We're flying all the way to Llano for sugar. Great. I thought there was a war on." He stopped and turned back to the corridor. "Sugar?"

She smiled and nodded.

A few minutes later, Adam exited his quarters fully dressed, armed, and pulling on a pair of fingerless leather gloves. Only Coraline was waiting for him. "So, tell me again, Baby Sister, why are we taking two aircraft and an armed contingent to Llano, Texas to pick up sugar?"

"Sugar is a cat, silly."

"Eli's old cat? Is she still alive?"

"Very much so."

"Why now? I'm sure she's found a good home by now. It's been over a year!"

"Let's go grab a bite and I'll explain it to you, Gulliver."

Again, Adam snatches the wisp of a redhead off her feet and sets her on his shoulders for the trip to the galley. He began leaning this way and that as if he were going to topple with her weight, as she laughed, screamed, and giggled. Rounding a corner, he was met head-on by his mom, arms folded, looking very.... motherly.

"What are you doing at this hour of the morning?" she asked with eyebrows raised.

Just then, Ranger Hollings stepped out of Evelyn's quarters.

Coraline sang, "Awkwaaaard."

Evelyn blushed, pushed the Ranger back into her quarters, and just left it with a simple: "Carry on."

Adam looked up at Coraline's smiling face and said, "We won't mention that."

She winked and laughed more.

As they entered the galley, Hayley and the others were leaning over the counter that separated the kitchen from the serving area eating breakfast tacos. There was a plate there with more tacos for Coraline and Adam.

"So, what's the plan?" Adam asked as he handed Coraline a breakfast taco.

Madison replied, "It's a simple snatch and grab. We fly to Coraline's old stomping grounds and call for Sugar. When she comes, we pick her up and skedaddle. We won't be on the ground for long."

"How do we know she'll come?"

Coraline explained, "The neighbors who took Sugar into their home moved further into the Void when the war started. One of their sons happens to be in the Texas Militia camped at the base of this mesa. He said their dogs and Sugar ran off before they left and they didn't wait around for them. We're going to rescue those animals.

"Dogs too?"

"Why not?"

"Yeah. Okay, Baby Sister, but only because you asked."

"What, you don't like dogs, Gulliver?"

He just shook his head and said, "Nah. They taste terrible."

Coraline, Sarah, Jennifer, Madison, and Hayley all reached out and swatted him a good one. And just for good measure, Lilly came around the corner and smacked him with her spoon. "Ju behave, Gigantor. Dios mio.... tasting dogs. Shame on ju."

"Okay, okay! I could develop a taste for them if it's that important to you!"

Whack! Went the spoon again.

"Okay! Okay! Let's get moving."

Remo Three touched down quietly on the front lawn of the now-empty home as Flyers Two and Three drifted silently overhead. Madison and Jennifer spread out to either side of the aircraft and waited as Coraline and Adam walked to the front porch of the home. There were no animals in sight, but they could hear dogs up and down the road barking. The sounds of screen doors opening and banging shut could be heard as neighbors went outside to investigate the cause of the ruckus. Soon whole families were outdoors pointing at the saucer-shaped aircraft parked on their ex-neighbor's lawn and the two floating fighter aircraft above.

Jennifer spoke into her comDev, "Well, so much for our secret mission."

An old woman carrying a large cup of coffee, hair rolled up in curlers and large fluffy bunny slippers walked from the house next door and asked Madison, "Are you the new neighbors?"

"No ma'am. We're here to fix the water heater."

"Oh. Okay. That's nice," the woman answered as she turned to walk away. Waving to the neighbors across the street she yelled, "It's okay. They're fixin' the water heater!"

Hayley overheard the conversation in her headset. She laughed, "Surely, they didn't buy that!"

"Believe me, I've seen worse. Remind me to tell you about the bobcat."

Coraline waited for a moment, then tilted her face to the sky and closed her eyes. With hands out, she opened her lips and released what sounded like a high-pitched trill. This went on for a least a minute before a calico cat broke from the bushes across the street and ran straight to Coraline. Trailing her swiftly were two large German Shepherds and a Dalmatian. The large dogs would have bowled her over in the excitement of their greeting had she not held up her hand and stopped them. They obeyed that hand gesture and sat immediately. Taking Sugar into her arms, she kissed and stroked the cat who assuredly recognize her as 'family.' Speaking to the dogs, she said, "If you guys need to go potty, do it now. We're going to take a trip."

The three canines ran to the fire hydrant on the corner and took turns doing their business as Madison and Jennifer laughed.

Jennifer said, "That's a pretty good trick, there, Baby Sister. You'll have to teach me that one. Now, let's load 'em up."

Coraline ran for the aircraft with Sugar and the dogs

following her single file. Madison shrugged her shoulders and said, "Mission accomplished. Let's go home."

When Remo Two and two Flyers reentered the landing bay, standing on the flight line was Alex, Eli, Evelyn, Ranger Nick, and Trevor Brice with arms folded and waiting patiently. The aircraft touched down and the door opened as the engines hummed down to silence. Sugar came out first and ran straight to Eli, who wrapped his arms around her, burying his face into her fur.

Evelyn waited for Adam and his armed escort to reach her group and asked, "Am I to understand you took two Flyers and Remo Three all the way to Llano to pick up a cat?"

"Well, yeah. That kind of sums it up, Mom." They all nodded in agreement.

Jennifer added, "It was actually a reconnaissance-in-force, Evelyn. We were..... uh... practicing... uh... yah. Never mind."

Madison turned to Jennifer and said, "You know, you need to practice that technique on people OTHER than Evelyn Walsh."

"I reckon so," Jennifer answered staring down at her boots.

Evelyn took a tablet from Trevor Brice and pointed at it, "Hayley, XO Brice here tells me you signed out three aircraft for a practice mission and you come back with a cat." Just then, Coraline and three dogs exited Remo. "And two, no, three dogs. Would you like to explain yourself?"

"Well, really, it was, well... good training," Hayley responded.

"And fresh air...," said Sarah.

"Solid tactical move...solid," said Adam.

Evelyn tried hard not to laugh. "Well, as long as there's a good reason," she said looking Adam in the eye. "Carry on."

Alex had to add his two cents: "And get those dogs off of my flight deck."

Sarah was awakened by a long deep tone coming from her console. Looking at her watch she noted she had napped for an hour and a half in the late afternoon. She had been forewarned by Alex to catch a good nap before mission start time. She sat up in bed and placed her feet directly into her boots already wrapped up in her flight suit. All she had to do was stand and pull her flight suit up and she was good to go. She picked up her Glock and press-checked it once before gently sliding it into her holster. She placed a communications device onto her flight suit, checked the mirror once, and walked into the corridor.

There were groups of people in twos and threes, heading in the direction of the flight deck. Nobody was in a hurry, but all were moving with a purpose. Excited tones punctuated their conversations. When she entered the flight deck she realized she had never seen such hustle and bustle as was going on at this moment.

Scientists, soldiers, and technicians were gathering in groups as aircraft crews moved as quickly as they could to pull the empty ordinance racks away from the fighter aircraft while others were staging racks of missiles. Nick and Alex gave her the thumbs-up just before turning to a group of soldiers gathered around a table loading up their battle gear with ammo, grenades, and specialty items.

One group stood out from the others. Adam and several scientists from Research and Development clustered around a rather large device Sarah recognized immediately. Seeing it was confirmation to all that war was upon them. The craft was roughly twenty feet square with four oddly shaped corners. She recognized each device on the corners as a copy of their first satellite Hermes, only larger. The four were connected by a honey-combed framework that held dozens of missiles. She began to do the math in her head of the thrust-to-weight ratio necessary to get something that large into orbit, but she checked herself. The hover technology did not depend on thrust; its movement through the skies above Earth only depended on the manipulation of the Earth's own gravitational pull. Even these thoughts had to be checked and replaced. She had a mission to accomplish.

Making a quick check on her own gear, she continued moving toward the newly refurbished Delta Flyer, but was stopped by one of the men from Ordinance.

"Sarah, be aware your ordinance for the Delta has increased significantly but should not change your aircraft's handling characteristics. I hope you remember your space-flight training."

She knew from yesterday's briefing her mission would take a different tack than the rest of the air team.

Hearing her name, she turned to see Hayley and Guan Yin approaching quickly.

"What's the plan, Sarah?" Guan Yin asked.

"I don't know. Alex will be here shortly to fill us in. I imagine we'll be briefed in the air. Do you know anything about why I might be taking a space flight?"

"You will be briefed. That part is true," said Adam in his deep voice, "but not in the air." They all turned to see him towering over them with hands on hips. Adam's face revealed an expression that conveyed a bit more worry than they had ever seen from him. Alex now approached and took a spot next to Sarah.

"We'll all be briefed in a few moments," said Alex. "But, as you all know, we have a special mission for Sarah. Your mission is in the opposite direction from the others. The Delta received some modifications since yesterday. It's now faster than anything on this planet. You'll definitely be needing that space-suit. You are going to deliver a message to the President who tried to have us killed in Waco. You'll be there and back before you know it. The Delta's payload will be three large missiles. Don't worry though..."

"I know. They won't change the flying characteristics of the aircraft. I got it. But if we're going to deliver missiles, wouldn't Zeus be a better choice?" said Sarah pointing to the opposite side of the landing deck. Every eye went to it.

"It would," said Adam, "but we need Zeus in the west. I'll be with Nick and the ground team."

Hayley took a step toward Adam and put her hand on his arm. "Wait...YOU are going in with the ground team? Mom will need you here!"

"Not this time. I'm playing chauffeur to Coraline and Eli. We go in behind the teams in the Beast."

"With the kids?" asked an astonished Hayley.

"We gather now. They'll explain it all." Adam said nodding toward the large doorway that separated the flight deck from the rest of New Castlehale.

Evelyn, Jennifer, and Maddie walked through the opening with a purposeful stride. As they approached, the teams who had been in their separate huddles moved closer to meet. Soon there were thirty or forty people gathered around Evelyn and the children. Ranger Hollings took charge.

"Ok, people, listen up. This won't take long. Each team here has a job, but our coordination must be near perfect for this to work. Our mission is simple. We are going to take the facility in Nevada where Dr. Tanner, the author of this war, lives and thrives. We are going to see to it he thrives no longer. The mission consists of three phases. Phase One: Distraction in the east. Sarah will pilot the Delta Flyer into space, make one orbit of the earth, take out several communications satellites, descend upon Washington D.C. and fire two of three specialized missiles. The first target will be the Pentagon. Number two will be 1600 Pennsylvania Avenue and number three will be fired at a communications array in Maryland. She will be in and out so fast their pilots flying air cover won't have time to blink before she's already on her way out. Nothing on earth can catch that aircraft," he said pointing to the Delta Flyer.

"Captain, are we planning to destroy the Whitehouse?" Hayley asked with a bit of dismay in her voice.

"No. These Mega-Hammers will simply knock out their electronics. You've used miniaturized versions of these missiles to great effect. These will be devastating. Admittedly, there is a slight chance these missiles may not totally disable those two hardened targets, but the psychological impact will be effective. They're our message to the new administration: Think twice before bombing our children.

"The third is a bona fide strategic hit. It'll blind them temporarily. It will keep them in the dark long enough for us to get in and get out.

"Phase one also utilizes our latest piece of technology. Zeus will take up a stationary position in orbit over Nevada, take out runways, here, and here," he said, using a laser pointer to highlight two bases near Area 51. "Primary, we want to make their runways temporarily unusable. Secondary, take out as many of their ready aircraft as possible. Especially these vertical take-off aircraft, here, and here. The Delta Flyer in the east and Zeus in the west will coordinate their tasks to take place simultaneously.

"These attacks will also serve as a distractor to another phase one objective. We will be using Meteor Crater as a staging area and rallying point should things go wrong. This will necessitate a ground-assault team taking the facility that overlooks the crater. The Meteor Crater museum has been taken over by a certain drug cartel known for human trafficking and gun-running. Arrangements have been made with law enforcement in Flagstaff to support us in this effort. When this facility is secured, our air assets, as well as those from Oklahoma, can converge on the staging area located at the floor of the crater.

"Phase Two: The air team will watch over us, while ground units hit Area 51 hard with two objectives: Eliminate the enemy and rescue the prisoners of this facility. Hopefully, Zeus will have ruined the nearby air base, but just in case, CPAG, (Central Plains Air Guard) has agreed to protect our flank with a squadron of fighters and come to our aid over the area if necessary. This squadron consists of older aircraft, but their pilots are top-notch. The same is true for the OAG (Oklahoma Air Guard).

"Phase Three is extraction of the prisoners. This could prove to be tricky, but we made arrangements with OAG to send two Ospreys to make that happen. Once they are airborne, they will fly directly to Junction where those rescued will receive medical attention and be reunited with their families, most of whom are living there now.

"That is an overview of the plan. The details will be provided by Coraline in just a few minutes. By the time she is done with you, you will know your part of the mission and that of every member of your team. So, if, God forbid, we should lose anyone, we will each know what we must do to cover for the other person."

Ranger Madison asked, "How sure can we be the prisoners of this place will willingly come with us? How certain are we they are not brainwashed like Charles Reynolds?"

"We don't know for sure. From the information we gathered from Charles Reynolds, Coraline is more powerful than all of them combined. To aid in convincing them, we will be bringing Charles Reynolds along with us," answered Nick.

"WHAT?" exclaimed one of the air crew who serviced Hedgehog's aircraft. "That guy killed Hedgehog! How are we supposed to trust he won't turn on us mid-mission? What assurances do we have that..."

He was cut short by the appearance of Charles Reynolds onto the flight deck, accompanied by Coraline and Eli. Every eye was riveted on the man as he approached. More than one person present considered drawing their sidearm, then wondered if they possessed the self-control to NOT shoot this man where he stood, but the sight of Coraline holding the man's hand belayed their gut. Those assembled made a path for the three as they approached. Coraline, Eli and Reynolds stopped when they reached the center of the group.

"I know what you are thinking," said Coraline as she looked around the circle. "You are wondering if we are making a mistake bringing this man with us. We aren't. Charles Reynolds is gifted. Enough that he was able to hide it from me when I first met him. He can't do that anymore. He has been...," she paused to look up at Reynolds, "rescued. Trust me in this. Alex, Ranger Nick, Madison, Jennifer, all of you, trust me."

Alex walked up to Charles Reynolds and looked him square in the eye, wishing with all his heart he had the gift of reading souls through the eyes. But he did not, so he decided to go along with Coraline's decision. He knelt down before her and took her hands. "I trust you, Little Ginger. Tell us what to do."

Coraline hugged Alex, then smiled at the assembly.

"Everyone take the hand of the person next to you. This will only take a minute."

Starting with the Walsh family and spreading out from the middle, everyone managed to be in physical contact so there were no breaks or gaps. Once they were convinced every person was included, Coraline took hold of Evelyn's hand and the process of moving the plan from Coraline's mind to the others began. When the minute was over, everyone knew their part of the plan and every other team member's jobs. There were side-effects no one expected. There were soldiers who now understood more about quantum physics than they could ever have imagined. Pilots knew ground unit tactics, air crews knew some kung fu, and every person there wondered why they now knew how to put together a great dish of beef and chicken enchiladas. Evelyn wondered this herself until she looked toward the end of the human chain and saw Lilly holding hands with the last person in line. A good number noticed it at the same moment, which caused a wave of chuckling to wash over the group.

"Alright, people! We all know our part. Phase one begins now. Delta is wheels up in eight minutes. Let's move it."

Alex walked with Sarah to the place where a crew was ready to help her complete her spacesuit with all the attachments. He kissed her one more time, then jogged away to his fighter. As she stepped into the suit, she noticed technicians and scientists were pouring over the Delta Flyer to make sure she was ready. Beyond them and closer to the flight doors, Zeus was hovering toward the opened doors. Soldiers and Texas Rangers were piling into Remo Two and Remo Three. Three was just placed on the flight line last night. Over the months, Coraline had 'trained' increasing numbers of new generations to work with the knowledge and experience of their parents and older generations. All personal manufacturing at New Castlehale had ceased and every soul, including children, were creating parts needed for the coming war. Manufacturing entities from all over the continent had been delivering raw materials to an airfield outside of Austin for months. Planes, satellites, missiles, and new technologies had been rolling out of their labs for weeks at this point.

From where Sarah was standing, surrounded by the space-team technicians, she could see the new Flyer Three which was to take the place of Hedgehog's flyer. The hedgehog painted on the nose of the aircraft gave her a sense of comfort. It was to be her flyer now. Her part in this was to complete her task in phase one of the plan, then come home, switch planes, and rejoin the squadron over the Nevada facility.

As she climbed aboard the Delta Flyer she turned briefly to wave at Alex, Hayley, and Guan Yin in their planes. There were other planes on the other side of the landing deck waiting for pilots. One was hers, of course, but the other would be... she stopped her thought when she saw Evelyn Walsh climbing into the cockpit of one of the other fighters. Sarah touched her communication device.

"Dice to Queen."

"This is Queen. What is it, dear?"

"What are you doing, Mom?"

"I'm going in with the squadron, sweetheart. I can do this. Coraline made certain of that."

"Are you sure, Mom? Once I'm done with Phase One, I'll be there. They may not need all of us!"

"No battle plan survives contact with the enemy, sweetheart. Remember that from your history lessons?"

"Well, yes I do. Shoot straight, Mom. I love you."

"I love you too, Sarah. You better get going. May the One be with you."

"And with you, Mom.... And with you."

After she got settled into the cockpit, the technicians strapped her in with care. One of the scientists tried to give her last-minute words of advice but stopped halfway through when he realized she now knew everything he knew. Sarah was polite enough to say, "thank you." As she started her engines and the canopy was lowering down around her, she wished she had eaten something. She found herself feeling hungry...for chicken enchiladas.

CHAPTER TWENTY-THREE
PHASE ONE BEGINS

The acceleration of the newly updated Delta Flyer created 3G-forces that pressed Sarah into her seat for a length of time she had never experienced. Only minutes earlier, as her Delta aircraft exited the landing bay doors, her thoughts were cast back to the first day she took the Delta up to operational altitudes and thought fondly on that exhilarating ride. She made several high-G turns that day, and although they seemed fierce, they didn't last long and could be alleviated simply by returning to straight flight. Now she was taking this spacecraft to escape velocities; she understood why these next several minutes would not be a fond memory. Her only consolation was the knowledge this was necessary to reach orbit. The g-forces reduced considerably soon, and stars now appeared more dazzling than she had ever seen them. It took a moment for this new vista to make a deep impression on her psyche before she realized she was now higher than she had ever flown.

"What am I thinking? I'm higher than any human has been in 60 years! Oh Phillip, I wish you could be here with me to see this! But... you probably see things like this every day. Still..."

Her mind was flooded with memories of videos displaying old space shuttles launched in the 20th century. It took over a million and a half pounds of liquid fuel, in addition to two solid fuel booster rockets at a million pounds apiece, to propel that heavy spacecraft into orbit! Of course, they didn't have fusion engines and anti-grav pads in those old systems. With the aid of the anti-grav pads, the Delta Flyer could go into space with the same amount of fuel it would take to make a cross-country trip. The new technology greatly simplified matters in reaching escape velocity and maintaining orbital velocity, even with course corrections, with little or no fear of running low on fuel.

Sarah pulled an object from her pocket and let it go right before her eyes to watch it float. The temptation to unstrap her harness to experience weightlessness was great, but she knew it would be detrimental to the mission at hand. Important targets were approaching fast, and this would be the first test in space of Artemis BS (ARBS). This was a miniature version of the Artemis System that protected New Castlehale from incoming missiles. The "BS" stood for "Baby Sister." It was Adam's idea.

The pure, brightness of the sunlight entering through the cockpit glass seemed harsh to her, but the pitch blackness of deep space and the dazzling stars in contrast to that and the looming Earth was something she later said, "changed my perspective of everything." She made a mental note: "When I get home I'm going to encourage every member of the family to do this at least once."

"Command to Delta Flyer."

"Go ahead, Command. I read you loud and clear."

"Roger that, Delta Flyer. Your trajectory is five-by-five. Sit tight for one orbit and you will begin your descent for the completion of this mission. Hermes will be on station to watch over you. Be advised, your first satellite target will be in range of ARBS in 22 minutes. Begin charging in 18 minutes."

"Acknowledged Command. Charge in 18, acquisition in 22."

"Delta Flyer, be advised: you will be passing over the east coast shortly. Enjoy the view, you won't see it again for 90 minutes."

"Roger that, Command."

Sarah switched through her systems, checking each one

for unusual readings that might be a cause of concern. There is no way she could possibly have memorized the parameters of every system on the updated Delta Flyer on her own. Since her connection with Coraline, she not only knew the numbers, she actually understood them and the ramifications of any change. Everything appeared as it should be, so she concentrated on the new ARBS. The power cycling system was prepped and ready for charging but would not take place until minutes before the actual utilization of the lasers. Enough of this looking at monitors. There was too much to see outside the glass!

"Delta Flyer to Command. Initiating a roll for reorientation of aircraft."

"Roger that, Delta."

Looking down on the planet, it was obvious she was passing the terminator, which is the line that separates the dark side of a rotating planet from the side lit by the sun. The terminator, which moves over the surface of the Earth traveling at approximately 1,036 miles per hour, falls behind quickly when one is traveling 17,000 miles per hour. These numbers passed through her head, of course, because the scientists she had been 'Coraline-connected' to had these numbers in their heads. She marveled as she considered the magnitude of these velocities. She was traveling 17,000 mph around the Earth, while the Earth was traveling 67,000 mph around the sun, while the sun was traveling 514,000 mph around the galactic center. All of a sudden, her current speed meant very little in light of the big picture.

"Oh, forget the numbers and enjoy the view," she said to herself.

"Delta to Command."

"Go ahead, Delta."

"Would it be possible for you to patch me through to Coyote?"

"Delta, please hold."

It must have been an unconscious force of habit, but while she was waiting for them to respond, she took a moment to check out her makeup and lipstick in a mirror. "You look pretty good for a woman with a bubble-head," she said to herself.

"Uh, Delta, can you repeat that last transmission? We didn't quite get it."

Flying 150 miles above the earth, it is not likely anyone saw how red Sarah turned at the realization she forgot to cut her transmission.

"Nothing. Forget it."

"Delta, this is Command. Be advised Coyote is under radio silence."

"Roger that, Command."

The converted military version of the Gulfstream business jet was flying west from its base in Washington D.C. to Nellis AFB near Las Vegas in Nevada. General James M. Prentice of Air Combat Command was nose-down in a tablet going over documents given to him by his staff. His usual scotch and water rested in the cup holder to his right. The term 'annoyed' was not quite strong enough to describe how he felt about the loss of so many aircraft in the past year, all during a mission kept secret even from the Commander of Air Combat Command. The newly sworn-in President was also in the dark. Somebody knew something about this secret mission and he was hell-bent to find out who. He knew now only what everyone else in the country found out through news media: that a combination of U.S. Air Force, and ground units launched yet another unsanctioned attack on locations inside the Void in violation of law. Now, every military base inside the continental U.S. was on war status, with no war declared. Nothing was making sense. At this point, not one U.S. base had been attacked or even threatened, yet there were military bases already declaring themselves for one side or another just like they did during the first Cultural War. All this began shortly before the death of President Taylor near Waco, Texas. Although he was instructed to investigate, he wasn't given enough information to put two and two together. As a result, he was beginning to believe the 'rogue general' theory in all this, because nothing else made sense.

"These are my aircraft we're losing and I don't even

know why! What the hell is going on down there?" he asked himself as he looked over another useless document. He barely heard the voice of one of his aides asking if he needed anything else.

"I'm sorry, Airman, what did you say?"

"Will there be anything else, General?"

"No, that will be all. Thank you."

The airman turned back toward the rear of the plane and drew the curtain separating the General's chair from his assistants and crew in the aft compartment. The General turned back to his documents as he nursed his scotch and water. He was known as an officer who became so engrossed in what was before him he often missed the conversation of those around him, so it was completely within character he was unaware of the small girl standing next to him. He only looked up when she cleared her throat. The sight of her beautiful little face surprised him. He asked, "Who are you?" and was about to call out to his assistant, but she reached out and touched the side of his head. That is all he remembered until he was shaken awake by the aide informing him they were only minutes from landing. In his unconscious state, he had been unable to see the child begin to glow as a glistening bubble formed around her and she floated up and through the ceiling of the aircraft. The men piloting the General's jet had been absolutely unaware mere feet above their aircraft was a strange-looking fighter jet. This jet was the recipient of that glistening bubble that carried Coraline safely from one aircraft to the other. Nor did they see Flyer One peel away to disappear into the night.

U.S. Military bases worldwide had been ordered to high alert, so Nellis Air Force Base in Nevada, under the command of General Timothy A. Mack, was no exception. All non-military traffic was forbidden entry. Air patrols were activated, gun emplacements were bolstered, and all personnel were at their post on alert crew. After receiving the message from the Pentagon, General Mack called a general meeting of every wing commander on base, which included air and ground units of the Marine Corps, Army, Navy, Air Force, and an assortment of special operations groups. The purpose of the meeting would be to brief the commanders on the current conflict taking place in the Void. The briefing will be conducted by five-star General James A. Prentice whose plane arrived only minutes before.

"Roger that, sir. Understood," said General Mack into his phone, then turned to the man to the right. "Orders. We're standing down. Recall all aircraft except for the AWACS; let's keep those flying. All *Ready Five* crews will stand down. Let's clear the flight line, and when I say clear, I mean clear! Not one soul will be allowed onto the runways. Do I make myself clear?"

"Yes, sir. General."

Colonel Stravinski made the call. It took only a few minutes before the word was being broadcast throughout the base. From the windows of the large meeting room, General Mack looked out over the runways of Nellis. It seemed apparent the large room was built to give attendees a grand view not only of the flight line, but also the sky including the zenith, due to the fact the glass was curved back over their heads allowing every attendee total view from horizon to zenith. The flight line that had been brimming with fighter aircraft in a state of readiness, along with the hustle and bustle of airmen driving trucks now began to resemble an ant hill disturbed by the toe of a boot. Aircraft were being pulled from the flight line. Hoses were rolled up, officers were pointing and shouting while truckloads of personnel were being move back to the interior of the base.

"What's up, General?" the officer asked.

"I don't know, Bill. But five-star General Prentice is due to walk in through that door any second now. We'll hear it all at that point."

"AttccnSHUN!" was shouted near the doorway. Every officer in the room stood at attention as General Prentice walked through and handed his hat to the man behind him. General Mack and his staff remained at the front. There were smart salutes exchanged before General Prentice said, "At ease, gentlemen," then turned to face the room. "Please be seated." He then turned back to General Mack and said, "General Mack, I apologize for keeping you in the dark, but I've just come from Washington and I believe there is a solution to this fiasco in the Void. There are a lot of lives at stake, and I'm not going to risk another pilot, soldier or crewman because of one rogue agent and officer."

"Did you say, 'rogue agent', sir?"

"I did indeed. Now, I take it, by the activity down on the flight deck this base is standing down from alert crew. Am I correct in this assumption, General Mack?"

"Yes, sir, General Prentice. You are correct."

"Now. I am going to ask a few simple questions, and I want simple answers. No explanations. No excuses. Understood?"

"Yes, sir. Clear, sir. Would you prefer we vacate the room before you ask your questions, sir?"

"No. These officers should know what's going on. They deserve to know the truth because shortly, they will need the truth to understand what is soon to happen. Now, General Mack, did you, or did you not authorize the launch of 15 Tomahawk missiles from this base, or the surrounding area, this past week?"

"Yes, sir. I did."

"On whose orders were those missiles launched?"

"They were ordered by President Taylor, sir."

"Did you speak with President Taylor yourself?"

"No, sir. I did not, nor did anyone under my command. They were ordered by President Taylor through one of the President's men whose name we confirmed as being attached to the President, along with the proper codes." The General was handed a tablet. He flipped through several pages and came to the information he needed. "One Dr. Harvey Tanner, from R&D Command, and confirmed by Major Barret Ratcliff."

"General, do you have a time stamp on that order?"

"Yes, sir. 2018 hours, the President's time stamp near Dallas, Texas."

"Are you aware, General, President Taylor died at 2008 hours?"

General Mack looked again at his tablet, then glanced at

his staff. The numbers didn't make sense. "The President died at 8:08 PM near Dallas, but ten minutes later, somehow still managed to give an order to launch 15 Tomahawk missiles on an undisclosed location inside the Void. The orders were to hold the launch until 2400 hours."

"Please be seated, General Mack," Prentice ordered. "What we have here, ladies and gentlemen, is a missile strike against U.S. citizens, inside the Void, contrary to the Cultural War Treaty which is bad enough. We add to that the fact it was ordered by the President of the United States, to be carried out by regular Air Force personnel and a special operations group headed by the man in charge of Research and Development Command. Now, we obviously cannot impeach President Taylor posthumously, but this Dr. Tanner and his associates are well within the reach of the arms of justice."

"Sir, has Dr. Tanner been relieved of his command?"

"No, he has not. This is the head-scratcher for me. I was notified only moments after President Taylor's aircraft went down. In an emergency meeting within minutes of his death, no one on the President's staff, the Vice-President or the Joint Chiefs of Staff mentioned anything about Taylor having this launch as a contingent to failure in the talks that went on in Waco at the Texas Ranger Headquarters. Yet, this Dr. Tanner, who obviously knew about the order, failed to mention it during the meeting, in which he took part."

"Sir, was he pressed on the issue after the launch was initiated?"

"No, General. He was not because the only thing we knew was you launched those missiles. The President did not want to move on this until we knew who we were dealing with. Incompetence makes us all look bad. The President, his staff, the Joint Chief, and you. We only had your word on who issued that order, that is until I was twenty minutes out of Nellis`. All the documents we needed were laid in our laps through an anonymous source. We made a quick check and were able to put two and two together. This was a continuation of the unauthorized entry of government forces into the Void a year ago. The conspiracy that began in Washington has engulfed R&D Command."

"What's going to happen now, General Prentice?"

"I'll get to that, but first let me say President Cott received a call from the Void, the very people President Taylor spoke with before his death, and they have suggested a course of action. The President agreed with it. I dare say nobody here is going to like it. Hell, I don't like it, but I do believe this is the best route to preventing a repeat of the Cultural War. There are too many military bases already picking sides in the coming war. The price we are going to pay for that tonight might seem steep to some of you here, but to me, this is simply more practice for our engineers."

"Engineers, sir?" asked General Mack.

"Yes, sir. That's what I said. What we are about to witness should be very interesting," he said as he checked his watch. Then walked over to the windows to check on the progress of clearing the flight line. "General, I would suggest you get on the com and get that flight line cleared a lot faster than is happening right now. We have about fifteen minutes."

"Fifteen minutes until what, sir?"

"Never mind that, General. Get those people moving! Now. Whatever aircraft or other materials they have not cleared from the flight line, will be left behind and all personal must be away from that area exactly 15 minutes from now. Not one soul. Do you understand, General?"

"Roger that, sir."

"Good. Then, I noticed there were refreshments being staged outside in the corridor. Please have them brought in, and let's have a bite before the show begins."

Staff wheeled in carts loaded with a large assortment of food. General Prentice seemed more than eager to fill a plate with delights before moving to a spot near the windows. Every officer in the room seemed as eager since none of them had eaten dinner before being summoned to the meeting. A lot of questions were murmured throughout the room as the five-star up front chowed down, seemingly oblivious to the chatter going on at his back. He instead seemed fixated on the activity below. Occasionally, he would glance at his watch and shake his head.

Finally, the last of the aircraft were removed from the

flight line with only a few officers waving frantically to the stragglers. Within a minute the entire area surrounding the runways were cleared.

"General Mack, how strong is this glass?"

"That glass has withstood a thousand sonic booms, sir. May I ask, sir, what exactly is it we're going to see?"

"What you are about to witness is the prevention of a war. This base launched Tomahawk missiles on Junction, Texas last year, as did several other bases across the country, without the authorization of the President, that we know. Just a few short days ago, this base launched 15 more to a location in the Void. It has been substantiated that the culprits who ordered up those missiles ordered them under wrongful pretexts, deceiving and controlling the late President Taylor. These same culprits are about to receive just recompense for their actions, but not by us. We are to stand by," and here he checked his watch one more time, "and allow our runways to be destroyed."

"Say what?" came out of General Mack's lips before he could check himself.

"You heard me right. We are going to stand right here and watch our runways destroyed."

"But our AWAKs will see them coming long before they reach here!"

"And we will do nothing about it. That is, if we could do anything about it. General, we could launch every plane on this base, and it would not prevent what is about to happen. These people have technology far beyond anything we possess and yet were fair enough to warn us ahead of time. Gentlemen, it's time. Three, two, one..."

Instinctively, every soul present took a step forward. Missiles from high zenith screamed in at fantastic velocities, and, in one-second intervals, violent detonations marched their way up the runway until it was utterly destroyed. The accuracy was perfection, one officer noted under his breath. When it was over, the five-star General turned to those in the room.

"Ladies and Gentlemen, I have been getting requests for a few years about the need to upgrade the runways at Nellis Air Force Base. Half that work has just been done for you.

Enjoy the new runway, people."

With that the General turned one more time to inspect the damage and shook his head.

"Damned impressive, that."

General Mack's assistant leaned into his boss and whispered, "Sir. Permission to speak freely?"

"Go ahead."

"Well, sir," the colonel said, "this whole thing smells. I don't believe we'd be overstepping if we were to contact Washington about this. Sir, no disrespect meant, but it could be General Prentice is the one who has been compromised. It's too late for these runways, but it would be better to know, sir."

The General took a long hard look at General Prentice standing nearby, then turned to the colonel. "Do it quietly."

CHAPTER TWENTY-FOUR
METEOR CRATER

Sarah had settled herself into this mission with a whole heart. She felt a calmness she hadn't felt in ages. She felt it had to do with the magnitude of the task given her and the awesome opportunity to see things no other human being had seen in many decades.

"Void Command, ARBS is charged and ready for Target One."

"Roger that, Delta. Stand by."

Although the ARBS was completely new to Sarah, she understood every procedure in bringing the system online, and she knew the range and limitations of it. If the ARBS worked as well as everyone thought, it would increase her chances in air to air combat, should that present itself. Even though the Delta Flyer retained its plasma cannons, those would not have near the effect of this system for destructive combat capabilities.

"Delta, you are in range of Target One."

"Roger that, Command."

There was no heads up display for this system. It was all contained in her headgear. As she looked around the cockpit, the headgear superimposed objects in orbit with her in 3d. Some flashed by, while others appeared to be moving slowly either along with her or on an interception course. Target One was highlighted in a deep red, while the others were blue. This was going to be easy she thought.

"Command, I have acquired lock on Target One."

"You are clear to fire, Delta."

To either side of the nose of Delta were new additions to the aircraft that seemed to be bulges. The covering on the port side retracted, revealing what appeared to be a great big eye that rotated quickly through up and down, left and right calibration movements. Once Sarah had acquired lock on Target One, the firing solution came rapidly. When she triggered the system, she didn't see a ray or a flash, as one might have expected from an earthbound laser. The target, a satellite of some importance simply fell apart, having been hit several times. It began to spin as whatever propellant had been placed within, escaped quickly.

"Target One has been destroyed, Command."

"Roger that, Delta. Stay alert for Targets Two and Three."

"Copy that, Command. Delta out."

Sarah was grateful to be occupied with eliminating the satellites because the thought of not making a precise reentry over her target made her nervous, even though she knew Command would walk her through the numbers. She wasn't worried about launching the missiles necessary to accomplish her mission, but the task of egress from the area was filled with unknowns. Were F-40s in the air? Were they staged to pounce? Her Delta could outrun anything they sent up after her, but air-to-air missiles were a different matter altogether.

"Command, Targets Two and Three have been eliminated."

"Roger that, Delta. Enjoy the ride until we contact you."

The smoke was still rising from the craters created by the incoming missiles when Colonel Stravinski spoke softly to General Mack. "A word, sir?" The General nodded and took a few steps back from the windows to hear what his officer had to say.

"General, sir, are you buying this explanation from

General Prentice?"

"Colonel, I have my doubts, but I wasn't going to voice them out loud. Talk about a Dr. Strangelove scenario, rogue generals and agents. Our orders to launch the Tomahawks were legit on every front. We followed orders, yet we lose our runways as a consequence."

"My thoughts exactly, General. Why didn't the people who destroyed our runways simply use those missiles against Dr. Tanner and the eggheads at R&D Command, sir? I'll be damned if we have to sit back and take what's coming to them."

"There's more to it than we're being told here. I'll ask the questions," said General Mack before returning to General Prentice's side.

"Sir, permission to ask a few questions?" Mack asked quietly.

"Permission granted, General. What's on your mind."

"Well, sir, we launched those Tomahawk missiles in good faith, following authenticated orders, yet we are paying the price for someone else's treason."

"I understand that, General Mack. You and your staff have already been cleared of any wrong-doing in this. So, there will be nothing negative on your record or any officer under you."

"With no disrespect, General, we are relieved to hear that, yet it is still us who paid the price," General Mack said, nodding toward the smoldering runways.

"Let me ask you a question, General Mack. How many advanced aircraft have we lost in the past year over the Void?"

"Too many, sir. Most of our aircraft that have gone into the Void never returned. But in that too, sir, we were under orders."

"There is your problem, General Mack. You are too focused on whether you are considered to be at fault. Forget that notion. What the President is focusing on is the fact every military incursion into the Void has ended up in abject failure. One rogue general concocted the idea and executed the battle of Junction and lost. The officers and soldiers who carried out those orders lost the battle and many lost their lives, yet only the general is breaking rocks at Fort Leavenworth USDB. The General leaned close to his subordinate and said, "Did you know to this day, he doesn't remember why he did it?"

"No, sir. I did not. What's up with that?"

General Prentice simply shrugged. "But I don't need to remind you that aircraft from this base were sent back into the Void on a weapons free mission just days ago. Again, a failure to execute," he said as he seemed to be looking a thousand miles away. "Fault? It doesn't matter. Our fault, your fault, my fault, Tanner's fault, right now we need to understand we are dealing with a force that is technologically head and shoulders above anything we can throw at them. We know they've got anti-gravitation hover technology our eggheads can't even comprehend. You just saw what they did to our runway and all we could do is stand back and watch it happen. They've got laser platforms in space."

General Mack's jaw fell open.

"That's right. I personally viewed a video of their 2-megawatt anti-aircraft lasers taking out our Tomahawk missiles. They didn't miss once. My guess is the missiles we just witnessed were probably their old technology. We were told they have large laser systems in orbit. Jeez Louise, our U.S. Space Force ceased to exist during the Cultural War, but these guys somehow have total air and space superiority while we're still trying to keep the lights running. We kicked a hornet's nest and now their anger towards us is near seething rage. From what I've learned, they could have destroyed this entire base, while the best defense we could offer is to climb under a rock and hope we can dig fast enough. The runways sir, were a small price to pay for our intrusion into the Void. Fault? Let's concentrate on surviving this."

"Thank you, General Prentice. Where do we go from here?"

"Where? Nowhere. R&D Command is about to lose their bacon and our instructions are to ignore any request they make for backup. It's time that facility was closed for good. The public no longer has the stomach for extraterrestrial stories about Area 51. Time to end it. Dr. Tanner has been told by the President that if he refuses to release his prisoners immediately and turn himself in, they will do nothing to stop these Defenders of the Void from getting their justice."

"Sir, how did they respond?"

"They haven't. I'm guessing this Tanner character, whom the late President Taylor put so much stock in, has something up his sleeve he believes will cancel out any technological advantage the Voiders possess."

"Nothing makes sense anymore, General Prentice. We've got Washington trying to tamp down a rebellion of rogue 'generals and agents,' while trying to tamp down aggression by the forces inside the Void. We've got air and ground bases picking sides willy-nilly and patriot states closing down their borders to blue states. From what I've read about the Cultural War and what brought it about, this seems more chaotic than that!"

"General Mack, I agree with almost everything you said just now, except the forces inside the Void have yet to be the aggressors. We have been the aggressors."

"What are your orders now, sir?"

General Prentice turned to his subordinate. "My best guess is these 'Defenders' just want to be left alone. I can't put my finger on the whys, but it's my gut sense. My fear is, after they get a taste for knocking over military installations, they may not want to stop. Power does that to people. So, as for orders, fix those runways, arm up, gas up, gear up, and be ready for anything. Move your vertical take-off fighters away from here. Hide them. You saw the accuracy of their missiles. You can't shoot what you can't find."

The sentries on the roof of the Meteor Crater souvenir shop weren't paying the least attention to what was going on around the center. Both were well armed but had set their rifles aside for whatever nonsense they could concoct in their drug-induced state. Neither of them noticed three aircraft move in silently from the northeast, barely feet above the earth. Alex, Hayley, Madison, and Nick moved quickly to a hiding place in the northeastern parking lot area.

"I count two sentries on the roof. This is something I can take care of," said Nick as he removed his backpack.

"Uh, Nick," said Alex. "I think if our plan is to get up there quietly and undetected, we better let Hayley take this. She's kinda made for this. I know you're like bulletproof and all, but what we need here is absolute stealth."

Hayley raised her eyebrows and nodded as Madison acknowledge it with a hand on Nick's arm and a reassuring smirk.

Every eye was on Nick's watch as he was checking it while saying, "Sounds like a plan. Hayley. Let us know when we're clear." When they looked over to Hayley, she was already gone. They couldn't see where she had gone or how she was going to get to the roof. Madison was scanning the area between them and the tourist center with her night vision and came up with nothing. "Daaannnng," was all she could say.

On the roof, one of the sentries was singing an old song about the YMCA, with accompanying arm and hand gestures, while the other laughed hysterically. Mr. Laughter was trying his best to shield his lighter from the wind to fire up another hand-rolled smokable. The singing stopped.

"Don't stop now, butt-face! Your singing was fixin' to sound better!" the laughing man said as he looked up.

Standing over him was a tall, slender figure dressed in black. A swift kick to the head put the man out. Pulling something from a pouch, she pressed it to his neck. Hayley touched her comDev and spoke.

"Sentries are asleep. Move up."

"Roger that, Slice," said Alex as he, Nick and Madison moved to cover the distance between the parked vehicles and the tourist center. The Meteor Crater Natural Landmark Museum was a favorite tourist attraction for hundreds of years until the Cultural War broke out. With bandits running free over the area for decades, who wanted to risk encountering them just to see a crater. Taken over by the cartel and used as a sleepover for their cross-country

211

criminal activities, it was a favorite drinking hole for a vast array of nefarious types. A long list of sheriffs and their posse had tried time and time again to remove them from this important landmark but were out-gunned at every turn. Previous assaults had been met with rocket-propelled grenades and heavy machine-gun fire that drove them back in every instance. Top-notch snipers had been able to whittle on the bandits little by little, but they could not stay in the area for long because of the bandit patrols and their use of night vision equipment. The cartels had the money to maintain better equipment than local law enforcement. On this night, however, night-vision technology would only have worked if it were actually being used.

Nick and Madison moved directly to the tourist center while Alex made his way to the south side that faced the mile-wide crater itself. Using his own night vision, Alex was able to spy a group of four sitting next to a BBQ grill on the outside observation deck.

"Coyote has eyes on the north side observation deck. Four bandits. No other activity."

"Roger that, Coyote. Ranger One inside the facility moving west. No activity here."

"Ranger Two moving east through facility. Common room contains approximately 15 individuals, mostly children and a few babysitters watching a movie. I've seen this one. They are only about a quarter of their way into it."

"Coyote, this is Slice at the top of the radio tower. Can you see me?"

Alex used his night-vision to see his sister atop the tall tower on the western edge of the parking lot.

"How'd you get up there so fast?" he asked.

"Ninja magic, of course, silly."

"Yah yah.... what do you see?"

"It appears our bandits are all at a bonfire approximately a mile northwest near Meteor Crater Road. It looks like quite the party."

"This is Ranger One. Coyote, do you need help with the four?"

"Negative, Ranger One. I got this."

"Roger that, Coyote. You're on your own. Ranger Two,

212

wait for me and we'll detain the movie-goers. When we've tied up loose ends, I'll notify Queen. Roadrunner is on his way now with the Flagstaff Sheriff and a posse. They'll take over up here. Slice, be our eyes in the sky here for a few more minutes, please, ma'am?"

"Affirmative, Ranger One. Slice out."

Standing straight up from his concealment, Alex walked, bold as brass, right up to the four sitting on the observation deck. The one with his back to the canyon saw him first but sat there wide-eyed. The others got the hint and turned around to see a tall, smiling man in a flight-suit holding two automatics.

"Howdy, barbecuers. As much as I hate ruining your meal, I'm afraid I must. Those of you who don't want a hole in your forehead, raise your hands now."

They all raised their hands immediately.

Meanwhile Nick and Madison stood just outside the common room. The smell of popcorn wafted through the small opening Ranger Madison peeked through. She held a finger up to her lips, indicating they should do this quietly. Nick acknowledged with a pat on her shoulder and a smile. They opened the door to find the room mostly filled with children. Three women seated comfortably in recliners were the only adults there. Two were fixated on the movie; their cell phones placed on a table between them, while one played a candy game on a tablet. Not one soul took notice of the two camouflaged warriors standing behind them.

Madison's hand moved slowly over the coffee table and removed the two cell phones and placed them in a large pant pocket. The babysitters remained glued to the movie as Nick pulled out a small device and pressed it to the neck of the woman playing on her tablet. She experienced instant sleep. Both Rangers applied the devices to the necks of the two remaining adults with the same results. Madison again pressed her finger to her lips and nodded toward the door. They backed out together and closed the double doors. Removing a couple of large cable ties from a pocket, Nick secured the door from the outside. A child was not going to leave that room, and the adults would sleep for hours.

"This is Ranger One. Movie-goers secure. Report."

"Slice has eyes on bonfire. No unusual activity."

Alex's transmission began with lip-smacking noises, followed by a gulping sound. "Coyote, sitting here enjoying a beer and some barbecue on the observation deck. Come join me while we wait for the cavalry."

"Coyote, stay where you are. Slice, plant a camera and then come on down. Meet us on the observation deck."

"Roger that."

When Madison, Nick, and Hayley walked onto the observation deck, they found Alex chowing down on beef ribs while four men lay asleep, side by side.

"You are one magnificent example of a pig, brother," said Hayley.

"Join me? Even ninjas need sustenance," he replied with a smile.

"Ranger One to Queen."

"This is Queen, go ahead."

"Bandits are bunched up at a bonfire about a mile northwest of crater, near the main road. We have detained their babysitters and children in the common room. They are enthralled in a movie. We are free to engage bonfire."

"Roger that, Ranger One. Queen to Roadrunner."

"Roadrunner, go ahead."

"Meteor Crater visitor center parking lot is cleared for landing. What is your ETA?"

"Five minutes if I step on it."

"Roger that, Roadrunner. Step on it. Queen to Coyote."

"Coyoffy hew," he said with a mouth full of BBQ.

"Coyote, as soon as Roadrunner arrives with Sheriff Williamson and his crew, you, the Rangers and Slice will get airborne and we'll deal with the bonfire party."

"Woger dat, Kween."

Hayley, who was nibbling daintily on her beef rib, paused to say, "Do you actually allow Sarah to see you eat like that? And stop drinking that beer. We have work to do."

"Whaaa??," he said as he took another large bite of the well-cooked BBQ.

ANDREW C. RAIFORD

CHAPTER TWENTY-FIVE
NINJA MAGIC

Remo Two was almost overloaded with the sheriff's deputies. Unfortunately, some had not showered in days, which made the flight from Flagstaff distasteful. From the pilot seat, Adam turned to address the group behind him. "Two minutes out people. Check your gear. Here's the situation: The Crater Center is taken. Prisoners are detained. My sister just informed me there are about a dozen children in the common room watching a movie. They are unaware anything has happened. Their babysitters are asleep, as are the sentries on the roof and four on the observation deck. As soon as we touch ground we'll have air cover. The remainder of the bandits seem to otherwise be engaged at a bonfire party down near Meteor Crater Road. Sheriff, I suggest moving quickly to cover the north entrance. For those who will proceed down to the bonfire, there are vehicles in the parking lot for your use. Please approach lights out and wait for instructions from Alex before moving in. In that satchel right there, you'll find three pairs of night-vision goggles, compliments of New Castlehale."

The young Sheriff Kyle Williamson sat shaking his head saying, "You guys accomplished in one evening what four previous sheriffs and myself have been trying to do for decades."

Adam kept his attention focused on the controls as they made their approach to the Crater Center's parking lot. "We've had the same problem in our corner of the Void until about eight years ago. I understand the problems. We don't want to invite help from the outside, because once you do that, the floodgates are open that will eventually allow Feds to come and go. It's all in the Treaty."

"But what about the Crater Center?" the sheriff asked, stretching his neck to get of view of the terrain below. "How did you get close enough to make it happen?"

Adam just smiled and said, "Luck, and ninja magic."

"Ninja magic?"

"It's a long story, sir. But I will say my sister Hayley can gain access into any place you can imagine, and she always comes out without a scratch on her. I hope you get to meet her."

Remo Two set down swiftly and gently on the parking lot north of the tourist center. Adam shouted, "Door will open to the north, ladies and gentlemen. Thank you for flying with Walsh airlines."

***

Stuart "Stu" Barber had inherited the leadership of this particular group of bandits who made the Meteor Crater Natural Landmark Museum their home. The tourist trap, now renamed Barberville by the cartel, came to him when his older brother Vince was picked off by a Flagstaff sniper earlier in the year. Being afraid of his brother's fate, he only ventured out of the building at night. His spy network indicated Flagstaff lawmen lacked the technology necessary to see in darkness. It was his idea to throw a bonfire party this far out from Barberville. In truth, the truckers who delivered the wood would only venture as far as the entrance of the museum at the intersection of Meteor Crater Road. They dumped it and high-tailed it out of there as quickly as they could. But Stu took credit for the decision, nonetheless.

There were lawn chairs of all make, shape, and form surrounding the mountain of logs stacked twenty feet high. Once they put a flame to it, it grew quickly and before long, the heat was such that no one could easily approach it. As a result, booze had been flowing for hours, the music decibel levels approached the threshold of hearing damage, and stupidity was stacked as high as the wood itself. Several revelers had to be extinguished after dancing too close to the flames to impress others. One or two individuals were thoughtful enough to have brought first-aid satchels in anticipation of the danger, so once the burned bandits had been put out and cared for, the dancing, shouting, and shooting guns in the air continued. Stu took mental notes on those who wasted the most ammunition.

The party was in full swing when eerie lights appeared in the sky above. The bluish color created a strange and frightening aspect to the surprise. Every bandit ran for their weapon but were too frightened to pull the trigger on the unearthly aircraft. Stu turned the music off and craned his neck this way and that to figure out what was hovering over their heads. Every ear listened intently for the sound of the whirling blades of a helicopter, but none came. Instead, a deep vibrating hum pulsed through the air. Fear gripped the entire assembly, causing them to move closer to Stu. Blinding lights suddenly burned from the sky, causing the bandits to shield their eyes. Temporarily blinded, they could only guess five or six objects circled them emitting the eerie throbbing. The large saucer-like craft moved directly above while the remaining four circled them.

"People of Earth," came a voice from the sky that sounded particularly feminine. The bandits got the message loud and clear. They were not dealing with law enforcement; these were visitors from another world! They looked at each other in a mixture of wonder, fright, joy and terror."

"People of Earth, we come in peace. Before we greet you face to face, you must lay down your primitive weapons."

"Eat shit, ET! We're not laying down our weapons! We don't take orders from you," Stu yelled at the top of his voice.

Evelyn cut power to speakers, then switched over to communicate with the other aircraft. "They meet an alien race, and all they have is: You're not the boss of me?" They were all enjoying a huge belly-laugh. She switched back to the loud speakers.

"We are saddened," said the loud voice from the sky. "We had hoped for peaceful relations between your planet, which seems to be mostly men and our planet, which is mostly females. By refusing to lay down your weapons, you have become enemies of the Xanthall Empire, of the Thrayb Galaxy. We regret you must all die."

The majority of the men threw their weapons away from them. Some even turned to their girlfriends or partners to remove any pistol or knife attached to their belt and thew them to the pile. Two or three men approached Stu and pleaded with him. "Stu, think about this. They need men, and if they like us, these aliens might give us stuff!"

"Yah, Stu... they're all women! Come on, dude!"

"They might be naked!" said the largest one.

"Buck naked!" echoed another.

Stu's face revealed a stunned incredulity. "You two are about as dumb as a tick on a howler monkey! If we lay down our guns, they'll kill us anyway!"

"Dude, look, we've already tossed our guns and we're not dead yet," said the large one.

Stu turned to see the large pile of rifles and pistols lying near the fire. He closed his eyes for a moment, then, in an attitude of forced resignation, he too walked over to the pile and dropped his weapons. First his rifle, then his handgun, then finally his large knife was tossed into the dirt. Those who had not dropped theirs did so now that the boss led the way. Turning to the men, he said, "They better be naked."

The voice from the sky boomed, "You have chosen wisely. Now. Gather together; kneel and greet the Queen of the Xanthall Empire."

Remo Two landed quietly and gently to the side of the fire opposite the pile of discarded weapons. The other four aircraft repositioned in order to bathe the saucer in light. All thirty-two bandits huddled together and knelt facing the spaceship from another galaxy. Accompanied by the sound of gases being released, the door opened slowly, followed by the ramp extending to the ground.

Three or four seconds of inactivity passed, which heightened the sense of expectation all around. Then,

Hayley and Madison stepped into the doorway standing side by side, wearing flight helmets of unique design, each carrying a copy of Adam's laser rifle. They moved slowly down the ramp to the desert floor. Madison gracefully removed her helmet and dropped it to her feet, then tossed her hair as if she were starring in a shampoo commercial.

The group of bandits seemed to be collectively holding their breath. Then, Evelyn stepped into the doorway. There was an audible gasp from the group of men kneeling before her.

"Bow to the Queen of the Xanthall Empire!" demanded Hayley who was barely succeeding in her attempt not to laugh.

Every mother's son and daughter pressed their head to the dirt. Fear and shock gripped them. They kept their heads down. Stu was the first to raise his head, only to find himself looking down the barrel of Sheriff Kyle Williamson's 12-gauge shotgun. Suddenly the lights changed and it became obvious to all that the aircraft over their heads were fairly terrestrial in nature. Some stood up to run only to be checked by men and women of the Flagstaff posse who threatened them with large automatic weapons.

The sheriff said, "Mr. Stuart Barber, you and yours are under arrest. You will be transported to the Flagstaff jail until we figure out what to do with you."

A caravan of vehicles from Flagstaff could be seen snaking their way up Meteor Crater Road as the process of handcuffing the prisoners began. Hayley turned to her mom and said, "Your majesty, Prince Adam of the Xanthall Empire tells us the runways at Nellis are toast. The other, uh, Xanthall aircraft are moving into place on the bottom of Meteor Crater. Also, Princess Sarah is leaving orbit to make her run."

At that moment, Stuuart Barber decided to make a dash toward Evelyn to choke the life out of her. He was on his feet before anyone could react and was almost on top of her, when Hayley intercepted him. His forward momentum worked against him as Hayley stepped into his path. Grabbing him by his belt and shirt, with a twisting motion, she turned him upside down and slammed him into the dirt with such a thud that all breath escaped him. When he opened his eyes, he found a sword pressed to his throat.

"You do not want to make enemies of the Xanthall Empire!"

After the deputies handcuffed and removed Stu, Sheriff Kyle put his hand out to Hayley. "You must be the 'ninja magic' your brother Adam spoke of on the way here. I can't tell you how pleased I am to meet you."

Hayley removed her helmet and smiled at the cute sheriff. She shook his hand and blushed.

"Delta to Command, initiating reentry in five, four, three, two, one, firing retros."

"Roger that, Delta. Recommend using hoverpads to slow your rate of descent. There is no need for a burn. Bring her in gently until you reach altitude of 60,000 feet. Check your waypoints."

This part of the flight took longer than Sarah would have liked, but she understood the need to keep her velocity in check on the way in. Once gravity took over, the hoverpads were able to keep her descent to a pleasant glide. During this period, she had plenty of time to run systems checks on all three EMP missiles. Thinking back on the first test of the large EMP they detonated over the desert, she remembered how powerfully effective that particular missile turned out to be. She also remembered it was during that test Hedgehog spoke his first words after over a year of silence following the death of their parents. Thinking of Hedgehog almost made her wish the missiles she'd be unloading on the D.C. targets were high explosive in nature rather than the electromagnetic pulse type. Almost. It took a recollection of Evelyn explaining what she was doing was merely a distraction to what was going to be done to those who actually did kill Hedgehog.

"I can't wait to get back in my fighter for some payback," she said to herself.

The time went faster than she thought as she glanced at her altimeter. As she neared 60,000 feet, she began double-checking every system on the aircraft.

"Command, Delta Flyer at 60,000 feet. Initiating engines, making my dive."

"Roger that, Delta. Good luck. May the One watch over you."

"Thank you, Command. The One and Hermes will suffice," she said with a smile.

The lights over the east coast of the continent made a beautiful picture as she made note of her next waypoint. The three mission targets were lined up nicely on her chart. The first two missiles would be fired within seconds of each other, the third would be a minute later, then it would be one mad dash for home.

"Command I am on approach to the first target. Charlottesville on the left and Richmond on the right. Altitude 25,000 feet."

"Roger that, Delta. Be advised, Hermes indicates you are being intercepted by three Federal fighter jets."

Sarah glanced at her display to take note of the three aircraft, two behind and one coming on headlong. Without thinking about it, she activated the Delta's Artemis BS laser system and began the calculations for a firing solution for the first two EMP missiles. Knowing in very short order she may not have the opportunity to launch, she began planning for an early firing solution.

"Command, intercept acknowledged. Calculating firing solution. Activating ARBS."

"Delta, there may not be time. Suggest you bug out."

"Roger that, Command. I am advised," she said but her intentions screamed otherwise. Then came the warning from the intercepting aircraft.

"On guard, delta-winged aircraft on heading 29.26 degrees, you are intercepted by armed Air Defense fighter. You have been intercepted. Work east...immediately. Your current heading takes you into restricted airspace. Come up on frequency 121.5. Rock your wings in acknowledgment and turn to heading 110 immediately."

Sarah responded with, "Air Defense fighter, say again," just to eat up the precious few seconds she needed for gaining firing solutions.

The reply from the Federal fighter came immediately. "On guard, delta-winged aircraft on heading 29.26 degrees, you are intercepted by armed Air Defense fighter. You have been intercepted. You are entering restricted airspace. Work east immediately. Rock your wings in acknowledgment and turn to heading 110 immediately or you will be fired upon."

Firing solution was set. ARBS system was locked onto aircraft ahead of her. She only had seconds to fire ARBS, launch the missiles and bug out. During the few seconds the laser system was concentrating on the interceptor, the doors beneath Sarah's Delta aircraft opened and dropped two missiles, each independently programmed for their target. As soon as the doors were closed, she went full-throttles as she turned east and pulled back on the stick to gain altitude. She felt quite certain the few second burst from ARBS was more than enough to develop stress fractures in that aircraft, resulting in catastrophic failure, therefore no chance of missile launch. The two remaining aircraft at her six o'clock turned with her in pure pursuit but were falling well behind. Both Federal aircraft fired short-range air-to-air missiles as soon as they realized their target launched missiles.

Knowing that the use of the ARBS system on missiles approaching from directly behind was problematic, if not impossible, she had to make a hard turn and hold it long enough for the system to acquire the incoming target. As this was taking place, the following fighters could easily close the distance for more effective shots. The Delta Flyer had an advantage the enemy fighter had no way of anticipating. Sarah turned her nose straight up and utilized her hoverpad technology which made her craft nearly weightless. She accelerated to speeds unknown to her enemies below as she rolled her craft to place the lasers in perfect line-of-sight to the approaching air-to-air missiles. Nothing could touch her now, but there was little consolation to the fact she failed to fire her third missile on the communications center in Maryland. Soon she would be in orbit again.

"Delta to Command."

"Command here, Delta. You don't have to tell us.

Hermes caught everything. The good news is you are beyond your pursuers reach. The bad news is, you're done there for now. You'll make reentry over New Mexico and bring Delta home."

"Roger that, Command. What's the verdict on the EMPs?"

"Delta, both birds reached their targets. 1600 Pennsylvania Ave. is dark, Pentagon seems unaffected. Didn't do neighbors any good though."

"Roger that, Command. Patch me through to the Queen?"

"Affirmative, Delta. Please hold."

Sarah wondered how it was her aircraft was spotted so quickly when she dropped from orbit and hoped to get some answers from the science teams. She felt assured any of their fighters would not have been spotted.

"Queen to Slice. How are you sweetie?"

"I'm good. I guess you know already I was not able to complete the mission."

"We are, and I just heard back from the science team. The consensus is the delta wing design is a problem, no matter what we paint the plane with. Berry in aeronautics has already suggested a redesign. Says it would require more resources than we have on hand though. As soon as this mission is over, I'll make a requisition to our material suppliers for what we need. Come on home, darling."

"What are my orders, Mom? What happens when I reach New Castlehale? Am I too late to join you?"

"We'll see, Slice. I'll let you know. We are about to commence phase two."

"Mom, remember one thing. I still have one mega EMP on board. If you'd like me to deposit this thing anywhere between the west coast and home, let me know."

"Thank you for that reminder, Slice. I'll let you know within the hour if there is a change."

"Roger that. Slice out."

CHAPTER TWENTY-SIX
PHASE TWO BEGINS

The view from the bottom of Meteor Crater was otherworldly. The crisp dome of stars overhead seemed almost artificial in conjunction with the nearly 600-foot walls of the crater. Scattered about the bottom of the crater were the advanced aircraft of New Castlehale, which included their fighters, both Remos and Adam's desert vehicle. Also present were two Ospreys on loan from the Oklahoma Air Guard.

A large group of soldiers, airmen and crew stood around the circle of mission leaders seated on whatever could be scrounged for this purpose. Among them were a few camping chairs which were stowed away by Adam for his mom and siblings. He, of course, made sure April had one. Adam was proud of the transformation she had made in the time since she and her family had become a part of New Castlehale. He thought he had never seen her look so beautiful as she did at this moment, cradling a weapon of her own design. Evelyn noticed, even in the dim light of their makeshift camp, the way Adam looked at April. This too was something she would have to wait and worry about later. The task at hand was worrisome enough.

The Sheriff of Flagstaff leaned forward to make a point. "Ms. Walsh, I know you could have found a staging area in this desert to land these aircraft, but you chose to put your mission, the lives of your family, your soldiers and pilots at risk by doing us this favor. We've tried for ages to take this place from the cartel and failed. If there is anything we can do to repay you, please let us know."

"Please, call me 'Evelyn'. We had fortune on our side, Kyle. Who knew the bandits would throw a party a mile from their base?"

"And who knew the Queen of Xanthall of the Thrayb Galaxy would show up to help!" laughed Nick. "I've seen a lot of strange things in my years with the Navy and the Texas Rangers, but I've never seen anything quite so.....bodacious. Next time the opportunity arises, I want to be the Emperor of Xanthall. I'd love to step out of Remo and dare them to shoot me."

"Well, that's all fine and dandy for you, Mr. Bulletproof!" chortled Adam. "By the way, I've never actually seen that happen. You wouldn't want to give the Sheriff here a demonstration, would you?"

"Bulletproof?" asked Kyle.

"There will not be any shooting Nick tonight," Evelyn answered crisply. "At least by any of us. However," she said eying Nick with delight, "the security detail at Area 51 may feel differently."

"Aw, Mom! Come on! You got to shoot him in Waco!" said Adam with a smile.

"Let's not talk about that," mumbled Nick.

Madison raised her hand and said, "I shot him 3 times. Just so you know."

"Let's not talk about that either," Nick said with an 'I-am-the-boss-of-you' look, raised eyebrows and all.

"Bulletproof?" Sheriff Kyle asked again.

Eli and Coraline stepped into the circle. "He is bulletproof. I've known for a long time, but it was his secret to keep. I have my gifts," she said as she gracefully floated into the air about six feet, then set down gently into the circle. "Nick has his gift. He is almost indestructible."

Nick seemed surprised by this and had to ask, "Almost?"

"Yes. Almost. We will have a talk later," Coraline said with a smile.

Nick beckoned the children to him by opening his arms.

"Have I told you recently how much I love you two," Nick said smiling proudly at them. The three of them hugged for a moment.

Almost every eye in the circle was on Evelyn now, with smiles that said, '*I told you he was a good guy!*'

Alex had to be the one to interrupt the sweet moment. "Alrighty then! We are wheels up in less than fifteen minutes. Let's get a situation report. Adam, an update on Sarah?"

Adam, who had taken April by the hand, let it go and sat up straight. "Sarah dropped out of orbit and was immediately intercepted by Federal Air Forces. Our only guess about how they glommed onto her so quickly is she entered the restricted airspace right in front of them. Washington must have had the whole east coast put on alert. Three advanced fighters pounced on her, but she managed to destroy one with her lasers and also launch two MegaHammers before she disengaged. Her chosen method of escape was to re-enter orbit. So, both the Pentagon and the White House were introduced to our EMP missiles. We're not sure the Pentagon was affected at all, but the White House went dark. Message delivered. Sarah is about to drop out of orbit again over the west coast and is headed our way. The question we have to answer right now is: Do we need her to deliver that final EMP on top of Area 51 on her way home? Pros and cons?"

"Pro: they would be blind to us. All their cameras, night vision, plasma rifles and any security devices would be disabled. We could walk right in," suggested Hayley.

"Con. Any door with an electrical lock would remain locked. We have people to rescue," said Nick.

"Can we blow the locks?" asked Adam.

"More explosives to carry and we don't have a door count. Pete, you were in there. Any idea?"

"Most of the doors I saw would open with a boot. I only saw a few cells meant for prisoners. Each had multiple security devices. Some had several. But the locks themselves were only designed to hold the iron bar in place. Too much telekinesis happening to not lock those bars down."

"I can open those doors," said Eli timidly.

226

"A power grinder might be handy to bring along," suggested Pete.

"I can open those doors," repeated Eli just a little louder.

Evelyn held up her hand to prevent Pete from continuing. "Eli, dear, what did you say?"

"I can open those doors."

Every eye was fixed on him. Those who did not know him or had seen the things he could do were especially puzzled. Ranger Nick dropped to one knee in front of Eli.

"Eli, are you sure you want to do this? I seem to remember it was painful for you when you cut through the chains the day we rescued your mom. You may have to do that many times inside the facility."

"I remember the pain too. But I've learned a lot since then. It doesn't hurt anymore."

"Are you sure?"

"I am."

Pete, uncomfortable with the prospect of bringing children along, asked, "Whoa, wait. I'm not sure I see what Eli can do in a situation like this. Sure, he heals people, but healing won't open steel locks."

Nick looked around for something they could use for demonstration and spotted a stack of metal fence posts that had been used in a mining venture. He picked up a six-foot post and carried it back. Gripping it in his strong hands, separated by two or three feet, he held out the post in front of Eli, who reached up and grabbed it with his little hand. There was a brief white-hot glow; then, with dripping metal falling to the earth, the metal post was cut into two pieces. Nick made sure to watch Eli's face as he performed the task. There was no sign of pain whatsoever.

"That didn't hurt?"

"Not a bit."

Nick turned and pointed to Adam. "Contact Sarah. Let's drop a Hammer on these bozos. Let's saddle up, people!"

The darkness of the meteor crater was broken by the lights from the New Castlehale aircraft lifting skyward. Adam was hoping the entire squadron would travel in formation as he played Wagner's Ride of the Valkyries through the communications channel, but Nick overrode that notion. The fighters did not stay in formation with the Remos, the Beast and the two Ospreys. They had work to do making sure the skies were clear, so they roared ahead of the pack. This did not prevent Alex from taking Adam's idea of broadcasting the Valkyries over the fighter com-channel.

The flight to Area 51 did not take long given the maximum velocities Alex and the squadron of flyers could attain. It would take another 10 minutes for the Remos to catch up and even more for the Ospreys that were lumbering away at a mere 450 mph.

Hayley came over the channel.

"Uh, Coyote...we are entering enemy airspace. Can the Valkyries. We don't need the distraction."

"Roger that, your ninja-ness. Coyote to New Castlehale Command."

"Command here. Go ahead, Coyote"

"Let's have Zeus take out those runways as we make our approach, but not before Dice drops her package. Timing is essential."

"Roger that, Coyote. She's making her run now. Zeus will be timed appropriately. Trust us. We can handle the math."

"Right. Sorry Command."

"Dice to Command. Hammer release in five, four, three, two, one. Missile away."

"Roger that, Dice. Nicely done. Exfil heading 085. Go buster. Zeus is about to throw bolts."

Evelyn glanced at her radar. Hermes II, being tied into their onboard tracking systems as well as those of Zeus, revealed the current position of all her aircraft as well as the danger zone that signified the area that would be affected by Zeus' rain of missiles.

"Queen to Dice."

"Dice. Go ahead, Queen."

"Dice, if you are heading back to base to swap aircrafts, you may as well stay put. By the time you get back here it will be over."

"Queen. Negative on return to base. I don't need to slip into a fighter. I may not have air-to-air missiles, but I have one helluva laser that works even better. I will be on your six shortly."

Evelyn was also happy to see how well Sarah was doing. A time for mourning would come, she knew, but for now, Sarah was proving herself.

"Command to air squadron. Zeus is throwing bolts. Confirm visually."

The night took on an eerie glow as missiles dropped from the sky like lightning. The entire area lit up as the runways outside Area 51 were destroyed. Only two or three aircraft were in the process of taking off from the small base; the rest that remained on the flight line were destroyed. Alex, Hayley, and Guan Yin moved in quickly to destroy the aircraft that took flight. Anti-aircraft batteries lit up the night, but it was obvious they were having difficulty pinpointing attacking aircraft.

"Coyote to Command, Zeus was on target, Zeus was good."

"Thank you, Coyote. Recalling Zeus for rearming. Command out."

"Slice to Dice. These anti-aircraft batteries are prime targets for ARBS, wouldn't you say?"

Sarah smiled.

"Roger that, Slice. Dice to Command. Permission to go weapons free."

"Queen to Dice. Weapons free is affirmative."

The Delta Flyer flew beneath Evelyn's aircraft with a burst of acceleration. Sarah worked feverishly locating each anti-aircraft battery, as well as missile launchers with the help of Hermes II, which locked onto the origin of every burst made from ground level. Amazing even herself, it was mere moments before she had them plotted and the ARBS system stoked and ready to fire. Streaking in at low altitude, she left a path of destruction behind her. As fast as her on-line computer could identify and fire the laser, the batteries were rendered inoperative beneath her.

"Slice to Dice. I'm on your six. Let's make another pass, just to be sure."

"Warning. Ground to air missile locked on," came through their comDevs. Hayley went left as Sarah banked right. The missile followed Hayley. Her flyer spewed chaff and flares as she sought to escape the missile. The missile exploded harmlessly near the flares.

"I'm getting good at this," she said to herself.

"Coyote to fighters. Remos are on approach. You know your places. Dice, with Slice. Follow her lead."

"Roger that, Coyote. Dice out."

Alex banked Flyer One to offer cover for the Remos and the Beast coming in low from the east as Hayley, Sarah, and Guan Yin descended to the roof of the main facility. It only took a few bursts from their guns to clear the roof of snipers. As each aircraft touched down, beginning with Hayley's, the canopy would open, the pilot would exit the craft and then the fighter would automatically ascend into the air to take up watch over the area on autopilot. What made tonight different from previous missions was control of the plane taken over by a remote pilot seated in one of the simulators back in New Castlehale. Coraline's information exchange created new pilots chosen from the families living in the underground complex.

Hayley and Guan Yin helped Sarah remove her spacesuit, and she soon stood on the rooftop wearing her comfortable spandex uniform. Something was missing, though. She checked for her handgun and spare ammo and ran her hand across her sword. What was it? Following Hayley and Guan Yin's glance, she looked down to be reminded she didn't have shoes. The heavy space boots she had removed were much too clumsy to wear in personal combat.

"Sarah, you didn't put shoes in your flight bag?"

"Apparently not," she said poking around in her flight bag.

"Nothing in the Delta?" Hayley asked glancing at Sarah's flyer.

A look of hope poured out on Sarah's features as she exclaimed, "YES!"

Sarah climbed back into the Delta Flyer and came back down with the exact same pair of blue denim cork shoes with laces that tied about the ankle, she wore the day she and Alex almost had their first kiss.

"You're going to wear those?" laughed Hayley.

"Better than going barefoot!" said Sarah as she strapped them on.

Guan Yin smiled as she said, "They are very nice, Sarah. They look good on you."

Hayley nodded in agreement, "Let's do this!"

As soon as they were away, the Delta Flyer closed up and ascended into the darkness.

Dr. Tanner, Major Ratcliff and four others had been in a meeting when the building shook and the electricity suddenly went out.

"What the hell was that?" someone shouted. A quick check proved even their cell phones were inoperable. Major Ratcliff drew his sidearm and manipulated the light attached to the picatinny rail below the slide. Dead.

"That was an electromagnetic pulse. We need to get those generators back online," he said as he felt his way to the door.

"I'm coming with you," responded Dr. Tanner. "The rest of you stay here."

When they entered the corridor there were soldiers moving about using cigarette lighters to illuminate their way. The Major led Tanner to a panel in the wall and opened it. Inside was a wire cage with electronic devices inside. The Faraday cage had effectively protected the devices from the electromagnetic pulse. Feeling around for a flashlight, he tested it, then used it to illuminate the hall.

"You, Sergeant!" shouted the Major. "Get over here and take some flashlights. Take a detail downstairs and get those backup generators online. This key will open the panel on the south wall. Replace the electronics card on the generators with the ones you'll find in the wire cages there. Be quick, Sergeant. In that same room, there is another panel filled with working comDevs. Distribute those. When you get those generators online, sound red alert. You know the drill."

The floor and walls began to shudder. The muffled sounds of far-off explosions made everyone stop what they were doing. Fear filled their eyes as they glanced at the ceiling. Deep rumblings increased and became so intense it became difficult to walk a straight line, yet Dr. Tanner and the Major made every effort to make a run for the floors below. Dr. Tanner took the lead as they made their way to a stairwell.

Major Ratcliff's men who were outside the building when the attack started were frantically pushing their way back into the structure. Wounded soldiers were being dragged into the building. The volume of incoming fire was overwhelming. Two dozen Area 51 security officers covered the door with the intent of killing anything that entered. Interior lights flashed on again. Apparently, someone restarted the generators, but the guards didn't feel any safer. The light only made them visible.

A thunderous explosion blew the doors off their hinges and through the smoke and flame came a man armed with a squad automatic plasma rifle. The exchange of gunfire was deafening as the 25 guards opened up on the man who stood his ground and never budged. More than a few soldiers wondered if they were shooting blanks. Fear filled their hearts as the man's withering gunfire found every soldier firing their weapon. Then, the queerest thing happened. When the few remaining soldiers had emptied their weapons, sheer fright and terror prevented them from being able to replace the magazines.

"Lay down your weapons and you will live. Fire one more shot and you will die."

Most threw down their weapons and stood up. One battle-hardened veteran was on his feet moving directly toward Nick, belching full-auto fire from his rife. He did everything he was trained to do correctly. Nick hesitated for a moment as he admired the man's courage. Captain Hollings regretted having to put the man down, but he had to do it. IIe shouted a new command.

"Lay down your weapons and you will walk away from this alive. Do it now."

It was obvious some of the security detail had never fired a shot in a hostile environment before today. One or two wept and thanked Nick as they passed him. New

Castlehale soldiers cleared each person for weapons as they passed through the doorway. Nick stood alone, surveying the foyer. He shook his head as he walked over to where the last brave guard had fallen and turned him over.

"Forgive me," he whispered to the man. "It's war, and you were on the wrong side. Rest in peace, brother."

On the floor above, one security officer looking through the partially opened door had witnessed the events below as two of his buddies listened intently to the gunfire. The eyewitness said, "We should just walk down there and give up."

"Ratcliff would have our heads. Are you kidding me?" said another.

"You think those guys downstairs care a lot about the Major right now? You are aware there were twenty or thirty guys guarding the entrance below. They didn't do so well."

The sound of footsteps coming up the stairs outside the room startled them. All three raised their rifles as they backed slowly from the door; beads of sweat poured down their brow. One began to shake. The utter silence of the room was broken when someone standing behind them cleared their throat. Turning slowly, their sight was met by three women in black holding samurai swords poised to strike. One of the men fell to his knees and placed his hands on top of his head, another attempted to bring his rifle to bear, while the third froze in place. The one who raised his rifle died quickly. The fight was over.

Hayley's eye caught the motion of the doorknob turning and prepared to draw her pistol. Slowly the door opened with the groan of old hinges, and in walked one of the most magnificent creatures anyone at Area 51 had ever laid their eyes on. Jennifer looked like death competing in a beauty contest. Wearing a vest that barely covered her chest; her hair in dreadlocks, face painted in diagonal white stripes which contrasted nicely with her chocolate skin, and carrying her large rifle, she knew she aced her first impression.

"Jennifer. You don't need that rifle," Sarah laughed.

"You could kill them on looks alone. You look scary, sister. I'm just saying."

More gunfire could be heard below them. Jennifer pulled two sets of temporary cuffs from a pouch and bound the soldier's hands behind their backs after searching them.

"Come with me, gentlemen, we're walking out the front door where you will be cared for along with the rest...," she broke off as she spied the headless body at her feet, "... who still have their heads." She led the men down the stairs to waiting sentries. After leaving the two men with their guards, the four women headed back into the building to do some exploring.

CHAPTER TWENTY-SEVEN
MAJOR UNDERESTIMATION

The largest laboratory in the facility had been cleared of all the usual equipment. Gone were the beakers and Bunsen burners, centrifuges, and microscopes. The walls were now lined with computers, monitors, and electrical control panels that serviced a large glass sphere suspended above the floor. In the center of the device was a man strapped to a y-shaped apparatus, connected to electrodes.

"Mr. Paden, you have not been forthcoming with me, and frankly, I'm disappointed in you. We spent many days and weeks implanting all those electrodes in your brain, your chest and back and you assured me we would be alerted to the presence of your daughter when she came within hundreds of miles of this facility. And now, my delightful device is dead. You failed to tell me about the EMP missiles. You and Heather both assured me this device would work to my advantage."

"We lied," Paden laughed.

Dr. Tanner's face revealed a deep embarrassment. The lab assistant standing nearby looked away because of it. He didn't want to be a part of what was most likely going to take place next. He knew Dr. Tanner's calm exterior hid a rage that would soon be unleashed.

"What else did you lie about?" he snapped. "You told me your daughter's powers are far beyond mine, and yours, and anyone else in our care. Did you lie about that?"

"No. I did not. Coraline is more powerful than you can imagine." He coughed and gagged most uncomfortably in his weakened condition. His appearance was haggard and emaciated. After composing himself, he lifted his head. "She is here," he said looking up at the ceiling. "I can feel her. You will be powerless before her."

"Dave, Dave, Dave... that is where you are wrong. You see, I have you..." he said as the doors opposite him opened. He looked up to see several people leading Heather Hollings into the room. She appeared to be dressed for travel and despite her handcuffs, she appeared happy.

"Hello, Heather. You seem to be in a festive mood tonight, but I assure you, things are not going to turn out the way you think they will."

Heather's eyes narrowed even though she retained her smile. Tanner always had difficulty reading her expressions. It had taken him some time to realize he couldn't trust anything she told him. She was so accustomed to fooling the people in whose horrible care she had been under most of her life that hiding the truth became a part of her daily existence.

"You do realize, my dear, the only reason I have kept you alive is you are simply a card to be held. I don't care about your gift. Frankly, I never did. I don't care about your insight into the future and I certainly don't care about your brother. When he walks in that door, he will do anything I tell him to do because I have you," he paused for effect, "and I have him. Nothing else matters. Your life doesn't matter and our friend David's doesn't matter. I am the only one who matters at this moment because I can do this."

He held out his hand and flames leaped from it. "They will obey me, or I will turn you and David here along with everyone in this chamber, except myself of course, into smoking cinders in mere moments. I, too, have my gifts. And my gifts trump yours."

David Paden began laughing. It was a weak, pitiful laugh, but it was directed at Dr. Tanner, nonetheless. Tanner turned to address him.

"Ah, David, I'm sorry. I almost forgot you were tied up.

You there," said Tanner to one of the researchers, "Remove him. A pity I could not demonstrate its power. It would have magnified David's power and added to my own. I hadn't considered an EMP taking out this lab's generators as well as the ones upstairs. An oversight on my part, but only a minor setback."

He turned to one of his assistants and said, "Put those clothes on him. And you, let's loan Heather one of our backpacks. That one right there. Put it on her now."

Heather continued to smile as she allowed the backpack to be placed upon her.

"Ms. Hollings, I know you are holding onto a hope that your life is about to change for the better, but I assure you, it is not. I'm actually sick of seeing that stupid grin on your face, and I am looking forward to the time, which will be soon," he said glancing at his watch, "in which it will be wiped from your face."

"I'm awfully sorry, Tanner, if my smile offends you, but know this. What is about to happen is more monumental than you can conceive. I know what you have in mind. And you are sadly mistaken if you believe you will walk away from this. There are some very angry people, nearer than you think, on their way down here right this minute. When they get here, the last thing you will have on your mind is my 'stupid grin.' Prepare to meet your betters."

Tanner turned his back to her. He did not like what he just heard and was not about to let her see he was shaken. He thought for a moment, then, rather than attempt to verbally rebut her response, he simply walked up to her and slapped her face so hard she lost her feet. His colleagues were shocked and stood staring with disapproving looks. One of his senior associates turned and walked out of the room.

"You're losing friends fast, Tanner," said David. "If you weren't a coward, you'd remove my inhibitor and we'd have at it. Gift against gift."

Tanner made a mad rush to where David stood and put his face an inch from his nose. "You think I'm stupid, do you? I should just crisp you up right this minute. I still have Goldilocks there to obtain their obedience. Why do I need you?"

In a fit of anger, he turned and threw a fireball across the room burning two of his own guards in a horrendous death. Then melted the doors on the opposite side of the room in flames of such heat he came near to scorching every person in the lab.

"They won't be coming through those doors," he said with a manufactured grin.

"My daughter won't need a door," said David.

"And how is it you know so much about your daughter?" he said in another flash of anger. "You haven't seen her since she was in diapers!"

"Let's just say we share a garden."

Moving through the halls, Madison, Nick, and Pete cleared each unlocked room as they proceeded. When the lovely Ranger reached out to grab a doorknob, she froze in place. Nick noticed her hesitation and moved close. Communicating with her eyes and a head shake, she whispered, "You're bulletproof. You go first. Something about this I don't like."

Nick nodded and signaled for her to back up a bit and keep an eye on the hall. After moving to a safe distance, she covered the doors they had yet to check as Pete covered the rear. Nick reached for the knob and gave it a turn. The explosion blew him off his feet and through the opposite wall onto his back. The ferocious blast was the signal for the rooms yet checked to pour forth soldiers. As soon as they stepped into view Madison and Pete opened up with their weapons. Nick was struggling to extricate himself from the sheetrock and wiring while trying desperately to hang onto his large weapon. He gave up trying and with wiring wrapped around his head and dust in his eyes, he held his weapon at arm's length and began spraying a horrendous volume of bullets down the hall. Madison dove into the room that was the origin of the blast. She was on her feet immediately and briefly poked her head into the hallway. Something strange was happening. It was as if everything were happening in slow motion. She could see the bullets in flight headed toward her; she had plenty of time to pull her head back to avoid being hit. This was something completely new to her, but she chalked it up to the adrenaline of the moment. Holding her plasma rifle out at arm's length, much in the same way Nick was doing, together they drove the soldiers into retreat.

Madison checked once to ensure the hall was clear, then ran to help Nick get untangled from the mess using wire cutters from her belt. Immediately turning her attention down the hall again. When Nick stepped up behind her, instead of the expected tap on the shoulder to move forward, she felt his hand grip her. She turned and saw what Nick was focused on. Behind them, Pete was on his back in a pool of blood. Moving quickly, Nick ripped a first-aid bag from the back of his belt and knelt over Pete. His eyes were open, but he was not breathing and had no pulse.

"He's gone," Nick said with frustration, mixed with anger. Madison placed her left hand on his arm as she covered the hall with the gun in her right.

"Let's finish this."

Removing the empty drum magazine from his weapon, he replaced it with another with a hard tap. "For Pete's sake," he said.

"For Pete's sake," she responded. "I'm really pissed off now."

The sound of weapons-fire came from an adjacent hallway ahead, obviously from the group that retreated from this hall. Nick trotted forward and poked his head around the corner to see a dozen men attempting to bring their guns to bear on a threat blocking their way, but they were too tightly packed to use them effectively. He wondered what was going on until he saw the flash of a short sword arc briefly above the men's heads. Long guns were being discarded for sidearms and knives in the tight space available. Nick and Madison did the same and joined the knot with the same weapons. The two men in the rear turned to see Nick approaching and managed to swing their 9mm handguns and squeeze off a round or two before he was upon them, but promptly found their handguns

239

snatched from their grasp and used as bludgeons to beat them over the head.

Madison stood on top of the men who had been knocked unconscious to see what was going on up ahead. She was just in time to watch Jennifer physically pick a man up over her head the throw him through a glass window. Sarah, Hayley, and Guan Yin were shredding the men before them with short swords and well-placed kicks. An immense man of considerable bulk tried to use his weight and size to overpower Guan Yin with hopes of pinning her to the floor. The momentum that moved his mass was just the playground Guan Yin needed to guide him into a particularly stout metal door-jamb. His lights went out on contact. Another man tried to follow up his friend's attack with one of his own. A spinning heel kick ended that notion. When the fight was over the two New Castlehale teams stood together covered in blood and sweat, staring at the lone survivor of the soldiers lying on the floor. The poor man had his hands up, begging not to be killed. Hayley ignored him for a second to speak to Nick.

"What now?" she asked.

"We need to find Tanner. Find Tanner; we find the prisoners."

Jennifer asked, "Where's Pete? He knows every inch of this place."

There was a moment of silence, then Madison spoke the words.

"Pete didn't make it. We'll have to figure it out on our own."

Jennifer's eyes filled with tears and she grasped at something to say but it wouldn't come out.

"This man should know," Nick said pointing to the man on the floor. "Chances are he knows his way around here. If he doesn't cooperate, then we'll let Jennifer pull his right arm off and beat him with it."

"I'll do it too," said Jennifer as she savagely pulled the man to his feet.

Sarah began plucking equipment from the man's vest. She tossed his ammo, knife, and handcuffs onto the floor and emptied his pockets. When she was satisfied that he was clean, she pushed him once for good measure. Jennifer had him by the scruff of the neck and whispered angrily into his ear, "Test me, little man, and you'll wish you were one of your friends here," as she pointed to the pile of dead on the floor. "Do you understand me?"

He nodded vigorously.

"Where's Tanner?" she asked.

"Stairs to the right, down three floors, turn right, second door on the left," he said shaking.

Nick asked, "Where are the prisoners?"

"Stairwell to left. Down two floors. Cells on that floor."

Hayley drew her sword and took a couple of steps toward the man. "I think he's lying."

"I'm not lying! I'm telling the truth! It's just like I said! Please don't kill me!"

Jennifer looked down at the soldier's BDUs and noticed a large wet spot. Everybody had to look.

Nick nodded, "I think he's telling us the truth."

Hayley sheathed her sword and asked, "So, what now?"

"We'll split up. Maddie, Guan Yin, and I will take the stair to the right to Tanner. Hayley and Sarah will take the stairs to the left to the prisoners. Secure that floor while Jennifer takes Mr. Pisser here upstairs to be added to the detainees and then return with Adam, Coraline and Eli to see to the prisoners. If the perimeter is secure, send a squad down here to make sure the building is clear. We're not leaving anybody behind, dead or alive.

"Command Base to Coyote. Be Advised. Hermes II has detected military aircraft gathering 200 miles southeast of your position."

"Command, feed me that information. What are we looking at?"

"Coyote, we count thirty fighter aircraft, plus tankers and AWACS in the sky over Edwards Air Force Base. Also, be advised bombers have been launched from Missouri. We cannot tell you their intentions. Both groups are in the air, but neither are headed your way."

"Roger that, Command. What is the status on Zeus?"

"Zeus is being rearmed now. ETA to your position is one hour."

"Zeus in an hour. Acknowledged. Command, tie me in with New Castlehale Remote-pilot Squadron leader."

"RS leader, here."

"Squadron leader, I want Hayley's Flyer on my wing. Bubbas form up on my six by twos. I want lights out. No active radar. Trust Hermes. He will not steer you wrong."

Alex watched as his mom and Adam maneuvered for a landing just outside the main building. It was apparent by the swift collapse of Area 51 ground troops Dr. Tanner and Major Radcliff had not planned well. There was no longer an exchange of gunfire.

"Coyote to Queen. Be careful down there, okay?"

"Roger that, Coyote. I'm landing alongside Roadrunner. Will release my craft to New Castlehale control. Don't worry; I have plenty of protection. I'm safer than you are at this moment."

Alex glanced to his right and saw Hayley's flyer pull in next to him. It was strange not seeing a pilot, but he understood there was a definite advantage to remote-piloted fighter jets. The greatest advantage came from not being affected by g-forces. These planes could take a lot more g-forces than a human could possibly withstand.

Jennifer pushed the man before her as they ascended the stairwell. At the landing she opened the door and shoved the soldier through just as three men were about to enter the stairwell. Two of them nearly lost their feet as the third pushed out his pistol and fired at Jen from only three feet away. Stumbling backward at the sight of the gun muzzle saved her from catching a bullet in the face, yet she ended up on her back. She had the presence of mind to maintain her grip on her rifle, switch to full-auto and let loose a torrential volume of gunfire that killed her prisoner and two of the men. The third man's gun was stripped from his hand by a bullet from her rifle. The man took note of the fact

Jennifer had emptied her magazine, smiled, drew a large knife and dove at her.

She barely had time to discard the rifle before blocking the fist that contained the knife with her left hand as she landed a right fist on the man's cheek. Stunned, he rolled past her and down the stairs. Jen hoped this was the end of the fight, but the man was back on his feet in an instant and rapidly moved towards her again. She drew her own knife and this changed the situation entirely.

"You've never met a fighter like me," he said as he moved closer.

"Apparently I have, since I see my knuckle-prints on your face, dip-shit."

"I know who you are," he said. "I've read all about you. You think you can beat me, but I've trained thousands of men to fight."

Jennifer read the name tag on his uniform and her face brightened. "Major Ratcliff! I was hoping to run into you. I've left a few of the men you've trained dead on the floor. I don't suppose you are going to be any different."

With great care, she backed into the hallway where the three soldiers lay dead. Ratcliff took this as a sign of fear, but her purpose was to give herself room to maneuver, which the stairwell did not afford. Acting more quickly than she anticipated, the Major made a swipe at her face with his large blade. She managed to grab his wrist, pivot on her feet, and then shove her right elbow into his ribs. The gut-wrenching sound of the wind being knocked from his lungs was music to her ears. Not letting go of his left wrist, she pushed forward throwing him to the floor with a thud. He did not rise immediately.

"How's that training working for you now, Major?"

Slowly, he stood and took a deep breath. Then, in a convulsive shudder, he shook it off. Again, they began to circle each other. She lunged in for the attack this time. What began as a feint transitioned into a large swiping backhand with her knife, followed immediately with a return swing to the left. Instinctively taking advantage of her overextension, the major came up with his knee into her right side and smashed his fist into her face, knocking her to the floor. With a raised boot, he intended to stomp her head, but instead had his legs kicked out from beneath him. In his attempt to stop his fall he placed his hands out before him, yet when he hit the floor face first, the very knife he was holding cut him across the forehead.

They were both on their feet quickly and breathing heavily. Ratcliff wiped the blood off of his brow, understanding the implications of being the first to be cut. The statistics were looking bad as he recalled his own training lectures. For the first time, there was fear in his eyes, along with a good amount of blood.

"Somehow, I feel like I need to wipe the blood from my knife, but look at it, Major. There ain't none." She held her blade up to inspect it. "You must have cut yourself. Is that a part of your training?"

They say the eyes are the windows to the soul, and in this case his were filled with anger. His motion was quicker than she anticipated. He threw his knife at Jennifer who was still holding her knife high in a mocking attitude. The Major's knife stuck deeply into her shoulder just inside her vest, causing her to drop her knife and stumble to the floor. Rather than make a rush to take advantage of her situation, he made an effort to reach the rifle dropped by his fallen soldier. Turning to deliver the finishing shot, his eyes rested on the muzzle of .45 automatic. The bullet that exited the barrel went through his forehead, and thus, the man who had trained thousands died at the hands of the celebrity from Junction.

Jennifer let out a cry of pain as she struggled to her feet and moved over to where the Major had fallen. Spitting on his corpse, she calmly said, "I'd say you underestimated me majorly."

Her instinct was to pull the hilt of the large knife protruding from her shoulder, but the pain was excruciating. Judging by the blood loss, she knew if she didn't find help quickly, she'd go into shock. Turning toward the foyer, her way was blocked by five figures silhouetted in the blazing lights from outside. Three adults and two children. The room swayed, and she passed out.

CHAPTER TWENTY-EIGHT
TANNER'S FOLLY

Maddie, Nick, and Guan Yin moved down the hall to the door they were told opened to Dr. Tanner's laboratory. As they neared the door, it opened. The man in a lab coat who exited the lab was startled by the weapons pointed at him and threw his hands up.

"If you are looking for Dr. Tanner, he's in there. I'm fed up with his barbarism. Whatever you do to him is okay by me. I'm leaving. If that's okay by you."

The three Defenders stepped aside and let the man pass between them. Nick took a knee as he covered the door with his rifle. He touched his comDev.

"Ranger One to Slice. Situation Report."

"Slice here. There were only three children in the cells. According to them, the rest were removed a couple of days ago. The children do not know where they were taken."

"Roger that. Deliver them to the Osprey crew and order them to leave as soon as they're ready to lift off. All ground forces are to board now. And Slice, find your mom. I have a feeling we're going to need Coraline and Eli down here."

"Will do. Slice out."

"Ranger One to Coyote. Situation Report."

"This is Coyote. Our Hermes satellites indicate warplanes are being launched around the country. I suggest you wrap things up and we retreat as soon as possible.

Command is in touch with friendly forces and they too are putting aircraft in the air. There are two friendly squadrons headed our way now. Zeus is moving into orbit."

"Roger that. Ranger One out."

The expression on Nick's face told Maddie he was concerned. "Let's finish this. There are a lot of New Castlehale lives on the line here. Ready to move?"

Maddie placed her hand on the doorknob and turned to Nick. "You go straight, I'll take right, Guan Yin, take left. For now, use your gun, please."

Guan Yin, who had her sword in hand, held it before her eyes with a disappointed sadness at forsaking it for a gun. Her response was so swift and graceful in returning her sword to its sheath in one fluid motion that Maddie smiled and said, "That's amazing! How do you do that without cutting yourself?" She then turned to Nick, "Ready to catch more bullets?"

Nick rolled his eyes and nodded. "On three. One, two, three!"

Nick was through the door as soon as it was opened. As predicted, the soldiers in the room fired upon him as he pressed forward. He couldn't help but notice the more he was shot, the less the impacting bullets hurt. He could feel them hit but were no more bothersome than being splattered by a paintball gun. His return fire was withering as the opposition sustained serious losses.

Maddie, whose attention was focused to the right, squeezed off round after round, being careful to fire only at those who fired upon her. She had enough presence to note the people in lab coats who had no weapons. Again, she experienced the sensation of everything happening in slow motion, but this time noticed her own movements seemed normal to her. Bullets were traveling only six or seven inches per second! She could have grabbed a bullet out of the air if she so desired but remained content to simply dodge them. One of the first projectiles she studied closely appeared to be headed directly for Guan Yin. Acting instinctively, she used the shoulder stock of her rifle to deflect its trajectory. Understanding her rifle stock was plastic, she curiously inspected it to check for damage and saw there was merely a dimple. Beginning to understand the nature of her new gift, she turned and ran past Nick to address the remaining targets. Maddie was moving faster than the eye could detect, yet she felt she was moving at normal speed. It was only when the danger had passed that she experienced the sensation of returning to normal human space-time. It was exhilarating to say the least.

From Nick's perspective, he watched as men he had not fired upon fell to the floor left and right. Then, Maddie suddenly appeared ahead of him with her rifle at low ready. "How the hell did you get in front of me?" he asked.

Shrugging off his question, she pointed to a place below a large glass sphere suspended above the floor. Lying on the floor were two individuals, a man and a woman. Nick carefully slung his rifle across his back as he walked toward the two.

"Heather?" he asked.

"It's me, Nick. It's me," she said as she pulled herself to her feet.

They fell into each other's arms. "I'm so sorry it took me so long to find you," he whispered.

"I understand, Nick. I knew exactly when you would come, but it's not over yet," she said nodding toward a large control panel. Slowly, a man in a suit came out of hiding. Nick, Maddie, and Guan Yin quickly turned their weapons upon him.

"And this," the man said with a smile, "is what is called a Mexican standoff."

Nick lowered his rifle and took a few steps toward Dr. Tanner. "I've been in Mexican standoffs, Tanner, and they didn't look like this. You see, we have weapons and you don't. This looks more like a firing squad to me. You're just target practice."

"Nick, take him serious," Heather warned. "He can fry us all. He's gifted. Pete told you about it."

"Oh. Yah. I remember now. He can burn people. Pete did tell me about that. Speaking of Pete, you're going to pay for his loss."

Tanner stretched out his arms, his hands glowing white hot, as he took two or three slow steps forward. "It's true. All

I have to do is will it, and every person in this room becomes cinders in moments. Everyone except for me, of course." The look on Tanner's face was enough the infuriate the Ranger.

"You're welcome to try that theory out on me, FryBoy," Nick said as he moved closer to Dr. Tanner.

Tanner thrust his hands forward, resulting in a scorching inferno that engulfed Nick completely. The others recoiled due to the searing heat yet could see through the ravenous blaze the Ranger continued to stand erect. When the flame subsided, the Texas Ranger casually dusted himself off with his hands and laughed in Tanner's face. Dr. Tanner looked none too pleased. Every lab assistant hovering over their instruments dropped what they were doing and ran straight for the exit. Maddie stopped the first one before he reached the door.

"Leave this building immediately. An aircraft up top is waiting to take you to safety. If you want to live, get on that plane," she said as they raced past her.

"A true Mexican standoff then," said Tanner. "I can kill every person in this room except you, and you would no doubt kill me, but you won't try because you'd lose your sweet sister and your friends, not to mention Coraline's father here."

Every eye went to David Paden.

"I am Coraline's father," he said nodding.

"Your daughter is here," said Nick.

"I know. I can feel her presence."

"Then you possess her gifts?" Madison asked.

"Some, but not all. Some different. I'm not as powerful," he said with a touch of pride. "When she's here, she'll prove it to, uh, what was it you called Dr. Tanner? Fryboy? I like that." He laughed, but then grimaced as if something hurt terribly. Despite being driven to his knees in pain, he struggled to say more when Tanner cut him off.

"Coraline will do what I say unless she wants to see her dear old dad incinerated. Heather, tell these people exactly what you know to be the truth."

Heather had wrapped her arms around David Paden, and in the process felt a plate-sized metallic object attached to the center of his back. Placing her head against David

Paden's, a rush of information flooded into her brain. After only a second or two, she understood Dr. Tanner's brazen courage that enabled him to stand confident in such a crowd of dangerous individuals. Heather was able to put together the information conveyed to her with the information her own gifts had revealed. She made eye contact with Tanner and smiled sorrowfully. "Not every person here will get out of this room unharmed. But it will surprise you to know who. I've seen it," she said. "But prepare yourself, Dr. Tanner, to pay for your folly. Coraline is at hand."

The lights went out as the entire building began to shake with the force of an earthquake. Flashlights were lit to reveal the large glass sphere in which David Paden had been suspended swaying dangerously. Everyone moved away from it.

The arrival began with a flash from a small hole forming on the ceiling of the laboratory. The white-hot glow grew larger and larger as a jet of sparkling dust and dirt shot downward, hitting the top of the glass sphere, much like the sparks created when a diamond cutting wheel slices through steel. When the perfectly circular hole grew to twelve feet in diameter, it was obvious a devouring high-energy shape was lowering itself into the room. The complex faceted surfaces caused everything it touched, including the glass apparatus, to be shredded to smaller and smaller pieces until they appeared only as smoke and heat, all of which were drawn up into the hole that was left in its wake. When it settled to the floor of the laboratory it began unfolding, revealing a sphere within that contained a group of human figures resembling beings of light and energy. The sphere came to rest on the floor as the energy field dissipated, leaving Coraline, Eli, Evelyn, Adam, Jennifer, and April standing at center.

When the smoke cleared, the darkened lab was illuminated by a brilliant light emanating from the freshly drilled shaft leading to the surface. It was an eerie sight, even for Dr. Tanner who had lived his entire adult life dealing with people of extraordinary powers. Coraline moved slowly over to her weakened father and put her arms around his neck. The two held each other for a few moments, then she turned to Heather.

"I'm sorry for what you have been put through, Heather. Your brother has sacrificed much to find you. We are going to make that right."

"Thank you, Coraline. I knew you could come for us. Is this the boy I foresaw?" she asked nodding towards Eli.

"Yes. This is Eli, he.."

"Yes, yes, fine, fine, fine, we are all now introduced," interrupted Tanner. "Now shut up and listen for once in your short life. This is why I hate children so. They tend to prattle."

"We're very sorry, Dr. Tanner, if we're boring you," said Evelyn as she stepped in front of Coraline.

"And you are?" he responded, shaking his head. He did not like being interrupted.

"I am Evelyn Walsh."

"Should I have heard of you?" he asked with eyebrows raised.

Nick and Adam, along with Jennifer, Hayley, and Sarah all nodded their heads saying things like, "Pretty much," and, "Yup, probably so." Nick was the one who spoke directly to Tanner.

"Well, yah. I'm pretty sure you would have heard of her since every one of the setbacks you've experienced lately were all her."

"And The Defenders," Evelyn added.

"Ah. Humble as well as beautiful and smart. I won't be savoring the moment I burn you into dust," he said, but then paused. "Well, on second thought, I might just fry you right now. I'm surprised Major Ratcliff didn't put you down upon your arrival. He really has a bone to pick with you."

"I hate to break it to you, mister, but I put your pet soldier down earlier. He was a hot-head, so I air-conditioned it with my forty-five here," Jennifer said, waving her pistol in the front of her face. "The only bone-picking in his future will be done by worms."

Tanner held a surprised expression for a few seconds, and said, "I thought he was better than that. Oh well, on to business. I will make a proposal, Coraline, to which I'm sure you'll give me a counter-proposal. Then I will reply, 'Do you want your dad to die?' As you can see, I've been thorough in my planning."

Eli, who was visibly shaken by what Dr. Tanner was saying said, "Coraline, I could stop his heart right this second. Then we could just go home."

"What a delightful child you are, Eli. Yes, I'm sure you could, but it's lucky for David Paden there, and the rest of you, you didn't. You see, I have attached a device to his back that will activate the second my heart stops beating. Mr. Paden and I are inexorably linked to this life. You couldn't possibly understand what this device does even if I explained it to you."

"I do understand it, Dr. Tanner," said Coraline. "I understand it because my father understands it. You believe the device will transfer all of my father's gifts and any gifted person nearby to you, making you more powerful and killing him in the process. But I'm afraid that is not going to happen, because you are wrong about how the device works. My father built this device. He did not tell you what the device actually does."

"That is utter nonsense, child. I know how it works because another who lived in this facility looked into your father's mind and confirmed to me that he was telling me the truth."

"Are you referring to Charles Reynolds?"

Tanner's expression conveyed confusion, shock, and anxiety all at once. He moved his mouth, but no words came forth. Finally, with much effort, he answered her question. "Yes, Mr. Reynolds has been a great help to me in preparing for this final meeting. If you think he is on your side, you are sadly mistaken. You see, he, like you, has the capability of only showing what he wants you see. You only believe you have subdued the man. You have met your match little girl."

Nick nodded to Madison who touched her comDev and spoke, "Hayley, could you bring Charles Reynolds down, please?" It was only a matter of seconds before three figures descended on rappel lines from the opening in the ceiling, touched down softly onto the lab floor and detached. Hayley and Sarah stood slightly behind Charles Reynolds who stood facing Dr. Tanner.

"Ah, my friend Charles, it's good to have you home," said Dr. Tanner who tried to sound as sincerely as possible.

"Stuff it, Doc. This is not my home," he responded.

"Nonetheless, you assured me, before you let these people turn you, that the information from David Paden was true. Whatever you tell me now does not matter."

"But it does matter, Dr. Tanner. I was wrong about the extent of information I can gather from a gifted person. I was so used to gathering information from normal people, I overestimated my abilities. The girl is absolutely correct."

Dr. Tanner looked as if his entire world had crashed before him into a pitiful heap at his feet. Staring at the floor, he began to sweat and his eyes bulged as the realization he had been wrong about a very large number of things washed over him. Every person there knew that it was a dangerous moment and expected him to react as he did. In precaution, many of them took several steps back. Coraline, who was standing next to her father, waved Madison to herself and took her hand as soon as she could. The three of them stood together hand-in-hand as Heather continued to support David Paden.

Suddenly, the room was bathed in a golden light. Everyone, except for Dr. Tanner was standing within the glow as silence enveloped them. It was as if they had been transported to a different dimension. They all looked at one another, puzzled at what was happening to them. "Don't be afraid," Coraline said. Her voice sounded almost muffled as if there was a total absence of solid material in their small world to reflect her voice. "I am borrowing Madison's gift for a moment to save your lives. Dr. Tanner cannot hear me and for now, he can't even see us because we are living at a much greater speed than he, but in a matter of minutes, he will notice something has changed and will most likely react by energizing the device on my father's back."

Madison understood what she was talking about immediately. "Coraline, can we disable the device in our current state? We'd be done before he even knew what was happening."

"The device cannot be disabled without killing my father. All I can say is this; If you are not gifted, once the device is activated, you will die instantly. Those who are not gifted must leave immediately. Return to the surface as quickly as you can and move away from the facility. I can give you about two minutes from now. Run now, as quickly as possible."

"But what about the rest of you? What will happen to you?" Evelyn asked.

"We'll live. I don't have time to explain. Run. Now."

Adam, April, Hayley, Guan Yin, Sarah, and Jennifer turned and sprinted out of the lab, followed directly by Evelyn. Coraline watched until Evelyn had exited the laboratory.

"Gather as close to me as you can. I will try to protect you, but just in case, Eli will stand with us and heal us as fast as we are harmed. It may hurt, but do not let go of the person next to you. I asked the gifted to stay because there is going to be an energy transfer that can be handled by those who are gifted, but it is not easy. The more of us there are, the easier the transfer will be. I should have asked Hayley and Jennifer to stay, but they are not quite aware of their gifts yet."

Heather, Coraline, Eli, Nick, Maddie and Charles were huddled together around David Paden, who cried out in tears, "There is no guarantee you will not all be changed or harmed. Perhaps you should all go now. Leave me!"

"That's not going to happen, Daddy," Coraline answered. "Trust me!"

It was obvious to all in the room Dr. Tanner's movement was almost imperceptible. Logic dictated his mind would also be working at a snail's pace. The sphere of energy that enveloped them all, causing them to experience life at nearly light-speed, was beginning to fade. Once they returned to normal space-time, they could only continue to cling to one another and hope for the best.

The glow diminished and suddenly Dr. Tanner realized there were fewer people in the laboratory than only moments before. He looked behind him and strained his neck to see where they could be hiding, but there were none to be found. He also noticed those who remained were bunched up around Coraline's father.

"Where did your friends go?"

"Which friends are you talking about?" answered Nick.

"Do not make me angry or Paden will pay."

"If Paden pays, you pay, Tanner."

This obvious fact disrupted every thought in Dr. Tanner's brain. He began to pace back and forth like a caged animal, desperately trying to form a plan, but the turmoil of being thwarted thus far made it difficult to latch onto one coherent thought. Everyone watched him patiently, hoping his indecision would give the others the time to reach the surface and board an aircraft. He would begin a sentence only to stop and rethink. Finally, Coraline said to Eli, "Everyone is out. Do what you said."

Eli spoke, "What's the problem, Tanner? Cat got your tongue?"

"Shut your mouth! Where did the others go? I demand you answer me immediately or I will energize the device!"

Eli's intense dislike for this man was demonstrated by his response. "Pull the trigger, butt-bag, and watch what happens. Never mind, I'll pull it for you."

Dr. Tanner clutched his heart as Eli concentrated on shutting it down. "NO!" he screamed as he slumped to the floor, gasping for breath. His device was triggered, which led them to believe that Tanner was no longer alive. Panels set high in the walls began to glow and beginning with a low-pitch hum, the room began to vibrate, then shake. David Paden's head wretched back and his back arched in pain as he let out a mournful scream. The sounds intensified as they went from a vibrating hum to the sound of a hurricane descending upon the space they occupied. Coraline's energy field contained the group in a chaotic swirling vortex, as everyone there reacted much the same way David did. Faces to the ceiling and arched backs, they all screamed as the room around them began to disintegrate. Panels were ripped from the walls to be sucked upward through the opening in the ceiling. Chairs, desks, anything not bolted down were swept up into the opening and turned to dust. Had it not been for the protection Coraline afforded them through the energy field, they would have been swept up also. Even with Coraline's protection it took great effort to hang onto one another. Dr. Tanner's body was lifted into the air and burst in an explosion that took out half the building, yet the flames were directed at David's device. They managed to burrow through the energy field and wrapped him, as well as Heather in white hot flames. Those hanging onto her screamed all the louder.

Nick and Eli seemed less affected by the pain than the others, as electrical currents traveled from person to person with crackling snaps and loud buzzing bursts. But Eli was losing strength rapidly as he healed them at nearly the same rate as the currents could burn them or short-circuit their nervous systems. Nick gripped him, as well as those around him with all the strength he could muster as the intensity and chaos increased. "Eli! Be strong!" he shouted, but his voice was barely audible over the deafening roar and the powerful forces at work.

The white hot flames that engulfed David and Heather grew and encompassed the entire group. Screams and shouts increased to the point even Coraline wondered how long the others could withstand this torture. Suddenly, everything went blinding-bright and silent.

CHAPTER TWENTY-NINE
THE CHOICE

Circling the complex, Alex observed a group running from the main building to board Remo. The doors closed and the saucer-shaped craft lifted gracefully into the air and turned southwest. The Ospreys, which had gathered the ground forces, prisoners, and rescued children were already wheels up and headed for Junction.

"Queen to all aircraft. Clear the airspace above this facility for two miles. More if you can. Do it now. I mean now. Do not delay."

"Coyote to Remote Squadron leader, you heard the Queen. Yank and bank. Let's clear this airspace. Climb to 12,000 feet. Converge on me."

Alex banked his aircraft and pushed the throttles forward. The acceleration pinned him back into his seat, but he felt no effects of the intense g-forces. Ever since Coraline healed him and prepared him for the dogfights above Kermit, he had not felt the effects of g-forces at all. He recalled how Hedgehog had passed out while seated behind him, yet he stayed alert and in the fight. Once he gained altitude and leveled out, he searched for his squadron. To his great surprise, they had already formed up behind him. Apparently, Coraline's knowledge transfer to the remote pilot team had been effective.

It was mere happenstance Alex was not looking in the

direction of Area 51 when a blinding white-hot flash came from that direction. Alex had instinctively dropped a filter on his flight helmet to cover his eyes, yet he could see little detail as the area was bathed in brilliant light. After a few seconds, he banked to the left for a better view. A ring of fire, emanating from the hole which Coraline cut to descend into the complex, rushed across the surface of the Earth, destroying everything in its path. It took a full minute before the extent of the damage was apparent. A deep crater was all that was left of the complex. In the exact center of the crater was a ball of light, too bright for even filtered eyes to observe.

"Coyote to Queen."

There was no response. Alex knew Remo could not possibly have made it far, so he checked his radar display being supplemented by data from Hermes in orbit above. The information relayed to him via satellite was very sketchy at the moment. Whatever was disrupting his communications was most likely interrupting Hermes also. It took twenty seconds before his screen cleared up enough to locate Remo. He was happy to see whoever was piloting was wise enough to move the aircraft behind the protection of the hills to the southwest. His comDev indicated someone was trying to contact him, but all he could hear was a garbled voice drowned in static.

"Coyote to Command."

There was a reply but the voice was still garbled. He tried several channels, but nothing. Returning to their designated mission channel, he heard a voice, but not much clearer.

"This is Coyote. Say again. Repeat your message."

"This is command base. Zoom out your display. I repeat. Zoom out your display."

Alex followed the command and saw aircraft converging on their location from every direction. Friendly aircraft came from the north and east, as enemy aircraft approached from the southwest. The data from Hermes showed him the location of every New Castlehale asset. His squadron trailed him; Remo was hidden behind the hill; The Ospreys with ground troops were enroute to Junction and would soon have the protection of the Texas Air Guard. There was but one airborne craft hovering alone, and that was Adam's Beast, which also happened to be the only non-stealth craft in the air. Enemy radar would have already seen it.

"Coyote to Roadrunner."

"Roadrunner, go ahead," replied Adam in a transmission that was still static-laced.

"Roadrunner, you better do something with the Beast. It's low-hanging fruit."

"Roger that, Coyote. Remote landing it now."

A tone sounded in Alex's flight helmet as a hypersonic missile streaked across the sky and destroyed Adam's beloved Beast and scattered its pieces across the countryside. Alex didn't waste another moment before he began barking out orders.

"Listen up, Defenders. So much for our deal with the Feds. We're at war. Remote Squadron, kill your engines, hover and turn into the enemy. Do not show them a hot tailpipe. Hermes can see them, but they cannot see us. You are weapons free to the southwest. Let's give them some of this. Fox two!" he said as he fired off two missiles.

From the relative darkness, missiles streaked away into the night to hunt down the incoming warplanes from the southwest.

"Coyote to Delta Flyer. Use your lasers to thin the herd a bit. Go buster and blow through them."

The Delta Flyer's fusion engines came to life and accelerated as it flew straight at the oncoming squadrons. The calculations necessary to fire the lasers at multiple targets were being accomplished by computers at New Castlehale and fed to the pilot by a team of weapons officers seated nearby. In quick succession, federal aircraft fell from the sky. Those that were missed or simply passed up turned to follow the Delta Flyer, but at the speed she was traveling she was out of visual range and invisible for all practical purposes.

"Command to Coyote. Federal F40s are approaching from the west. CPAG will engage. OAG is entering airspace now. Zeus is in orbit and is minutes from firing position."

As the converging enemy warplanes filled the sky, they

launched missiles and used their guns in a deadly aerobatic ballet. While the numbers belonged to the Federal aircraft, the technology belonged to The Defenders as all of their planes had access to the information fed to them by the orbiting satellite Hermes. Regardless of the advantages and disadvantages, aircraft from both sides were falling from the sky as the air battle intensified, with the exception of the flyers built by the New Castlehale air teams. The hovercraft technology allowed their planes to maneuver in ways even the agile F40 warplanes could not anticipate, yet as more and more fighters appeared, the sheer numbers made victory questionable for The Defenders.

"Command, we're in a fur ball here! Where is Zeus?"

"Coyote, Zeus will be iffy in this situation. You are very close."

"Try one and see how it goes, Command. Pucker factor is high here."

"Roger that, Coyote. Hermes is chatting with Zeus. Launching now."

From high in orbit, a single missile was launched and sped toward the relatively jumbled mass of warplanes. Hermes had locked onto one particular bogey and fed coordinate changes to the missile as it neared its target. When the missile was one second away from hitting the target, another aircraft flew directly into its path and was destroyed instead.

"Command! You did it. Splash one bogey!"

"Affirmative, Coyote. But that was not the bogey we had targeted. That could just as easily have been one of ours."

"Acknowledged, Command. Go after stragglers, AWACS, and tankers. We'll take care of the fur ball."

***

"Where are we?" Eli asked no one in particular. He could sense the presence of others, but he couldn't see anyone in the whiteness.

"I was hoping you'd know," replied Madison. "Coraline?"

"I'm here."

"Where are we?"

"I think I know, but I'm not sure. Give me a minute," replied Coraline from nowhere they could see.

Nick's voice came from whiteness, "Heather, are you here?"

There was no response. The utter silence of this white world was absolute. After what they experienced moments before, one would think they should at the very least, have ringing in their ears. In comparison, the sound of a voice was almost shocking.

"David, can you hear me?"

No response.

"Everyone who can hear me sound off," said Nick.

Coraline, Eli, Madison, and Charles all answered. There was no response from David Paden or Heather Hollings.

Madison asked, "Coraline, can you help us out here? Where are we? How do we get out? Can we return to where we were? Is it safe to return to where we were?"

"Give me a few more moments, please," replied Coraline.

Out of respect for Coraline and her gifts, everyone waited. There were many questions, but more than one noticed wherever they were, there was one other person who didn't answer besides Heather and David. Dr. Tanner was not answering either. They each wondered if, when the whiteness became something else, something tangible, were they going see the three of them dead? Asleep? Unconscious? The imagination can play games with a brain with no input. The only person thinking positively about the situation was Coraline, who finally spoke up.

"Here we go," she said, as the whiteness faded and color made its way into their world again. The five found themselves standing on a large circular green lawn, surrounded by perfectly trimmed hedges and the rose-bush lined path. Eli and Charles recognized the place immediately as Coraline's garden with its deep velvety-blue, star-filled sky surrounded by an unending golden glow on every horizon. Also unmistakable was the marble-like dais in the center of the lawn, book-ended by two large fruit-bearing trees. The mystery of the missing Heather Hollings and David Paden was now partially solved. Floating above the dais was Heather holding David Paden in her arms. The scene resembled an angel bearing an unconscious saint into Heaven. The difference was she seemed to consist entirely of flame and molten hot metal that ebbed and flowed from head to toe. How could she touch him and he remained unburnt? Why was she holding him? Was he alive? Was she alive? They gracefully floated together ten feet above the dais. Only Coraline climbed the steps. She walked beneath them staring intently, wondering if there was anything she could do to help her father or Heather. For the first time ever, Nick saw she was as perplexed as the rest of them.

"What's happening here, Coraline?" asked Eli. "They are both alive, I think. I can feel them."

"I feel it too," she said, "but we need help."

"Help from whom?" asked Nick. "We are all they've got. Who can help?"

"The One can help, if you ask," came a voice from behind them.

The sight that met their eyes as they turned sent ripples of emotion through them. Feelings of awe, shock, fear, and hope poured over them as a radiant being approached them with slow, sure steps. His features were concealed in light as he walked between them to approach the dais steps. Coraline and Charles simultaneously acknowledged the being by speaking his name, "Messenger."

"Did you call us here, Messenger?" asked Coraline.

"I did not. You rode here on pure thought, with the aid of these gifted," he said motioning toward the entire group with his palm up. "On the hope of escaping the evil one."

"I must assume you are speaking of Dr. Tanner," said Nick.

"You are correct," said the Messenger as the glow about him subsided, and the detail of his features became clear to all. His face was the portrait of kindness, yet revealed power and an ageless depth of understanding. And his bearing made you feel he might have been a witness to every major event since the beginning of the world. Somehow, he seemed stern and encouraging at the same time. His eyes spoke the truth as he scanned each face. "Unfortunately, for him, his self-deception had a deleterious effect on his well-being."

Madison nudged Nick and whispered, "I think 'deleterious effect' is a fancy way of saying he exploded."

Messenger looked directly at her and continued. "But his desire to inflict pain on others has not yet ripened." He glanced at the two figures hovering above them. "There is one who will shortly cross the threshold into the Realms, but which one of them has not been determined."

"Who will make the determination?" asked Nick who never took his eyes from his sister. Worry was painted across his features. He had fought so hard all these years and hoped he might have more time to spend with her than the brief moment they had together before the device was activated.

"These are mysteries even Messengers long to understand. We see things from a different perspective than you, yet some things, such as determination and free will, puzzle us as much as it puzzles mankind. For many centuries, books have been written on this subject, and yet every one of them fails to contain the wisdom of the One."

Eli smiled and asked, "You read our books?"

The Messenger looked into the boy's face with a fascination that surpassed any seen on Earth. "Yes, Eli. Many of us read them. I find them intriguing and disappointing. One day, my kind and yours will stand together and learn from the One who will reveal all."

"Messenger, why are we gifted?" ask Madison, who moved a few steps toward the ancient being.

Slowly he turned to her and produced a smile. "Madison Jameson. You have proved to be one of interesting qualities. Your question is fair. I, like you, do not possess full knowledge of the dealings of the One, but one thing we know about you; your love for Coraline and Eli and those helping them is without limit. Since the night you met Coraline on the road, you have been unwaveringly faithful to her. The answer to your question is simple. Humans have given themselves over to the evil of this planet. Many are unable to discern good from evil. Hate from love. What once was good and right has become wrong. What once was wrong has become right. It has become commonplace for evil to kill and destroy for things as small as having a different opinion.

The last great war thinned the ranks of the evil, but war can never solve a spiritual matter completely. Many were given gifts to protect the innocent. There may be a question in your minds of how war can solve anything, yet even among my kind, we have been at war with evil since their leader was cast down. The universe is in one unending struggle. War in the heavens, war on the earth. This is the reason some are gifted."

"But, Messenger, some of the gifted are evil. Dr. Tanner was evil! At one time, Charles here was evil!" said Nick who pointed at Charles. No one had noticed Charles had been kneeling with his head bowed since the Messenger arrived. They all stared at him, including the Messenger, who walked over to Charles and beckoned him to stand.

"My dear Charles. Stand. For all has been forgiven," he said as Charles looked the Messenger in the face. Messenger never took his eyes off of Charles as he continued to answer Nick. "You are correct, again, Nicholas. Even the gifted have choices to make. There are some who, like the rest, were born with their power, yet sought to use it for selfish gain. Dr. Tanner was one of those. As I mentioned, there are Messengers who have chosen likewise. The war between the good and the evil has been a constant for many millennia. War is not an evil in and of itself. It is the hearts that start them that are the greatest evil."

"Then, you are on our side?" said Eli.

Messenger smiled at Eli's comment. Turning to him, he took a knee before the boy. "You have ever been a delight to us, Eli. Your purity and love is known in the Realms. But, in answer to your question, no. We are not on your side. You are on ours. Many wars have been fought on Earth, each warring party claiming the One was on their side, but the One does not take sides. You must take the side of the One."

Eli squinted his eyes at this answer. "Then how can you tell who is on the side of the One?"

"By their love. The one who hates cannot know the One."

"But, Messenger, we have killed people in our defense! We didn't want to, but we did! Is that love?"

"Sometimes it is. We did not give you your gifts to entertain yourself and others. It was done for the very reason evil must be suppressed during these dark days. You have done this and yet maintain your love. It is for this reason Coraline was sent back after having been in the Realms."

"Coraline has been to the Realms?" Charles asked.

Coraline showed no discomfort at being the focus of attention at this moment. Rather, it seemed as if she had been hoping for a moment such as this to give insight to those she loved into the bigger picture. "Yes, I have been to the Realms many times."

"Coraline is special. There are few like her," said the Messenger.

"Are any of those close to us?" Nick asked.

"Yes. There are two others with you, like Coraline, yet neither understand it yet." The Messenger paused. "Soon. Soon."

Coraline placed her hand on the Messenger's sleeve. "Two others? You and I have shared in many conversations recently. I'm surprised you did not mention this."

"It was not yet time," he answered. "Yet, I feel you already have a suspicion in your heart as to the identity of the first."

Coraline studied each person nearby. Her mind then went to two others, perhaps three that could have been here with the others. Hayley and Jennifer were two that crossed her mind, but it was the third that made her pause. When she turned to the Messenger, he was nodding.

"Say it, little one," he said.

"Evelyn Walsh?"

The Messenger continued to nod. "Your feelings on this matter are accurate. Again, we go back to the night on the road when you all converged. The Rangers, the Walsh family, and you two were brought together there for your first meeting. Much has changed since that night. But you, Coraline, recognized something in Evelyn from the very first moment."

"Did we know one another in the life before?" Coraline asked.

"Yes. She was your mother in two of your re-insertions, but neither of you remembers it. And were it not for the accident, you would have been born to her in this lifetime."

"Are there such things as accidents?" asked Eli.

For the first time in Coraline's experience, she saw the Messenger laugh.

"Always the deeper questions, Eli. You are a joy. We will call it an 'accident' for human purposes. Eight years ago, Charles Walsh was killed in his laboratory by a fusion energy experiment. To say it as briefly and simply as possible, the ripping of space/time that killed him also had an effect on the potential mother. I will use the simplest explanation I can give so you will understand. Evelyn Walsh's knowledge was imprinted on the incoming Coraline, who was appointed to be her child. Instead, Coraline was born to Teresa and David Paden. Yet, Coraline was born with every drop of Evelyn's scientific knowledge. She is in every way Evelyn's daughter, yet in every practical way, she is Evelyn herself. This may be confusing to your minds, but Evelyn is the source of Coraline's emotional makeup, as real as the connection to her physical parent, Teresa. David, here, was chosen to be her father, partially because of his gifts."

Madison knelt before a tearful Coraline. "How does this make you feel, Coraline?"

"Happy. I have wondered why I was so drawn to her. There was always the powerful connection I felt every minute I was with her. I secretly suspected this, but I thought it was only because I was wishing and hoping it was true. Now that I know it is, I feel complete. Happy."

It wasn't Nick's intention to break the intensity of the moment, but he felt the issue of his sister and Coraline's father needed to be moved along. "Messenger, what happens now? What happens to us? What happens to them?" he said nodding towards the hovering Heather and David.

"The answer begins now," said Messenger. "Coraline, come to me."

He placed his hand on top of her head. The glow with which he entered the garden grew again, but this time enveloped both of them. The radiant golden aura intensified, then Messenger disappeared leaving Coraline wrapped in light. This lasted only a few seconds before she returned to her own state.

"We must act quickly if we are to save Heather or my father."

"What do you mean Heather OR your father? Can't Messenger save both?" asked Nick.

"Messenger is exactly what his name means. He is a Messenger. He cannot decide. The choice of who stays and who moves on to the Realms will be theirs. We cannot make the choice for them. Follow me. Run!"

Coraline ran to the beginning of the rose path and waited for the rest to catch up, then held out her hands for others to take. They huddled in a circle holding tightly to the person next to them.

"They are here," Coraline said, looking back at the dais. Heather and David Paden were surrounded by a dozen or more glowing beings. Coraline and all her group stared in awe, but only for a few moments before they were covered in a vortex of images and light. As they were being transported away from the garden, Nick mouthed his sister's name.

"Heather."

CHAPTER THIRTY
TWO FROM THE ASHES

The skies above Remo Two were filled with aircraft locked in close aerial combat. Adam watched the progress of the battle from a hand-held tablet receiving data from Hermes, while Evelyn kept her eyes to the sky above using a night filter on her helmet. Hayley had climbed to the top of the hill with Guan Yin and Sarah to keep an eye on the crater left by the explosion. In the center, there remained a bubble of light. April and Jennifer stood guard outside of the aircraft

"Queen to Ranger One. Come in Ranger One."

No response.

"Queen to Ranger Two. Maddie, please answer."

"Queen to Slice."

"Here."

"Can you see what's happening down there?"

"Affirmative. Nothing to report. Just that ball of light."

"Keep us informed."

Adam let out an exasperating gasp. "Mom, according to Hermes, the feds are losing more planes than we are, but they have the numbers. We can't last a lot longer, and Zeus can't help when they are so close together."

Evelyn ripped the flight helmet from her head and answered Adam with equal frustration. "We still have hope. They don't have AWAKs. They lost their tankers. We can stay in the fight longer than they can. They've got to be close to running out of fuel, right?"

Adam nodded his head. "Correct. But the same is true with our allies. They're also close to bingo fuel. Something has to happen soon, or we're toast."

Evelyn got that look on her face that indicated she had to make a timely decision that crossed the line of her comfort levels. She understood completely ordering her planes back would expose them and whatever was happening in the center of that crater. The mere existence of the light at the center of the crater told her Nick, Coraline, Eli and the others were alive."

"Queen to Slice."

"Slice. Go ahead."

"Stay where you are, we'll pick you up."

Adam looked up in surprise. "We're leaving?"

"We're going to the crater."

They boarded Remo and took off immediately. Skimming close to the rocks and earth they set down on the top of the hill and briefly opened the door for the three women to board, then made a straight line to the center of the new crater.

"Set down right there, Adam, and stay at the controls. We may have to leave in a hurry."

It wasn't until they landed that they could grasp the power of the explosion that took place here. The crater was deep and large. They felt fortunate to be alive. They had just opened the door when the brilliant ball of light suddenly disappeared, and in its place was a huddle of humans beings in a group-hug. Evelyn found she couldn't run fast enough to reach the survivors.

"Nick!" cried Evelyn. Reaching the group, she put one arm around Nick's neck as she gathered Coraline and Eli into the other.

"Where is Heather and David Paden?" asked Hayley.

"They are being cared for! We can't stay here!" said Coraline in an anxious tone. "We've got to get away from here! Far away as fast as we can!" She looked up into the sky and said, "Send our allies home!"

As they ran to board Remo, Evelyn spoke into her

comDev: "Queen to Command. Newcastle aircraft, form up on Remo. Allied aircraft, return to base. I repeat. Allied aircraft, return to base."

As soon as the door closed, Adam instructed everyone to buckle in and prepare for a rough ride. Once he was assured everyone was secure, he turned Remo eastward and threw the throttles forward. Nick and Madison had experienced this g-force party once before during their previous visit to this area, so they knew what to expect. The inside of the aircraft was filled with grunting and the noises one would make trying to catch a breath. Jennifer was the only one willing to speak.

"I really need to go to the bathroom."

Glancing off of his left and right wings, Alex noted the two remaining New Castlehale aircraft were Hayley's Flyer and the Delta Flyer. All the rest had been destroyed during the air battle, yet the loss was less painful knowing none of them had human pilots on board. With a touch of sadness, Alex had to accept the fact the future of the New Castlehale Air Force would be remotely operated aircraft. He knew a good amount of time would be spent rethinking aircraft design to accompany this advancement. But now was not the time. To his relief, the dots on his display that represented enemy aircraft were headed back to their own bases. Yet it would only be a temporary respite according to the signals sent by Hermes. More squadrons from the west were moving towards Area 51. Alex chuckled and spoke his thoughts out loud. "You're going to find nothing but a crater there when you reach it. That and Zeus waiting for you."

"Coyote to Command."

"Command, go ahead."

"What kind of reception can Zeus give the incoming bogeys?"

"Zeus has a lot of lightning left, Coyote, but not enough to handle what's coming."

Alex and the remaining flyers met up with Remo, taking up positions left, right and behind.

"Coyote to Queen. What's the plan?"

"Coyote, we're setting down at the coordinates I'm about to transmit. You and Delta Flyer land beside us. Flyer Two will maintain a position 1000 feet nearby and turn your cameras toward Area 51. Transmit to Remo."

"Roger that, Queen. Flyer Two, you heard the Queen. Acknowledge."

"Roger that, Coyote. 1000 feet."

Traveling one mile every 7.2 seconds, it did not take long for the four aircraft to arrive at the designated coordinates, a relatively flat area behind a range of high hills. As soon as Remo set down, Jennifer shouted, "I gotta go!" as she pounded on the door switch. Before anyone else could unbuckle their own harnesses, she was out the door and sprinting toward a large boulder.

Charles Reynolds smiled. "When you gotta go, ya gotta go."

Nobody was in much of a laughing mood. The two people who were the reason for this mission had been left behind, and no one, with possibly the exception of Coraline, knew why.

"Where's she going?" asked Alex as he stuck his head inside the door Jennifer had vacated only moments before.

Eli answered, "She had to go."

Evelyn said, "Come in and be seated." Then she turned to Coraline and asked pleadingly, "Sweetheart, can you catch us up on what you know?"

"I'm a bit curious myself," said Nick, "and I was there!"

"I can show you. Everyone take hold of each other."

When they were all connected, Coraline revealed everything she learned at the meeting with Messenger, including the part about her relationship with Evelyn. There were more than just the facts of their reinsertion into this world. The memories of every previous lifetime were revealed. This was Messenger's parting gift to Coraline before he left. They remembered everything. They remembered their families, the time periods, the successes and failures, the good and the bad. It was a lot of information to share, but they all saw it. They even got a glimpse of the Realms. When the sharing was over there were many tears between Evelyn and Coraline as the two held one another. There was an awesome, solemn shock for the others at having seen the Realms, the Messenger, and the group of Messengers that surrounded Heather and David. But something was missing and they all wanted answers. What was to become of Heather Hollings and David Paden?

The door of the aircraft opened and Jennifer stuck her head in to take in the scene of obviously impacted people.

"Did I miss something?" she asked.

The humor of the situation snapped them all out of their info-shock. Coraline looked almost embarrassed with an I'm-sorry-you-missed-out look on her face. She reached out to take Jennifer's hand and Evelyn intercepted it. "Can we all see it again?"

Coraline smiled and nodded vigorously. Everyone touched the person next to them and they saw it a second time. When all was revealed, it was the vision of the Realms that affected Jennifer the most. She cried as she told them how much her father and mother spoke of Heaven when they were alive. "It's a real place. As real as this!" she stated with stunned conviction to the others. They all nodded in agreement.

Silence permeated the aircraft when the sky outside lit up with another bright white flash. Adam turned to the display receiving live stream from the remotely operated aircraft above them. He switched it to a monitor set into the wall of the aircraft for the passengers to see. There was nothing but white for a moment, but it faded quickly. A large translucent dome began to spread out from Area 51. Lightning bolts burst from the source, as the scenery surrounding the dome was distorted. It was as if gravitational waves were bending light in every direction.

"Adam, what is our exact distance from that?" asked Evelyn quickly.

"Distance, 21.4 miles," he answered.

"According to what the Messenger communicated, 20

271

miles was good enough. We have room for error."

"There is no error.....Mom," said Coraline, looking directly at Evelyn.

Alex nudged Hayley in the side with a large smile as they quickly accepted the fact they truly did have a baby sister! Together they watched with interest as the dome continued to grow, getting closer to their location.

Madison spoke up for the first time since entering the aircraft, "I would close that hatch if I were you, Jennifer. I don't know if it will help or make any difference whatsoever, but I'd feel better if it were closed."

Jennifer touched the door controls, but more gently than she did in her haste to leave. The door closed and seconds later the fading dome passed over them with a deafening roar. It did not sound like what you'd expect from an extremely large explosion. It was tonal in nature, such as the Doppler effect one would expect from a passing synthesized pipe organ playing its lowest notes at high decibels. When it hit, the video feed from the aircraft overhead temporarily distorted and spun as Flyer Two was tossed several hundred yards. It was the hoverpad technology that saved it from being cast onto nearby rocks. Once Flyer Two had regained stability, the video feed of the sky in the direction of Area 51 returned. Nothing to see.

"Roadrunner to Flyer Two. Climb to 3000 and let's get a close up of that crater."

It took a minute before they got an image, but the results were disappointing.

"Command to Roadrunner. Be aware enemy aircraft continue making their way to the site. Whatever we do, we should do quickly."

"Command, this is Roadrunner. Engage Zeus. Instructions for Flyer Two. Land on our coordinates immediately. Relinquish remote control. Command, instructions for Delta Flyer: Take control of Delta and stay on our six."

Adam turned to the crowded passenger compartment and began laying out a course of action. It was usually Evelyn or Alex and sometimes Nick who took this role of command. The beauty of the Walsh family is when a need arises, nobody really minds the person with the greatest overall picture of events takes charge. This is a part of the respect they have for one another. Nick was glad to see Adam take this moment by the horns.

"Alex, you and Sarah to Flyer One. Hayley and Guan Yin to Flyer Two. Go before us. Keep under the radar. Everybody else buckle in. Remo will follow at a safe distance. We're going to move to ground zero. Some of you survived the first explosion, there is no reason why we should not find the others there also. Coraline, am I right?"

Coraline nodded. "There are answers in the crater."

The four pilots boarded their planes and lifted into the air. Adam watched as they moved quickly toward the deepened crater and he followed them in, while keeping a distance.

As the four aircraft approached the area only 30 feet off the ground, they slowed to watch the progress Zeus was making with the federal aircraft. Missiles streaking in from high overhead were taking out enemy warplanes one after another. Whether it was the confusion of having missiles appear from nowhere or the loss of so many of their pilots, the surviving aircraft turned tail and bugged out. This gave Adam and Alex the opportunity to head straight to the center of the crater unencumbered by threat. Their hope was to find Heather and David Paden just in the same way Coraline and the others appeared after the first explosion.

"Roadrunner to Coyote, stay on station. Watch our backs, brother."

"Roger that, Roadrunner. Slice, let's keep our eyes peeled."

Evelyn took Nick's hand as they approached the glow at the center of the crater. Everyone followed closely, with Coraline on Evelyn's other hand. Together they watched as the glow intensified to a blinding brilliance, then disappeared. What was left was the warm glow of a flaming figure. Nick recognized his sister immediately. With trailing flames, Heather moved towards them slowly as if walking were something new.

"Heather? Are you okay?" asked Nick.

"I am better than okay, Nick. I am.... changed," she

responded in a clear voice.

"Where is David?"

"The decision has been made. David has moved on to the Realms," she responded as she looked to the skies. "There is more concerning this, but I must pause to tell you that you are all in danger here. I will take care of it."

"Queen to Coyote. What's our situation?"

"Bogeys are inbound. They will be on top of us in minutes. Zeus is returning to base. We have no cover. We have no support. We are sitting ducks. We need to wrap it up and bug out."

Heather's feet left the ground as she floated skyward with an urgent suggestion. "Evelyn, I will take care of this. Land your planes now."

"Queen to Coyote. Land those planes here immediately. Do it now."

Heather ascended with the speed of a missile leaving a flaming trail behind her. She reached an altitude of 15,000 feet within seconds and then halted her ascent. The intensifying reddish-yellow flames emanating from her body could be seen for many miles. The incoming pilots were perplexed at the thought of a missile launching from a place that appeared to have been nuked. But, they had orders to shoot down anything in the sky above Area 51, so six fighters locked missiles onto the stationary burning object miles ahead and fired. Heather saw them coming and smiled. After half a lifetime of being cruelly treated by government researchers, she was getting some type of payback. The missiles slammed into her with great force, but any damage that should have been done to her, took place at the origin of their launch. Six fighters exploded in balls of flame. The remaining pilots searched frantically for the source of the missiles that must have struck the other planes but found none. In the absence of a foe besides the flaming object ahead, they too locked onto Heather. For every action, there is a reaction. This is a scientific norm. But the reaction to force directed at Heather took place at the origin of that force. Missile for missile. Bullet for bullet. Anything done to damage her, damaged them. This too was a parting gift from David Paden. Every federal fighter was destroyed.

"I've got some power here," she said out loud as she studied her flaming hands.

"How can I burn and not be consumed?" she thought. "This must have been a result of the device on David Paden's back. But can I turn it off? How do I do it?" She pondered it intently, and in doing so, the flames went out. She was happy to see she was able to control it until she realized she was free-falling to earth. It was an exhilarating feeling, but she knew she had to do something quickly or die. "Wait. Can I be killed? Wouldn't the force of the ground hitting me be directed back at the ground?" Not willing to test that theory just yet, she willed the flames back. As soon as she was alight, she flew directly to the center of the crater, being very careful not to land on top of her rescuers. Flying did not come as naturally to her as it did to Coraline when she discovered her ability to create wings like a bird. She hit the ground harder than she really wanted to and created her own little crater. The whole group cringed when they watched the botched landing. Climbing out of her crater, she stumbled towards the group, still covered in flame. Nick ran forward to meet her.

"Are you alright, Heather? That was a horrible landing!" Nick said half worried and half laughing.

"I'm fine. I'm not used to flying. Would you do me a favor?"

"Anything, Heather. Just ask."

"Would anyone happen to have an extra set of clothes for me? I can turn these flames off, but I'll kinda need something to put on. I'm pretty sure when I go to flames, well, my clothes kinda do too."

Hayley chimed in immediately. "I do! I keep a personal bag in my flyer. I hope you don't mind wearing spandex."

"Believe me, it'll do until I get something that's more....me. But before I do that, I must finish what I was going to say before the planes showed up."

Everyone gathered around her, staring at the awesome, flaming woman.

"I am to tell you that David Paden was given a choice and he chose the Realms. He asked me to tell Coraline that he will be able to visit her anytime in her garden. He made this choice because of a special set of circumstances that has only happened once before in the history of humankind. I can't explain it nearly as well as this one could, so I'd like to deliver the package."

"The package?" Coraline asked, "What package?"

"You'll see. Please remain where you are."

Heather floated into the air and held her arms skyward. The air above her seemed to boil and suddenly turned to light. The sound of it was like a rushing wind as the light got wider and brighter, then there was a brief flash and the doorway above her head went brilliant and a body was ejected from it. The ejected person was flailing his arms trying to land in a way to do the least amount of damage. Adam instinctively intercepted the falling person and caught him in his arms. He had his back to the group when he made the catch, then turned slowly to reveal the person in his arms.

"*Hedgehog?*"

There was a concerted rush to him as his feet were gently lowered to the ground by a dumbstruck Adam. Sarah's face flowed with tears as she plowed into him, covering him with kisses and hugs. A few of them reached over her to touch him for no other reason than to confirm he was real. There were simultaneous shouts and questions.

"We thought you were dead!"

"How are you here?"

"Where have you been?"

"How is it you are alive?"

Hedgehog just smiled and cried, mainly because everyone else was crying. The light reflected off of every tear before him, which caused him to ponder the source of the light. He turned to see a flaming woman floating gently to earth and his jaw dropped.

"Who is that?" he nearly shouted.

Nick responded, "Hedgehog, meet my sister Heather. She's the one we'd been planning to rescue for some time."

"*She* needed rescuing?" said Hedgehog.

Being careful to keep a safe distance from the others, Heather took a few steps toward him. "Initially. Yes. I needed to be rescued from Dr. Tanner. I saw this coming.

But I did not see you, Hedgehog. You are an anomaly. And I'd love to talk more with you about this," she said sincerely. "We cannot stay here much longer. More planes are coming, and I'd rather not have to destroy them," she said looking to the skies. "We must return home. Hayley, may I borrow those clothes now?"

Hayley motioned for her to follow. Every eye followed the flaming sister of Nick. Seeing someone burning with flame is an uneasy experience even if they are totally unaffected by it. Once the two were hidden from view behind Flyer Two, it was obvious her flames had gone out when they found themselves standing in almost pitch-black conditions. Flashlights came out, and those who were riding home aboard Remo entered the aircraft and began buckling themselves into the seats. Nick waited at the door for his sister. When she approached Remo, Nick noticed she appeared ten years younger than she did when he saw her in Tanner's laboratory. He took her in his arms once again.

"Let's go home."

CHAPTER THIRTY-ONE
BREAKFAST OF CHAMPIONS

Lilly, of the wooden spoon, seemed to be more affected by Hedgehog's return than any of the others. Since the moment Remo entered the landing bay, she had not stopped crying. But her tears did not prevent her from preparing a huge breakfast for the family. On this morning, the kitchen overflowed with volunteers from the New Castlehale community for the purpose of feeding the soldiers and Rangers who returned home before Evelyn and the core leadership. The temporary helpers prepared breakfast tacos, coffee and cinnamon rolls for the groups huddled together in the landing bay awaiting debrief. Finished with that task they assisted in serving breakfast to the Walsh family. Kate Jennings, who normally helped Lilly with the meals, could not bear to leave Eli's side for a moment. She had hugged and kissed him so many times he was seen wiping tears from the top of his head with a napkin.

The one person in the galley who should have been most distraught after the events of the past 12 hours sat next to Adam humming and swinging her legs under her chair as she spread butter and jam over her toast. Many at the table looked at her and mourned the fact she had lost her real father. Most at the table projected deep emotional feelings of 'aloneness' onto her, but these well-intentioned emotions were misplaced in this situation. They were unaware of the promise of the Messenger that she could visit her dad anytime in her garden. This was the very best outcome as far as she was concerned. Her father was safe and secure in the Realms, while she had unlimited access to visit him in a place that existed outside of the space-time continuum. Coraline was content.

"Are you going to be alright, baby sister?" Adam asked lovingly.

She looked up with a smile that expressed a new appreciation for her beloved 'Gulliver', as she was fond of calling her giant brother. "I haven't lost him, you know," she said.

Adam tilted his head in the direction of Hedgehog seated next to Sarah and said, "I can't argue with you there, baby sister. Nothing is as it seems to be these days. I wonder if everyone else is as weirded out about it as I am. Am I wrong to feel that way, Cor?"

Coraline whispered to Adam, "Everyone is wondering about Hedgehog. But the explanation is simple. I'm sure he'll get around to telling it. I don't want to take that away from him."

"So, you know?" Adam asked surprisingly.

"Of course, I know, Mr. Brute Squad!" she giggled.

"Don't call me brute squad. Just because you're such a delicate little butterfly, the rest of us don't have to be tiny-winged fairies," he said as he wrapped his arm around her head and poked it with his huge finger.

"What are you guys going on about?" asked April.

"Abumm finnnk he nogha bwuhh sqahhh."

"What did she say?"

Adam chuckled as he let go of her. "I think she said something about eating a buttered beef quad. You should stick with your bread and jam, little fairy, or you'll be as big as me."

"One day I'll be as big as you."

"Nuh uh."

"Yah huh."

April smiled to herself. She remembered what it was about Adam that made him so desirable when she first met him but realized it was mostly superficial. He was tall, strong, and handsome! He was also very famous the night she met him in Austin. Still is. But she could now see that all those things are just what they are; they aren't WHO he is. He's a family man through-and-through, and her mother pointed that out to her.

"He loves his mother, misses his father, and cares for his family and friends more than he cares for himself. And I think he cares for you. If I've ever met a person like him, I can't remember when," said her mother. "Hang onto this guy."

"I intend to," she said to herself, as she felt a little hand take hers. Looking down to see Coraline's hand holding onto hers, she glanced at the child who winked at her.

Heather sat quietly beside Eli who seemed intent on making sure she had plenty of food and drink. He would jump up and refill her cup before it was half-empty. Coffee was a special treat for her since she was without it for decades. He'd put things on her plate that she didn't ask for, but she knew better than to eat the usual breakfast foods placed before her. One doesn't need to be clairvoyant to understand the body takes time to get used to eating things other than the gruel she had been fed. The fresh fruits on the table were her favorites. In spite of Eli's hovering, she did love the attention she was getting. There was a lot that would take some getting used to. What she would enjoy most is the freedom to do what she wanted, when she wanted to do it.

The glances she received from people around the table indicated she was a complete mystery to them. Some of the faces were just curious, while others were awed. The demonstration of her new powers during the night probably cemented that into their brains for some time to come. Eli mostly just smiled at her as if there was a kinship others couldn't understand. At one point, when she acknowledged his adoring gaze, he held his finger up till it glowed red hot, then dipped it into her cup of coffee, instantly heating it to near boiling point. She in turn held her finger up, thought about it for a few seconds, then shook her head.

"I should wait till I'm outside to try that," she said

smiling. "I'm not sure I could control it."

"I think that would be best," said Kate Jennings.

"Ms. Hollings?" said Eli. "Coraline and I can show you how later. We might be able to help you with that."

"Thank you, Eli! I would love that! It's very sweet of you to offer. But Eli, please call me Heather."

Jennifer and Madison spoke softly with each other at the end of the table. Jennifer's whisper intensified for a moment.

"She said what?" asked Jennifer.

"She said, and I quote, 'I should have asked Hayley and Jennifer to stay, but they are not quite aware of their gifts yet'. She must know something we don't. You must have a gift like mine! Like ours!"

"But I haven't felt anything!" Jennifer responded, flexing her fingers before her face. "Tell me about yours again."

"Have you ever been in a situation where everything seems to move in slow motion? Think about it." Madison whispered.

"Well, yes. Remember the night in Junction when we were in danger of being overrun by the feds? Our bunker was hit by rockets and you and I were thrown to the ground? Everything about that was in slow motion. I dragged you across the ground to put some space between us and the bunker, knowing it might be hit again."

"Like it was yesterday," said Madison. "Did I ever thank you for that?"

"Only a hundred times," Jennifer chuckled.

"Well, imagine being able to control slow motion at will, but you can move regular speed while everything else was slowed down."

"What good would that do? I don't get it."

"Look at your plate."

"I'm looking at it. What am I looking for?"

"Keep looking."

Madison caused time to stand still for herself in the room. Looking around the table, everyone seemed to be frozen in place. Some had forks to their lips, others in mid-sip with their coffee cup, while others were frozen in laughter or mid-speech. The only one in the room moving at her speed was Coraline. The beautiful child waved and said, "I'm glad to see you're getting the hang of that."

"You can see me!"

"Of course! Your gift was imparted to you when Eli and I healed Alex near Kermit. You were holding him."

"Then, can you tell me about Jennifer's gift? She must have received it when you and Eli healed her knife wound at Area 51."

"Yes. She should be able to become invisible and walk through walls."

"Does she have to become invisible to walk through walls? Or can she walk through walls whether she's visible or not? That's an important distinction!" said a concerned Madison.

Coraline laughed her infectious little giggle. "Sorry! I see your point. Only when she is invisible can she pass through things, and things can pass through her."

"Bullets?"

"Anything and everything."

"Oh, she is going to love this!" screeched Madison. "How does she do it? Just a thought?"

"We'll talk about that later."

"Alrighty then! Thanks! I better get back!"

Madison looked around the table and spotted a plate of bacon. Picking up four pieces, she placed them on Jennifer's plate before she returned to normal space-time.

"Whoa!" Jennifer exclaimed. "You also have the gift of making food appear?"

"No, silly. I can move at lightning speed. I grabbed a handful of bacon and dropped it onto your plate before you could blink your eye. Get it?"

"That is very cool, Maddie. If I had my druthers, I'd kinda like to be bullet-proof like Nick. Half the enjoyment would be seeing the look on the bad guy's face as I strolled over and ripped the gun out of his hand and shoved it up his..."

Madison interrupted her, "Chill, sister. I know what your gift is."

"Whoa, wait. You told me just a few seconds ago you had

no idea what my gift is. You said Coraline must know something we don't."

"I did. But in the time I grabbed that bacon to put on your plate, I also had a conversation with Coraline."

"What? You are really freaking me out!"

"It's true. Here's what she said."

Madison explained what she knew to Jennifer as the breakfast sounds of clinking dishes, glasses, pots, and pans continued. Cholo refilled cups and put out new pitchers of juice. At one point he was engaged in conversation with Heather, offering to fetch anything she wanted; Heather explained Eli was taking very good care of her. Cholo was in the process of listing off everything that was good to eat in the kitchen when he felt the instructional whack of Lilly's wooden spoon.

Everyone stopped whatever they were doing and became silent when Evelyn, Nick, Hayley, and Alex entered the galley.

"This morning we conferred with the President, our Governor and other Texas leaders," announced Nick.

"Can we trust the President?" Madison asked. "We made a deal with them, albeit subversive, when Zeus destroyed the runways at Nellis, and they attacked us anyway."

"We made mention of that to the President, and he assures us his forces are standing down, what's left of them. We gave them a significant thrashing over Nevada, thanks to Heather, Alex, and Zeus. They lost a large number of fighters and support aircraft with little to show for it, not to mention a large hole in the ground where Area 51 used to be. He is not interested in continuing the conflict, and it is not in our interest to thin their military any further. They still need to protect the borders and coastlines from foreign intruders who will try to take advantage of this internal conflict. The Texas Border Patrol has already engaged armed groups coming up from the south this morning. The intruders were soundly defeated by the TBP using the relatively new Police Battle Cruisers (PBCs), not to mention the fact the State Guard has been flying constant patrols along the border since this thing flared up. In addition, twenty minutes ago, we repositioned Zeus and Hermes to an orbit over the border area. Very little will get through. Hermes II is over us, and Hermes III is over the Dallas/Ft. Worth area. There will be a Zeus II and III by the end of the week."

"What did the President say about the prisoners that were taken away from the Area 51 before we got there?" asked Madison. "Now that we have the upper hand in negotiations, it makes sense to me we should be able to see them freed."

"We brought that up. He is going to get back to us," answered Nick. "For now, we are going to have to trust he is negotiating in good faith. But in light of our current situation, there will be a change in our policy regarding the sharing of technology. Evelyn, would you care to address this?"

She nodded and took a step closer to the table. "Within the State of Texas, we will begin upgrading allied armed forces to include fusion power and hoverpad technology. This will take place in stages. The first to receive our advanced weaponry will be Texas Rangers and the Texas State Troopers. Each of their headquarters will have landing pads. We'll have quick-reaction forces located all over the state in case of emergencies. With fusion engines and hoverpad technology, it will be cheaper to put Rangers and Troopers in the air, than use gas-powered vehicles on the ground."

"On top of this," Nick added, "we will build a fleet of upgraded Zeus satellites, with Hermes and Artemis technology built-in. New Castlehale alone will have access to these satellites. They will only be deployed over the continental United States. Alex suggested we name this effort *Operation Second Amendment*."

"Where are we going to build these things?" asked Madison. "I pay attention during important conversations, and from what I've gathered from Adam, Alex and Evelyn, this facility just barely has the capacity to keep us in the fight. We're fortunate to have what we have! We'll need new facilities."

"Madison is absolutely correct," Adam responded. "We don't have that capacity here, so a new plant will be built near Buchanan Lake. Training for staff members and engineers will take place here at New Castlehale. The Governor, Major Johnston, Major Carol Peters and General Stokes are all in agreement to location and mission."

"Wait, Adam, how do you know this?" asked Jennifer. "You've been sitting here with us while Evelyn and the others were in Command Central making plans! How could you know what was being said in there?"

Adam rose from his chair and cleared his voice. "Many of you know that special gifts, similar to Coraline's, have been given to others. Nick is bulletproof. Madison moves like lightning. And now, I have been given the gift of being able to hear things spoken in other locations. I came to breakfast just to prove it."

"*No way!*" shouted Jennifer. "*That* is fantastic!"

"I'm pulling your leg," he said as he pulled an earbud out from his right ear. "I listened in with this."

The room exploded with laughter. Coraline and Eli laughed the loudest, and Jennifer laughed the least.

"I owe you one, Adam. I really do owe you one," she said as she pounded her fist into her other palm. Adam laughed, but did so with a little gulp.

"Anyway," continued Adam. "I came to breakfast instead of going to the meeting because I preferred to be here with my baby sister and the rest of you guys. But, I still heard every word said in Command. Details of the new facilities will be hammered out after the upcoming wedding ceremonies."

"The *what*?" blurted out an astonished Jennifer as she stood up. "If you're pulling our leg again, I *will* climb over this table and thump you!"

Nick put his arm around Evelyn. "He's one hundred percent correct. Evelyn has agreed to become my wife, and, of course, you are all invited to the wedding."

There was a round of applause. When it ceased, Coraline said, without even looking up from her plate where she was running her tiny finger across to pick up the traces of butter and jam, "I thought I heard Gulliver say *ceremonies*, plural."

"Uh, yes. I misspoke. There will not be plural ceremonies. There will be one double ceremony."

The room was filled with multiple gasps, 'what?', and 'huh?'. When Sarah kissed Alex there was yet another round of applause.

Hayley walked to the end of the long table and leaned forward, resting her hands on the tabletop. "Now that we're all up-to-date on the war, our deals with the State of Texas, and the nuptial bliss-to-be, there is one mystery we are all interested in being enlightened." She looked directly at Hedgehog.

Hedgehog, who had been relatively quiet during breakfast, leaned forward and smiled.

The morning sun had already begun to heat the dirt and ash of the massive crater left behind by the splitting of space/time and the device that had been attached to David Paden. Fires that were scattered across the landscape, spewed toxic fumes as they consumed the materials thrown from the blast site. Most of the construction materials had been incinerated to ashes lay in heaps almost as far as the eye could see. One such heap began to stir as something buried within struggled to gain the surface. A charred hand pushed the ash to one side, followed swiftly by an arm, a head, shoulders, and torso. Fighting to free himself, the disfigured man screamed as he finally pulled himself out of the ash and rolled down the incline to lie face-down in the dirt and dust. With great effort, he pulled himself to his feet to survey his surroundings.

Dr. Tanner, a frightening caricature of his former self, tottered as he began to walk across the barren wasteland. Gone was the pristine suit. Tattered shreds of melted fabric stuck to his skin. His destination appeared the be the broken remnants of a stairwell belonging to a structure which stood several hundred yards from where the main facility previously existed. The building in which this stairwell had been a part had been sheared off at ground level. When he reached the spot, he found the steps led down into darkness. From his hands sprang flames of fire which lighted his way as he descended into the belly of the ruins.

CHAPTER THIRTY-TWO
EXPLANTIONS

In the silence of the galley, the scraping sound produced by Hedgehog's chair being pushed back was harsh. He moved to the end of the table and cleared his throat. Work in the kitchen stopped. Every ear was tuned into Hedgehog's voice as he spoke.

"Some of what I'm going to tell you is not first-hand knowledge, but what was told to me. I gotta be honest, some of you look a little scared. Some of you are wondering what it's like to come back from the dead. But I'm going to start by telling you straight out; I did not die."

"But we were there," said Hayley. "We watched your plane explode. How could we be wrong about that?"

"She's right, Hedgehog. I mean, we saw what we saw and couldn't come to any other conclusion. In the end, though dead or alive, we're glad to see you now," said Sarah.

"I thought the same thing, guys," Hedgehog answered. "I thought I was dead. I was on approach to the mesa, and the next thing I knew I was in a white world. There was nothing to see but bright whiteness, then someone spoke to me. It was Messenger. He said I was in the Realms and my mom and dad would be waiting for me. My first thought was I must be dead, because mom and dad were. Then I could see them far off! I waved to them and they waved back! Messenger told me to wait where I was until it was time. I don't know how long I was there. It could have only been a couple of minutes, but it could have been more. Time is not a big thing in the Realms, I found out later.

"Somehow, I kinda got sucked into a garden where I saw Coraline and Sarah, and well, all of you saw that part already. I really did think I was dead. After I left them, it was the Messenger who told me I didn't actually die. That seemed weird to me, but he explained it happened a couple of times long ago, where live people were taken into the Realms. He said I was snatched right out of my flyer just before the explosion took place. And, well, ended up in the Realms."

"When you say *Realms*, are you really talking about Heaven?" asked Rita.

"I am! I talked to a lot of people who had different names for it. I heard it called *Paradise*, *Zion*, *Tiāntáng*. One guy called it *Abraham's Bosom*. Yeah, that was weird, but everybody gets along there, so I didn't mind the differences."

Jennifer asked, "So, umm, Hedgehog, did you see...I mean...happen to run into...you know...the Big Cheese?"

Hedgehog and Coraline laughed at exactly the same moment. "I did see the One, if that's who you mean. And I doubt anyone there refers to him as *the Big Cheese*. There was a lot of activity around him though. There were Messengers coming and going constantly. The One appears as a blinding light and was constantly surrounded by thousands of Messengers and people with wings."

"Are you sure he was the One?" asked Evelyn.

"I was told what I was seeing was actually him, but that I would not be speaking directly to him before I left. A glowing guy walked me around, explaining things. He was the one who led me over to I see my parents and brother! That was great! They were glad to see me, though somehow they already understood I wouldn't be staying. After hanging out with my family, the glowing guy took me around and introduced me to a lot of people. Whenever we came across Messengers, they would reach out and touch me. I didn't get it, but nothing that happened there came close to being bothersome. OH! And I was quite surprised to run into Ranger Pete! I thought he was still down here with you guys.

By the way, he said to tell you he's better than fine."

Madison's eyes were filled with tears when she asked, "Hedgehog, did anyone explain to you why you were saved and sent back?"

"I asked the glowing guy that question, and he told me I still had work to do."

"What work is that?" asked Eli.

"He said I'd figure it out."

"Something about this doesn't exactly strike me right," said Jennifer, shaking her head.

"Jennifer, we got Hedgehog back! There's nothing wrong about it!" responded Sarah with some emotion.

"Why does Hedgehog get a second chance when many haven't! Most don't actually! Please, don't get me wrong. I'm as glad to see Hedgehog as anyone here, but there are others who weren't given that break. Pete is one. My parents! Eli's dad. Loads of people aren't given that chance! Hedgehog, even your parents and brother!" Jennifer said in tears.

"I would like to answer that question," said Coraline.

Hedgehog was glad for the spotlight to be turned from him. "Please do, Coraline. I know the answer, but you'll say it much better than I could."

Coraline stood up on her chair; something she was not used to doing. "The question of *second chances* and *breaks* is only meaningful in a universe where life and death are not the same thing. Hedgehog's experience is another proof that death is a gateway to another life. Is Pete alive? Yes. Just not here. To those living on this earth, he seems dead. Jennifer's parents, Eli's dad, along with my father, are all very much alive. The words 'break' and 'second chance' mean little or nothing to them. Being in the Realms *is* their break."

"Coraline is correct," said Heather. "Coraline's dad and I were there together. We saw the very things Hedgehog told you about." She turned to look at Hedgehog. "I also saw the One. But in our case, the One spoke to us. We learned the same war that is happening down here against evil is taking place on a plane unseen by us. The One chose many thousands of years ago to utilize his Messengers in this war. He has Messengers whose power is second only to him, and some that are not. They are all engaged in this war. He has appointed gifted humans to make a difference on our plane of existence. Of all those gifted, Coraline is the most powerful because she is the keeper of the keys. As you know, she can turn on dormant gifts in others. Within this room are fighters who have been gifted. Eli can heal with a touch as well as command over the elements of earth, wind, fire, and water. My brother Nick is nearly indestructible. Madison can alter her existence in time. Charles, who is not in this room, has retained his gift of suggestion, despite having misused it for the enemy. All has been forgiven. Go easy on him. Others in this room are gifted but have yet to discover them."

"What about yours?" asked Nick. "Can you tell us about yours?"

"I am not yet aware of all my gifts. When we pulled together to protect ourselves from Dr. Tanner's lunacy, I was the one in contact with the device he created. Dr. Tanner thought any of the gifts present at the time the device was activated would be transferred to him automatically, but he was wrong. One of David Paden's gifts was to allow special abilities of others to replicate and flow through him to be amplified to meet the need of the moment. All of our gifts were amplified and flowed through him to me. The One explained these things to me. Then he blessed me with other gifts. He said my gifts would make me..." she paused uncomfortably, "the ultimate protector."

"Protector of who?" said Hedgehog.

"You."

"Me?"

Heather looked around the room as she thought carefully about what she was going to say. The decision to speak it aloud had been weighing on her the entire morning. "Well, you... and my children."

"Holy Schnikes! Are those three children we rescued.... are they...?" stammered Hayley.

"Yes. They are waiting in the corridor."

Trevor and Ruth Brice, who had been standing at the door, made beckoning motions to someone nearby.

"Meet my children, Wolfgang, Max, and Callista."

Three children ran into the galley shouting, "Mom!!

Mommy!!" They glommed onto Heather and loudly related to her the events of the past 12 hours.

"We flew in a flying saucer!" shouted the seven-year-old twin boys.

"Two ladies with swords let us out of our room!" the youngest, a tiny girl of three, stated emphatically. "Those ladies!" she said pointing at Sarah and Hayley.

"That's right sweetheart. Those ladies' names are Hayley and Sarah."

Callista ran over to the '*ladies*' and hugged them.

"Did you have a nice ride in our flying saucer?" Sarah asked.

"Mmm hmm! It was fun, but they made me stay in my chair with my belt on cause the plane was doing this!" Callista answered as she made her hand go up and down.

"That's right, darlin'," said Hayley. "They make me wear a seat belt too. They keep us safe when the plane does that."

In the meantime, Madison moved over to Coraline and whispered in her ear, "Coraline? Did you know about this?"

She nodded affirmatively and whispered in return, "Yes. But it wasn't my story to tell."

"Fair enough, but do you know who the father is?" Madison asked with raised eyebrows.

"Yes. Heather Hollings is my step-mom."

Madison, who had been leaning over to speak to Coraline, stood straight up to process that bit of information. Then leaned over again to ask, "Does Nick know all this?"

"He knows everything."

Sitting on top of the mesa that was home to New Castlehale, Charles Reynolds was sure he was at least four feet from the precipice. Not being as sure of himself with heights as Coraline or Eli, he felt more comfortable away from the edge, but he did enjoy the view. Occasionally, he would toss a rock over the side as he cursed himself and the mistakes he felt marred him for life.

"The One may forgive my stupidity, but humans are not

quite so magnanimous," he said as he chucked a rock as hard as he could.

"You don't give us enough credit," said a voice behind him.

Turning, he viewed two individuals standing nearby. He instantly recognized Coraline's bare feet to identify her, but the flight suit worn by the second person only narrowed his guesses. He couldn't see their faces because the sun had risen to a place directly behind their heads.

"Hi, Coraline. I mean it. My encounter with the Messenger was, well, life-changing to say the very least, and the offer of forgiveness for my actions, as horrible as they may have been, was humbling. But, unlike this family, the Messenger had no stake in the game. As much as I appreciate what he said to me about the One, it was your lives I nearly shattered."

"We *are* the One's stake in the game," said Hedgehog.

The sound of Hedgehog's voice brought Charles to his feet. He had hoped not to do a face-to-face with the boy for at least a day or two. He needed at least that much time to formulate his thoughts before making his case.

"When we harm one another, we harm the One. There's no getting around that, Charles," Hedgehog offered.

"I know. I know. And I've been sitting here all morning trying to conjure up excuses, but I always come up with nothing; I have none. '*I was on the other side*' is a weak argument for blowing up kids. I don't know what to say, except I am sorrowful to the point of being sick. I don't know how I'll be able to remain here among the people I harmed the most. I could go live in Junction, but I'm afraid I won't get a great reception there either. I don't know what to do."

"Then stay here," said Coraline.

"That's right, Charles. Stay here. We forgive you," Hedgehog said, hoping to assuage his guilt, but realized Charles would need something more specific. "*I* forgive you. You're one of us now, not only on this plane of existence, but on a much higher plane. And as far as the family goes, they have forgiven me for things that would have made lesser people crap their pants."

Coraline laughed. "Nobody came close to crapping their pants, Hedgehog. So, you stole a fighter jet! They got it back all in one piece!"

Charles Reynolds chuckled, "You stole a flyer?"

"Yah, it's true. And they punished me by building me a better, faster flyer with a Hedgehog painted on the nose! So, you see, Mr. Reynolds, if there is any place you want to be, it's in a family that can overlook mistakes. Besides, if *I* can forgive you for blowing me up, they pretty much *have* to."

Coraline put her hands on her hips and said, "But that's the point, Hedgehog! You weren't blown up! All Mr. Reynolds did was blow up your flyer. You stole a flyer and he blew one up, so I think you two are like two peas in a pod."

Coraline always had a way of viewing things that, once stated, set the world aright, and this time was no different. Hedgehog and Charles exchanged glances that said it all. They each realized they had more in common than they thought.

"That settles that then!" said Hedgehog as he put out his hand to Charles. It was accepted.

"Well, now that we've got that ironed out, do you think Lilly might have some leftovers from breakfast?" asked Charles.

"We're way ahead of you," said Coraline, as she handed Charles a paper bag with three breakfast tacos. "Bacon, egg and cheese, if my mind-reading is still working correctly."

"You bet it's working! Thank you!" Charles replied gratefully.

"Well, you two enjoy the view," said Coraline, "I have an appointment with the ladies."

She walked back to the small house to take the elevator down, but before she entered, she looked back to see Hedgehog and Charles sitting side-by-side at the mesa's edge.

Hayley, Madison, and Jennifer decided it was a great idea to take some drinks, a few snacks, and four picnic chairs, as well as check out one of the Remos, for a jaunt down to the Texas Militia encampment near the base of the mesa. Jennifer's suggested activity was to watch the construction crews. Madison and Hayley agreed wholeheartedly, but really were more interested to see Jennifer's reaction to the hard-hatted men working onsite. From their vantage point, they could see all the foot-traffic coming in and out of the location of the barracks and headquarters. To the west there were already landing pads going in. A long line of concrete trucks were waiting their turn to pour for the runways and helipads. The State of Texas had spared no expense in supplying materials and labor for this effort, which was quite generous considering the fact that according to the Cultural War Treaty, anything they built inside the Void would no longer belong to the state, nor be under its control. It was an act of good faith by the current Governor.

"Hey there, Mr. Universe! You are lookin' fine in that Home Depot tool belt!" Jennifer yelled to one particularly large man on his way to work. He stopped, pulled off his shirt and flexed his muscles in a typical Mr. Universe pose. Madison and Hayley turned red and palmed their faces as Jennifer '*woo-hoo'd*' like a school-girl.

"You do realize," Hayley said as she held back tearful laughter, "this sort of thing has been looked down on for almost a hundred years, Jennifer?"

"Anyone who wants to complain, well, they know where to find me," Jennifer replied as she waved furiously at the men.

Madison looked at her watch. "Why did we come out here when we knew good and well that we're supposed to be meeting with Coraline?"

"She said she'd find us, no matter where we were," said Hayley. "This is as good a test of her tracking abilities as any."

Madison surveyed the landscape with binoculars and stopped when her gaze crossed the top of a three-story building under construction. At this point, only the steel frame of the building had been built, so the sight of the girl standing on the highest beam was a bit disconcerting. "There she is," she said handing her binoculars to Hayley.

"What's she doing up there?" Jennifer asked in mid-wave at more workers.

The three looked at each other as Madison asked, "You don't suppose she wants us to come up there, do you?"

"I doubt it," responded Hayley.

When they looked again, Coraline was gone, and all three were on their feet in a second. "Where'd she go?" Hayley nearly shouted. "She didn't...."

"I'm here," came Coraline's small voice.

Jennifer nearly jumped out of her skin. Seated nearby at their feet, facing the same direction, Coraline sat on the ground hugging her knees as she watched the large machinery working nearby.

"Holy Guacamolies, child! You nearly gave us a heart attack!" said Jennifer. "How did you get...I mean, hardly a second went by and...this is going to take some getting used to. People disappearing and popping up here and there. Bacon appears on my plate. Hedgehog back from a big bright hole in the sky... a flamin' lady...what's next?"

"What's going on here?" asked Coraline.

"We were curious about the progress on the new base, so we came down to see the work," said Hayley.

"And the workers. Right Jennifer?" Madison added with a smile.

"Yup. Checking out the workers," responded Jennifer looking in the opposite direction.

Half of Coraline's fun is pretending she doesn't understand things adults believe would go over her head. It was a part of her childish charm. But, she winked at Madison and said, "Well, if you feel the workers are all checked up on, now would be a good time to talk."

Hayley said, "We have Remo checked out for the afternoon. Let's get out of here."

Coraline pointed to the top of the hill some miles off and said, "Let's go there."

Hayley began folding up the chairs they had carried with them as Madison closed up the cooler. Coraline was looking this way and that for one last look at the construction site. She took notice of a stack of folding canopy tents and smiled. When she turned back to the three women they were waiting for her.

"You guys are still here?" Coraline said.

"Well, you're coming with us, aren't you?"

"No. You go. I'll meet you there," Coraline said with a smile.

"But..." Jennifer started.

"I'll meet you there!" Coraline laughed. "Honest!"

The three adults left the child seated on an empty orange bucket. As they walked to their aircraft, they'd look back occasionally to see what she was up to, and every time she was still seated, waving. Upon entering Remo, Hayley took the pilot seat while Madison took the co-pilot seat. Jennifer, the last to enter the aircraft, kept her eyes fixed on Coraline even as the door closed.

"What's the deal, Jen? You don't believe she'll be there?" asked Madison.

"I don't know what to believe any more. Just get there as fast as you can. I'd like to be sitting on the ground before she even gets up off that bucket."

Hayley sped off toward the mesa in the distance as Jennifer held on tightly to the braces. Making their approach to the indicated mesa top, they were amazed to see Coraline seated on the same bucket in the shade of a folding canopy that had already been staked to the ground. With smooth landing accomplished, the three of them stayed where they were, in silence, mouths open, and watched the little girl singing her heart out.

"How does she do that?" asked Jennifer.

"Think about it, Jen. Remember my bacon demonstration this morning? That might be a bit of a clue."

"What bacon demonstration," asked Hayley. "I'm feeling a little behind the learning curve."

"Well, my dear sister, you are about to receive the education of your life," said Madison.

CHAPTER THIRTY-THREE
A SLEEPLESS DAY

President Cott walked into the Cabinet Room in the West Wing of the White House, and, as usual, everyone stood immediately. In every other meeting he'd attended since he took office a short time ago, he would enter, they would stand and before he was halfway to his seat, he would say, 'Please be seated'. There was much on his mind and he missed the opportunity. He didn't realize they were still standing until he was in his chair. He simply motioned for them to be seated. More than a few glances were exchanged.

"General Clayton, there is a large hole in the ground where Research and Development Command used to be. I would like to know how," asked Cott.

"Sir, R&D Command came under attack shortly after General Prentice was at Nellis Air Force Base. He ordered the base to stand down while the runways were destroyed. He informed the officers in charge that a deal was struck between you, sir and the '*so-called*' Defenders in the Void."

"Tell me something I *don't* know, Clayton. I already know *why* it disappeared. I would like to know *how*. General Prentice made that deal apart from me. When the General's plane touched ground at Andrews AFB, he was immediately placed under arrest. Interestingly enough, he had absolutely no recollection of his trip. It was then we knew for sure what we were dealing with. Apparently, one of those 'gifted' individuals Dr. Tanner had been telling us about for years is responsible for that memory wipe. The last time I spoke with Tanner, he informed me this conflict is swiftly moving away from our usual methods of making war. The problem is, Dr. Tanner disappeared along with the rest of Area 51."

"Sir. We may be able to shed some light on that."

"Mr. Samuels, who is the 'we' you are referring to?" asked President Cott.

"I apologize sir. I am referring to the Department of Defense. The work being done at the Research and Development Command was a black project funded by the DOD and directed by the CIA. According to Dr. Muller, most of the assets under Dr. Tanner's leadership have been moved to a secondary location."

"Who is Dr. Muller?"

"I'll let her explain it to you directly, sir."

The woman seated directly behind Mr. Samuels stood and turned toward the head of the table. She pulled on her well-pressed jacket and adjusted the frilly ends of her white blouse. "Mr. President. I was sent to R&D Command recently on an intelligence gathering mission."

"Dr. Muller, I apologize for being in the dark here. I'm new to this job. Who are you, and who sent you to R&D?" asked the President.

"I work with the CIA and I was sent to gather information from Dr. Tanner after a part of his project was compromised in Oklahoma," she responded.

"Ah, yes. That particular institution's function was to hold innocent Americans hostage in order to keep their experiments under control. Yes. Everyone knows about this now. Tell me about these *assets* that were moved. Are we talking about *people* or *prisoners*?"

"Sir, the answer to that question depends on who you ask."

"I'm asking you."

"Sir, it has been determined the people who were detained in this project were risks to national security. From that perspective, I think it reasonable to call them...*assets*. Their families, who were liberated from the facility in Oklahoma were definitely *prisoners*."

"Tell me about the *assets*, Dr. Muller."

After clearing her throat, she opened up a simple pencil notebook and began. "Dr. Tanner moved thirty-one gifted individuals to location #2, feeling his location was compromised. Five *assets* remained behind with Dr. Tanner. We do not know yet, what became of Dr. Tanner or his assets. Several of his lab assistants surfaced in Austin a few hours ago and are being debriefed now. They did manage to say the entire facility was stormed by military personnel. They were placed on an aircraft that flew directly to Junction, Texas, then on to Austin. They claim three of Dr. Tanner's assets - children - were on that flight to Junction, where they deplaned. The lab assistants indicated Dr. Tanner had become extremely unstable, forcing them to flee. They have no knowledge of events after their aircraft exited the area."

"Do we have any idea of what gifts or powers the three children possessed?"

"No, sir. That knowledge resides with Dr. Tanner."

"Do we have any idea of what gifts or powers the people who were moved to location #2 possess?"

"I do not have that information, sir."

"Who does have that information, Dr. Muller?"

"I do not have that information, sir."

President Cott ran his fingers through his hair and turned to his National Security Adviser. "Carl, what do you know about this?"

"I know as much as you do now, sir."

There was a pause while the President contemplated all he'd learned. Dr. Muller had returned to her chair.

"Okay. Back to my original question, General Clayton. How is it that there is a giant hole in the ground where Area 51 used to be?"

"We don't know, sir. We have a team on the ground there right now. All they can tell us at this point is that it was not nuclear. It doesn't even show evidence of being a conventional explosive. If it was a part of the hoodoo bullshit that took place at that facility, there may not be anyone left to explain it, unless we pay this Evelyn Walsh a visit in the panhandle of Texas," said General Clayton.

"I'm going to look you straight in the face and warn you and every other person in this room. If there is any clandestine attempt to contact or attack the people in the Void, outside of my knowledge, you will be tried for treason. If there is any 'visiting' that is going to take place, it will be at our discretion. Is that clear?"

"Crystal clear, sir."

"Good. Dr. Muller, please stay behind. The rest of you are dismissed."

Coraline, Hayley, Jennifer, and Madison sat in the folding chairs that had been placed in a circle under the shade of the folding canopy. Only moments before, the four of them had leaned forward to touch their heads together so Coraline could relay to them the information and instruction they needed to understand their newly acquired gifts. Now finished, no one spoke as a soothing wind flowed across the top of the mesa. It seemed more appropriate to sit back and contemplate the information that rushed through their minds at the touch of the red-headed child. Glances were exchanged between them. Occasionally, lips would begin to formulate words, but none came. Five minutes may have passed before anyone spoke.

"I'm at a loss for words," said Hayley. "This is hard to wrap my head around."

Madison answered, "I'm kinda glad I stumbled onto my gift in the field. It would have been almost impossible to wrap my head around it being delivered through a fire hose."

Jennifer sat staring at Coraline. Several times she started to ask a question but stopped, realizing there were better questions. Every question she came up with was more or less a 'me' question. Realizing the gifts were not about the possessor, she finally asked, "Are we born with these gifts?"

"You asked the right question, Jennifer," Coraline said. "The answer is 'yes,' according to the Messenger. By asking that question, you get the answer to the question you almost asked, which was 'What did I do to deserve this?' We are born with the gifts, so you obviously did nothing to *deserve* it. Very few have them, and some of these go their entire life and never access their gifts. These few require a 'keeper' as Heather mentioned to you all earlier. I am the keeper."

"I want to make sure I got this straight," said Hayley. "I can teleport to any location I can see or a location I have visited before."

"Correct."

"It doesn't matter how far away it is?"

Coraline shook her head, "It doesn't matter."

"May I try this now?" Hayley asked.

"You do not need my permission but be clear on this. You cannot teleport to an unseen place you have never previously visited."

Hayley brought to her mind the vision of standing on the rooftop of the temple where she learned kung-fu in China. She wasn't exactly sure how to activate this power, but the mere thought and desire transported her instantly to the place she fought with Master Cheng atop the monastery. The Texas panhandle warmth was replaced by the howling cold wind of the high Himalayas. There was no activity on the roof, which made sense as it was the middle of the night. She walked to the edge of the roof and looked down into the courtyards below to see the occasional warrior making nightly rounds with his torch. Satisfied at the accuracy of her teleportation, she again visualized the mesa where she had sat moments before with her friends.

The sound of her appearing was something akin to the electrical spark made by an electroshock taser. Jennifer jumped slightly. "So, did it work? You disappeared quickly!"

"It worked, Jen. I stood on the roof of the Chinese temple where Sarah and I studied recently. Next time I do that I'll make sure to dress appropriately and remember what time it is in China."

Madison laughed. "You could have picked a place here in Texas that was a bit closer. That was a huge leap of faith for a first-time try."

Hayley turned to Jennifer. "Your turn!"

Jennifer looked a little shaken as she glanced once more at Coraline for support.

"Don't be afraid, Jennifer. Just begin with a visualization of being invisible. The moment you..."

Jennifer disappeared.

"Am I invisible?" she asked. "I can still sorta see myself."

Coraline was laughing, which set the others to doing the same thing.

"Don't laugh. Just tell me if you can see me!" Jennifer insisted.

"You are completely invisible to us!" remarked Madison. "Now, you should test that walking through walls thing! Take a run through Remo there!"

Jennifer got up out of her folding camping chair and moved it back a few feet. To the others it seemed to move all on its own. She walked over to the aircraft and began by putting her hand through the door and withdrawing it. As she held her hand out before her, she noted she seemed to be translucent. Then, taking a deep breath, she walked completely through the aircraft and came out on the other side. The others could hear her exultation from where they sat. Jennifer ran back and forth through Remo several times before she ended up at her chair. Again, visualizing the change, she reappeared near the others.

Coraline was still laughing. "That worked just fine!" she said.

Madison pointed out everything she wore on her person disappeared also. "Your Walther .45 disappeared right along with the rest of you. Try it again but with your gun in your hand."

Jennifer drew the double-stacked PPQ from her cross-draw holder and disappeared again. "Can you see it?"

"Nope. So, your gift, like mine and Hayley's, allows you, Jennifer, to carry things invisibly. Hayley can transport herself and whatever she's carrying, while I can move quickly with a rifle in my hand. I proved that back at Area 51. My question is, can we take others with us?" They all turned to Coraline.

She sat up straighter and folded her hands. "The short answer is yes. But you must be very careful doing it. Anything you drop or let go of is no longer under your power. This includes people. A person Jennifer let's go of, will become visible. Madison's works exactly the same way. Anything she lets go of reenters normal space time. Hayley is not likely to drop anything since her teleportation is instantaneous, but yes, she can take someone by the hand and teleport them."

"Madison told me earlier not only can I pass through things, but things pass through me. That works for the person I'm holding onto also?" Jennifer asked.

Coraline nodded.

Jennifer handed her gun to Hayley and said, "Shoot me!"

"I don't want to shoot you!" Hayley responded, offering it to Madison.

Madison took the weapon and laughed saying, "I'll do it!" Pointing the muzzle of the handgun in a safe direction, she asked Jennifer, "Where do you want it?"

"Well, Maddie, at least wait until I'm invisible! I'll disappear and you shoot where I was, okay?"

"Okey doaky!

Jennifer disappeared, and Madison took aim where she had been standing a second before and fired twice.

"Did it work?" asked Madison.

There was no answer.

"Jennifer, did it work?" Madison shouted. Still no answer.

Suddenly, Jennifer appeared, but she was lying on her back with her arms spread wide and eyes closed. Madison and Hayley both leaped forward to check her wounds. Coraline stayed seated with squinted eyes.

"Jennifer! Where are you hit? Jennifer!" Madison screamed.

Jennifer opened her eyes and screeched, "*Gotcha!*" as she quickly got to her feet.

"AAAACCH!" yelled Madison. "You're lucky I don't beat you for that!"

Hayley took it upon herself to bring the conversation back on topic. "Here's how I see it. We need to work through a strategy to use these gifts as a team. For instance, I should always know exactly where Eli is, so anyone who is wounded can get help immediately. We should work on moving as a unit through different scenarios. We each have a talent that will be useful for escape and evade, taking prisoners, or protecting our friends and family. This is a total game changer. This will make us almost unbeatable!"

"Almost," said Coraline. "Until you run up against an enemy also gifted. We are moving along nicely. But I'm afraid Dr. Tanner's gifted prisoners may be moving along also."

"What makes you say that?" Madison responded.

"I shared our story and information with Heather on the trip home, and she shared what she and her children knew about the experimentation Dr. Tanner practices on his prisoners."

Jennifer smirked, "Don't you mean, *used* to practice?"

"No. I believe Dr. Tanner is still alive," Coraline answered. "I spoke with my dad this morning. He also seems pretty sure Dr. Tanner survived the explosion."

"But how can that be?" said an exasperated Madison. "How could he possibly have survived that? You saw the results of that blast! There was nothing there but one great big bloody hole in the ground!"

"You survived it. We all did," said Coraline calmly.

"But, but...we had your protection. All of us."

"Dr. Tanner may have *been* his own protection," Coraline injected.

"Would Nick have survived that explosion outside of the protection we had as a group?" Madison asked.

"I think he would have, but I can't say for certain," Coraline admitted. "To be fair, I can't say for certain Dr. Tanner is alive. It's just a guess."

Jennifer listened to what the others were saying, but her thoughts were on the original issue; the idea there may be enemies that are gifted like them. "Coraline, should we be afraid of these people in Tanner's group? Charles Reynolds was in there too, but he's on our side now. Couldn't the others be like Heather? She's been there since she was 15 years old, and yet never cooperated with them!"

"Wouldn't it be nice to have this information *before* the lull in the war is over?" asked Hayley. "I mean, look at us! We've got the means of finding out where the new location is! Jennifer can get into any building on earth and bring us along! We can find out once we get to that location; there would be no need to escape and evade. I know my way home! In a flash we'd be standing in New Castlehale's landing bay! Who knows? We may even be able to get inside. I latch on to some and deliver them to their families, if they have family in Junction!"

"I love the way you think," said Madison. "Question. Have you ever been to Washington D.C.?"

"Oh, hell no!" said Jennifer. "Why would I want to visit that snake pit?"

"I'm talking to Hayley!" Madison laughed. "If she's been there, she can take all three of us there. We can all hold hands and stroll into any building or office we choose. For that matter, we could take Coraline with us and walk right into the Oval Office and find out from the President himself where the new location is, then wipe his memory of ever seeing us, and *voila*, we're home free!"

The four of them sat in silence for a minute until Coraline spoke up. "I'm game, but only if Mom and Nick approve it." But then she added, "And we wait until after the wedding. I'm going to be busy this evening and tomorrow getting things ready for the ceremony."

"You're the wedding planner?" blurted out Jennifer.

"Yes. I've already run it by Mom."

Madison could hardly contain her happiness as she squeezed Coraline in a hug. "I love it when you call Evelyn Mom. I can't tell you how happy it makes me."

Hayley insisted, "Makes 'us', Maddie. I love that I can call you baby sister, and it be true."

Coraline's eyes welled up with tears at hearing what they had to say. "I know now it is true. But, really, you all have treated me and Eli like family since the day we met. Adam has loved me and looked after me like I really was his baby sister since that day. You all have. So, since I've been here, I have felt the love. We know more now, but the love has always been there."

"And always will be," said Jennifer. "Now, let's talk about our costumes!"

"What costumes?" asked Coraline.

"Our super-hero costumes, silly!" said Jennifer who seemed perfectly serious.

CHAPTER THIRTY-FOUR
A NEW DIRECTION

The double-wedding invitations were delivered to the living quarters of every family in New Castlehale announcing the marriages of Ranger Captain Nicholas Hollings to Evelyn Walsh and Alexander Walsh to Sarah Stark. Along with the invitation were some very interesting instructions. The first concerned attire. It simply stated that dress for the occasion will be 'dressy casual'.

The second set of instructions also had to do with attire. Those attending the ceremony were asked to envision the very best wedding attire that they could conjure up in their minds. If they wanted, they could go online to get ideas or remember a dress or suit from a movie or any catalog they cared to use, but the point was to find the perfect dress or suit, no matter the cost, and keep that vision in their mind when they show up in their dressy casuals. More instructions would be given there.

Andrea Trevino, the head of New Castlehale Research and Development stopped Coraline in the corridor that evening.

"Any dress?" she said, knowing that the strange request in the invitation probably would involve the small red-headed child.

"Any dress at all. All I need is to get that visual from your mind, and that is what you'll be wearing to the ceremony. Trust me."

"Ok. Then, there is one dress that I saw a woman wearing at the fancy reception we attended in Austin last year. I thought it was the most beautiful dress I had ever seen. It must have cost a fortune! Can you get that dress?" Andrea asked in a tone of voice that indicated she should have started her question with, *Yah, right.*

Coraline laughed, "Of course! All you have to do is picture it in your mind, and I'll see it." She held out her little pointer finger and held it a few inches from the scientist's forehead, then said, "Ready?"

"Yes."

After a second, Coraline stepped back and said, "You're good to go. I'll see you at the wedding!"

Coraline repeated this process several times that evening for those who couldn't possibly wait to find out how this was supposed to work. They understood the meaning of dressy casual; they just didn't see the relevance of filling your mind with beautiful clothes. Several teenagers stopped her in the corridor, and like Andrea Trevino, they asked her if the invitation really meant *any dress.*

"Show me what you have in mind," was Coraline's reply. "May I touch your forehead?"

"Uh..... Yes," said the young girl with hesitation.

Coraline instantly withdrew her finger and asked, "Did you happen to run this by your mother?"

"No. I didn't. But I was interested to see if this were something you could do."

Coraline laughed. "It is certainly doable, but I'm pretty sure I'd be in deep doo-doo with your mother. Tell you what I'll do. I'll show this to my mom and get her opinion. After all, it is her wedding."

The three girls looked at each other and indicated that that was fair enough.

Breakfast began that day, much the same way it began every morning. Adam and Coraline were the first to arrive and proceed with their usual ritual. Adam would toast

Coraline's bread and reach to the middle of the table to fetch butter and jam while Coraline sipped on her juice. When the bread made the springy ejection sound, he would quickly grab the toast, place it on a saucer and hand Coraline a butter knife. She would spread her butter and jam as Adam went on and on about something new. April usually entered mid-ritual, grabbed herself a cup of coffee, and sat next to Adam.

"How did you sleep last night?" Adam asked April.

"I was totally amazed how I could get home at oh-dark-thirty yesterday morning, go directly to my room, shower, change clothes, and go directly to work without feeling exhausted!"

"I don't think anyone slept when they got home," said Adam. "There were debriefing meetings, video conferences and people just hanging around talking, but I doubt that anyone went right to sleep when they got home."

"Coraline, what did you do when you got home yesterday morning?" April asked.

"Oh, this and that. Spent some time with Hedgehog. Talked to my dad. Met with Hayley, Madison and Jennifer, then a lot of wedding stuff."

Adam leaned over to Coraline and said, "Touch my forehead and see what I want to wear to the wedding."

She reached up and touched him and instantly saw Adam wearing a costume of a large yellow chicken. When Adam saw the look on her face, he laughed.

"Don't tempt me, Gulliver. If you want to look stupid, I can put you in this," she said as she touched his forehead again. Adam saw himself wearing a sparkling green strapless gown and a purple feathered pirate hat.

"Oh, you nailed me, baby sister. That's even better than my big yellow chicken."

Coraline smiled at him as she held her buttered toast to her lips and in a muffled sing-song fashion, she sang, "Don't tempt me, Gulliverrrrrr."

Alex and Sarah strolled into the galley feeling very pleased about themselves and plopped down across the table from Adam. There were 'good mornings' exchanged over the sound of glassware and dishes. Alex looked up to find Lilly standing over him with a dumbfounded expression on her face. She banged a large platter of eggs and bacon onto the table giving the impression she was none too pleased.

"Dios Mio! Alex! What are you two doing here? It's bad luck to see the bride before the wedding! You should know these things!" Lilly cried out.

"Lilly! Lilly! Relax. That superstition is antiquated moose-poop!" said Adam, who had gotten up from his chair to fill a pitcher with juice and had the misfortune of making that comment as he passed her.

WHACK! Lilly's spoon found its mark on Adam's arm. "Don't you antiquated moose-poop me, Mr. Gigantor! This is tradition a thousand years old! It's what is done!" Lilly said shaking her spoon at Adam.

Coraline leaned over to April and whispered, "She mostly only whacks *him* with that spoon. I think she loves him a lot."

"I'd hate to see what she'd do to him if she hated his guts," said April in a half giggle.

"Lilly," said Alex, "that old custom of not seeing the bride before the wedding came from the time when most marriages were arranged and the two had never seen each other. They didn't let the groom see the bride beforehand because they were afraid if he saw her and didn't think she was pretty enough, he'd run away. It was a denigrating practice that probably never contributed to the longevity of a marriage. I've already seen Sarah, and I'm absolutely sure I'm not running. Ok, mostly sure."

"Lilly, whack this man with your spoon for me, please," said Sarah.

Just about that time, Evelyn and Nick walked into the galley. Lilly took one look at the couple and threw up her hands, broke into Spanish and headed back into the kitchen area.

"What's Lilly upset about?" asked Nick.

Alex shook his head and said, "I'll explain it to you later. She'll get over it. She'll whack Adam a few more times and she'll be back to her old self. Right Adam?"

"It's easy for you to say, brother. I'm the one she

310

whacks."

"But you're so big! You can take it," Alex said as he popped a piece of bacon into his mouth.

Hedgehog, Eli, and Rita came running into the galley as if they'd been racing to breakfast. The three of them moved to the remote end of the table and continued whatever conversation they were having. Meanwhile, out in the corridor, Jennifer, Hayley, and Madison were plotting.

"I'll go in first, invisible and sit down in that first chair on the wall side. Then, I'll let you know when and give a countdown, and you two pop in. Madison, take the second, and Hayley take the third. If we do this right, we'll all appear at the same time," Jennifer said in a whisper.

Becoming invisible, she didn't even bother using the door. She walked right through the wall and headed for her seat. Waiting a few seconds for Lilly to empty her hands as she set another platter on the table, Jennifer then gave the word. The electroshock sound that resulted from Hayley's transporting was slightly louder inside the galley than it was outdoors. The combination of the sound and the women's sudden appearance made Lilly scream, caused Alex and Nick to jump to their feet in an instant, while April turned over Adam's juice.

"Where did....? How did you just...? Dios mio," Lilly yelled. She was almost in tears as she turned to go back into the kitchen.

Evelyn watched Lilly over her shoulder, then turned to the table. "I think we all need to go easy on Lilly today. She's having a tough time. Too many changes all at once, what with weddings, people coming back from the dead, all these super-powers being flaunted," she said looking at the three ladies at the end of the table.

"Sorry, Mom."

"Yes, sorry Evelyn," said Madison and Jennifer almost simultaneously.

"Anyway," Evelyn said addressing the entire table, "let's catch each other up on the latest. I'll go first. The Governor assured me last night that a cease-fire is in effect. He is hoping that it will continue, and quoted the classic Latin phrase, *Si vis pacem, para bellum*, which, as most of us know means, *if you want peace, prepare for war*. So, we will continue to update our defenses and push out new technologies. Just this week, our Research and Development has made a major breakthrough in wireless energy transmission that will enable us to connect our settlements in the Void, to supply free energy. This is huge. Thanks to Coraline, the information sharing that took place between all of our scientists has increased our creativity a hundred-fold.

"As of today, we will begin selling some, not all, of our advanced technology to selective buyers. The state of Texas, backed by several Texas energy concerns, will begin the work of switching the state from a fossil fuel-driven electrical grid to one driven by our fusion generators. The generators themselves will be totally under our control. The energy companies' role will be to plug into it for use in their electrical grids. This is huge. Our entire state, as well as the Void, will run on cheap energy. And although we are willing to sell to other states, they will have to jump through some hard hoops to acquire it. The Governor warns us that this is inviting bad press, but I told him that we're willing to take that chance. You see, they are free to concoct any lie about us they want; they just won't do it using our electricity. Free energy to households in Texas and the Void will likely result in a substantial increase in quality of life for all. It will mean more jobs and lower prices for goods. If they want to be a part of that, they'll have to make some concessions.

"On the New Castlehale front, with regard to the wedding ceremony, preparations are going well. Guan Yin is on her way to Austin to pick up the Governor and his wife. They will be arriving shortly before 1100 hours. The other Remos are picking up the caterers and food for the reception."

Alex injected, "Remote Squadron piloted flyers are escorting Guan Yin to and from Austin. XO Brice also made sure that all flights have a security detail on board."

"Hermes I and II will be on station above Austin and this facility. Nothing will get through without us seeing it first. Zeus is fully-armed and on station. We don't want any surprises today," Adam said as he pushed his food around his plate.

Nick stood to speak, "General Stokes' Osprey will be arriving this morning from Ft. Hood and land up top. Ranger Major Johnston and Carol Peters of the State Troopers will be catching a ride with her. Their Osprey will land up top at 1015 hours. XO Brice will meet them and an escort detail will give them a quick tour before the wedding. We promised them a peek at our new Artemis system."

"On a more personal matter," he continued, "today is my last official day as a Texas Ranger. I sent Major Johnston a letter of resignation and it was accepted. I can't see myself gallivanting all over the State for Major Johnston and be Commander of Military Assets here at New Castlehale. I predict I'll be busy enough right here for some time to come. Also, I believe Sgt. Jameson has an announcement of her own. Sergeant?"

"Thank you, *Commander*," said Madison with a flourish on the rank. "I am, as of today, a field agent for New Castlehale Special Operations Group. I have tendered my resignation with the Texas Rangers also, and it was accepted late last night."

"You're not interested in being a pilot, Maddie?" Hedgehog asked with a note of disappointment.

"Oh, I'll be a pilot, but not with the fighter squadron," she said with a smile. "We can thank Adam for proving that hoverpad technology works just fine on ground vehicles. Flying cars will be the thing of the future. We'll be the first to get them, after Adam of course, who lost his beloved Beast back at Area 51. I saw the schematics for the prototype. It's a doozy. They'll be starting on that this week!"

"Who will be in the Special Operations Group?" Hedgehog shot back.

Hayley and Jennifer waved their fingers at Hedgehog and smiled back in a way that communicated to everyone there that they were thrilled about the prospect.

"Can I be a part of that group?" Hedgehog asked.

"NO!" shot back Alex and Sarah at the same instant.

"I will not lose my best pilot when we've got trouble brewing," Alex said as he stood. We've got an Air Wing to build and I need my best man to lead the new Angel

Squadron. Put the idea of becoming a secret agent out of your head, Hedgehog. You've got better things to do."

Nick nodded in agreement. "Hedgehog, you're the best person for the job. You're our best pilot and, well, since you're the only pilot that has been to Heaven, we figure that the newly formed Angel Squadron will follow you to hell and back. No pun intended."

Rita never looked so pleased in her entire life.

Hedgehog looked back and forth between Alex and Nick with his mouth open. "So, wait, we're going to have more than just one squadron?"

"That's right. Take a look at the monitor on the wall there," Nick said as he pointed. What appeared to be a closed circuit camera down in the aeronautics lab was the frame of a new fighter being worked on by a team of scientists. "What you are seeing is the first of our remote fighters. Alex, would you like to explain the differences between the new fighter and our current models?"

"Sure. You may have noticed that this fighter is smaller than our current flyer and will be different in many other ways. It will have no cockpit. It will only carry two missiles. Gone are the plasma guns."

"Excuse me, Alex, but no guns?" asked Madison. "I'm no expert, but two missiles and no guns doesn't make a formidable fighter considering the planes we've been up against lately."

"That is true, but this plane will be armed with 700 kilowatt lasers; these are the same lasers we put on the Delta Flyer which were combat-tested by Sarah during the Area 51 rescue. This particular plane will have two thrust engines and a smaller unit deep inside the fuselage to power the lasers. Our entire inventory of future aircraft will have the same interchangeable engine components that can be swapped out in less than an hour. Due to its lightweight, the thrust-to-weight ratio is far better than any aircraft on Earth."

"Will they hover?" Hedgehog asked.

"Of course, but thanks to Coraline, our researchers have come up with a better, more efficient way to mount them on our aircraft. No longer will there be recognizable pads protruding from the bottom of the craft. They can now be built into the frame of the aircraft, making for a more aerodynamic design. These aircraft will give us air superiority in any situation, plus the fact that we will not be risking pilots. With our Hermes system of satellites, our remote pilots will be in constant communications with the aircraft. In other words, we can go anywhere. To ensure this, our Hermes satellites will have on-board ARBS systems. They cannot be destroyed by conventional means."

"How long to test flight?" Hedgehog asked.

"Not long. But we are quickly running out of metal for the planes we're cranking out. That is why we're making deals with the State of Texas. The sooner we get those materials, the sooner we can build several squadrons of these aircraft," said Evelyn.

Kate Jennings stood in the doorway of the kitchen drying her hands with a cup towel. Clearing her throat, she got Evelyn's attention. "Evelyn, what is our goal with all this military hardware? I understand that it has been invaluable in our survival recently, but with all our new allies, shouldn't we be reasonably protected by now?"

"That's a good question, Kate. The answer is, at this point, we can't totally trust anyone who is not New Castlehale or not living in the Void. This current governor, Aaron Hammond, is a solid ally, but he won't be there forever. No matter who is in office, we will maintain our strength, not only defensively but also offensively. They must know, from here on out and forever, that we will not be pushed.

CHAPTER THIRTY-FIVE
WEDDING

All the guests had arrived and were gathered on the transformed Landing Deck expertly decorated for the wedding ceremonies. Some of the non-residents of New Castlehale looked around and saw warplanes parked here and there and wondered if this really was a suitable spot to hold a wedding. They would have expected the wedding of someone as famous and important as Evelyn Walsh of The Defenders to one of the most famous Texas Rangers in that organization's history to take place in a private club with perfect lawns and peacocks. Just the thought of showing up in dressy casual was not something they would have chosen, but it was not their wedding. The only person there in a suit was the Governor of Texas, but that was his everyday garb, so no one faulted him. More than half of those in attendance still wondered about the request made for them to envision in their minds the perfect wedding attire, but they figure that if the gifted child Coraline had anything to do with it, it would be a fun twist to the event.

"Do you have your perfect wedding attire in your mind?" General Stokes' husband whispered to her as they stood in the crowd waiting for things to start.

"I do. Do you remember what the First Lady wore to the Military Ball six years ago?"

"Uh.... no. Remember? I wasn't your date at that event,"

he answered. "We've only been married five years."

"Sorry, hon. Well, it was a to-die-for dress. Why do you suppose they asked us to do this? I'm thinking that the red-headed child over there is going to project our thoughts onto a screen or something. Can't wait."

Nick Hollings, Evelyn Walsh, Alex Walsh, and Sarah Stark walked up the steps of a temporary platform together. When they turned to face those in attendance, they stopped and exchanged a few words with each other. Then Nick touched his comDev.

"May I have your attention, please? Evelyn and I, along with Alex and Sarah would like to thank you all for coming today to witness our exchanging of vows to enter into the bonds of marriage. At one point in our nation's history, the institution of marriage was considered an anachronism. It seemed too old-fashion and out of date to some, but not to us here in Texas. We kept the old ways and most of us here were raised during difficult times when it seemed appropriate to cling to the things that make for a stable society. Our parents taught us the old ways, and well, we turned out okay. If you are all ready, then we'll get this show on the road.

"XO Brice, is everyone present and accounted for?"

The XO punched something into his table and got a green light at the top. His only answer was a thumbs-up.

"Okay. I'm going to hand this wedding over to Coraline who will take it from here," Nick announced.

The wedding party exited the stage and stood near their family as Coraline walked up the steps. She reached the top and turned to those gathered.

"We made a funny request in the invitation that everyone envision their favorite wedding attire. I want everyone here to take the hand of the person standing next to them. Those on the right end of each row take the hand of the person behind them. The goal is to have every person in this area connected. No one should be left out. If you are not touching the person's hand close to you, you will miss out on the entire event. I will give you half a minute to make sure you are all connected. Now, I want everyone to stay connected and think about that dress or suit. When I say 'let's begin' I want you to close your eyes and keep that vision in your head for ten seconds, then open your eyes. Is everybody ready?"

Coraline looked around, and when she felt the crowd was ready, she said, "Let's begin," and quickly moved down the steps and took hold of Evelyn's hand. When the ten seconds were up, every eye opened and they found themselves somewhere other than the landing bay.

Coraline's secret garden had never quite looked this way before. The dais, which normally stood in the exact center of the large perfect lawn, was now set to one side. Even the two large fruit-bearing trees which stood to either side of the dais were moved with it, and instead of the lawn, the most exquisite floor ever seen covered a circular area. Each tile was several meters square and inlaid with diamonds, rubies, pink garnet, abalone shell and green onyx, all set in a sunburst pattern that was a mesmerizing delight to the eye. Nick and the others who had been to the garden previously, recognized the difference in the dome above. In addition to the star-filled night and accenting dawn-like horizon, a large ringed planet poked halfway over the horizon. A sun's rays filtering through the planet's rings cast an ever-changing display of golden bursts and refracted colors that danced across the gem-inlaid floor. Most of those gathered were transfixed and silent as they took in the scene around them. General Stokes turned to her husband and pointed at the floor saying, "Now we know how they can afford 1 megawatt laser systems."

Nick had made sure that his old friends Shifty and Doris, along with their grandson Jimmy, could be in attendance. They had ridden in style with a detail of Texas Rangers to New Castlehale and put up for the night there. Jimmy was almost a head taller than the last time Nick had seen him. Shifty commented to Doris that Nick must have married into money. Doris elbowed him.

The bridesmaids, separated from the body of attendees by a high rose bush hedge, held hands as they all stared at the scenes around and above them. Jennifer, Madison, Hayley, and Heather were stunned as they took in this world created from Coraline's mind. Eli, who was the ring-bearer, had seen it a number of times, yet even this amazed him.

"It appears you spared no expense, little flower girl," said Madison to Coraline. The beautiful red-haired girl's face revealed a deep satisfaction for the changes she'd made to her no-longer-secret garden.

"Speaking of expense, look at us!" squealed Jennifer as she felt the fabric on her dress. "We look like a million dollars!"

They wore identical elegant, Bordeaux dresses, with asymmetrical necklines, pleated bodices and ruched waistbands. Coraline, on the other hand wore a simple, floral-patterned, summer dress and, true to her nature, was barefooted.

Heather was speechless as she laughed and spun like a schoolgirl. "Did you know that until today, I have never worn a dress in public? Of course, I haven't really *been* in public, have I?"

"Public or not, Heather, you do look great in that dress!" said Madison.

Heather was beside herself. "I thought the casual dress that Evelyn gave me to wear at the reception was wonderful, but these... these are the most beautiful dresses I have ever seen!" she said.

Hayley hugged her new step-aunt and said, "You look absolutely beautiful, Heather. There's a mirror over there. Let's go see!"

Sure enough, a dozen paces from them, stood a full-length mirror, large enough for all four to stand side-by-side. Eli, who was able to sense the joy emanating from these women, just stood back and smiled.

"Oh my God. We *do* look like a million dollars!" said Madison.

"Look at us! Even my zit is gone!" noted Jennifer.

"My sword would have clashed with this dress, I think," said Hayley with a grin. "It's a good thing you didn't include it, Coraline."

They all laughed at the absurdity of the thought.

"Are you all about ready?" came a voice from the corner of the hedge.

They turned to see Sarah and Evelyn. Sarah wore the traditional white wedding gown, but this particular dress was far from ordinary. All one would have to do is to search the internet for 'most expensive wedding dress' and this one would be close to it. As long as every detail of the dress was in Coraline's mind, she could make it happen here in her garden. The only downside to the arrangement is that she could never save this wedding dress for future use of a possible offspring. They all understood this and accepted it. There was too much happening in the world to worry about a future dress choice. It was the light-pink hair that had the ladies gawking. Tiny white flowers had been braided throughout her hair and the effect was stunning!

Evelyn was beautiful in a lab coat or combat gear on her worst day, but today, she would give a runway model competition in her wisteria gown with its off-the-shoulder neckline, banded sleeves, and trumpet skirting. The 3D tulle and organza texture embroidery caused the dress to swish as she moved.

"Okay, we just got demoted to looking like $599.95," Hayley said to the others. "You two look like a gazillion dollars!"

"Thanks to Coraline!" said Evelyn. "Consider the hundreds of hours she saved for everyone here, just getting dressed!"

"Mom, don't get all practical on your wedding day," said Hayley laughing.

"It's just about time now," said Coraline. "You all know what to do!"

The low tones of reverberating horns sounded from nowhere in particular. The vibrations of the notes could be felt in one's chest. Every eye turned to the dais to see a lone, bearded figure in robes appear from thin air. Those who speculated that this person would officiate the wedding were correct, but the identity of the man was a mystery to all but Nick and the others who were present in Dr. Tanner's laboratory at Area 51. Everyone moved quickly to the stone benches that appeared instantly at the sound of the horns. There may have been some hesitation by those who stopped to decide whether to sit on the bride's side or the groom's. But within minutes, they had it sorted out.

Nick and Alex entered the stage from unseen steps on the back side of the dais. Behind them appeared Texas Ranger Major Samuel Johnston as Nick's best man, and Adam as Alex's, and three groomsmen behind them. The youngest of the groomsmen was Hedgehog, who spent more time waving at people in their seats than anything else. Once in place, a trumpet fanfare sounded in perfect musical harmony announcing the beginning of the ceremony. Everyone turned their eyes to the only path that exited the area to see the bridesmaids lined up. Heather was first to enter, followed by Madison and Jennifer, then Hayley, who was Evelyn's and Sarah's maid of honor. The fanfare stopped and the music changed to a processional as they walked onto the diamond-inlaid floor. Once they reached the front, instrumental music stopped altogether and a thousand choral voices began to sing an excerpt from the Hymn of the Cherubim as the ring bearer and the flower girl entered in single file. The singers were unseen, but the effect was awesome.

The basket of flower pedals that Coraline carried resembled every other basket seen in every other wedding, but something strange and magical happened when she tossed the rose pedals. They did not float to the floor as gravity normally requires. They floated into the air and circled the aisle in which they walked. The brides walked in together, unescorted, and proceeded slowly to the front. When they reached the dais, rather than walking up the stairs, the very tile on which they stood began an ascent to the top of the stone structure, carrying them slowly to stand next to their grooms and the man who would perform the ceremony.

"We are here today to celebrate the joining of Nicholas Hollings to Evelyn Walsh, and Alex Walsh to Sarah Stark," said David Paden. Coraline had never felt so happy in her entire life.

CHAPTER THIRTY-SIX
SPECIAL OPERATIONS

In the months following the wedding, New Castlehale had indeed taken on substantial changes. Even Alex mentioned that it took some effort on his part to get used to seeing the continual traffic coming and going through the landing bay doors. Prototype aircraft, as well as Remo deliveries, were in constant motion through those formerly secret doors. Uniformed security details scrutinized every person exiting each incoming aircraft. Even Adam's vehicle was inspected upon reentry through his tunnel. Only now, he had to share it with arriving officers from the Militia camp at the base of the mesa. He felt lucky to keep his own personal parking space, though. There were changes throughout the complex.

Gone was the small house atop the mesa that for decades acted as a secret entrance to the facility. In its place was a steel and glass structure that acted as an entrance for visiting dignitaries to the underground complex. Several landing pads were hastily built for these visits. No one could get to the top of the mesa by vehicle without first passing through several checkpoints down the long winding road. XO Brice had built up quite a large security force made up of personnel from his former Militia company. This meant building more living facilities near the Militia base and a means to sustain such a force.

Adam and April busied themselves packing supplies into the back of the latest version of the Beast. The latest iteration of the flying vehicle was every bit as formidable as the one lost over Area 51, but it appeared to be much more aerodynamic than its predecessor. The two, accompanied by April's mom Ruth, would be flying out to the new manufacturing facility near Lake Buchanan first thing in the morning.

"Look at that," said April as she pointed to the three aircraft coming through the doors within feet of one another. "I think that Alex would probably have something to say about that. Those remote pilots are taking a risk bunching up like that."

"Oh. That. That's something new one of my teams has been working on. The 'remotes' no longer have control of their aircraft once they enter the canyon. Landing and parking is done automatically now. Once the console indicates New Castlehale has taken control, the remote pilots just get up out of their seats and walk away. It takes some of the fun out of it for the pilot, but after being on patrol for hours or coming back from combat, they're mentally exhausted," Adam said watching as each aircraft was stacked one atop the other in the newly designed hanger.

"You want to go catch a movie?" he asked April.

"I do, but I think we may have to hold off on the popcorn just yet," she responded as she pointed to Alex standing in the entrance to the landing bay waving them over.

"I wonder what this is about," said Adam.

Alex met them halfway. "Brother, something has come up and you should be there when they discuss it."

"What's up?"

"We're called to the conference room. I'll let Nick explain it," Alex answered.

"Adam, this is your mom, could you come to the conference room, please," came over his comDev.

He touched his com badge and responded, "Will do, Mom. Alex has already told me. We'll be right there."

April showed no disappointment at the interruption of plans and smiled. "I'll walk with you and leave you at the door. Holler at me when you're ready, Adam. By the way, Alex, how's married life?" she asked.

"Married life is great! You two should try it?" Alex replied turning a statement into a question.

"Pressure... pressure," muttered Adam.

"To answer your question, Alex, we've actually talked about it and decided to not even address it until we've spent more time together," said April. "As beautiful as your wedding was, we're going to take it slow for a while. My parents and yours agree with that. Not something you jump into with haste."

"Thank you, April," responded Adam, who couldn't conceal the look of pride that he felt at being so close to someone on the same page. "I couldn't have answered that better."

"I know," she said with that devastating smile as she walked away.

The two brothers stood watching her walk away. "Dang, Bro. I'd hang onto that woman. She's a keeper," said Alex looking up at his little brother.

"Boy howdy," was his only response.

Nick got up out of his chair just as soon as they entered the room.

"We received intelligence this afternoon that should be acted upon as soon as possible. We'd like everyone's input. Shall we begin?"

"We're still waiting on two others. Andrea Trevino is on her way up from the labs, and the XO's shuttle just arrived in the landing bay," said Hayley.

Jennifer leaned over to Madison and whispered, "Oh my God. I was in such a hurry I didn't even put my pistol in my holster. I feel naked. Would you mind fetching it for me, please?"

Madison looked down at her empty holster and said, "That's gotta be a first. Is there anything else you'd like me to fetch for you, your highness? A sandwich or a milkshake?"

"Don't get persnickety with me, Maddie. Will you get it for me or not?"

"I already have," said Madison whose elbows were now on the table with her chin resting on her hands."

Jennifer glanced at her holster to see that her gun was already there. "How... when... Oh, never mind."

When the XO and Andrea Trevino arrived, Nick walked to the monitor on the wall.

"We received information this morning that confirmed the rumor that Dr. Tanner was alive and well. An asset within the CIA has given us the name of a person who has been ordered by the president himself to take control of Tanner's project."

"Didn't the President assure us that Dr. Tanner's project was shut down?" Heather asked.

"Apparently, he lied," answered Evelyn. "And we're going to find out what is happening."

"What's the plan?" Adam piped up.

"The plan is simple. Hayley will transport Madison and Jennifer to Washington D.C., where they will infiltrate CIA headquarters, find the office of Dr. Muller, gather as much intelligence on her and her activities related to location number two. They will *only* gather information and return here where we will decide on a plan of action."

"Hayley, have you been to Langley?" Andrea Trevino asked.

"I went to Washington D.C. when I was a kid with my dad. I distinctly remember going to the Lincoln Memorial, so I can transport there. Once there, I'll find my way to Langley. Shouldn't take long. Once there, I'll transport back here, gather up these two beauties, then, together we'll transport directly to Langley. Jennifer will get us into the building. Madison will do a quick search of the floors, find Dr. Muller's office, and together we'll thoroughly pick through everything in there. Once we've found what we need, we'll transport home."

"Do you know how large that place is? A search could take days! Hell, weeks!" said the XO. "I've been there and it's a maze of offices!"

"Even if you do find it, how likely is it that Dr. Muller will have anything in her office that would lead us to the location? I would think not very," said Alex. "You might do better taking Coraline along to extract the information from her brain, then zap home!"

"That's not going to happen," said Evelyn. "We are not going to send Coraline into CIA headquarters. No."

"We'll go with my original plan," said Madison. "Our best guess is that Dr. Muller's office will be in this building here," she said pointing at the monitor screen on the wall. "I should remind you, there will be cameras everywhere, and I do mean everywhere. This shouldn't be a problem if we remain invisible as much as possible. Hayley, you're up first. Good luck."

"How do I look?" Hayley asked, spinning on her heels to show off her dark blue pantsuit. "I do want to blend in."

"You look like you fetch coffee for the boss," said Jennifer.

"Speaking of *fetching*, if I were you, Jen, I'd find something more professional to wear than those cargo shorts. We may not be invisible every second, and well, you're not going to blend in looking like this," Madison said, looking Jennifer up and down.

"Can if I want to! Nobody needs to see me and they won't if I don't let them." Jennifer said folding her arms and sinking back into her chair.

"Alrighty then, suit yourself," said Hayley. "No pun intended. I'll leave here as soon as it's dark on the east coast."

The Lincoln Memorial had only a few night-time visitors, so no one noticed her sudden appearance between two pillars, nor heard the distinctive snap that occurred at transport. Walking into the well-lit interior of the memorial she found herself once again standing before the statue of Abraham Lincoln. It had been many years since she last occupied this spot, but because it was in her nature to soak up information, she could quote the words inscribed in stone above his head. Turning her head, she also remembered the exact words of the Gettysburg Address, but she walked over to take a look at them. She could almost feel her dad's presence as she read them again. A flood of memories swept through her mind, including her mom's recent remarriage.

"You'd approve of him, Daddy. He's a lot like you," she whispered out loud.

Turning to leave, she took the steps down to the walk, then perused her surroundings to make sure she wasn't being watched. The tourists seemed to be absorbed in doing touristy things; most were busy with taking selfies and photos of the memorial itself. Hayley's focus was drawn to a family attempting to flag down a passerby to take a photograph that included all of them. Moms and/or dads tend to be left out of family photos. The dad's request was soundly rejected by two people too busy to be bothered, but the third, a lone man, acquiesced. When he had control of the camera and the family was all arranged nicely, the man shouted, 'Thanks for the camera, idiots!' and turned to escape with the expensive camera in Hayley's direction. As he approached at a run, she stood in his path. Laughing, the man made a leaping jump with his boot extended in hopes of planting it directly in her chest. The outcome was entirely other than he had hoped. With only a slight sidestep and a hook kick, her foot connected with his chin, which resulted in knocking him unconscious before he hit the ground with a sickening thud. Another consequence was that the very expensive camera which had been tucked under his arm was making an arch through the air with hard concrete as its likely finish. Without even thinking, Hayley performed what her martial arts master called the '*ability to be not there.*' Only in this case, it was the ability to *be* there; the camera was firmly in her grip before she realized that she had thought it through. Turning the camera over in her hand to check for damage, she looked up to see the family, which had moments before been frozen into inaction by the audacity of the street thief, running toward her clapping and shouting.

"I've never seen anything like that!" gushed the mom. "That was amazing! Thank you!"

There were slaps on the back and handshakes repeated by every member of the family. "You knocked him clean out!" and "How on earth did you do that?" were shouted and repeated.

"I've been working out," said Hayley as a-matter-of-fact. "Would you like me to take your picture with the Memorial behind you?"

"Well, yes! As long as you include this loser it!" said the dad.

At that the entire family lined up behind the unconscious man and posed as if they were on an African big game hunt. No one had to remind them to smile. They were all laughing when Hayley took the photograph. Hearing sirens approaching, Hayley looked to see the security camera on the light pole that must have alerted them. She turned to the dad.

"I don't want to be here when the police arrive. Would you mind telling them that I had to be somewhere?"

"Of course. We'll just say he tripped when you stuck your foot out, which is exactly what you did."

"Thanks! Enjoy your visit!" she said as she disappeared behind the bushes.

With a snap she transported to the roof of the Lincoln Memorial and paused to look down upon the scene of the crime. As soon as the man regained consciousness, a policeman had him in handcuffs and walked him to an awaiting squad car. His partner was writing down details from the family, who all seemed to be speaking at the same time. When Hayley was assured of a good outcome, she removed a pair of binoculars from her satchel and moved to the opposite side of the roof. Getting her bearings, she remembered that her destination was just over six and a half miles away, but there was no way she could see Langley from the top of the memorial. The solution was quite simple in her mind; jump from building to building along a 130 degree heading, and she'd be there soon enough.

After a dozen jumps from one roof to the farthest within sight, she soon found herself standing atop the tallest building of CIA Headquarters. Remembering Madison's warning about cameras, she immediately transported herself to the darkest corner of the parking lot below her. Inside the security office, a young officer pretending to watch the monitors caught something in his peripheral vision on one of the cameras, but by the time he looked directly at the screen, everything seemed normal. He watched it for a few more seconds, then went back to his cell phone to continue his game.

Realizing that the roof above would probably be the best place for them to start, she transported herself back to her quarters at New Castlehale. Pulling off her shoes and placing them neatly beside her dresser, she fell back into her comfy-chair, and pulled the footrest to her with her toes. With a sigh of relief, she kicked up her feet and touched her comDev.

"Maddie, this is Hayley."

"Hayley! Are you back already?"

"I am. It went well. I can take us in first thing in the morning."

"Well, I've been thinking about that," Maddie said with a tone of concern. "Are we sure that we want to be there when the halls are filled with people coming and going? Wouldn't it be easier and safer to go in tonight when most of the employees are home in their beds?"

"Does it make a difference when we're going to be invisible *and* be able to pass through solid objects, which I might point out, includes people?"

"Ugh. That's hard to visualize. Should we test that out before we go to find out if the person we pass through senses anything? Hang on a sec, let me ask Jen if she has done that."

There was a period of silence. Hayley took the pause to snatch a small square of dark chocolate from a bowl on the small coffee table next to her chair. Unwrapping those little chocolate squares was like Christmas every day, she often thought. And that was exactly the thought that was going through her head when Madison and Jennifer appeared right in front of her.

"Excuse me?" said Hayley as she bit into the square. "I don't recall hearing a knock."

"Sorry, we should have," said. Jennifer. "Promise it won't happen again. But we did test the walking through people theory on the way here. We passed right through

Adam and April kissing in the corridor. They didn't react in the slightest."

"I'm not sure that's a good test. You could throw firecrackers into the corridor and not break the moment for those two," Hayley laughed.

"Well, one thing for sure, it proved that Adam is, for all intents and purposes, over his infatuation with our lovely Junction Queen here," said Madison.

"Oh, shut *up*," responded Jennifer. "I think it's high time that the three of us find ourselves dates."

"Well, Jen, there's a whole camp full of men right at the base of this mountain," said Hayley. "What about that huge Hunky McHunkster that you like to 'woo-hoo' at on his way to work down there. You've been hootin' n hollerin' at him for months now, but you never walk over to talk to him."

"That's just havin' a little fun, Maddie. You know that," responded Jen, a little red-faced.

After an uncomfortable, short silence, Madison continued with the original question of whether to go into the CIA headquarters at night or in the daytime. "There is more room for error with a building full of employees if we go in during the day. I'm for going in right this minute. Jen, you're the one who will get us in there; what do you think?"

"Let's do it now. I'd like to get it over with."

"Okay. It's decided then," said Hayley. "I'll let my mom know, then change into different clothes, and we'll be on our way."

The three women appeared with a snap on the roof of the CIA Headquarters. None of the cameras covering the roof could possibly have picked them up since they were invisible during their transport.

"Okay, this is not the building we need to search. Let's go that way and find the building we need to be on," whispered Madison. Together they walked hand-in-hand to find the building they needed.

"That's it! Two buildings over."

No sooner had she said it than they were standing on the

other roof.

"Ugh! Can we like say 'three, two, one' before we do that? It throws a hitch in my giddy-up when you do that with no warning," said Jennifer.

"Sorry. I'll remember that," said Hayley. "Maddie are you sure this is the building?"

"Pretty sure. Let's get down to those steps there on the left."

"Three, two, one." Snap.

Standing at the entrance to the three-story building, they could see two guards occupied a desk behind the bullet-proof glass; one engrossed in his cell phone while the other clicked through security camera feeds using the keyboard before him. Without hesitation, Jennifer led the group through the glass, desk, and guards and entered the first office they could find.

"I'm up," said Madison. "I'll search this whole building before you can say, "Peter Piper picked a peck of pickled peppers."

"We'll hold you to that, Barbie. Peter Piper picked a ..."

"Okay. Muller's office is on the second floor. Let's go," said Maddie who seemed a little winded.

"Why are you out of breath? You're already faster than lightning. You didn't run, did you?" asked Jennifer.

"I was hoping to be back before you got to Piper, but something slowed me down," Madison replied.

Taking the staircase, they moved up one floor. Hayley noticed the key fob reader on the door to the second floor had been ripped out. "No wonder it took you so long to get back to us, Maddie. Did you do that?"

"Oh. That. Well, yes," she answered.

"If we'd all gone together we could have walked right through that door! What if someone comes through and sees that?" asked Jennifer.

In an instant the fob reader was reassembled to its former state, even though it was now non-functional. "There, good as new. Can we go now?" Madison retorted.

Entering Dr. Muller's office, they released one another.

CHAPTER THIRTY-SEVEN
TRAILING

"Look, she rates her own restroom!" said Hayley opening a door. "She must be important."

Going through every drawer and cabinet, the three searched Dr. Muller's office for anything that might lead them to location two. Every framed photo and diploma on the wall was photographed, as well as every document on her desk.

"I'm not sure we're going to find anything if we can't get into this computer," said Madison. "Perhaps if we..."

Voices could be heard right outside of the office and the door rattled slightly as the keypad was being manipulated by someone trying to get in. Hayley backed into the restroom and closed the door, while Madison reached out to take Jennifer's hand to disappear. Two people walked in, one of them obviously Dr. Muller.

"They will ask about us sooner or later," said the person walking directly behind the middle-aged woman. "If Tanner hadn't shown up, you'd be running that whole show."

"I know. I know. How many times do you have to remind me? But he did show up," said Muller.

"He did," nodded the other, "and butt-ugly too! He looks like the wiener that was left on the grill. Did he ever tell you what happened?"

"I asked. He didn't want to talk about it. He apparently

had his ass handed to him on a great big platter out there at Research and Development. Let me give you a bit of advice. Don't ever bring it up to him. He spirals into a depressed pile of worthlessness, then gets mean. You don't want to be anywhere around him when he gets mean."

Jennifer and Madison stood in the corner of the room watching the interaction between the two and trying not to breathe too hard.

"Owen, where's Charlotte?" asked Dr. Muller looking a little concerned.

"Right where we left her. Outside the door."

"Well bring her in!"

Owen opened the door and looked down the hall a few paces to find the teenager leaning listlessly against the wall.

"Charlotte, would you step into the office, please?" Owen beckoned.

Slumped shoulders and head down, the girl's body language screamed the fact that she was nowhere she wanted to be. Her hair was disheveled and her hand-me-down clothing was wrinkled and threadbare.

"Charlotte, do try to keep up with us when we walk. Okay? I don't want to have to fetch you every time we turn a corner. Do you understand?"

Charlotte nodded her head without looking up.

"I only brought you here to meet some people, but you must listen to what I say and obey me quickly. Sit in that chair," Muller said pointing to a chair against the wall. Jennifer and Madison were on the opposite side of the room watching carefully.

"Someone has been in this office," muttered Muller aloud as she opened her desk drawer. "Someone has searched this office! Charlotte, come here! Find who has been here! Now!" she scolded at the girl.

Charlotte cocked her head to one side, first this way, then that. She touched the desk, then bent her head down to sniff its surface. Moving around to Muller's side of the desk she smelled each drawer, then every object on the desk. From there she moved to the cabinets and walls, touching each photo and object on the shelves. Madison and Jennifer had to do some twisting the turning this way and that to stay out of her reach, while Muller and Owen looked on. When the disheveled girl got to the bathroom door, she reached the doorknob, then stopped, stood straight, then pointed at the door as she looked directly at Muller.

Owen reached inside his waistband and pulled out a snub-nosed revolver and put his hand on the knob. With one swift motion he pushed his way through the door with his handgun out before him.

"Nobody here. Are you sure this girl is going to impress anyone in the morning?" Owen said as he holstered his weapon.

"There is no doubt that there has been someone in this office, and I intend to find out who. Charlotte, how many people besides us have been in this room today?"

Charlotte held up three fingers. "Three? Surely three people could not get in here undetected. Are you sure?"

Charlotte nodded without looking up.

"Well, I need documents," she said as she sat down before her computer monitor. Jennifer and Madison moved as silently as they could to be in a position to catch the password being typed but didn't get it. The printer that Madison had her rear end pressed against made a few sounds before it began printing off pages. Again, they moved away from the desk to escape detection. Muller stood up and leaned over the printer as if to will it to print faster. Moving to put distance between them and the doctor, both Jennifer and Madison were shocked to find Charlotte looking directly at them. Her eyes went from one to the other as her lips formed a smile for the first time since she walked into the room. To their surprise, Charlotte put her finger to her lips before resuming her eyes on the floor body language.

"Are we coming here tomorrow?" asked Charlotte.

"Charlotte, why should you care where we are going?" Owen asked.

She shrugged her shoulders and kept her eyes to the floor.

"It's okay, Owen. Charlotte is just curious, aren't you Charlotte? You've been good today, and I hope you are good tomorrow when we meet with doctors."

Charlotte nodded.

Gathering up her papers, she tapped them on her desk and stapled them before stuffing them in a manila envelope. "No. We are not coming here tomorrow. We're going to a new place."

"Are we flying home tomorrow?" Charlotte asked without looking up.

"You are full of questions today, Charlotte! Yes, you're going home tomorrow, but we must meet people first. We'll eat some lunch and then go home. Now be quiet and stop asking questions," said Dr. Muller.

"Okay. I like Andrews Air Force Base. They have good snacks," Charlotte said looking directly at Madison.

Dr. Muller, Owen and Charlotte left the office and closed the door behind them.

"Where do you suppose Hayley's got off to?" asked Jennifer.

"If I were her, I'd be outside the front door waiting for us. I think we should head that way. We have all the information we need to find the second location of Dr. Tanner's group," said Maddie.

"What? You're not thinking about stowing away on Dr. Muller's ride home! At best it's probably a small private jet! I doubt that we'd get away with that," said Jennifer a little surprised.

"We'll figure that out after we find Hayley. Let's get out of here."

The two held hands and walked through the door, down the stairs and out the front entrance. Hayley was nowhere to be seen. They searched the rooftop without success, then realizing that she wouldn't show herself until they did, they became visible. Hayley popped in, took their hands and they all found themselves back in Hayley's quarters at New Castlehale.

"Sorry that I had to buzz out of there so quickly, but there wasn't any place to hide inside that bathroom," said Hayley. "What'd you find out after I left?"

Madison and Jennifer recounted everything in detail as Hayley listened patiently. When they were done, Hayley slapped her communications badge. "Hayley to Command."

"Remote viewing."

"What does that mean, Heather?" Jennifer asked.

"Remote viewing is the ability to see things without actually being there," Heather explained. "Charlotte has the capability to look, if she so desired, inside our labs and watch our science team put together an engine. I was in a cell next to her for a couple of years. She often described places outside of Area 51, both here in America and overseas. Her body was a prisoner, but her mind was not. Apparently, a part of her gift includes the ability to see you, Jennifer. The good news is, she is not a great fan of Dr. Tanner. So, based on what you have told me, she was trying to help you. She let you know when and where they are flying out tomorrow. That's no small thing."

"How can they use her against us?" asked Hayley. "If she's not a Tanner-fan, can they force her to reveal our secrets?"

"Tanner has a gifted truth-sensor that he used when Charles Reynolds wasn't around. The truth-sensor is more accurate than a polygraph. They tried hooking me up to lie detectors, but I was able to defeat them because I was aware of what they were doing. If they put this guy in the room with a gifted, he can tell whether they are telling the truth, mostly," said Heather.

"Mostly?" Nick said.

"Those with mental powers can feel him boring into their heads and put up a defense or send him down a rabbit hole. Those with no gift or physical gifts alone stand no chance. Charlotte is young and may not yet be able to withstand his assault, and it is an assault. They would be able to at least tell if she was fighting them. When we fought them, there were severe penalties."

Nick growled under his breath. His jaw was set and his eyes spoke volumes. "We are going to go in there and bring all those people out. We are going to end the Tanners and the Mullers."

"Remember, Nick, that we've already given it our best shot, and Tanner is still alive," Evelyn said. "We've got to think this one out."

Madison said, "I agree with you, Evelyn. Even though we succeeded in getting Heather out of there, we did miss the chance to end Tanner. But look at what we have now! Heather is more powerful than Tanner could imagine, due in part to David Paden's sacrifice. Hayley, Heather, Jennifer, Nick, Eli, Coraline and I can accomplish anything we set our minds to. We can go in there and stomp the ever-lovin' dog-sh..."

"We can't," said Coraline.

They turned to see her standing at the end of the table. "We can't go in with power and hope to win against Dr. Tanner. My dad told me that even though there are gifted individuals like Charlotte who would love to see Tanner fail, there are also those who believe in his goal with all their hearts."

"Well, baby sister, does your dad know details of who and what we're up against?" Adam asked.

"He does, and now I do. I spoke to him when this meeting started. Some of the group removed from Area 51 are powerful. Only two of us at this table would stand a chance against their best. The smartest thing most of you should do is run away. What concerns me most is the fact that they know where we live, and we have no idea where to find them."

"Something we're going to remedy tomorrow," said Hayley.

Evelyn sat listening intently to every word spoken as she stared at her folded hands on the table. After some discussion, she spoke up.

"I'm going to put on my scientist hat now. Jennifer, you and Madison should report to Research and Development as soon as we're done. I want to know if you two are detectable in any way. You may be invisible, but the question I want answered is, *can you be detected outside the visual spectrum*? I'm talking x-rays, ultraviolet, and everything in wavelengths that won't kill you. I want to know if there is a substance you can't pass through. There are questions we need answers to about Madison, such as, is there any way you can be detected as you move lightning speed through their complex. I'm going to get Andrea to the labs tonight, and together we're going to take a look at you. The sooner you get in there, the sooner you can catch some sleep before you go tomorrow."

"Alex," said Nick, "Let's reposition Hermes to cover eastern U.S. We've got to be able to move coverage as quickly as possible. Park Zeus over the central states. When that plane takes off tomorrow, we want to follow it wherever it goes."

"You got it. It may be wise to send up Delta Flyer. Delta is undetectable at high altitude; she can shadow that plane and go wherever it goes. Let's call it insurance."

"Make it happen! We'll meet again at 900 hours tomorrow."

The view from the top of the control tower at Andrews Air Force Base was impressive as the three women watched the air traffic come and go.

"Are you sure they are flying out on that plane?" Jennifer asked.

"As sure as I can be," said Madison. "You were with me when we read the passenger manifest over that guy's shoulder. That is the only Gulfstream being prepped this morning. And the best thing of all, we know it's destination. Minot, North Dakota."

"If my memory serves me right, Minot is an Air Force Base. Aren't they more likely to take a military jet? They could be packed onto a military aircraft like that C-130 there," said Jennifer.

"We are talking about someone important to the President of the United States here, Jen. They are not going to be 'packed' onto a C-130, hon. Besides, that's a gunship. See the howitzer poking out the side? The government uses Gulfstream jets to move their VIPs around. Trust me."

"We'll find out soon enough," said Hayley. "There they are!"

Binoculars were brought to eye level. They easily identified Dr. Muller and Charlotte walking toward the

Gulfstream parked on the tarmac. Two people exited the aircraft to meet their passengers. As Dr. Muller shook hands with the two, Charlotte turned and looked directly at the three sitting on top of the control tower and waved.

"Okay, this is really creeping me out," said Jennifer. "I think I may have tinkled myself a little."

Hayley sang, "Too much information!" as Madison laughed.

They watched the aircraft as it was closed up and taxied to the runway. As soon as it was in motion, Hayley announced, "It's time to get out of here. Ready? Three, Two, One."

Zap.

Appearing in the Command Control room, Hayley walked directly to her station and sat down. Monitors came to life as she made the call. "Officers to command. The ball is in play." Madison and Jennifer stood over her shoulder as she brought up a readout from Hermes over the east coast. "It should be any moment."

Adam and Alex walked into the command center and took their chairs. Adam took a few moments to get on the same page as his sister, then announced, "Hermes team, watch for our signal. Hayley will designate target."

Hayley's monitor revealed every plane in the air on the eastern seaboard. She switched it to the main wall monitor. As soon as the aircraft that they witnessed moving down the runway only seconds before took to the air, she marked that signature for tracking. "Hermes team, we are looking at a military Gulfstream 850. According to the flight manifest, destination is Minot, North Dakota. We'll know soon enough if that is the case. Regardless, let's move both Zeus and another Hermes to that location immediately. East coast Hermes, shift with the target."

Alex spoke into his headset, "Landing bay, Delta is clear to launch. Angel Squadron, man your stations."

Nick's voice came over the loudspeaker, "Special Operations Group, you have ten minutes to gear up and come to the ready room."

It was an interesting looking bunch that showed up to

the SOG ready room. Nick, Hayley, Jennifer, Madison, and Heather walked into the room wearing light grey and black camouflage, form-fitted uniforms.

"Tada! Superhero costumes!" said Jennifer.

"We do look quite... fetching," said Heather. "Are you sure that when I do my flame thing that these things won't burn up and leave me in my birthday suit again?"

Nick answered, "I had the same problem catching plasma rounds. They burnt my clothes off and I ended up almost naked. We've tested these. They work. Ok, people, let's get started. What you see here is Minot Air Force Base. I've been in and out of there a hundred times. It remains the home of the global striker force. Being filled with mostly bombers and missiles, it seems an unlikely spot for Dr. Tanner to set up shop. My guess is that it was picked for its remote location, but knowing the commanding colonel there, my guess is that Tanner's new facility is somewhere off base. Dr. Muller's aircraft continues on this heading."

"Do we have a plan?" asked Madison.

"We do. Hayley and Jennifer will take our fastest aircraft and fly directly to Minot. They will jump from their aircraft at 35,000 feet and land on top of this building."

"Nick, why that building? The control tower is on the south side of the runway about a mile from that structure," said Madison.

"You'll have to tell me one day how you know these things, Maddie. The reason I chose this building is that small aircraft are almost always directed to this tarmac. Every time my unit made a stop at this base, we taxied to that area. We deplaned and were picked up here for transport. I saw several Gulfstreams parked there. Let's call it an educated guess. From this roof you should be able to see Dr. Muller exit her aircraft. Follow her to their destination. Confirm it and get back here. You're going to be our transport. Any questions?"

"Uh.... Yah," said Jennifer. "I heard you say that we're going to jump from our airplane at 35,000 feet and land on top of that little building."

"That is correct."

"I've never parachuted from an airplane in my entire

life. I don't know how they work and I certainly wouldn't know how to steer one. Have you gone wackadoodle?"

"That would be 'have you gone, wackadoodle, *sir*', but you're assuming that you'll be using parachutes. You won't."

Madison leaned over and whispered in Jennifer's ear, "Feel free to tinkle yourself."

CHAPTER THIRTY-EIGHT
CHARLOTTE'S WEB

"Command, we are nearing our destination, and not seeing a break in the cloud cover below. Can you tell us what the surface visibility is at Minot?"

"Uh, Slice, this is Ranger One; you'll have to contact Minot control for that information."

"Oh, that'll work! 'Minot control, we're invading your military installation and would like to know what your surface visibility is, so we don't take a nose-dive onto your tarmac.' I think you're going to have to do better than that."

"Slice, we're guessing that the surface visibility is about 500 feet."

"Guessing? Can you be more accurate?"

"Command to Dice, report."

"This is Dice. Slice you have nothing to worry about. I've been monitoring Minot and you've got at least a 500 foot ceiling."

"Thanks Dice. Command, I owe you one."

"What does that mean?" asked Jennifer.

"It means that we're going to have to keep our eyes peeled for the ground. We won't have long to transport once we've cleared the cloud cover."

"Well, 500 feet doesn't sound too bad."

"Keep telling yourself that."

"Command to Slice."

"Go ahead, Command."

"Dr. Muller's plane is on approach now."

"Roger that, Command."

"Okay, Jen, brace yourself. It's going to be a cold dive. I'll keep an eye on my altimeter. I'm going to hover directly above Minot and we'll bail out together. Are you ready?"

"As ready as I'll ever be."

"Command, we're hovering above the coordinates now and I'm opening the canopy."

A freezing rush of wind filled the cockpit as the canopy rose. They wore space suits similar to the one Sarah used in her orbital flights, so the cold was not as bad as it would have been otherwise. After they had unbuckled themselves, they moved cautiously to a place above the wing, being careful never to let go of one another.

"Jennifer, you're crushing my hand! Hold firmly, but please try not to break every bone there."

"Oh. Okay. Sorry. Are we going to go on 'three'?"

"On three. Ready? One, two, three!"

Hayley, having skydived on many occasions, felt exhilaration at the free fall. Jennifer, not so much.

"Jennifer. Jennifer! Listen to my voice."

"I can hear you!"

"I know you can hear me, but I want you to listen. Calm down. Do what I do. Spread your arms and legs out just like me."

"Shouldn't you be watching for the ground?" cried Jennifer.

"We have a couple of minutes before that. But, by spreading our arms and legs we can slow our descent."

"Like this?"

"You've got it. Now, I will keep an eye on my altimeter and know exactly when we're close. The second we see ground, I will transport us to the surface. We will stand up, get our bearings, and transport to the place we need to be. Do you want to make us invisible now or later?"

"Later. I want to be able to see you."

When they broke through the clouds, Hayley realized that they were lower than 500 feet. SNAP. When they opened their eyes, they found themselves lying on their stomachs somewhere between runways.

"Jennifer?"

"Yah?"

"We're visible."

"OH!"

After doing their disappearing act, they were able to get their bearings quickly. They immediately transported to the roof of a nearby building. From that vantage point, they spotted the Gulfstream jet that carried Dr. Muller and Charlotte coming in for a landing. The distinctively shaped tarmac where the taxiing aircraft would be parked could be seen off to their left, as well as the rooftop of the correct building.

"It might be tricky keeping up with the car that picks her up. So, just hang on. We'll do the best that we can."

They transported at least ten times from rooftops to sidewalks and back again following the automobile. When Hayley realized that their prey was leaving the base, they transported to just about any place they could where they could keep eyes on the car. Jennifer was pleased when she realized that their destination was only a few minutes from the base at a large farmhouse with an even larger barn. They transported to a spot just feet from the car when it pulled up to the front porch of the home. When Charlotte exited the vehicle, she stopped and looked straight at the two invisible invaders. She seemed quite surprised to see them but smiled when she did.

"Stop daydreaming, Charlotte. Let's get a move on," said Dr. Muller. The two of them went up the wooden steps of the home and entered.

"What do we do now?" Jennifer asked.

"They said that we should get back immediately, but what do you say we stick our heads inside for a quick look-see?" said Hayley.

"Hmmm. I'm not usually the sound of reason in just about any situation, but I'd say we best do what they say. You know, get back home."

"Come one! What's the use of having super-powers if we can't use them? If anything goes wrong, we'll just zap out of here."

"Okay, but just a look," said Jennifer with a tone of doubt.

Hayley led the way up the steps and looked inside through the windows. It's an uneasy feeling standing before an open window, even when you are invisible. As the two of them watched Dr. Muller and Charlotte through the large picture window, a large guard surprised them when he moved quickly to the window with a pair of binoculars. Both froze in spot until they realized that they indeed were totally invisible to the man. He could easily have been studying Hayley's forehead with those binoculars if one went by outward appearances. Their preoccupation with the man in front of them almost made them miss Muller's exit from the room. Charlotte was looking back at the window as she was pulled along by the hand. The last thing they saw of her was a smile as the door closed behind them.

Moving along the porch, Hayley and Jennifer entered the house through the closed front door. They tried creeping along silently, but the old wooden floors of this farmhouse creaked and groaned under their weight. The guard, who had been perusing the countryside with his binoculars, set them aside and took a few steps in their direction. He stood there for at least a count of twenty, then moved back to the window.

"Let's get out of here," Hayley whispered.

The problem with transporting is that you both exit your location and appear at the destination with the distinctive 'snap' that sounds on both ends. Whether the guard would make anything out of it on his end was just mere speculation, but the sound did indeed alert all those standing in the command center at New Castlehale when they appeared.

"Do we have a location?" asked Evelyn.

"We do. A farmhouse outside of Minot Air Force Base."

"How was the landing?" Nick asked.

Hayley walked to him and flicked his forehead with her finger. "I told you I owed you. We were about 200 feet off the pavement when we transported. It was close. *Very* close."

"So, what's the plan?"

"We go in tonight. No warplanes. No troopers. It will not be a military operation. Only a few of us will be transporting there. We go in, gather those who want out, and transport back," said Nick.

"Back where? Here? I would not recommend that," said Madison.

"No. We transport them to Junction. We've already made the arrangements to house them and reconnect them with their families. Bringing them here might prove to be problematic should even one of them be loyal to Dr. Tanner," said Nick.

"Who is going in?" asked Jennifer.

"Hayley, Madison, Jennifer, myself and Charles Reynolds," said Nick.

"Not me?" asked Heather.

"Not you, Heather. I'm hoping we can pull this off with as small a team as possible."

"Wait. Earlier Coraline said that there were only two of us who might be able to stand up to their strongest gifted. She didn't name names, but I'm pretty sure that she was referring to herself and me. What will you do if you run into the very powerful?"

"I figure if we do, we can run, as Coraline suggested. Hayley can transport out and take anyone close by with her. Jennifer can disappear and walk out of there with whoever is closest. Madison can be gone before they can blink. And, well, Charles and I will have to hope we're close to one of those three. I'll pair up with Hayley. Charles can pair up with Jennifer or Madison. Easy peasy. Any Questions?"

"Well, yes," said Evelyn. "Heather, you grew up with the gift of being able to see things that haven't happened yet. Can you bring that gift to bear on this mission? Can you see, at all, what we're running into?"

"I'm sorry, Evelyn. I wish I could help, but ever since Area 51, my visions have disappeared. I can read thoughts and sense things about people as well as I ever could, but I haven't had a prescient vision since that day. I don't know what happened."

"I do," said Coraline. "You experienced a major gift-dump that day. All of my father's gifts were transferred to you. Some of my gifts, Madison's, Nick's, Charles', and even Dr. Tanner's were all mixed and mashed and placed on you. I am not aware of all that you will be able to do, but only time will tell. I doubt that you lost your ability to see future events, but it may be diluted by all that has been placed on you, and it may take some time to resurface."

"With the gifts I know about, I think that I may be able to help this team. I've been practicing my control for the past couple of months. I can control my flight. I can control my flames. I think I can help. Besides, if there is an attack by someone stronger than these guys, I seem to have the ability to use that power against them. In my mind, I'm the perfect weapon for this job. Nick, big brother, let me help."

***

"What did the President think of our little wonder here?" Tanner asked.

"He was suitably impressed. He showed some concern when she described the exact contents of his desk in the Oval Office. And if that weren't enough, she told him that a congresswoman in Michigan owns a warehouse that is full of mail-in ballots. You can't imagine how interested he was to hear that."

"Excellent, Dr. Muller. We'll have him in our back pocket like his predecessor. Taylor was a fool if there ever was one and this one will be no different. Charlotte, you did well. Tell me now what you saw in New Castlehale. Did you look at the maps on the ride home like I asked?"

"I can't see inside that place, Dr. Tanner. I try, but I can't. There is something blocking me."

"Nonetheless, I want you to keep trying. Is that understood?"

Charlotte nodded.

"Are the other's prepared?" Dr. Muller asked.

"They are always prepared, my dear doctor. This time, when they show up, there will be a reception committee waiting. We are going to end Evelyn Walsh and her pets once and for all. Now, Charlotte, tell me again who and what you saw in Dr. Muller's office."

"I saw two people in the office. Both invisible to Dr. Muller and Owen, but I believe only one of them was gifted that way. The other seemed to be along for the ride. They made sure that they maintained physical contact. I do not know if the other was gifted."

"And the one in the bathroom?"

"The one in the bathroom was there one moment and gone the next. I don't know how. When we got to the airport this morning, I saw all three on top of the Control Tower. I waved to them."

"And you saw the same women on our porch this afternoon?"

"Only two. The invisible one, and the one that must have been in Dr. Muller's bathroom. They must believe that I am here against my will."

"Good. Good. I want you to take a walk around the house. I want to know if they are still out there," said Dr. Tanner. "If they are there, make them believe that you are here to help them."

Charlotte got up to leave, glanced once at Dr. Muller, then exited the room.

"Dr. Tanner, what if they bring David Paden along with them? And Heather also! Their numbers are growing! We know now, that besides Coraline, Eli and Charles Reynolds, they have the invisible one and possibly two others. We don't know how they may be gifted."

"Dr. Muller, you worry too much and too often. What does Heather do? She's a fortune teller at best! But apparently, she doesn't do that very well, or else they wouldn't be nosing around here. David Paden may not even be alive. The device I placed on his body most likely killed him when it was activated. What other powers do they have to oppose us? Invisibility? Our counter to that just walked out the door. You worry too much."

"Should I remind you of what happened after you lost consciousness at Area 51? One of them was powerful enough to destroy dozens of aircraft that were sent to finish them. Apparently, all of them were powerful enough to survive the explosions that left a crater hundreds of feet wide. So, yah. Why should we worry?"

"Sarcasm does not become you, Dr. Muller."

Charlotte walked a large circle around the farm house. She stopped to look at the large, barn-like structure several hundred feet away to see if there was any activity there. No one stirred. When she turned to continue her walk around the property, there was a distinct snapping sound that drew her attention. Turning, she found herself facing six individuals, dressed alike.

"Hello," said Charlotte.

"Hi Charlotte. My name is Hayley. You saw me earlier today."

"I saw you. And that one. And that one," she said pointing to Jennifer and Madison. "Hi, Heather. I'm glad you lived. I don't see David Paden. Did he die?"

"Yes, and no. It's hard to explain, but he is no longer with us," Heather responded.

"Do you know why we're here?" asked Nick.

"I do. It won't be as easy as you think. Not all of us want to be rescued. I told him...Dr. Tanner. He's inside and he's expecting you. You might be able to kill him because he's an idiot. That is why I drew you here. But you may not be able to kill his faithful. That's going to be harder."

"We're not here for anyone but Dr. Tanner, Charlotte. We have no desire to kill any of you. We'd like to take you home to your families," said Nick as he came closer to Charlotte.

"That's a lie," came a voice from the porch. In his own mind, Dr. Tanner's smile was as winsome as ever, but in reality, his face was a misshapen horror of blistered flesh and stretched facial muscles that barely covered his teeth. The very sight of him made Heather take a step back. He moved slowly toward the group, removing his gloves as he walked. "I'm sure you do have a desire to kill, Nick Hollings. I can see it in your eyes. Oh. Are you still angry with me for taking your sister? I don't see her boyfriend, David here, so I must assume he didn't make it out of my laboratory in Nevada. So sad. And what of your three brats, Heather? I kept them alive only because I was hoping you and David would join me. I regret not burning them to cinders."

Jennifer succumbed to Tanner's strategy to make them angry. "Shut your mouth, Tanner. Oh. I'm sorry. You don't really have one anymore! It's a good thing we're not here for a beauty contest because you'd lose."

"Nice," replied Tanner. He pointed to Nick and said, "But I was hoping to make this one angry, but I can see I failed miserably. You see, I want you to die first, so your sister has to watch."

About thirty individuals appeared from thin air behind Dr. Tanner. Ranging in ages from 12 or 13 years old to 35, they mostly wore the same frightened looks on their faces. The two or three standing closest to Dr. Tanner looked very pleased with themselves. "I'd like you to meet some of my friends, Texas Ranger Hollings. These are the very ones you came here to kill."

"Don't listen to him," Nick shouted to the assembled. "He's lying to you. He took you from your homes, your families and friends and imprisoned you. He told you that if you did not cooperate that he would do harm to your families. We rescued your families last year, and they are all safe. You can return with us, and we'll reunite you with them. But this one," he said, pointing at Tanner, "only now does he call you friends because he knows that your gifts can be used to accomplish his bent goals. We are here to stop him. You all see Heather here. She was one of you. She is safe now and being away from Dr. Tanner has made her more powerful than he could imagine. You see Charles Reynolds. He was one of Tanner's chief henchmen. He will tell you that we mean none of you harm. It is this man we are after. This man will answer for his crimes. We are going to give you a chance to switch sides. Anyone tired of being used by this man, step over to us. Do it now."

CHAPTER THIRTY-NINE
A NEW BEGINNING

There was a lot of discussion going on between those standing behind Tanner. Several seemed to be pleading with those around them, while others did a lot of pointing or pushing. It was obvious to everyone that there was dissension in the ranks. While this was happening, Nick whispered something into Heather's ear.

"Enough! Enough of this!" yelled Tanner. "Any of you are free to step over to their side! But know this; you will die with them this day! Nothing will save you! Go and join the fortune teller and the mind reader! Let's see how well they protect you!"

Heather burst into a human-shaped inferno and rose slowly into the air. Having learned to control her flames she made them look spectacularly dangerous. "Before any of you make your decision, I invite the strongest among you to take your best shot at me. You! There! I'm talking to you! Do your worst! Use whatever dangerous gift you think you have to make a dent! Do it now!"

The person she addressed was the one she remembered fearing the most before she was rescued from Area 51. It was obvious by the look on his face that he thought himself invincible. He looked at Tanner for approval, which was received with a nod, and stepped out rolling up his sleeves. Nick motioned everyone in his crew to step back a number of paces. When those standing behind Tanner saw Nick and the others backing away, they did also.

"So, the fortune teller can make flame and fly," he said trying to get a laugh out of those present, but the only person laughing was Tanner.

"Here's my best shot!" the man who thought he was invincible yelled as he thrust his arms forward and a bolt of lightning came from his fists and struck Heather directly in the chest.

The expected result did not take place on her but on him. He burst into flames and ran away screaming in pain until he dropped and smoldered on the gravel driveway. Dr. Tanner was frozen with shock and indecision and didn't notice that more than half of his friends ran to Nick's side. His powerful followers however did not freeze, and immediately they began lobbing torrents of flame, earth, electricity, shards of jagged ice and any other projectile or force field they could muster at Nick and the others. Hayley, Jennifer, and Madison disappeared to prevent being struck by the weaponized objects. Charles' life was spared only because he was standing directly behind one of the defectors whose only gift was to put up a force field. He had no offensive gifts with which to engage in battle, so he asked if he could stick close to her.

Most of the Tanner's loyal followers directed their powers toward Heather, who, as far as they knew, was their greatest threat. Tanner himself assaulted Heather with a volume of flame and heat that surpassed anything he had accomplished in the past, but it was turned back upon him. If it were simply a matter of withstanding his own heat, he would have come out unscathed, but returned with it were the accumulated powers of everyone targeting her. Several of Tanner's loyal followers lost their lives directing their powers toward her, being burned to a cinder by the very power their leader was throwing.

A man who seemed to be in his mid-twenties morphed from his human form to that of a monster standing thirty feet tall and went directly for Nick. Besides being bullet-proof, Nick's only power came from the muzzle of a plasma rifle. At the onslaught of the fight, he was able to withstand the blunt force of being hit by large rocks that appeared from thin air and pummeled his body, but the approach of this gargantuan beast put fear in his eyes. He stood his ground, firing his rifle into the towering threat, but was back-fisted by the creature and thrown far into the field across the fence.

Hayley saw what happened and transported herself directly into the monster's path, holding her sword out to the side in defiance. Surprised by the sudden appearance, he reached out and snatched up a farm tractor to use as a cudgel. If one could call the monster's facial expression a smile, that is what was painted across his countenance as he tried to hammer her into the dirt. With a snap, she disappeared. The creature looked left and right to find her, but, to his surprise, she was perched on his shoulder. With the flash of steel, she positioned her Japanese sword and drove it into what she figured was an ear and disappeared again. The beast reeled and stumbled this way and that and crushed several of his fellows as he fell dead upon the ground.

The battle was taking place in slow motion for Madison who moved and fired at the greatest threats with her pistol until something hit her in the head, knocking her to the ground. When she shook off the shock, she saw that there were two teenage girls moving as rapidly as she among the slow-motion combatants. Holding hands, the identical girls rushed at her as she struggled to her feet. Having dropped her pistol she braced herself for the collision that was sure to come. Her attempt to duck came too late; she was solidly clotheslined by the pair; flipping backward in a dizzying spin, she hit the ground hard on her back. One of the girls returned and pinned Madison's hand to the ground with a large knife. With a scream she returned to normal space-time. Her attackers did likewise, laughing as they moved to finish Madison with fresh knives. From behind them, Jennifer appeared out of nowhere, using her fists as hammers to knock them both off their feet, she then dove for Madison. As soon as she touched her friend they both disappeared.

The twin girls, still smarting from Jennifer's blow, used

their powers to follow Madison, who they assumed returned to lightning speed. Looking left and right, in the slow-motion world, the two girls could not find their prey. One of the girl's face went white as she realized she was being restrained. She could not move her hand which was being forcibly dragged upward. She felt a sharp pain as she was released. Looking at her own hand, the girl discovered that it had been impaled by the very knife she had used on Madison. A voice came out of nowhere. "How's it feel, little girl? You see, you're just fast. But we're fast *and* invisible. The next knife will appear through your throat if you do not leave immediately. Both girls turned and ran toward a nearby building as fast as their legs could carry them.

"Thank you! I thought for sure they had me," said Madison.

"You're welcome!"

"I know it's stupid for me to say, 'you came out of nowhere', but what were you doing before you saved me?"

"Well, I found out that I really can't do a lot with invisibility except to pop up behind people and knock the snot out of them. I don't really feel good about shooting these kids, so I just put a little persuasion to their jaw. Well, except for Dr. Tanner there. I snuck up from behind and gave him a swift kick to the gonads. Look, he's still curled up in a ball!"

Madison would have laughed harder, but her hand was bleeding profusely. Jennifer produced a large bandage and wrapped it up as best she could. When finished, she asked, "Are you good to go? Your pistol is lying on the ground over there. I think a bullet hole in their foot might take them out of the fight, don't you think?"

"I think so."

Jennifer disappeared to continue her attacks, while Madison went to find Nick, who had not returned to the fight since being launched over the fence by the giant. She returned to normal space-time and helped him find his feet. "Are you going to be okay? You look a little shaken there."

"I'll be fine. I just needed to catch my breath. What happened to the giant?" he asked craning his neck to see what was going on.

"Hayley showed him the error of his ways."

Together they moved back to where Heather still battled with the more powerfully gifted. Many were dead on both sides, including Charlotte, Charles Reynolds and girl protecting him. Other's had given up and walked away, some wounded, others just frightened by the ferocity of the fight.

"Stop! Stop!!" Dr. Tanner screamed at the top of his lungs.

It took a few moments, but soon all fighting ceased. The moment there was quiet, Dr. Muller came out of the farmhouse and stood behind Tanner. After she whispered something in his ear, he smiled and became more confident than ever.

"You cannot win this, Mr. Hollings. We could go on for hours, but eventually, you will lose because you cannot match us, in spite of your sister there," he said pointing to Heather.

"I disagree, Tanner. Look at your numbers. You've lost followers while we've gained. I'm not sure what exactly you are a doctor of, but it obviously isn't math," said Nick.

"You really think you did well, don't you, Hollings," he laughed. "Heather seems to be the best that you have, and yet you cling to hope for victory. I have news for you, Ranger. These you just fought are my second string team. Please, meet my A-Team."

Two men and a woman strolled out of the farmhouse, all focused on Heather who continued to hover fifteen feet above the ground. Their bearing was one of absolute confidence as they walked forward.

"Heather, I want you to meet your executioners. Hollings, you should say good-bye to your sister now, while you have the chance. We'll get to the rest of you later."

"Dr. Tanner, if you think these three can defeat me, please let them get to it so that we don't have to listen your prattling," said Heather, whose flames increased tenfold.

The three didn't wait for Dr. Tanner's word. Their attack on Heather was ferocious with no warning whatsoever. The first shot a white hot ray from her hands at Heather, which, when directed back to its origin was deflected by a force field generated by one of the men. The other hurled nearby objects at her, such as the tractor used earlier by the giant, as well as the body of the giant itself! Fence posts, automobiles, weathervanes, as well as nearby boulders, everything sent to hit her deflected off to be propelled back to the person who sent it. Nothing that hit her phased her at all. When the three saw that their best efforts had no effect, they stopped. Tanner watched the efforts with interest.

"I see now, Heather. We truly cannot defeat you, but I see that your powers are only defensive. You were able to hold these three off, but you were unable to harm them. Is that it? Is this the best that you've got?"

Heather looked to Nick for guidance, and Nick had nothing to say to Tanner's assessment of the situation.

Tanner continued, "As long as we don't attack her, she cannot harm us. But this will not prevent us from harming these," he said pointing to Jennifer, Maddie and the others.

Heather said, "Tanner, are you willing to bet your life on those observations. After all, you have only seen a little of what I can do. Are you willing to take that chance?"

"I am. You forget, Heather, we have studied you for decades and I know when you are bluffing. That's right. You may be able to send out a flame or two based on what I know about the device I attached to David, but that will not help you here. So, Nick, you have ten seconds to get every one of them down on their knees before we start on you, and you will not last a second when we do." The three who had attacked Heather moments before lined up against the entire group standing around Nick.

Just as they raised their hands, there were bright flashes 500 feet above their heads in the clouds as two bright, glowing objects broke through and hurled themselves toward the gathering. Coming to a halt over Nick and the New Castlehale team, they appeared as balls of energy, but that faded as they became more human in shape.

"Hello, Dr. Tanner. Time has not been kind to you, I see," said Evelyn.

"Speaking of time, yours has come to an end," said the voice of a child.

"Ah, Evelyn Walsh. I see that you too have managed to

obtain some power, along with this child of yours," said Tanner. "Will we have to repeat the demonstration of my most powerful to you? It hardly seems necessary; you cannot possibly stand up to them."

"Dear Dr. Tanner, you are suffering from apophenia. You see facts where you wish to see them, even though they may not exist," said Coraline. "We are here to."

Her sentence was interrupted by a powerful blast from the woman standing behind Tanner. The deadly ray never quite reached Coraline who seemed to be protected by a shield not seen. Coraline did not react, but Evelyn did. She pointed her finger at the woman who was instantly wrapped in a boiling mass of interrupted space/time. It grew until it engulfed all three of Tanner's most powerful minions, and Tanner himself was sucked into it, powerless to react in any way. It intensified until every molecule in their bodies were scrambled and exploded. Tanner was no more. There was no trace that he had ever been there moments before.

The only sounds that could be heard were the blowing of the wind, and the flames emanating from Heather, who then settled to earth and extinguished herself. Patting down her body, she made sure that her flame-resistant clothing had worked. It did.

"I'm sorry, Coraline. I reacted, and well, I haven't gotten the hang of controlling these new powers," said Evelyn. "I didn't mean to disintegrate them all. Sorry." She turned to Nick who had a confused look on his face and shook his head in disbelief. "Oh. That. Coraline and I have been busy lately. It appears that I had this buried deep but never found it until Coraline did a little 'drilling' to strike oil."

Eli, who had been brought back to the scene by Hayley, knew exactly what she meant by that. He walked over to Madison and took her by the hand, which healed instantly. She leaned over to him and asked, "What's apophenia?"

He shrugged, "It's a Coraline thing."

President Cott finished his press conference in the Rose Garden and walked toward his office with the First Lady.

She gave him a kiss on the cheek and continued to the family residence. As he opened the door to the Oval Office, he turned to the Secret Service detail and said, "I'll be working here for a while, see to it that I'm not disturbed," then entered. Seated in one of the armchairs was a striking woman with white-blond hair and hazel eyes.

"Uh...Ms. Walsh, nobody told me you were...who let you in?" the President stammered.

"I know this is a surprise, Mr. President, but I would not have come if it were not important." She put out her hand to shake his. When he took it, he found himself in a different room, in a different place. It was a wooden structure built to hold small town meetings, and the people gathered in the room looked exactly like small town people, except for those standing on the stage at the front of the room.

"What is this place and who are you people? I demand that you return me at once! I'm the President of the United States."

"Mr. President, meet The Defenders of the Void," said Evelyn.

It was an impressive group of people standing near him. If it were not for their commanding presence, they would have looked like ordinary citizens. He knew they were not. The intelligence gathered on this family had been very accurate. He walked up to the largest one of the bunch and said, "You must be Adam. I've got a building full of engineers who would love to make your acquaintance."

He moved down the line.

"Hayley and Sarah," he said with some apprehension. "I knew you by your swords and well, by the security feed that we saw from the Rangers Headquarters. Perhaps you'd like to train my Secret Service personnel?"

"You must be Alex. The flight suit. Dead giveaway. You cost us a lot of planes and pilots."

"Hedgehog? I thought you were dead."

"I get that a lot."

"Jennifer McKellen. Did you really kick Dr. Tanner in the... nevermind. Your reputation proceeds you."

"Rangers Hollings and Jameson. You two have uncovered a lot of corruption. I enjoyed watching the videos of the awards ceremony last year. Impressive.

"Ah... Major Johnston, I recognize you from the debrief of our team."

"Mr. President, I want you to meet Coraline and Eli," said Evelyn with a touch of emotion.

President Cott stood over the two children studying them closely for a few moments, then said, "You must be the children that started this whole mess. It wasn't your fault. Nobody holds you responsible. Most of those that caused you harm are now in prison or," He paused to look at Evelyn, then continued, "gone from us. You have lost loved ones, I know. There have been grievous losses on both sides, but it's over.."

With that, he turned to Evelyn and said, "I hope there can be peace between us."

"There can be, Mr. President. These people you see here are the families of the children that were stripped from them and placed in your facility at Area 51 and the one in Minot. Many of these family members were held hostage at your facility in Oklahoma. We rescued them, and we rescued most of the children. We must have your assurances that the practice of removing gifted children from their homes will cease. We are now requesting reparation payments for these families. We are asking for funds to build a school here in Junction to teach and train those so gifted if they choose to join us. Can we be assured you are willing to help us in this, sir?"

"I will try to the best of my ability to fulfill your request, Ms. Walsh."

"It's Hollings now, sir. Evelyn Hollings."

EPILOGUE

Workers moved quickly to gather up as much of the wreckage strewn across the desert landscape surrounding Area 51 as they could before they were discovered. They knew they would pass a cursory inspection, based on the fact that the aircraft they were operating from was a C-130 Hercules with American military markings.

It was obvious that there were several types of aircraft present among the rubble, but they grabbed as much as they could anyway. Individuals would drag or load heavy parts onto all-terrain vehicles and take them directly to the large aircraft where an Asian military officer would inspect each part.

"That is an F40 part. Throw it in that pile." He would say most often. And as ordered, the workers would throw the parts into the pile indicated and head back out for more.

Two workmen drove up and showed the individual a part that was totally unfamiliar. It was a disk-shaped object with much of the electronics still intact. The man seemed excited as he ordered the men to load the piece onto the large aircraft. Following the workers up the rear ramp, he stood looking at what they had collected thus far. Two of the larger parts looked like engines of some kind, but he had never seen anything like them. He made a snap decision and yelled out in Chinese, "Call everybody back, we're leaving. We have enough."

He was saluted and the process of getting all of the teams back to the aircraft began. None of what was happening here made sense until the Chinese officer handed the only American present a briefcase full of money.

"Have a safe flight home, Captain Zhang. Your

transponder should get you past all of our installations and Coast Guard," said the Air Force Major.

"Thank you."

About the Author

Born in Houston, Texas, Andrew Raiford was raised in a family of seven brothers. Most of the action and adventure that dominated his young life sprang from the imaginations of the brothers Raiford. Since there was no limit to the stories they could create through their play-acting, it was not uncommon to have Daniel Boone not only be attacked by bears or red-coats, but also Nazis and/or extraterrestrial conquerors. Imaginative eight-year-olds care nothing for history.

During his young adult years, Andrew took on some very odd jobs to keep his young family fed. For two years he was a real cowboy who rode, roped, and pushed cattle on a large ranch nestled in the snow-capped mountains of northern California. After moving back to his home state of Texas he worked in the printing business as a journeyman pressman, and later in gun sales, and corporate security. He even worked in church ministry as a pastor for ten years during the period that he and his wife raised five talented children. Those offspring would later become the inspiration for Andrew's first novel, Void of Power – New Generation, which surprisingly contained no Nazis or extraterrestrial invaders.

Now residing in Liberty Hill, Texas, he spends most of his life behind a keyboard. His wife Beverly, retired from the insurance industry, is his first-line manuscript editor before they are sent to a professional. Andrew recently stated that of all he has accomplished in his lifetime, writing is the most therapeutic, relaxing, and satisfying.

Made in the USA
Coppell, TX
19 March 2021

51939856R00203